JOIN THE AUTHORS
ENOUGH OF JA...

'A compelling and deliciously dark story of murder and secrets'
Claire Douglas, *The Couple at Number 9*

'Jane never ceases to surprise me'
Emma Curtis, *Keep Her Quiet*

'Jane is so very good at creating characters who get right under your skin'
Teresa Driscoll, *I Am Watching You*

'Jane Corry is the new queen of the psychological'
Kate Furnivall, *The Guardian of Lies*

'Grips with menace and dread, yet touches the heart'
Nicci French, *The Favour*

'Few writers can match Jane Corry'
Cara Hunter, *Hope to Die*

'Yet another twisty, exciting book that I couldn't put down'
Heidi Perks, *The Other Guest*

'Jane Corry writes consistently enthralling stories about the dark side of family life'
Peter James, *Picture You Dead*

'Jane Corry's psychological novels have sold more than a million copies so far'
Sunday Express

'Fans of psychological thrillers will be hooked after the first page'
Closer

ABOUT THE AUTHOR

Jane Corry is a former magazine journalist who spent three years as the writer-in-residence at a high-security prison. This often hair-raising experience helped inspire her *Sunday Times*-bestselling psychological dramas, which have been translated into sixteen languages and sold over a million copies worldwide. This is her tenth novel.

www.janecorryauthor.com

THE STRANGER IN ROOM SIX

JANE CORRY

PENGUIN BOOKS

PENGUIN BOOKS

UK | USA | Canada | Ireland | Australia
India | New Zealand | South Africa

Penguin Books is part of the Penguin Random House group of companies
whose addresses can be found at global.penguinrandomhouse.com

Penguin Random House UK,
One Embassy Gardens, 8 Viaduct Gardens, London SW11 7BW

penguin.co.uk

Penguin Random House UK

First published 2025

001

Copyright © Jane Corry, 2025

The moral right of the author has been asserted

Penguin Random House values and supports copyright.
Copyright fuels creativity, encourages diverse voices, promotes freedom
of expression and supports a vibrant culture. Thank you for purchasing
an authorized edition of this book and for respecting intellectual property
laws by not reproducing, scanning or distributing any part of it by any
means without permission. You are supporting authors and enabling
Penguin Random House to continue to publish books for everyone.
No part of this book may be used or reproduced in any manner for the
purpose of training artificial intelligence technologies or systems. In accordance
with Article 4(3) of the DSM Directive 2019/790, Penguin Random House
expressly reserves this work from the text and data mining exception.

Set in 12.25/14.25pt Garamond MT Pro
Typeset by Jouve (UK), Milton Keynes
Printed and bound in Great Britain by Clays Ltd, Elcograf S.p.A.

The authorized representative in the EEA is Penguin Random House Ireland,
Morrison Chambers, 32 Nassau Street, Dublin D02 YH68

A CIP catalogue record for this book is available from the British Library

ISBN: 978–1–405–97529–2

Penguin Random House is committed to a sustainable future
for our business, our readers and our planet. This book is made from
Forest Stewardship Council® certified paper.

MIX
Paper | Supporting
responsible forestry
FSC® C018179

To my family

Prologue

It's an unusually warm summer evening at Sunnyside Home for the Young at Heart. Everyone agrees it's the perfect end to the annual barbecue and how lucky it is that the rain has finally stopped.

'What a beautiful building – such lovely period features,' the relatives had marvelled, gazing at the original nineteenth-century chandelier hanging from the embossed ceiling in the music room. 'Did you know the house has been in the family for generations? And the grounds! As for the private beach, well really!'

'I wasn't sure whether to come,' said another. 'Not after everything in the papers.'

'Me too,' added someone else. 'We're still wondering whether to take Mum out, yet she seems so happy here.'

But they've left now, some in their flash cars or taxis and one or two on foot to the station.

If you listen carefully, you can hear the sound of the sea in between Claudette's soft strains of George Gershwin's 'Summertime' drifting through the French windows leading from the lounge.

Most of the residents have gone to bed – it's 9 p.m. after all – but a few stragglers remain. We are the only two left in the garden, taking an evening stroll under the moonlight.

'No one came to see me,' says my companion, as I push her wheelchair along, past a burst of yellow and orange roses.

'I'm sorry to hear that,' I say, although I'm not.

'You're a good carer, Belinda.'

I'm used to such compliments. 'Thank you,' I say.

There is silence for a moment.

Then 'What A Night!' bursts out. The beat is faster. Louder. And somehow dangerous.

No one is around. This is my chance.

BANG!

The sound of the gun is deafening.

PART ONE

The Stranger in Room Six

I see everything in this rambling old manor, from conversations whispered in grand, mahogany-panelled rooms, to private meetings spied through diamond-paned windows.

It may have changed over time – today, the wide Victorian staircase stands tall, adorned with a Stannah stairlift – but this house has survived centuries, and its secrets with it.

Most people are here for respite care: old age, illness, injury. I'll admit my own strength isn't what it was. But despite appearances, I'm here for another reason – a mission far more complicated – and, like my fellow residents, I'm running out of time.

I've got a bad feeling about this job. If I don't come back with the goods, I'll be dead meat. And so will little old Mabel Marchmont.

I

Belinda

Fifteen Years Ago

Beads of sweat roll down Gerald's forehead. It's not an attractive look. In fact, I observe (as I have done many times earlier in our marriage) that it's quite a repulsive forehead, full stop. Red and rather wrinkled, like a newborn baby. A leathery forty-nine-year-old one.

'Nearly there,' he gasps.

Oh, for God's sake! Just get on with it. It's not like he doesn't know *how*. But my husband has always been so particular. Why hadn't I noticed that before the children, when there had been time to get out?

His breathing is becoming increasingly ragged. 'Come on, come *on*,' he urges as if he's on a horse – something he'd never dare do in his life.

I try to distract myself, letting my mind wander back over the years, as it has been doing more and more recently. If it hadn't been for my mother nagging and nagging about settling down with someone who had 'prospects', I would have waited until I'd found someone who had set fireworks off in my heart. Just as . . .

No, I won't think about him. Not now. Not ever. Not even after the letter, which has been pulsing a secret excitement through my body ever since it fluttered unexpectedly onto the hall mat.

Sometimes I can't believe that Gerald and I are actually coming up to our silver wedding anniversary. Twenty-five years of utter boredom and loneliness. If it hadn't been for our daughters, I'd have left long ago. Maybe when they're both at university I'll finally do it. Take the plunge and go.

I know, deep down, that I don't mean this. It's just something I say to reassure myself that things might get better one day. I've seen enough from my small circle of not-very-close friends to know how divorce shatters a family. One has a son who dropped out of college; another whose daughter chose to live with her father and his new girlfriend. It broke my friend's heart.

I'd die without my girls. So, instead, I just stay here and pretend everything is fine until Gerald finally –

'I'm there!' he explodes. 'I've got it! Nine down is "antipathy"!' He glances at his gold watch with a gleam of satisfaction. 'Done it! In only nine minutes and forty seconds.'

'Well done, dear,' I say quietly, watching my husband as he folds up his *Times* neatly before rising from the breakfast table.

'Thank you,' he says, as if taking a bow. 'See you tonight – 6.30 p.m.'

Of course, that's when he's always home from his job as an accountant: 6.30 p.m. on the dot, every day apart from 'high days and holidays', as he puts it.

How bloody boring can you get? I'm not a swearer but sometimes the situation calls for it.

I wait, heart in mouth, for him to close the front door behind him (*'I'll do it, Belinda. You'll damage the catch again'*). Then I go up to my drawer and retrieve the letter that has dominated my thoughts since it arrived last week. I absorb the hue of the dark blue ink again, allowing myself to savour the delicious pleasure of his distinctive writing.

I hear the words in my head as if Imran is here to say them himself.

'Please ring me. I can't wait to hear your voice.'

'No,' screams the sensible voice inside me; the one that wants to hang on to the safety of the table for four; the casserole I'll prepare later this afternoon for family supper at 7 p.m. sharp.

But why not? *Why* can't he be allowed to hear my voice? *Why* can't I give myself permission to hear his? What *is* it about first love that just won't go away?

I reach for my mobile.

Nine down has done it for me.

Antipathy. What supreme irony! Isn't that what I've been feeling for Gerald for twenty-five long, uneventful years?

Enough is enough.

If I don't do *something*, I might just murder my husband.

2

Of course, I tell myself as I dial the number at the bottom of Imran's letter, I don't mean it. I wouldn't dream of hurting Gerald; it's just a turn of phrase. Nor, as I've already said, would I ever leave him.

One ring.

It's not 'just' that I'm terrified of wrecking my children's lives, although that is a major part of it. It's because I'm scared. How would I manage on my own? Apart from university, I've never lived on my own. Crazy as it sounds nowadays, I'd gone straight from my mother's house to my husband's.

Besides, I couldn't hurt him. Gerald might be boring; pedantic even. But there's something inside me that flinches at the thought of his face crumbling if I told him I wanted out. Even though we are totally incompatible.

Two rings.

Mind you, I'm pretty sure I'm not the only one to feel like this, judging by the conversation at book club. It's become part of our language.

'*Oh Alan/Douglas/Clive . . .*' one of the 'girls' will say with a sigh. Then there'll be some story about how the offending husband hadn't put the car in the garage so it needed de-icing or had left his muddy shoes on, leaving footprints on the new expensive carpet or had failed to book the usual family trip to the Dordogne on time and now the ferry was full.

That's when we all roll our eyes in sympathy, knowing that the complainant is just like the rest of us, and it isn't a big deal. Not really. Not compared with the thought of being a 'single mother': a phrase our own mothers used to whisper in hushed voices, as if this was the worst – the very worst – thing that could happen.

We might criticize our men, our marriages. But in the end we go along with them because it's so much safer and kinder than the alternative.

Three rings.

But would it hurt – would it *really* hurt – to hear Imran's voice if no one else knew? The temptation is just too much . . .

I think back to our Oxford days. To those heady long summer evenings when we'd lie in his narrow bed in the men's hall (or he in mine in the women's). But then he'd flown home to get married, and I'd sloped back to my mother because I couldn't afford a flat on my tiny salary, and it was as though Imran had never existed.

Until his letter arrived last week.

I've been treasuring the pale blue envelope ever since, so that now and then I can reread it. Of course, I tell myself in my stronger moments, I won't respond. What good would it do?

But one little phone conversation . . .

Don't I deserve that? It's not as though I'm going to do anything.

Four rings.

He's not answering. It's not meant to be.

I put down my mobile.

My knees are trembling so much that I can barely stand up. This isn't me. I like to think I'm pretty fit; in fact, I play tennis three times a week and often choose singles over doubles so I can get more exercise.

But doubles in marriage isn't what I thought it would be.

There's no passion. There never has been. It's a comfortable routine. A secure pattern of him going to work and coming home; me looking after the girls and the house (*'There's no need for you to work, Belinda'*); badminton, tennis; and my book club meetings, although Gerald isn't keen on my going out on winter evenings. (*'Don't you want to stay inside and watch* Morse *on video with me instead?'*)

It sounds old-fashioned and it is. I often think that Gerald should have been born in a previous decade.

I look at my mobile again. Surely Imran will see the missed call? Then again, he won't know it was my number. I'm not even sure how he got my address, unless it was through the university alumni society.

Still the phone remains resolutely silent. He's not ringing back. Not yet, anyway. And even if he were to, is it possible that I've read too much into his words?

I smooth the crease of the paper and read it again. It's not so much a letter as a three-line note, although it is written on Basildon Bond paper:

It's been a long time. Things have changed in my life. Can we meet? How about dinner on Tuesday night in London? I'm going to be there for work. Please ring me. I can't wait to hear your voice. x

Then he'd put his phone number.

'*Things have changed in my life.*'

What does that mean? Is he divorced? No. He'd often told me that he couldn't do that in his religion. Has he changed his mind? Is he widowed now? The thought makes my heart thump with excitement, which, in turn, makes me feel horribly guilty.

'That's wicked,' I tell myself sternly. Maybe it's as simple as Imran moving back to London with his job. That's it!

He'd want me to meet his wife. Probably his children. He's bound to have them. They'd all sit there and make polite conversation. Gerald would have to come too.

I couldn't take that. I know I couldn't. Why haven't I ever been able to get Imran out of my head? Is it because Gerald simply never measured up to that rush of first love; that bolt of electricity when Imran would take my hand as we'd walk across the quad to lectures; that 'Oh my God, he's kissing me!' when our lips had first met during the freshers' summer ball; the way he ran his fingers through my hair ('*It's like spun autumn gold, Belinda*'); that terrible agonizing emptiness when he'd left after graduation.

Is that why, despite being married now to a perfectly decent man, I can't stop dreaming of a parallel universe where someone had *really* loved me? Really listened to me, *desired* me.

Why do we make such hasty choices in our youth, without realizing the impact they have on later life?

I jump. My mobile's ringing! A number I don't recognize. Imran must be calling back; he would have guessed it was me. Guiltily, I stuff the letter into my pocket, as if someone is watching.

My heart is thudding so violently that it threatens to leap out of my chest. What am I going to say? I think back to the last time we saw each other, my things packed up waiting to go. His trunk already at the porter's lodge. His eyes on mine.

The lie I had told him.

Shaking, I press green to accept on my mobile.

'Is that Belinda?'

It's a woman's voice. Sharp, clipped, official.

'Yes,' I say shakily. Could this be Imran's wife wondering who just called him?

'Your husband's behaviour towards Karen is disgusting,' spits the voice.

'Karen?' I repeat. 'I don't understand.'

'Come on. They're having an affair. Don't pretend you don't know.'

I'm so stunned that I'm certain I've misheard her. This must be one of those awful hoax calls.

'They've been seeing each other for years,' she adds.

I don't normally get angry. But I find myself shouting now. 'Get off this phone now or I will report you.'

'Then you'll be sorry,' says the voice coldly. 'I'm a friend of Karen's. And I don't like to see her being messed around.'

There's a click as the woman rings off.

3

The phone rings again within seconds.

'Right – I really *am* reporting you,' I'm about to say.

But he gets in first. 'Just me.'

My husband always uses that phrase on the phone. It irritates me beyond measure, though I can't pinpoint why.

'I believe I left my sandwiches behind.'

My husband wants to talk about *sandwiches* when a stranger has just called to say he's having an affair?

The girls and I are always teasing him for his frugality, but his request brings life back to normality; to an ordinariness which, a few minutes ago, I'd been whining about, and yet now feels decidedly comforting.

I'm about to tell him about the prank call. He'd know how to deal with it. Gerald is good at that sort of thing. But his voice interrupts my thoughts.

'Can you leave them at reception? Sorry, dear, I've got a meeting to go to.'

Then he rings off before I can say goodbye.

Dear? That's not what my husband usually calls me. He'd said it with such warmth, too.

Of course Gerald isn't having an affair. He isn't like that.

And nor am I.

Carefully I rip up Imran's note into long, tidy strips and put them in the bin.

'*Be grateful for what you have.*'

That's what my mother had told me after Gillian, my first, was born and I couldn't stop weeping. 'You and Gerald have a child together now. Children need security and your husband can provide that.'

Now, as if on autopilot, I put the breakfast things away, make the beds, slip into my spring coat and leave for Gerald's office. It's not far, just a brisk twenty-minute walk into the pretty Hertfordshire town where we've lived since the beginning of our marriage.

Despite my earlier conviction that the call was a hoax, I still can't get those words out of my head. *'They've been seeing each other for years.'* That was impossible. Surely.

When my father left us, my mother would mutter how *'the quiet ones are the worst'*. But just because Dad had been like that, doesn't mean Gerald is the same, does it? Gerald may be what you call a quiet man, but he's also steady and dependable. In fact, isn't that why I accepted his proposal so eagerly? Besides, it wasn't as if I could marry the man I really wanted . . .

The office is in the centre of town. Maybe I'll suggest that the two of us share the sandwiches in the park nearby. That will give me time to explain the silly prank call and let Gerald sort it all out.

'I've brought my husband's lunch in,' I tell the receptionist when I arrive. She's sitting rather casually with her legs crossed on one side of the desk, reading a magazine.

I don't think I've seen this girl before. If I had, I'd have remembered her startling emerald green eyes which match her pointy shoes; the kind that make you wonder how anyone can walk in them.

'I'm afraid Mr Wall has gone out.'

So that meeting he mentioned must be an external one.

'What's your name?' I hear myself asking.

'Penny.'

I feel a flash of relief that it's not Karen, although of course it wouldn't be, because there is no Karen. Is there?

'Well, Penny, I'll just sit in my husband's office until he comes back.'

I head for the door with 'G. Wall, Senior Partner' on it and sit at the desk, trying to get my thoughts straight. But I can't, not without talking to Gerald.

My eyes fall to the framed photograph on his desk: one I'd taken of Gerald and the girls last year, smiling on a boat in the Scilly Isles.

My heart thuds with guilt, thinking of how I'd tried to speak to Imran earlier this morning. What kind of hot bed might that have stirred up? Thank goodness he didn't answer.

Next to the photograph is my husband's diary. I turn to today's date. *11.15*, he's written. There's no client name. No location.

He'd have left early to get there on time. Gerald's always been punctual. It was one of the endearing habits that drew me to him – that sense of security – before it became irritating.

I sit for a while and then, unable to resist, I open his filing cabinet. I don't know this Karen's surname but just in case, I look under 'K'. There's nothing.

Even so, something niggles.

Then I turn my attention to Gerald's desk, a handsome piece of oak furniture with brass handles. I open the top drawer. It has more files, each neatly organized. I flick through them. They appear to be clients' accounts. The same goes for the other drawers, but as I close the bottom one, I notice an envelope sticking out from a folder.

It's unsealed and its condition suggests it's been opened several times. Inside is a photograph of a woman with long blonde hair who is, at a guess, in her thirties. She's smiling at the camera and has a slight gap between her teeth.

Mouth dry, I turn it over.

With love, Karen x

4

My husband keeps another woman's photograph hidden in his desk.

My skin goes cold. I want to be sick.

I shove it back into the drawer, as if that will make it disappear, but I can still feel the tarty blonde grinning back at me.

I sit there, rocking myself back and forth, numb with disbelief and confusion. So the caller this morning was right. Gerald was – is – having an affair. When had Gerald planned on telling me? What am I going to tell the girls? What is going to become of our family?

Then the anger kicks in. How dare he ruin our lives when I have been hanging on, putting up with our mutual irritation and lack of affection, determined to keep our marriage going for the sake of our children?

Eventually I compose myself, just enough to walk past the receptionist and give a little nod. I can't say anything in case I burst into tears. I need to hold it together for now. I'll go home and make shepherd's pie with crispy potato on top, the way we all like it. I won't mention the call. I won't rock the boat, won't make the same mistake my mother did when she'd discovered my father's affair. I'll turn a blind eye and hope that this transgression, for surely that's what this is, will pass.

It might sound old-fashioned, but it will be better for everyone. I'm not allowing my children to grow up without a resident father like I had to.

In a daze, I make my way down the high street. But as I pass Marks & Spencer, I see Gerald walking towards me.

I find myself breaking into a run. 'I know,' I shout. 'I know about Karen.'

Part of me desperately hopes he'll deny it. But he doesn't.

His face looks as if he has stepped through an upstairs door to find that there is nothing between him and the ground, twenty feet below. 'I can explain,' he croaks.

So it's true.

'How could you, Gerald? How could you?'

He shakes his head. 'It's complicated.'

Then, to my astonishment, he bursts into tears and opens his arms to hold me. Gerald hasn't cuddled me for years. And he bloody well isn't going to do it now.

'Get away!' I scream, pushing him. 'I hate you.'

He falls sideways as if in slow motion. There's a crack as his head hits the pavement. Blood gushes out.

'Gerald!' I scream, dropping down to his side. 'Gerald! Oh my God. Gerald . . . Please! *Say* something.'

But my husband's eyes are open, staring up to the sky as if in surprise that his past has finally caught up with him.

5

Gerald's eyes are still open when someone helps me to my feet. His body lies motionless, blood streaming down the side of his face onto the pavement.

A man in a pale blue anorak is kneeling next to him, holding his wrist. 'I'm a doctor,' he says, looking up with anguish in his eyes. 'I'm afraid I can't feel a pulse.'

This can't be happening. I know people use that phrase all the time, but this time I really mean it. This just can't be real.

'She did it,' screeches a woman pointing at me. 'I saw her. She pushed him.'

It's the blonde from the photograph. 'Karen!' I gasp.

Tears are streaming down the woman's cheeks. 'You killed the man I loved.'

I feel like I'm in a crazy pit of madness.

'He's *my* husband,' I scream. 'And I didn't mean to hurt him. I was just angry.'

Of course I was. Who wouldn't be after learning their husband had been unfaithful? They'll believe me, won't they? They have to.

A police car is pulling up, followed by an ambulance. Again, I tell myself this can't be happening. Any minute now, Gerald will get up. He'll dust himself down (Gerald's fastidious about not getting dirty). He'll be a bit stunned after passing out, but his heart will be beating. We'll sort out the confusion over this horrid woman with the dark roots. We'll have to, for the girls' sake. Then we can continue with our quiet lives and I'll never, ever harbour ridiculous middle-aged dreams about Imran again.

But instead, two paramedics leap out of the ambulance. One starts trying to resuscitate him. My whole body shudders with terror as I watch. Eventually – I've no idea how long but it seems ages – he shakes his head. 'I'm sorry.'

Karen begins to wail, loud, high and hysterical. I want to cry but I can't, I'm too numb.

A crowd begins to gather. 'Why's that woman screaming, Mummy?' asks a child in a pushchair.

'Shh,' she says, putting a hand over his eyes and hurrying on.

They put a blanket over him.

I sink to the pavement next to the red shroud. Only a few minutes ago, I hated Gerald with all my heart. Now, I just want him here. We can start again. I'll begin to show more affection; he will do the same. We will learn from what we almost lost. Couples do that, don't they? This can be our second chance.

'Gerald,' I whisper. 'Speak to me, please.'

Above me is the same screechy voice. 'That's the woman you want. She did it. She murdered the man who loved me.'

I shake my head. 'It's not true. She's lying.'

Someone is putting their arms under mine and helping me up. They're lifting Gerald onto a stretcher. 'I'm sorry, madam, but we have to take the body away now.'

'It's not a body,' I sob. 'It's my husband. Please don't separate us. I need to ask him the truth. Find out what happened.'

'This woman needs to be arrested,' screams Karen. 'I saw the whole thing.' She looks around wildly, her eyes like a madwoman's. 'Who else did?'

'Me,' says a man with a ponytail, cautiously raising his hand.

'Me too,' calls out an elderly man leaning on his shopping trolley.

I watch, horrified, as a policeman starts to take evidence. 'I saw her pushing him really hard,' I hear the younger man saying. 'There was this horrible thump as his head hit the pavement.' He clutches his stomach. 'Makes me feel sick to think of it.'

'I didn't do anything wrong,' I say shakily. 'And if I did, I didn't mean to. It was the shock, you see. I found this photograph ... It looked like my husband was having an affair ... but he just isn't like that.'

'Come with us, please. We need to ask you some questions at the station.'

The station? I can't move. My legs won't work.

'Let me help you.'

The words are kinder than the tone of voice.

'My daughters. What am I going to tell my girls? I've got to ring them now.'

'You can make a call from the station.'

I have no choice. I lean against the policewoman as she helps me into the car. I feel everyone looking at me, as if the word 'criminal' is branded on my forehead.

Any minute now, I'll wake up. But as we drive through the leafy town, where no one murders anyone, I feel a cold calm descend on me as the truth sinks in. This morning, our lives had been normal. Now, my husband is dead. I am under suspicion, and everything has changed for ever.

6

At the police station, I'm taken into a room, empty aside from a table and two chairs. There's a plastic jug of water in front of me. My mouth is dry, but my shaky hands can't pick it up and I'm too nervous to ask for help.

On the other side is an unsmiling woman who says she is a detective inspector. She gives me her name but I'm too stressed to take it in.

'Do I need a lawyer?' I ask quietly.

'That's up to you,' she replies coldly.

The vice-chair of the tennis club is a lawyer. But if I call, the news will spread in seconds.

It will anyway, reasons a small voice inside me.

No. I need someone who really knows me.

Fortunately, I've always had a good memory. I've read that letter enough times to recall the number at the bottom.

'I'd like to make a phone call,' I say.

This time, he picks up immediately.

'Imran Raj speaking.'

A bolt shoots through me. I'd forgotten how chocolatey-rich his voice sounded. The voice that whispered in my ear while he held me tight beneath the sheets nearly thirty years ago.

'It's me, Belinda,' I whisper.

'You called!' The joy in his voice rings out around the room. The policewoman visibly twitches.

There is no time for formalities. No time to say, 'How lovely to hear your voice'. No time to tell him all the things

I've been saving up in my heart over the years in case – just in case – we ever had a chance to talk again. 'I need a lawyer,' I say instead. The words stick in my throat.

Instantly his voice becomes solemn. 'I don't understand. Why? Are you OK?'

'My husband, Gerald, has just died. They think I killed him, but it was an accident.'

'Belinda, is this some kind of joke?'

'No,' I cry. 'Just find me a lawyer. Please. I'm being held in a police station and I don't know who else to ask.'

'Where are you?' he asks.

I look at the policewoman opposite. 'Where am I?' I ask.

She writes down an address.

I try to repeat it, but my words come out wrong. She writes it down for me. I have to say the postcode twice because the words come out twisted. Mangled.

'I'll sort it,' Imran says. 'Are you all right?'

'No,' I say. 'I just want Gerald.' Then I burst into tears.

7

Of course, I still want Gerald. I want him to explain about Karen. But most of all, I want to see that awful, wrinkled forehead of his. I might not have loved him, but I just need things to be normal again.

'Just'. Such a small word that can mean so much and yet be utterly impossible.

The lawyer arrives. It's a man. He seems kind; gentle. In fact, he reminds me of my gynaecologist – something that might make me smile if it weren't for the circumstances.

Stammering, I tell him what happened. The anonymous phone call. The left-behind sandwiches. The office. The photograph. Coming across Gerald in the high street. Pushing him . . .

The lawyer listens silently, writing everything down. He says nothing but his face speaks volumes.

'You don't understand,' I say urgently. 'My husband wasn't the type to have an affair. That woman, Karen. She must have been out for his money. So, if he *had* strayed, well, it wasn't his fault. Gerald was sensible. Dull. Boring.'

He makes an 'Is that why you killed him?' face.

'I didn't want to hurt him,' I add hastily. 'I was just angry.'

I could also say that those dull and boring qualities, which had until today been so infuriating, now felt comforting. Grounding. Like rocks of stability that I would give anything to climb back onto.

'There were witnesses, you say.'

I nod. 'At least two men and . . . and that woman. Karen. I'm not going to be charged, am I?'

I'm conscious that my words are spilling out all over the place in my panic.

'Mrs Wall, your husband is dead. We're looking at a possible manslaughter charge.'

Slaughter? Visions of an abattoir come to mind. Then Gerald's blood, spilling onto the pavement, onto my hands. Onto my clothes as I'd leaned over him, begging him – screaming at him – to open his eyes.

They put me in a police cell. There's a raised block for a bed with a ripped plastic mattress. Nowhere else to sit.

I rock myself back and forth, hands cupped round my knees. Pictures flash through my mind like a horror family album. The hidden photograph in the desk. Gerald's shocked response – 'I can explain' – confirming my deepest fears.

A policeman comes in and takes me to a room marked Visitors. They're here! My girls! Elspeth runs up to me, buries her head in my chest. Stares up at me with tears in her eyes, begging me silently to fix it; make everything all right as I have done on so many occasions: lost school uniform; mind-boggling maths homework; a row with her sister. 'What happened, Mum?'

Gillian – always a daddy's girl – hangs back by the door. Her eyes are stony.

'There's a woman outside. She's telling everyone that you murdered Dad. Did you?'

A woman. Karen. The mistress.

'No, I promise. It was an accident,' I choke.

I try to explain but none of it makes sense. Why isn't Gerald here to answer the questions that crowd my head? How could he do this? How could I have missed the signs?

There's a knock on the door. 'You've got another visitor, but you're only allowed two at a time. They will have to go,' the policewoman says, nodding at my daughters.

'Who is it?' I ask.

'A Mr Imran Raj.'

I didn't expect *him* to come – just the lawyer.

'Who?' asks Elspeth.

Gillian scowls. 'He's the one who wrote the letter.'

My stomach sinks with apprehension.

'What letter?' asks her sister.

'The letter she was hiding in her underwear drawer. I found it when I was putting laundry away. Don't deny it.'

'I'm not,' I whisper. 'But it wasn't what you think. Honestly.'

8

If I'd married Imran instead, we'd be making love every morning just as we did in halls. We'd talk, really talk, in a way that Gerald and I had never been able to. The touch of Imran's hand would still send electric shocks of excitement all these years on. His voice would melt both my body and soul.

But now those chances have gone. I am here, a widow, on my way to the magistrates' court to plead guilty to manslaughter.

'That's my advice,' the lawyer had said. 'There were witnesses who saw you do it.'

'But I didn't mean to kill him,' I'd kept repeating numbly.

'That's why it's manslaughter and not murder,' he'd replied softly. 'With any luck, you'll only get ten years.'

Ten years? This can't be happening.

But I do what I'm told and am taken back to my cell for another night. Tomorrow, I'll be taken to the crown court to formally enter my 'guilty' plea.

It all seems so complicated, but I am too exhausted, too shocked, too worried about the girls, to hear some long-winded legal explanation. Instead, I sit on the stained mattress in the police cell, head on my knees, too stunned to cry. My daughters' faces swim into my mind: Elspeth with her 'please say this isn't happening' look; Gillian with her reprimanding glare and cold voice, as she interrogates me about Imran's letter. *'Is that why you killed Dad? So you could be with him?'*

In vain did I try to explain that the letter had meant

nothing. Yes, it had been signed off with a kiss, but he'd meant it in a purely platonic way. People do that nowadays, don't they? He was just an old friend – fine, ex-boyfriend – from university days who had got in touch out of the blue.

'But why did you ask him to find you a lawyer?'

'I don't know,' I'd said.

How could I explain to an eighteen-year-old – the same age I'd been when I'd first met Imran – that I needed someone who had *really* known me? Known the person I was before I'd married Gerald and tried to be someone else.

It doesn't make sense, not even to me.

I think now of Imran's face when I told him to leave the police station. The face I'd barely had time to take in: those same compassionate eyes; his aquiline nose; lips that had pressed mine so passionately all those years ago.

'Please,' I'd said. 'Go. I shouldn't have called you. The girls have got it wrong. They think you and I are having a thing.'

'But Belinda,' he'd said softly, 'we've always had what you call "a thing".'

'Then why didn't you stay and ignore your parents?' I'd wanted to say. 'Why did you leave for that bloody arranged marriage? Why didn't you stay and fight for me?'

If only I'd been braver.

If only he had been braver too.

Then he'd gone. And now here I am alone, about to go to court for a crime I didn't mean to commit. All because a husband I didn't even love had had an affair with another woman.

There's a certain irony there. Or madness, I'm not sure which.

'Belinda Honour Wall. How do you plead to the manslaughter of Gerald Arthur Wall?'

The court is almost empty. Just my girls with Gerald's brother, Derek, and a couple of reporters. Elspeth is weeping. Gillian is staring straight ahead, ignoring me.

Karen isn't here and nor is Imran. Of course he isn't. I'd told him not to come, hadn't I?

'Guilty,' I whisper.

My lawyer asks if I can be bailed until my sentence hearing comes up. The judge mentions a six-figure sum which is almost the value of our house. Gerald was always checking it against other properties in the local paper. Had he been doing that in preparation for leaving us, to see how much his share would be?

'I don't have that kind of money,' I say to my lawyer.

'Your friend Mr Raj said he was happy to put up whatever it takes.'

But how would that look to my daughters?

'No,' I say, shaking my head. 'I can't accept.'

'Belinda, if you don't take it, you'll go to remand prison until you're sentenced. Are you sure about this?'

I nod numbly. Anything is better than the girls questioning Imran's involvement further. I've already lost Gerald; I can't lose them as well.

'Belinda Honour Wall. You will be remanded in custody at . . .'

The words wash over my head. Elspeth's sobs have turned into wails. Gillian has her arm round her sister, leading her out of court without a backward glance.

I'm taken down the back steps of the building into a windowless police van, where I'm then strapped into a cubicle. Someone else is on the other side, hammering against the dividing wall. 'Shut up,' roars the guard.

'How long will it take to get there?' I call out nervously.

'About three hours.'

'How will my daughters find me?'

'They'll be given details in due course and you'll be told how to apply for visiting rights.'

Prison. Visiting rights.

The words fly around my head. I wish now that Karen had been in court so I could have yelled out to her, demanded to know exactly what was going on between her and my husband.

And in that moment, I feel that anger – the fury that had made me push Gerald – rushing back.

'You bastard,' I whisper. 'If you weren't already dead, I would *definitely* kill you.'

The Stranger in Room Six

We've all got our secrets, haven't we? After all, hasn't everyone made mistakes?

But I'll admit, when I was briefed for this job, I was gobsmacked. Sometimes, the worst criminals really are the people you least expect.

I'm under strict instruction that my target never finds out I exist: no direct approaches, no open threats. So I'll need to find other means, although that doesn't worry me. I've always been . . . How should I put it? Resourceful. Persuasive, even.

My boss and his boss say they 'chose' me because I'm 'good at this sort of thing', but I know it's never that simple. They've got things on me that could have me sent down for even longer than before. That's if they don't kill me first, and I'm not having that.

I'll do anything to save my own skin. Wouldn't you?

9

Mabel

Mabel can still smell her mother, though she hasn't seen her for eighty-four years.

Whenever her father visited France for business, he always brought back a bottle of Chanel No. 5.

'How lovely, darling,' her mother had said to Papa. 'Thank you.'

'May I have some?' Mabel had asked wonderingly.

'When you're older,' her mother had replied, but her father had given a quick wink.

'I think she can have just a tiny bit, don't you?'

So her mother had dabbed some onto her little finger and placed it gently behind Mabel's ear. She felt as if she might swoon with happiness.

'Thank you,' she'd said.

That was years ago: before the war. They'd lived in Chelsea back then. She'd always loved water and her favourite weekend pastime was to walk along the River Thames, holding Papa's hand and discussing landmarks like the Tower. 'I'm so glad that you share my interest in history, Mabel,' he'd often say.

Sometimes Mama came too but recently she'd been staying at home because she was expecting a present. 'Mummy says she's going to give me something that I'm going to love,' Mabel told Lizzie, her maid. 'I hope it's a pony.'

For some time now, Mabel had been begging for riding

lessons. 'Princess Elizabeth and Princess Margaret have been riding for years! I've been reading about it in *The Lady*.'

Mabel had always been an avid reader. She would fall on the magazine as soon as it was delivered.

'That girl won't take no for an answer,' her mother would say to Papa.

'She's got character,' he would reply. 'Just like you, my darling.'

Then Papa would hold out his arms and pull them both into a warm embrace. Everything was safe and easy back then, until the night in 1939 when they'd sat in front of the radio to hear Mr Churchill speak.

'Why are you crying?' she'd asked her mother.

'Just a cold, darling,' Mama had replied, dabbing her nose with a white lace handkerchief Aunt Clarissa had given her. Her mother's sister, who lived in Devon, gave everyone lace handkerchiefs for Christmas, which Mabel considered extremely dull.

Then, that evening, the doctor came. Mabel was told to stay in her room with Lizzie, but she could hear Mama crying and calling out. Her cold must have got worse.

'It won't be long now, miss.'

Then all of a sudden, Mabel heard a high-pitched wail. 'It's here!' Lizzie cried.

'What's here?'

'The miracle your parents have been waiting for, love. It's taken long enough. You're going to have a baby brother or sister! Isn't that exciting?'

Yes! This was much better than a pony. How she'd longed to have a brother or sister like all the other girls she knew. But when Mabel was shepherded into Mama's boudoir, she was met with a tiny red face that instantly burst into tears.

'It's all right,' said her mother. 'I know you're thirteen

years older, but soon you and your sister Annabel will be great friends.'

If only they'd had more time to get to know each other.

1941

Before Mabel knew it, the war had begun and Papa had left to 'do his bit' for King and Country. They all cried a lot then, including Annabel. Even the doll that Mama had bought her didn't help.

Then came the planes. Night after night, they would roar over the rooftops, while sirens wailed into the evening air, sending Mabel, Annabel, Mama and Lizzie running to the bottom of the garden to hide in the shelter that Papa had built a few weeks ago.

Then one night, there were no sirens. 'Thank goodness for that,' her mother said.

'But what if the planes come and we don't hear the warning?' cried Mabel.

'Don't be silly, darling. That's the whole point of sirens. We *will* hear them.'

'We need to go to the shelter; I just know it!'

'Honestly, Lizzie. That girl is so dramatic. Take her there, will you, to keep her quiet. I need to carry on nursing.'

'Please come too, Mama.'

'There's no need, darling, I promise.'

Mabel and Lizzie sat in the shelter 'twiddling their thumbs', as her maid called it. 'I'm meant to be meeting my young man,' she complained. 'I'll be late at this rate and . . .'

Then it came. The sound of planes.

The maid's voice was shaky. 'For the love of God. Where are the sirens?'

'Mama! I need to get her.'

Lizzie clung to her. 'You can't go out, miss. You'll get killed.'

Her voice was interrupted by crashing noises, screams. The din outside made Mabel's ears ring.

When it finally ended, the two of them crept out, hand in hand, too shocked to speak. Houses had been reduced to rubble. Bonfires lit the night sky, while children yelled and adults wept. Their neighbour was clawing through bricks, screaming out her husband's name.

'Where's our home?' Mabel whispered.

'Gone,' said Lizzie in a voice that didn't sound like hers.

'Where are Mama and Annabel?'

But the maid didn't answer.

'WHERE ARE MAMA AND ANNABEL?'

'God in heaven,' whispered Lizzie. 'They must be buried under all this.'

Frantically, Mabel tried to lift some rooftiles. 'Help me,' she called out. 'They're underneath. I know it.'

Side by side they worked, moving slabs, or trying to because most were too big and heavy. Around them, others were doing the same. Shouting. Screaming. Quietly sobbing. Names were being called. Joan. Tom. Harry . . .

'Mama!' screamed Mabel. 'Annabel!'

Men wearing uniforms arrived. A grey-faced man was being hauled out, limp and floppy.

'Don't look, miss,' pleaded Lizzie.

But she'd already done so. It was their neighbour.

'Ronald,' sobbed his wife. 'Ronald!'

Someone put a white sheet over him.

'But he won't be able to breathe if they do that,' implored Mabel.

'Too late for that, love, I'm afraid,' said a man in a tin hat.

Still, they dug. Mabel's fingers were bleeding. Her throat

was hoarse with shouting. 'It's no good,' said Lizzie tearfully. 'We can't do anything.'

'But we've got to.'

Then she gasped as a little arm poked up between some bricks. 'Look!' she said, pulling it out. 'It's Polly, Annabel's doll! My sister must be near here.'

'It doesn't mean she's alive, dear,' whispered Lizzie.

'She is! She has to be!'

Suddenly, there was another roar from the sky, followed by the screech of sirens.

'Jesus, Mary and Joseph,' Lizzie whispered, looking up at what seemed like a flock of birds in the distance. 'They're coming again.'

'Everyone to the shelters,' yelled the air-raid warden.

'We can't leave,' Mabel screamed. 'I'm looking for my mama and Annabel!'

'You've got to,' urged the man in the tin hat.

Then he picked her up and carried her, one arm flailing furiously on his back, the other clutching her sister's doll tightly.

'I'll come back,' she screamed at the rubble. 'I promise you; I'll come back!'

10

For the next two nights, Mabel slept on the crowded floor of the town hall, arms clasped round her sister's doll.

Then Aunt Clarissa arrived. She was younger than Mama, but much taller and not as smiley. Her long fur coat almost touched the ground while her mauve felt hat, perched to one side above her beautiful oval face, had a feather pointing up to the heavens.

'I suppose you'd better come home with me,' she said.

Mabel felt numb, as though she was here but not here. 'But how will Mama and Annabel know where I am?'

Aunt Clarissa's eyes fixed unwaveringly on hers. 'They'd have dug them out by now if they were still alive. I'm afraid we have to be realistic, dear.'

Mabel's bones and teeth began to judder. 'Can Lizzie come too?' she whispered.

'Who?'

'Our maid.'

Her aunt raised her eyebrows as though Mabel had said something very stupid. 'Do you think I can afford to feed two extra mouths? One is bad enough.'

'It's all right, love,' Lizzie whispered. 'I'll be fine, I'll find another job.'

Reluctantly, Mabel followed her aunt into a large, shiny black car with a badge on the front that said 'Morris 8 Tourer'. Her insides felt blown out, as if she had been hit by the bomb herself.

'Do you think it hurt them?' she whispered.

'They wouldn't have felt anything,' came the crisp reply.

For a second, Mabel thought she saw a tear glisten in her aunt's eye as she started the engine, but it disappeared as quickly as it had arrived.

'Now go to sleep. It's a long way to Devon. And don't sit so close. You stink from that awful place you've been sleeping in.'

The journey seemed never-ending; down roads that then led into such narrow lanes that they brushed hedges on both sides. Only Polly the doll gave Mabel comfort. It was almost like cuddling Annabel herself. She was so soft and warm. This made her cry all over again.

'For goodness' sake,' snapped her aunt. 'Stop it. How am I meant to concentrate with that racket?'

Mabel had never been to her aunt's house before, even though it had been Mama's childhood home too. As far as she could remember, such a journey had never been suggested and her aunt rarely visited them in London.

Then they turned a corner and Mabel gasped. 'Is that the sea?'

Despite her grief, she was mesmerized by the light glinting on the waves below. Mama had talked of swimming here when she was young. The thought made Mabel tearful again.

'I can't cope with any more of this,' said her aunt curtly. 'Everyone's upset but it's time you pulled yourself together. You've got the household to meet – the ones who haven't gone off to fight, that is.'

They were driving down yet another long narrow lane, lined by pretty cottages and a pub called the Seabeast's Head. 'Just as well there isn't any other traffic on the roads,' said Aunt Clarissa. 'I was only allowed to buy the petrol because you were an emergency.'

She took a sharp left before stopping abruptly at some

high wooden gates; the name The Old Rectory was carved into a stone pillar.

'Climb out and open them, will you?'

Then she drove through, leaving Mabel to run after her towards a large flight of stone steps and the biggest front door she had ever seen, with a knocker in the shape of a lion.

A girl in a blue-and-white gingham pinafore came running down, followed by two black dogs.

Mabel shrank back.

'Jasper and Bunty won't hurt you,' said her aunt. 'Come on now. Let's get you inside.'

Her voice seemed a bit softer now. Maybe she was tired and sad for Mama too. After all, they had been sisters.

'Where's the luggage, ma'am?' asked the girl, who looked about her age.

'Unfortunately,' said her aunt, 'there isn't any.'

'But...'

'Stop asking questions, Frannie. Just get my niece into the house. I've put her in the Red Room.'

Then Aunt Clarissa took a small silver flask out of her jacket pocket and tipped the contents down her throat. 'That's better,' she muttered to herself. 'God knows, I need something to get through this.'

It seemed Aunt Clarissa was definitely upset, despite her tough words. Mabel's own tears began to flow again as she followed Frannie upstairs.

'Is it true that the Germans got your mam and your baby sister in the Blitz?' asked the girl, turning round.

'Yes,' sobbed Mabel.

'Why didn't they get you too?'

'Because I was in the shelter with our maid. I wanted them to come but they wouldn't.'

'What about your dad?'

'He's away fighting Hitler.'

'Well, you'll be all right here. Just as long as the Krauts don't come over in boats.'

'How can they do that?'

'Because we're on the coast, course. Look!'

Frannie pointed through the window. Beyond the garden, Mabel could see the sea, like a silver brushstroke in the distance. It felt as if the house was surrounded by water.

'Don't go too close. Part of the beach is mined to stop the Jerries getting up. If you want to go exploring, wait for me. I can tell you the safe bits. You don't want to get blown up like . . .'

She stopped but it was too late. 'Maybe your mother and sister survived!' Frannie said instead, as if trying to make up for her lack of tact. 'You hear all kinds of stories. There was a street near Dawlish that got a direct hit, but this woman stayed alive under the rubble for five days and she was all right.'

Mabel gasped. 'Really?'

Supposing Mama and her little sister were trapped, desperately trying to breathe? What if someone had pulled them out and they were searching for her in London? They'd be frantic with worry. Why had she allowed Aunt Clarissa to bring her down here? She needed to go back.

Mabel turned and ran down the staircase.

'Where are you going?' thundered a voice.

It was Aunt Clarissa, standing at the foot of the steep wooden steps.

'Mama and Annabel might still be there under those bricks or in a hospital. I should never have left them.'

Hysterically, she ran towards the door and tried to turn the large ring handle, but it remained resolutely in place.

'For goodness' sake,' snapped Aunt Clarissa. 'They're dead. You just have to accept it.'

Then suddenly, the door opened, sending Mabel flying backwards onto the cold square flagstones.

A pair of tall, sturdy legs stood before her. 'What's going on here?' asked a kind, deep voice.

Mabel scrambled to her feet and found herself looking up at a ruddy-faced man, who instantly reminded her of Papa, though he looked a lot younger.

'You must be Mabel,' he said, putting out his hand. 'I'm so sorry you've been through such a terrible time. It's something that no child should experience.'

'She's not a child, Jonty. She's fifteen years old.'

'Come on, Clarissa. Cut her some slack. The poor girl's stared death in the face.'

'Aren't we all doing that, every day of our bloody lives?'

'Language, darling. Now stop panicking.'

'I'm not. But how can I look after her when we're so busy? We've got . . .'

He took her by the arm. 'Not here,' he said quietly. Then he reached into his pocket and brought out a sixpence. 'Frannie,' he said, 'after lunch, why don't you take Mabel to the sweet shop and then show her round the village?'

He pressed the coin into her hands as he spoke. 'There's a good girl.'

'Who's he?' whispered Mabel to Frannie as the drawing-room door shut firmly, leaving them in the huge hall, alone with the dogs sniffing for food.

'The Colonel. He lives in the manor down the lane. He's a friend of your aunt's.' She winked. 'A very good friend, if you know what I mean.'

No, but she didn't like to say so.

'He's really Lord Dashland, but everyone calls him "the Colonel" because of his bravery in the last war. Now come on.

Cook's got a rabbit; I can smell it on the stove. Then we'll buy some liquorice or toffee. What's your favourite?'

Reluctantly, she followed. Despite what her aunt said, Mabel knew Mama and Annabel were still alive. She could feel it in her bones. Somehow, they would find each other. Papa would be home soon after beating the Germans and then life would return to normal again. All Mabel had to do was get back to London. If only she knew how.

11

Mabel was still working out her escape plan over breakfast – a solitary occasion at the long mahogany table with just Frannie in attendance – when there was a loud knock on the door.

The dogs, who'd been sitting by her side hoping for a slither of bacon (there'd been a shortage in London after rationing started) leapt up and ran into the hall.

'Shhh,' said Frannie, running after them. 'You'll wake the mistress and then there'll be hell to pay.'

Mabel followed. A woman stood on the doorstep in a large floppy hat and skirt down to her ankles. She was carrying a woven bag and in it were some eggs.

'Here you are, love,' she said to Frannie.

'Thanks, but the missus hasn't left me any money and I can't disturb her.'

'What's new? You can bring it with you when you come home tonight.'

Then her eye fell on Mabel. 'Is this the maid then?'

Maid? She wasn't a servant.

'That's her, all right.'

Both spoke as if she wasn't present.

'Condolences for your loss.' The woman took off her hat.

'My mother isn't lost,' said Mabel firmly. 'Nor is my sister. They're missing but they're going to be all right.'

'Let's hope so, love.'

Then she glanced back at Frannie. 'I suppose you've been left in charge of her on top of your other duties?'

Frannie nodded. 'Me and Cook.'

'That's something.' Then the woman turned to Mabel with a friendly smile. 'We're making camouflage nets this afternoon if you want to join us.'

'What are they?' asked Mabel.

'Nets to hide buildings from Hitler. The idea is that his devil pilots look down and think it's just shrubbery or trees. Don't they have them in London?'

Mabel shook her head.

'Well I never. Anyway, school starts next week. You'll like that. You can meet some others your age instead of being all alone here.' She glanced disapprovingly up at the staircase and the dark forbidding portraits lining the walls. 'You'll be our first evacuee in the village. Mind you, I expect there'll be more before long.'

School? Mabel had never been to school before. She'd had a governess, Miss Butler. Where was she now? She might be standing on their doorstep – or rather the rubble that used to be their doorstep – wondering where they all were. Perhaps Mama and Annabel had turned up there too, dishevelled and confused but still alive. She couldn't stay here any longer, she had to find them.

'Where's the nearest station?' Mabel asked.

'Sidmouth,' the woman replied. 'It's a good forty-minute walk from here, though. Why?'

'I just wondered,' she said.

'Right. Well, I'll be seeing you later, love. Look after the maid.'

'I'm not actually a maid,' said Mabel hesitantly.

'Bless you. It's what we call girls around here. It's a term of affection. It can't be easy moving somewhere new after everything you've been through.'

Then she hugged Frannie, and Mabel felt a terrible aching chasm inside her. 'Is that your mama?'

'If you mean my mam, yes.'

A wave of jealousy swept over her. Frannie must have sensed it because she surprised Mabel by taking her hand. 'Come on, let's go down to the sea. It will make you feel better. It always does.'

Mabel allowed herself to be led away. Somehow, she told herself, she'd get to the station on the way back without anyone noticing.

'See that cottage?' pointed out Frannie. 'That belongs to the lacemaker. We're all a bit scared of her 'cos she can tell people's futures. My mam went to her just after she married me dad and the lacemaker said she'd be getting a big surprise. Then nine months later, my big brother was born.'

Frannie's face fell as she went on. 'Dan's in the army now, fighting for England. We haven't heard anything from him for five months. My mam's beside herself.'

'She didn't look upset,' Mabel heard herself saying.

'That's because she hides it. You've got to, haven't you? If we don't keep going, how are we going to expect our men to do the same?'

'My papa's in the army,' Mabel said proudly.

'Everyone's in something. At least they should be.'

'What's the Colonel in?'

Frannie snorted. 'He got some dispensation apparently, so he's not in anything. My mam reckoned he'd had enough of fighting in the last war and pulled some strings. You can do that if you're lord of the manor.'

They rounded the corner and Mabel stopped, stunned. Before her, the sea seemed to stretch on for ever and ever.

Then Frannie proceeded to take off her clothes.

'Someone will see you!' cried Mabel.

'Not likely. It's a private beach – part of the Sinclair Estate. Your aunt owns it, doesn't she? So we'll be fine. Come on!'

Looking behind her to check there was no one there, Mabel found herself peeling off her dress and her camisole top and stockings and then tiptoeing in.

'It's freezing,' she squealed.

Frannie chuckled. 'Only for a minute, then you get used to it. Just dunk your shoulders under.'

Ah! Mabel's breath was swept away for a few seconds. Then she found herself in another world. One where everything was spaceless and there was no war. No fear. No pain.

'Can you swim?' called out Frannie with a trace of panic, as though she should have asked earlier.

'Papa taught me', Mabel called back, catching up with her new friend using doggy paddle. 'We used to go down to this spot by the Thames.'

For a minute she was back there. Mama laughing and clapping from the riverside. The gay pink and yellow parasol over a picnic of salmon sandwiches. Happier days, before anyone mentioned Mr Hitler.

Suddenly, a roar broke Mabel's memories.

'What in goodness' sake do you think you're doing? This beach is out of bounds!'

Mabel turned, terrified. It was Aunt Clarissa, hand on her hips, face red with rage.

'But I thought it belonged to you.'

'That still doesn't give you any right to come down here. As for you, Frannie, you know the rules. I'd dismiss you immediately if I could find another maid. Back to the house this instant. Mabel, you're to stay in your room until I say otherwise. I have an important phone call to take and I need some privacy.'

12

How was Mabel going to get to the station if she had to stay in her room?

Furiously, she stomped into the intimidating Red Room, with its elaborately patterned peony wallpaper and thick scarlet curtains. She stood at the window, itching to escape, until half an hour later, her aunt strode in without knocking. A pink spot was glowing on each cheek as if she was excited or agitated.

'Did your telephone call go well?' asked Mabel politely. She didn't want to get on the wrong side of Aunt Clarissa again.

Her aunt's eyes narrowed. 'Were you eavesdropping?'

'Of course not. I stayed here as you told me to.'

'You'd better not be lying to me.'

'No, Aunt. I promise.'

'Good. Now, there are some rules you need to know, young lady. First, you must remember that Frannie is our only maid, now that the others have chosen to become land girls, or whatever they call themselves. She is not your play mate and I forbid you from becoming familiar.

'Secondly, I hear that Frannie's mother has suggested you attend the village school. This would be quite inappropriate. I will tutor you myself until we find a governess. I will, however, permit you to partake in the village camouflage netting activity this afternoon. We must show that we are doing our bit for the country. Is that understood?'

Mabel nodded, but as soon as her aunt had gone

downstairs, she grabbed Polly and tiptoed down the narrow backstairs, past the row of servant bells.

Frannie's mother had said the local train station was at Sidmouth. Mabel was sure she'd seen a signpost on the way to the beach.

It took a lot longer to walk there than she'd thought. Brambles scratched her legs and she was thirsty. Eventually she reached a brick building with a railway track behind it. There was no sign, but she recalled Papa saying that they'd removed station names to 'fox' the Germans. Oh, how she missed him.

'Excuse me,' she said to a man sat on a bench, dozing with his cap over his eyes. 'Can you tell me when the next train to London is?'

'Not until tomorrow now.' Then he looked at her suspiciously. 'Hold on a bit. Aren't you the young lady from the Old Rectory whose family were wiped out in the London raids?'

'No! Our house was hit but my mama and sister survived. I know they did. I have to find them. I just have to.'

Then she burst into floods of tears.

'There, there. Don't fret. I'll just pop into the office to make a quick call and check the times.'

Five minutes passed before she heard the clip clopping of a horse. 'Hello, Mabel. You've had a long walk, haven't you? I expect you need a lift home.'

It was Aunt Clarissa's friend, the Colonel.

'Thanks for letting me know, Sam,' he said, nodding to the stationmaster, who appeared sheepishly from the office. So, he had split on her.

'Climb up here on my saddle, Mabel,' said the Colonel. 'Bill will give you a leg up.'

'No, I'm going back to London. I need to get to my family!'

The Colonel sighed and dismounted. 'Let's sit here on the bench for a bit, shall we? Is that all right, Sam?'

The man touched his cap.

'The thing is, Mabel, you're right. Maybe your mother and sister *are* still alive. You do sometimes hear stories like that. But if they are, the first thing they'll do is contact your aunt. So if you go back home to the Old Rectory, you're more likely to be reunited faster.'

Mabel hadn't thought of that.

'My aunt will be angry with me,' she said in a small voice. 'She didn't like me swimming in the sea this morning with Frannie and she says I can't go to the village school. Instead, she's going to tutor me until she finds a governess.'

'Tutor you?' He roared with laughter. 'Clarissa doesn't have the knowledge or the patience. Let me have a word with her. I promise you I can make her change her mind.'

'Where have you been, you wicked child?' her aunt shouted when they got home. 'You frightened me out of my wits, disappearing like that.'

'Calm down, my dear. Your niece and I have had a little talk and she's not going to do it again. Mabel, may I suggest that you go upstairs to change? You'll still be in time to join the camouflage netting work party.'

He spoke as if *he* was Mabel's guardian instead of her aunt. She did as she was told but then couldn't resist tiptoeing downstairs and standing outside the library door, listening to the voices inside.

'There's no way you can teach the girl yourself, Clarissa. You'd be bored out of your skull. We've got so much to achieve and we're running out of time.

'Let her go to the village school,' he continued. 'She'll

make friends and it will take her mind off things. She thinks her mother is alive, for heaven's sake.'

'You're too soft, Jonty.'

'And sometimes I think you're too hard.'

There was a murmuring followed by silence.

'Very well,' she heard her aunt say eventually.

'Good, I'm glad we've got that settled. Time to get on with our work, don't you think? It won't be long now.'

Footsteps sounded and Mabel leapt back from the door and ran upstairs to her bedroom, shaking.

As for their work, what had he meant?

Then she realized he must mean war work. After all, everyone was fighting against Hitler, and since he was the lord of the manor, as well as a colonel in the last war, her aunt's friend would have a leading role. As for the 'won't be long now', he must be referring to the end of the war.

Then they'd all be together again. But what if Mama and Annabel *were* dead? Supposing Papa was killed too? Then what would happen to her?

13

Now

'Shhh, shhh. You've been having a nightmare.'

Mabel feels a hand taking hers, stroking it. For a minute, she thinks it's her aunt.

'It's all right,' continues the voice, much warmer and softer than Clarissa's. 'You're safe. There's nothing to fear. We're all here to look after you.'

Mabel opens her eyes. The horrid Red Room has gone. In its place is a cream bedroom with a television at the far end. There are two reclining chairs and a table with a fruit bowl on it.

'Where am I?' Mabel asks, her voice wobbly.

'In your room at Sunnyside.'

Sunnyside. Of course. Not the Old Rectory any more.

Mabel tries to focus but sleep blurs her vision. She can just make out a woman beside her, kind-looking, with sympathetic eyes, a touch of dark shadowing underneath.

'Who are you?'

'My name's Belinda. I'm a carer here.'

Mabel doesn't recognize her. 'Are you new?'

'I am indeed.'

'Do you live nearby?'

'I was lucky enough to get a room in the staff quarters, actually.'

Mabel snorts with amusement. 'Lucky? Most people can't wait to get out of this place when they finish their shifts.'

'Needs must,' says Belinda, smiling. 'Now, would you like a drink of water?'

'I'd rather have a large Scotch.'

'A large Scotch?' The new carer laughs as if she's said something funny.

'I mean it,' says Mabel, waking up properly now. 'You'll find the bottle at the bottom of the wardrobe. My brother set up an Amazon account for me, so I can order whatever I want. They don't let us have proper glasses because they're "too dangerous", so you'll have to use one of those awful beakers made out of plastic, or Bakelite as they called it in my day. Would you like one?'

'Thank you but I don't drink any more and even if I did, I'm on duty so I mustn't. Now, are you sure you're allowed a whisky?'

'I'm not a bloody child,' says Mabel. 'I don't mean to be rude but if you can't enjoy a decent drink at my age, when can you?'

The woman laughs again. It's a warm, tinkling sound. 'I take your point.'

'I'll have a bit more than that, thank you.'

'Better not, don't you think? It's medication time shortly.'

'Not for me. I refuse to be drugged like all the other old biddies in here. I've learned to grin and bear my pains like we did during the war. You had to get on with it then, you know.'

Mabel feels a tear begin to run down her cheek.

Belinda takes her hand again. 'Is that what you were having a nightmare about?'

'That and other things.'

'Do you want to tell me about them? It can help to share. I've done quite a lot of listening in my time.'

Mabel hesitates briefly. 'No, thank you. I'm quite all right.'

There's a knock on the door. It's the nurse on the drugs round. 'I heard you shouting again, Miss Mabel. How about a little shot to make you feel better?'

'You mean that bloody great needle that knocks people out? No thank you. I've told you that before.'

'I think Mabel feels a bit brighter now, don't you?' Belinda says, her voice kind but decisive.

The nurse shoots her a look, as if to say, 'Don't interfere.'

'Yes, I do,' says Mabel firmly. 'So you can take your medical wares away.'

The nurse's eyes fall on the beaker by Mabel's bedside. 'Are you drinking enough water?'

'Plenty, thank you. This flavoured stuff is absolutely delicious. Now please leave and shut the door after you.'

Then she turns to Belinda. 'Thank you. The staff here drive me mad. All we need now is for bloody Butlins Bill to come in.'

'Who?'

'Haven't you met him? He's the activities manager. Tries to get us to *do* things all the time. Comes up with games, quizzes, paper flower making – although half of the poor sods here are too arthritic to fold a petal – and storytime sessions. Though I don't mind those. If you sit at the back, you can catch forty winks.'

'Butlins Bill, I assume, is a nickname?'

Mabel snorts with laughter. 'One of my best! Apparently, he used to work for a bloody holiday camp. Sorry, I should tell you that I never used to swear.'

She takes a slug of whisky. 'But the older I get, the less I care what I say. Well, up to a point, anyway. The other thing that gets me about Butlins Bill is that he's always so jolly. You can't miss him, always in his spotty red bow tie. My aunt would have considered that very bad form.'

As if on cue, there's another knock on the door. A short man in a bowler hat and bow tie skips in.

'There you are, Mabel!' he booms as if surprised to find her in her own room. 'I've been searching for you everywhere!'

Then he takes in Belinda and sweeps off his hat before giving a short bow. 'You must be the new girl.'

Mabel makes a 'come off it' sound. 'She's hardly a girl. How old are you, Belinda? Fifty-odd? Fifty-five maybe?'

'Now, now Mabel. It's rude to ask a lady's age, isn't it? I was actually coming in to say that it's time for Claudette's concert. She's going to sing us some old-time favourites.'

Mabel drains her glass. 'Boring! Boring! I've heard them all before.'

'Actually,' says Belinda gently, 'it might be fun, don't you think?'

'Exactly! We need to get a move on!' Bill sings, the word 'move' a shrill high C.

'I'm not going to pop my clogs yet, you know,' huffs Mabel.

He drops to his knees. 'My dear lady. That's not what I was implying at all. Now perhaps your delightful carer might be kind enough to push you into the concert room.'

'I've got my stick, thank you. I'm perfectly capable of walking on my own.'

'But a wheelchair would be quicker, don't you think? After all, we're ready to begin!'

Then he scoots off ahead of them.

As Belinda wheels her along the wide corridors, Mabel does her guided tour bit, out of habit. 'The panels in this part date back to the eighteenth century and the concert room has a very fine chandelier that was installed when Queen Victoria paid a visit. I remember being mesmerized by it when I first arrived here during the war.'

Belinda's surprise is evident in her voice. 'You knew Sunnyside back then?'

'I did indeed. It was called the Old Rectory then. My aunt, who used to own it, took me in after my mother and sister died in the Blitz.'

'I'm so sorry.'

'Thank you.' For a minute, Mabel's eyes mist with tears before she wills them away again.

'What was it like to move here? Was your aunt good to you?'

'Let's just say that she was more interested in her social life. She would have big dinner parties, even during the war. All kinds of people came – one or two were famous actors.'

'Really? How exciting! Who?'

Mabel hears her aunt's voice in her head. *'You mustn't tell anyone about the people you've seen here, Mabel. It might jeopardize our war work. Remember – walls have ears.'*

'I can't remember,' she says, crossing her fingers. But she can. In fact, she can remember all too much.

Sometimes she fears her memories might drive her mad. Maybe she's crazy already.

14

The nightmares seem to go on and on. Clarissa is running towards her, knife in hand. 'If you don't do what I say, I'll . . .'

'NO!' she screams, sitting up, rigid with terror.

The door bursts open. 'It's all right, Mabel. You've had another bad dream.'

Trembling, she sees it's the new carer again. With a flood of relief, she remembers that Clarissa is long gone. No one can hurt her now.

But she can't stop shaking.

'Would you like a cup of tea?'

'I'd rather have my Scotch.'

Belinda laughs. 'It's only just gone 7 a.m., Mabel! In fact, I thought I'd pop in before my shift starts, so I could check on you. You can't start drinking at this time of the day!'

'I've had a tot or two earlier than that, I can tell you. Not just for the nightmares but for the tedium in this place. One can die of boredom, you know. In fact, I probably would if it wasn't for my friend here.'

She raises her voice. 'Alexa, who gave you to me?'

'I'm right here. But also in the cloud. Amazing!'

Mabel shakes her head with a 'don't you know anything?' expression. 'It was Harry, my brother. Or half-brother, I should say. If he wasn't such a busy man, he would visit me more often. When he does, he takes me for drives along the coast.'

She looks out of the window wistfully. 'I wish I could get down there more often. My aunt used to own that small private beach you know, and now it's mine.'

'Really?'

'Don't you believe me?'

'Of course I do.'

But she says it as if humouring Mabel; treating her like some of the other residents who make up things, either deliberately or because their minds are going.

'Well', continues Belinda, 'we should get you dressed so we can get out for an early morning walk before breakfast. How about this pretty skirt? The colour matches your beautiful eyes.'

'*Brilliant blue like cornflowers – always twinkling*', her Antonio used to say. Mabel pushes the thought of him aside and turns back to Belinda.

'Hah! Flattery gets you everywhere.'

'I mean it. Now, shall we get going?'

As Belinda pushes her chair through the grounds, Mabel lets out a sigh of relief. 'It's so good to breathe in the fresh air,' she says dreamily. 'Sunnyside can feel like a prison sometimes.'

The chair wobbles as if Belinda has taken her hands off the handles. For a moment, Mabel feels herself tipping sideways.

'I'm so sorry,' Belinda says, righting it again. 'I didn't realize the path edge was uneven.'

'Well, please be careful.'

'Of course I will. How clumsy of me.' Then, as if to hide her embarrassment, she adds, 'Aren't those beech trees beautiful?'

'Yes,' replies Mabel, still a bit shaky from her near-tumble. 'I remember when they were half that height. In fact, I knew the young man who trimmed them during the war. He was an Italian prisoner of war, actually. They helped maintain the land for us.'

'Weren't you scared of them? Being out in the open like that?'

'No, they were all very nice.'

Then Mabel leans forward in her chair, her eyes sparkling like a child's. 'Look! We're getting closer to the sea! I can breathe it. Smell it. You know, it was one of the first things I noticed when I came here during the war.'

She reaches out for Belinda's hand, her voice full of emotion. 'Thank you for bringing me out here, even though your driving skills could do with a bit of a polish. Often the carers are too busy. In fact, sometimes I feel like I'm going mad in that bloody house.'

Belinda squeezes her hand back. 'I'm glad to see you looking happier, but I thought you loved the place. Your face lights up when you talk about the past: the chandelier; the trees being trimmed by Italian prisoners; your excitement about the sea.'

Mabel's voice quivers. 'I do love Sunnyside at times but at others it brings back bad memories.'

'Maybe that's what leads to your nightmares,' says Belinda kindly. She hesitates before continuing. 'I used to work in a place where people had been through some very difficult experiences. Going back to their childhoods always seemed cathartic. I'd be very happy to talk about those things with you, too.'

'I'm not sure.'

'Or I could help you write your life story! That's another thing I used to do when . . . when I was a volunteer.' Belinda's voice seems to rise with excitement. 'You could leave your memoir for your children or grandchildren.'

'I don't have any,' Mabel says shortly.

'Oh! I'm so sorry, I just assumed . . .'

Mabel sniffs. 'Not everyone has children, you know. Do you?'

'Two daughters.'

'And are you close?'

'We used to be but . . . well, things are a bit different now.'

Belinda's expression darkens, and Mabel can't help but think there might be more to this woman than meets the eye. How intriguing!

'Well, why don't you tell me a bit about your life too?' Mabel probes.

'It's pretty dull, really.'

'I'll bet it isn't.'

A flush crosses Belinda's face, confirming Mabel's suspicions.

This is far more interesting than any of Butlins Bill's games! It would certainly pass the time to find out more about the new carer. She seems different from the others, though Mabel can't pinpoint why.

'I tell you what,' says Mabel, 'How about we each tell the other a bit about our lives? No one needs to go into things that they don't want to, but it's a way to pass the time. It will make a nice change to talk to someone younger. How old are you, if you don't mind me asking? I know Butlins Bill said it was rude to ask but I like to be straight about such matters.'

'Sixty-four.' Belinda flushes as she speaks.

'Hah! You're a spring chicken. I'm going to be ninety-nine on July the 12th, the day of the summer barbecue.'

'Ninety-nine. Wow! You don't seem it. What's your secret?'

Mabel touches her cheeks. 'I never listen to the news because it's too upsetting. I try to get as much fresh air as I can, even though I need a wheelchair outside. And I make my own facemask from honey and oatmeal. I learned that tip in a woman's magazine back in the fifties.'

'That's amazing. You could put that in your story.'

'You start yours first,' Mabel says firmly.

'We have to promise that we won't tell anyone,' Belinda says, sounding nervous.

'Naturally.' As for her own past, Mabel tells herself, she'll share the 'small stuff', as they say nowadays, but the big secret she'll keep to herself. Wild horses won't drag that out of her. It's more than her life is worth.

She claps her hands. 'Let's go then!'

Mabel has a delicious feeling that Belinda, with a slightly haunted look on her face, has got her own secrets too. She can't wait.

15

And so, their stories began. They talked in Mabel's room; they talked during walks through the gardens; sometimes they even talked in low voices in the canary-yellow library, surrounded by shelves of Rosamunde Pilcher and Maeve Binchy.

At first, the pace was somewhat halting, each of them being slightly nervous but also determined not to reveal too much. Mabel described the horror of searching in the rubble for her mother and sister, followed by her new life with her aunt.

'You poor thing,' said Belinda. She was so taken aback that somehow she found herself describing the shock of Karen's phone call and the terrible events that had led to her pushing Gerald.

Mabel's eyes had widened. 'You should have explained it was an accident.'

'I did,' said Belinda, 'but my lawyer still said it was manslaughter.' Then she went rather pale. 'But, please, you mustn't tell anyone. Remember what we agreed?'

'Of course, I won't. But does the manager know you were in prison?'

'No.' Belinda went bright red. 'I contacted someone I knew inside who was a professional forger and she made me a fake DBS certificate.'

'What's that?'

'It says I don't have any criminal convictions amongst other things.'

Mabel shivered. What would the law say if her own crime was discovered? Was it possible to send a nearly ninety-nine-year-old to prison?

Belinda, meanwhile, cursed herself for telling her story so readily. Was it because of nerves or because she wasn't very good at telling lies? Now, if Mabel blabbed, Belinda would lose her job – something she needed for reasons that no one would understand.

'You don't have to worry, you know,' Mabel said, noticing the concern on her companion's face. 'I like you and I want you to stay. Besides, I own this place. They have to do what I want.'

'You *own* it?' gasped Belinda.

'I knew you didn't believe me when I told you about the private beach. My aunt left me the whole estate when she died.'

Oh my God, thought Belinda. *So I've just told the owner of Sunnyside that I'm a murderer and that I'm working here under false pretences.*

If Mabel did let the cat out of the bag, Belinda would have to claim that the old woman was rambling. How could she have been so stupid?

Yet somehow, as time went by, the more they talked, the more each trusted the other, feeling as though a burden was being lifted. It had been so hard to carry the weight of loss and wrongdoing over the years. The wonderful thing about sharing, as Mabel pointed out, was that if one of them betrayed the other's confidence, it would be easy to get revenge by doing the same. It guaranteed silence on both sides.

Each woman turned out to be a good listener, neither interrupting the flow but waiting until the other had finished, either through tiredness (usually on Mabel's part) or because Belinda was needed elsewhere. Sometimes when that happened, Mabel would put her foot down and remind the interrupter that she owned Sunnyside, and that if she wanted Belinda with her all the time, that was her right.

Belinda might not know it, but she would never hear the whole story. Mabel was determined to keep that final secret until – and beyond – her last breath.

PART TWO

The Stranger in Room Six

So, little old Mabel Marchmont... Who'd have thought it?

At five foot two inches, bright blue eyes, auburn hair and in possession of her full mental faculties despite being ninety-eight, she appears the picture of innocence. But now I'm onto her, she had better watch out.

My boss has got me looking for a special item that no one has seen for eighty years. 'I never knew such a thing existed,' I admitted when I was briefed. 'The Second World War was so long ago. Does this stuff even matter any more?'

'No questions,' they told me. 'Just do it. We know she has what we need, so get it out of her – whatever it takes.'

Well. How difficult can it be to make an old lady squeak?

16

Belinda

Mabel and I have been sharing stories for three days. But then she asks me the question I've been dreading most. The question that conjures up my very worst memories.

'Tell me,' Mabel asks, her eyes gleaming with curiosity, 'what were your first days like in jail?'

That's not difficult. I remember as if I was there yesterday.

Prison, I learn, is full of people who insist they shouldn't be there, like the angry woman who'd been banging on the partition next to mine on the drive here.

'I'm innocent!' she protests, as we're shoved into a communal cubicle and ordered to change into oversized coarse navy tracksuits. 'They said I stole money from my company, but I didn't! What are they accusing *you* of?'

'Manslaughter,' I mumble.

The woman moves away. 'You're kidding me.'

'I pushed my husband by accident,' I add hastily. 'He fell and died.'

A fearful look comes into her eyes, as if I might try to do the same to her.

'I'm not sharing with her,' my reluctant companion protests to the guard when we find ourselves being taken to the same small cell. 'That woman's a killer. She'll hurt me.'

'I won't,' I say swiftly. I want to add that I am normal. That until a few days ago, I'd been a wife who was making the most of a marriage that wasn't satisfactory but not, with hindsight, totally unsatisfactory either.

Instead, I crawl into my bunk, put the scratchy grey blanket over my head, fold my arms and rock from side to side, black fears and terrors coursing through my mind. Nothing is ever going to be the same after what I've done. Never.

Gerald is dead. One of my daughters hates me.

I try to make sense of things as I lie there, blocking out women's shouts from the cells around me. When did it all start to go so wrong for Gerald and me? When he started the affair, did he return from work as usual? How could he, after something as huge as that?

Now I look back, I can see the signs, such as when he'd sleep in the spare room so he could 'get some rest' for work. Was that just an excuse to ring Karen? To tell her how much he was missing her? These thoughts drill into my mind; my whole life cast in a different light.

Somehow, I must have drifted off because I wake suddenly to an electronic click as our cell door opens. Women are outside, jostling in the corridor.

'What's going on?' asks my cellmate.

A guard comes marching up. 'Join the bathroom queue, ladies, or you'll miss the boat. There'll be a bell for breakfast soon and if you're late, you'll get a strike.'

'You'll hit us?' Quickly, I step back.

'Not that kind of strike. A black mark. Three and you lose visiting privileges.'

Everyone else seems to have a sponge bag. 'Didn't your lawyer tell you to bring toiletries to prison before your hearing?' the guard asks.

I shake my head.

'You can order one, but it will take time. Now get a move on.'

The lukewarm shower water dribbles. Thoughts whirl round my head. How are the girls going to manage at home? Will the law allow them to live on their own?

My lawyer said he'd send me paperwork so that I could give the girls access to the joint account that Gerald set up for 'housekeeping'. Of course, we left everything to each other in our separate wills. But can a murderer's wife inherit from her victim?

I feel too sick to eat but force myself to swallow a piece of cold toast. A woman with a shaved head and flame tattoos down both sides of her neck sits opposite, watching my every move. 'You're new, aren't you?'

I nod.

'What are you in for?'

'They say I killed my husband.'

This woman doesn't seem shocked like my cellmate.

'And did you?'

'I didn't mean to.'

'Hah! Sure, you didn't. My name's Chris, by the way. Let me get you a cup of tea.'

Gratefully, I cup my hands around the chipped mug. My hands are still cold from the shower. I take a sip. The warmth is comforting. When I finish, Chris and the other women roll around, laughing.

'Liked your tampon tea, did you?' one sniggers.

Have I heard her right? 'What do you mean?'

'It's Chris's present. She does it to all the new girls. She carries a used tampon in her pocket and dips it in before giving it to you.'

They've got to be joking, haven't they?

'Did you do the same to me?' whispers my cellmate.

They grin and both of us retch.

'And don't think about telling the guards,' Chris hisses. 'There are more of us than you and, trust me, this is nothing compared to some of the things we can do. You'll see.'

17

I'm allowed one call but after that I have to wait for my prison phone card, which will let me ring two numbers provided they've been checked and approved by the authorities. This can take 'a few days or weeks'.

Scared that Gillian won't pick up, I ring Elspeth. 'Are you all right?' I ask in a hushed voice; I'm in the wing office with a pimply youth officer sitting at the desk, pretending not to listen.

I can hear my daughter sniffling at the other end and my chest goes into freefall because I have done this. I have caused this pain to her.

'We're OK, Mum, but what about you?'

'I'm . . . I'm fine. Have you told school?'

'Uncle Derek did. But everyone knew already, Mum.'

Of course they did. It will have raced round the school circuit like wildfire. It might even have been on the local news.

The officer looks at the wall clock meaningfully.

'Are you managing?' I say urgently. 'Are you doing your homework?'

'What do you think, Mum?' retorts Elspeth, her voice distressed and high-pitched in a way that doesn't sound like my kind, gentle, younger child.

I don't know what to think about anything. But I know I have to try. There is the practical side to start with. 'I've applied for you and Gillian to access our joint account, but it might take time.'

Elspeth cuts in. 'It's OK. Uncle Derek's been going

through some of Dad's paperwork and found an account with his and our names on it.'

'Really? Did it have mine?'

There's a short silence. 'No.'

I gasp. Had he thought that if I found out about his affair, I'd clean him out?

'Is there enough for you to live on?'

'I think so. There's £170,000.'

£170,000?

How had he put that much away? What exactly was he saving up for? Had he hoped that the girls would go with him when he moved in with this other woman?

'You'll need to know how to pay the bills . . . Keep the house going.' I falter as I say this. Why hadn't I insisted on being more involved with the financial side of our marriage? Gerald had always told me 'not to worry'.

'Uncle Derek's helping; don't worry, Mum. Do you need anything?'

I vaguely recall that I'm meant to fill in a form if I want to buy basic items like deodorant and a newspaper, but no one's given it to me yet.

'Yes. Toothpaste and a toothbrush please.'

Elspeth sounds shocked. 'Don't they give you any?'

'You have to wait for everything here.'

'Time's up,' says the guard.

'They're making me go now. I miss you, Elspeth, I'm so sorry for everything.'

'Oh Mum, I miss you too. I would say "happy birthday" but . . .'

I'd forgotten. I'm forty-nine years old today, which means that if I get ten years, I'll be nearly sixty by the time I finally get out of here. Tears prick my eyes. 'Please tell your sister I love her too.'

That's when another voice takes over. 'It's Gillian. I don't want your love. You're not my mother any more. Don't try to contact me; I'll never forgive you for killing Dad. Not ever.'

Then the phone goes dead.

I can't get Gillian's voice out of my head. My older daughter doesn't love me any more and it won't be long until she turns her sister against me too. My girls are my world. What's the point in carrying on?

I'm told I have to work in the kitchen. I'm not allowed to use anything sharp 'because you're on a bloody manslaughter charge' so I'm on washing-up duty, but there's no dishwasher and there aren't enough drying-up cloths. The food makes me hungry and sick at the same time.

My cellmate won't talk to me. When she's not on her work party (the umbrella name for the different jobs we have to do), she sits on her bed, weeping, with a photograph of a little boy in her hand.

'Is that your son?' I ask softly.

She clutches the photograph protectively to her chest. 'I don't want you going anywhere near him after what you've done.'

I have become a woman I don't recognize. I am a murderess.

More paperwork comes: Imran has requested permission to visit me. I tick the 'NO' box. Of course I want to see him, but what's the point? What future is there for either of us in this?

Then I receive a message to say that my sentencing date has been brought forward. Before long, I will know my fate.

18

The day of my sentence hearing arrives and I can't breathe. Until now I'd hoped that someone might somehow say that yes, of course I'd done wrong, but that it was a mistake.

This can't be happening, but it is.

Chris, who gave me the tampon tea, slaps me on the back as I am led down the corridor, past the officer's mess and through the double-locked doors of the wing. 'Good luck with the new place.'

I shrink into my skin. I don't want people like that to treat me as one of them. Not long ago I was a mother who had dinner ready at 7 p.m. We'd sit round the table, the four of us, discussing our day.

Now Gerald is dead, I am facing ten years and my children are essentially orphans. I have ruined everyone's lives in two or three mad seconds. It is inconceivable.

As I'm taken into court, I see that both girls are there. Their faces are white and disbelieving. Gerald's brother is there too. Derek was never close to my husband, but he has his arms around both of my daughters, as if in protection.

I close my eyes as the judge speaks.

'Belinda Wall, I am sentencing you to fifteen years . . .'

Fifteen?

The girls will be thirty-one and thirty-three then. They might be married. They might have children. I will have missed so much.

What have I done?

Gillian stares at me. She mouths the words 'I hate you'. Elspeth buries her head in her uncle's chest, weeping.

I want to scream, to cry. But my throat has closed up.

Numbly, I am led through a maze of passages to a van outside and taken to another prison. This one is four hours away, according to the driver. How are the girls going to get here to visit? Will they even want to visit? Not Gillian, certainly.

I go through the same entrance procedure as in the holding prison, wincing as someone puts their finger inside my back passage to check I'm not hiding drugs. I am photographed. I have to sign paperwork. I am told that the few possessions I came in with will be given to me when I am released in fifteen years' time.

Then I'm taken to my new cell.

There's a woman inside, sitting on the bottom bunk, with hair tied back in a scrawny ponytail, playing loud rap on her radio.

'Meet Shirley,' says the guard with exaggerated politeness, as if taking the mickey. 'Shirley, this is Belinda.'

After he slams the door on us, the woman takes out a toothbrush from under her mattress and starts to chew the end.

'How many prisons have you been in before?' she asks between chews.

'None,' I say, trying to shout over the music. 'Well, only the one after they arrested me.'

'And what are you in for?'

'I killed my husband.'

Shirley holds up her palm and makes to slam it into mine. 'Respect!'

Respect?

'There are a few of us here. I did the same. The bastard tried to throttle me.' Tears glint in her eyes. 'I had a three-year-old.

Look. Here's a picture.' She pulls a battered photograph out of her tracksuit pocket. A toothy toddler grins at me. 'No one in my family would have him so he was fostered and then adopted. Now I'll probably never see him again.'

That's awful. 'I'm sorry,' I blurt out lamely.

'It's why I chew on this thing. It helps keep me sane. But don't tell any of the guards or I'll have to throttle *you*.'

I make a nervous 'I'm sure you don't mean that' sound.

The woman's eyes harden. 'I'm not kidding either. Now listen to me. I'm going to be nice to you because I can tell you're one of the soft ones. So here are some of the rules. Don't piss anyone off or God knows what will happen. Someone might try and skin you.'

My throat tightens. 'What?'

'Boiling water and sugar – the oldest trick in the book. The sugar makes it stick to your skin so it all peels off, bit by bit.'

Did I just hear her right?

'Oh, and don't get in with any of the gangs. They're always falling out or making hooch and then you'll be in even more trouble.'

'What's hooch?' I ask.

'Don't you know nothing? It's the nearest we can get to alcohol. They make it out of fruit, sugar and bread. To be honest, half of the murderers are in here because they were high on booze or drugs.'

I think back to the couple of glasses of wine I'd have with Gerald. I silently vow never to drink again.

'So,' continues my mentor, 'keep your head down and you might get out early for good behaviour. What did you plead?'

'Guilty,' I falter.

She shakes her head. 'Bloody daft.'

Perhaps it was, but as my lawyer said, I had no choice. The evidence was too 'overpowering'.

At lunchtime – macaroni cheese, which I've always disliked – I find myself the centre of attention.

'I'd like to kill my old man, carrot-head,' says one, leaning across towards me, her mouth open as she chews. 'Got any tips?' She seems deadly serious.

I try to ignore her, keeping my eyes directed steadily down at my plate.

Finally, my phone card comes through. I go to ring the girls during social hours but only one phone is working so the queue snakes down the corridor.

Eventually it's my turn. A combination of hope and fear makes me try Gillian first. She puts down the phone as soon as she hears my voice. I try again. The same thing happens.

I ring Elspeth. It goes through to voicemail. Is she busy or does she not want to speak to me either?

'Get a move on,' snarls the woman behind me.

I walk away, glancing into the communal sitting room with its worn carpet and TV that only works when someone bashes it. My cellmate is there. She waves at me to join her but I shake my head.

I have nothing in common with those women.

But you do, says a voice inside me. *You're a criminal. Just like them.*

19

I have nightmares about Gerald conspiring with other inmates to beat me up. I'm so scared in the morning that I refuse to leave the cell, despite being given a second strike. Three, and I go to Solitary. I stop eating. I stop drinking. How can I live without my girls? Will they ever forgive me?

Solitary means a bleak single cell without a window, for twenty-four hours a day. A kindly prison officer entreats me to 'eat something, love'. I can't. The weight drops off me and they have to find me a smaller-sized tracksuit. Then I'm called into a room marked Visits.

'Elspeth,' I whisper, too weak to talk any louder.

She looks older. Strained. 'You're so thin, Mum,' she says, making to give me a cuddle.

'NO TOUCHING!' roars the guard.

'Gillian wouldn't let me come before. Uncle Derek said we should cut ourselves off. But I still love you, Mum.'

Tears stream down my cheeks. 'Thank you,' I sob. 'Tell me, what's it like at home?'

'We've had to leave the house,' she whispers. 'Journalists kept knocking on the door. They wanted to talk to us but we wouldn't, so we're staying at Uncle Derek's.'

My heart sinks. Will he turn my younger daughter against me too? I try to remember that it's better for them to be with their uncle than on their own.

'Uncle Derek is arranging the funeral.' Elspeth's eyes swim with tears. 'We had to wait until the autopsy was carried out.'

The funeral? How could I have forgotten that there'd be one? I could blame it on the shock of Gerald's death but, to be honest, it's more the shock of being in here.

'I don't know if they'll give me leave to go,' I say, remembering how the other day a woman in the dining room was cursing everything in sight because she'd been refused permission to go to her 'nan's wake'.

Elspeth looks down at the ground. 'Uncle Derek thinks it's best that you don't because of . . . the situation.'

Of course. Why would he want his brother's murderer turning up at his grave?

'He says it will encourage more journalists to be there.'

I'm trying to summon the courage to ask the question that has been hammering in my head since this all began. 'Have you heard from . . .' I finally blurt out.

I want to say Karen's name, but I can't bear to taste it in my mouth.

My daughter seems to understand. 'That woman? No.'

Then a guard comes in and says it's time for her to go.

'Will you come again?' I beg.

Elspeth nods. 'But please eat. They told me you're refusing food. I don't want to lose you too, Mum.'

So she still cares. Tears stream down my cheeks in gratitude. 'Are you able to concentrate at school?' I ask.

Another nod. Her eyes are wet.

'And what about your sister?'

'She's working hard too but she won't talk about you.'

I swallow the lump in my throat. 'We all have our own way of dealing with things.'

'I said, visiting time is over!'

Elspeth clutches my arm. 'Will you be all right, Mum?'

'NO TOUCHING!'

'I'm all right as long as you two are,' I choke, desperately trying not to cry for her sake. 'I'm sorry about your father. I really am.'

Tears are rolling down both our cheeks now. 'I know you are, Mum. I'll come again as soon as I can.'

A guard leads me away. I walk with my head turned so I can see Elspeth's face for as long as possible. I keep staring until her brown hair turns into a speck in the sea of visitors and she disappears altogether.

When I get back to my cell, I find people coming in and out. 'Get her away from here,' snaps a guard to the officer beside me.

'What's happened?'

'Your cellmate's only gone and topped herself.'

An ice-cold shiver goes through me.

I'm ushered away, but not before I spot the pool of blood on the floor.

They take me to the guards' office at the end of the wing, where I'm told to sit down. The door is shut.

'Did your cellmate seem suicidal to you?' says the woman opposite me.

'No,' I whisper.

'What about the toothbrush?'

'The one she kept chewing?'

'So, you knew about it. Did you never think to tell anyone?'

'Why would I?'

'Because she chewed it down to a sharp point and then stabbed her own artery.'

I'm stunned into silence. How had I not known? '*It helps to calm my nerves,*' she'd told me. And, naive as I was, I'd believed her.

'Couldn't cope with the shame of embezzling funds from her boss,' the officer continued. 'One of the big papers was about to run a piece on her.'

'But she said she'd murdered her husband because he'd tried to throttle her.'

'Rubbish. Our Shirley was a big-time fraudster. Thousands, she got away with.'

'Perhaps,' I say, finding my voice becoming stronger, 'she killed herself because she couldn't live without her three-year-old.'

'Told you that one too, did she? There was no three-year-old. She just had a random photograph to get sympathy. A bit of a fantasist, you could say.'

I gasp. 'So she lied?'

'Takes one to know one,' says the officer chillingly. 'Come on. All that stuff about you pushing your old man by accident. You *wanted* him dead didn't you, Lady Belinda?'

20

It doesn't take long for 'Lady Belinda' to catch on. One of the guards clearly took against my 'posh accent', and now everyone uses it.

I try to ignore it but it rankles. My mother had always taught me to speak the 'Queen's English'. There had been no preparation at all for a life of crime. I count my blessings that she isn't here to see this.

As the days pass, I begin to wish I'd pleaded not guilty.

'You got bad advice,' says my new cellmate when I am naive enough to share this with her. 'Your lawyer should have said there were extenuating circumstances.'

She says the phrase with such fluidity and certainty that it's clear she's familiar with it. Word has it that this woman, with her steely eyes, is part of a much-feared family gang. This is her third time – or is it the fourth? – in jail. Opinion differs. People tiptoe around her. No one wants to get on the wrong side.

I might not have known my previous cellmate very well, but the horror of her death haunts my every waking hour. At night, she adds to my nightmares about Gerald.

'Shut up, for Christ's sake,' my cellmate complains when I wake screaming from a dream where my husband is bleeding to death on the pavement after slashing his wrists with a toothbrush. 'How am I meant to get any sleep?'

Rather surprisingly, I learn that she has a daughter, younger than Elspeth, who is expecting a child. 'I need to be with them,' she says. 'They'll need my help and protection.'

'Protection against what?' I ask.

She looks at me as if I've asked a daft question. 'From gangs or the authorities. You can't trust anyone in this life, Lady Belinda.'

What kind of world have I entered? Karen has ruined my life. She's ruined all our lives. And now she's disappeared off the face of the earth.

I feel so angry that, if she was here, I'd kill her.

'Stop it,' I say to myself. 'You're not like that.'

But the more I think about it, the more the idea takes hold. Karen needs to pay for destroying our family.

Imran has applied to visit several times now, and each time I tick the 'NO' box, with a heavy heart.

Then a letter arrives:

Please allow me to visit you. I expect you're ashamed of what you did but I am also certain – because I do still know you Belinda, even after all these years – that you didn't mean to hurt your husband.

How can he say that he knows me? It's been so long, and yet I suppose there was a time when he knew me better than anyone in the world. I think back to walks, hand in hand along the river in Oxford, his arm around me. I am leaning into his jacket, sheltering from the wind. I feel safe. Loved.

But I know now how dangerous a letter can be. If I hadn't been stupid enough to keep his first one, Gillian might not hate me as much as she does. I tear up the page, angry at myself.

Then I receive another visitor request. It comes through internal mail. This is different from post delivered from the outside, which is handed out every morning. You can tell who hasn't received anything from their dropped faces and the way they slink back down the corridor, in contrast to the ones who open their envelopes with a mixture of 'Bloody hell' and 'Yes!' at the news inside.

I look at the name on the *Request to Visit Prisoner* form. It says P. Black. I don't know anyone of that name. Supposing it's someone from the press who wants to berate me for what I've done? But then again, what if it's genuinely important? Against my instinct, I tick the 'YES' box.

For the next week, I shake and shiver, unsure if I'm ill or whether it's nerves.

When I go into the visitors' room, my mouth is dry with apprehension. Then I take in the petite woman with the smart, pointed lime-green shoes.

A shock of recognition shoots through me. This is the receptionist from Gerald's office, Penny. The woman I met minutes before pushing my husband to his death.

My visitor is visibly trembling. 'I've never been in a prison before,' she wobbles, looking around as though someone is going to attack her. 'But I had to come. I felt you should know the truth about your husband and Karen. Did you know they had a child?'

21

Mabel

1941

In Devon, each day seemed to blur into the next. Mabel would wake with a sense of peace, the sunlight streaming in through the tall diamond-shaped windowpanes.

Then the truth would gradually dawn. Mama and Annabel were missing. If she was honest with herself, they were probably dead. Papa was away fighting, and any minute now Mr Hitler might march up the beach towards the Old Rectory and they'd be murdered in their beds.

Or at least that's what the women talked about when they gathered at the village hall for camouflage netting afternoons or tended the allotments so they could 'dig for victory'.

Mabel had this vision of digging and digging until she found a Jerry underground whom she could knock on the head with her shovel. She'd never hurt anyone before in her life, but when she thought of Mama and her baby sister, she felt she could quite easily kill a German without any regret at all.

Throughout all this, Aunt Clarissa and the Colonel would hold long meetings late at night in the library, working out how they could 'get England back on its feet'.

Mabel knew this because, each night, she'd try listening at the door, thinking that if only she could help them too, then perhaps Aunt Clarissa wouldn't dislike her so much.

One evening, the door flew open. Aunt Clarissa was on the other side wearing a pale blue evening gown as if dressed up for a party. She was with a group of people that Mabel had never seen before – certainly no one she recognized from the village. They eyed her coldly, as if she shouldn't be there. 'What do you want, child?'

'I'd like to know if I can help you beat Mr Hitler,' said Mabel staunchly.

Aunt Clarissa's eyes hardened. 'What have you heard?'

Mabel felt her own voice waver. 'Only that you are working out how to get England back on its feet and destroy the enemy for ever.'

'Good girl,' said a deep voice from behind her aunt. It was the Colonel. 'Don't worry, Mabel. We'll let you know if you can lend a hand when the time comes. Now meanwhile, I'm afraid this meeting is private. Why don't you go out and check that Foam is settled for the night?'

Foam was an old carthorse who, to Mabel's delight, had been in the stables when she arrived. 'She's a safe ride,' said the rosy-cheeked elderly groom. 'I remember your mother riding her at your age, although your aunt wasn't so keen.'

A lump came into Mabel's throat. The thought of Mama having ridden the same horse made it feel all the more special.

Meanwhile, Mabel couldn't help wondering why Aunt Clarissa had never married. In the past, when she'd asked her parents why this was so, they'd gone quiet for a bit and then said she'd never found the right person. Maybe she'd found the right person now, Mabel told herself. On more than one occasion since her arrival, she'd noticed the Colonel's hand brush her aunt's.

The following morning, her aunt informed Mabel that they were expecting more company that evening. 'We don't want any disturbances. You're to have an early supper and bedtime.'

How disappointing! When her parents used to have dinner guests, she would be allowed to meet them in the drawing room in her best dress and with her hair plaited by Lizzie. 'What a charming girl,' the guests would coo. Her parents would beam down at her approvingly, and Mabel would feel warm and loved and safe.

'No, you certainly can't join us,' snapped Aunt Clarissa when Mabel expressed this wish. 'In fact, if I see you up and about, I will send you back to London immediately. Bombs or no bombs.'

'Now, now, Clarissa.' The Colonel turned back to Mabel. 'Your aunt doesn't mean it,' he said kindly. 'She just gets a bit agitated before people visit. In fact, it's really rather exciting to have a crowd. Just like the old days!'

Mabel recounted all of this to Frannie. The two girls had become fast friends, and were now up on the cliffs, looking out for U-boats. Everyone in town was terrified the Germans might invade by sea.

'What kind of visitors?' Frannie asked, intrigued.

'According to Cook, they're a mixture of wealthy farmers and people with titles. Rumour has it that there's even an actor,' said Mabel conspiratorially.

Her friend frowned. 'It's not right. We're meant to scrimp and save during wartime.'

Then, as they reached the cliff edge, she pulled some bracken across and revealed a gaping hole. 'Look!'

'A tunnel!' gasped Mabel. 'Where does it go?'

'Down to the main beach. Me dad and uncles have been digging it for ages, but it's nearly finished now. If the Germans land, the women and children can escape to safety on the fishing boats.'

'Can your mother sail?'

'She can row,' said Frannie staunchly. 'We all can. Course, I'm going to stay and fight them with my bare hands.'

'But you're a girl!'

'So what?'

It was another world. To think that not so long ago she and Mama and Papa and Annabel would spend their weekends walking along the river or in Hyde Park. And now she was here and they were gone.

'If my mother had gone into that shelter with me, she would still be alive,' she said in a small voice. 'And so would my sister.'

'So, you've accepted they've passed then,' said Frannie gently.

'I suppose so,' sniffed Mabel. 'Mama would have come and found me by now if she'd survived.'

Suddenly, she felt a pair of arms around her. Then Frannie stepped away, flushing. 'My mam says you're very welcome to come round for a cup of tea and scone one afternoon. But don't tell your aunt. She won't appreciate you coming to a humble place like ours.'

'I'd love to,' said Mabel, dabbing her eyes with a handkerchief. 'Thank you.'

That night, Mabel had an early supper and washdown at the sink – baths were restricted to once a week to save on gas. Then she spent the evening with her nose pressed against her bedroom window waiting for the guests.

By 10 p.m., she'd given up and gone to bed.

In the morning, her aunt's face was even more pinched than usual.

'Did your guests enjoy the dinner party?' asked Mabel politely.

Clarissa's lips pursed. 'That's none of your business.'

But when she marched out, leaving Mabel alone in the breakfast room, Cook got very cross. 'No one came! If you ask me, it's because of the petrol rationing. All that food wasted! It's a crying shame. The missus wanted me to bury it in the allotment instead of giving it away but that's because she doesn't want folk knowing she's entertaining when others are going hungry. It's all right for her lot. They don't know what an empty stomach's like.'

'I'll take it home,' Frannie said eagerly when Mabel told her.

'Let me help,' offered Mabel.

'You can bring it when you come for tea. Mam says to come this afternoon.'

When she got there, she found a cottage which was small in size but bursting with warmth. 'These are my brothers, and this is Grace, who's just turned four.' A pretty little girl with long hair ran up and danced around her. If Annabel had lived, she might have grown up into a lovely child like this. The thought brought a lump to Mabel's throat.

'It's so nice to be here,' she said to Frannie's mother.

'Ah, thank you. You're welcome any time. And you've brought a whole hock of ham! How very kind.'

Frannie's father was a large man who relied heavily on his stick, having been injured in the Great War. He sat in a big chair with an antimacassar on the back. They'd had them in London too. Mama had told her they were to soak up the men's hair oil.

Now, he sat forward in interest. 'Frannie told me what you said about your aunt's important visitors. Sounds like they were coming a long way. Did anyone mention a name or say if they were coming again?'

'No, I don't think so.'

'Ah, that's a pity.'

'Why's that?' Mabel asked.

'Just because then we can have more food if there's any spare,' said Frannie's mother quickly.

'I'll let you know if I hear anything.'

'Thanks love.'

It gave Mabel a nice feeling to know she was doing some good. That's what the war was all about, wasn't it? Those who couldn't fight were at least able to help in the war effort at home.

The following week, Mabel overheard Cook ranting to the groom in the courtyard.

'Another dinner party when the rest of us are rationing! She says it's for the one who was meant to come last time, that friend of the Colonel's. A real lord, apparently,' Cook sniffed.

Mabel flew down to Frannie's cottage. Her friend – or 'the maid', as Aunt Clarissa kept saying she had to call her – hadn't come into work that day because of a cold. But this news couldn't wait!

Excitedly, she banged the front door knocker. Frannie's mother opened it, wearing her apron.

'Aunt Clarissa's got a lord arriving tonight so there might be some spare food tomorrow!'

'Is that right?' said Frannie's mother. 'Thank you for telling us. I'm afraid you can't see Frannie. She's asleep. Poor lamb has got a nasty fever.'

Mabel was beginning to feel rather warm herself. That night, she woke feeling hot and bothered, after a dreadful nightmare in which there'd been lots of shouting. Then she realized there really *was* shouting downstairs. What was happening?

Shivering, she went to the top of the bannisters. Down below she saw a tall man she'd never seen before, being marched to the door, hands tied behind his back with rope. 'Please,' he called out. 'Help me, someone!'

'You've made a mistake,' shouted the Colonel, running after them. There was a panic in his voice that she'd never heard before.

'I hope for your sake you're right, sir,' said the policeman. 'You can clear it all up at the station.'

Aunt Clarissa was weeping, her hands over her face. After they left, Mabel flew down the stairs to comfort her.

'What are you doing here?' snapped Clarissa. 'I don't know what you heard but they've made a mistake.' Then her eyes widened. 'I need to tidy up the dining room.'

There were papers all over the table. 'Don't touch them!' she roared at Mabel. 'Just leave.'

On her way out, something glinted on the floor. Picking it up, Mabel saw it was a small red-and-black badge with a square design of interlocking lines.

'Do you want –'

'I said, get out,' yelled her aunt. Mabel ran back to her room. She would, she told herself, put the badge somewhere safe and give it to her aunt when she calmed down.

If only she'd handed it over immediately, life might have been very different.

22

At sunrise, when she couldn't sleep, Mabel tiptoed down the stairs and found Aunt Clarissa sitting in the drawing room overlooking the gravel drive.

'Has the Colonel come back yet?' asked Mabel.

Her aunt jumped. 'Goodness me, child. You scared me out of my wits. Go back to bed. I need some peace.'

'But has the Colonel . . .'

'I said, go back to bed. Didn't you hear me?'

Please may he be all right. Although he could be brusque when he wanted to, the Colonel was generally very kind to her. More so than her aunt, at least.

Mabel headed for the library to find a new book. Stories always helped her fall back to sleep, especially when she had nightmares of the Blitz. Suddenly, she heard the front door opening and voices in the hall. One was the Colonel's. Her heart lifted with relief.

'Jonty!' sounded her aunt's voice. 'Thank God you're back. What happened? What did they ask you?'

'Shhh, not here.'

'In the drawing room, then.' A door slammed and it fell quiet.

Later, when it was time for lunch, Mabel found her aunt looking much brighter. The Colonel, however, gave her a hard glare.

'If you wish to know something,' her father had advised, 'ask someone in a courteous manner.'

So she did.

'Why did the policeman take you away, Colonel?'

He continued chewing slowly, staring at her with cold grey eyes, before visibly swallowing. Then he leaned forward across the table so his gaze was locked with hers. 'It was just a misunderstanding,' he said coolly.

'Was it a misunderstanding about your friend too?'

'It was, actually, although he's rather upset about losing a small badge he was wearing. Have you seen it?'

Mabel was about to say 'yes' but then froze. What if they thought she'd stolen it? Would they believe her if she explained she'd wanted to hand it over but Clarissa had told her to leave?

'No,' she said instead, trembling inside.

The Colonel was giving her a hard stare. 'I didn't think so. Otherwise, I am sure you would have told us, wouldn't you?'

'Yes,' she managed to say. Then she ran up to her bedroom to find a safe hiding place for the badge. Somewhere no one would find it.

After lunch, when Mabel went out into the garden to gather flowers for her nature school notebook, she became aware of the Colonel behind her.

'Thank you for comforting your aunt when I was called away,' he said, his tone friendlier than before.

'I tried,' stuttered Mabel, turning to face him, 'but she wanted to be on her own.'

'Ah, that's because she was upset.' His eyes were fixed on hers again, making her feel extremely uneasy. 'You wouldn't want to do anything to upset your aunt, would you?'

'Of course not.'

'Because you're an orphan now – or as good as. And do you know what happens to orphans during the war?'

'No,' she said in a small voice.

'I'll tell you. They get given away to people who don't want them and don't look after them.'

How could a person be so nice one minute and so terrifying the next?

'Why are you angry with me?' she asked quietly.

His face softened again. 'I'm just reminding you of some facts. But I would like to know one thing. Did you tell the police we were expecting a guest for dinner?'

'No.'

'Then it must have been Cook.' He frowned. 'We can't afford any security breaches. She will have to be let go.'

Mabel couldn't be responsible for that! 'I might,' she stammered, 'have mentioned it to Frannie.'

'Our little maid?'

Our? The Colonel spoke as if he employed her too.

'We thought there might be some food going spare, you see,' she babbled. 'Like last time when I took it down to her family.'

'Last time?'

Mabel's mouth went dry. 'I gave them some leftovers to save waste like the posters say. I explained that some important guests of yours hadn't turned up.'

Something cleared in the Colonel's face.

'I see.' He patted her on the shoulder. 'That was very thoughtful. And you're right, we mustn't waste anything in this war. Not food. Or lives, unless it's absolutely necessary. Good. I think we've cleared up a few misunderstandings now.'

'Wait, please.' Mabel caught him by the cuff of his jacket. He looked down at her hand, surprised. Embarrassed she took it away.

'You said just now I was an orphan, "or as good as". But Papa is still alive.'

'Actually, he was shot down over Norway a week ago. He might have bailed out, but we don't know. Didn't your aunt tell you?'

'No.' Mabel put her hand to her mouth to stem the scream of horror and shock inside. 'No, she didn't.'

'Maybe she was protecting you.' The words sounded kind, but his voice had a hard edge to it. 'We will have to hope that your father has been taken to a prisoner-of-war camp, rather than . . .'

He stopped.

'Rather than what?'

'Well, there are stories of soldiers being shot on the spot: especially high-ranking ones like your papa.'

'Shot on the spot?' she repeated, stunned.

He patted her on the shoulder again. 'It's a mad world at the moment, Mabel. But you have your aunt and me. Just as long as you behave yourself, of course.'

Mabel sobbed all night. There was only one person who would understand and that was Frannie, but she hadn't been at work for two days now. Perhaps Mabel would cycle down in the morning and check she was all right.

The cottage door was ajar. There was no answer when she knocked so she just went in.

Frannie's mother was sitting in a rocking chair, staring out of the window at the sea.

Mabel had a sinking feeling that something awful had happened. 'Are you all right?' she asked softly.

She shook her head. 'Last night,' she whispered, 'my husband went out to get firewood and someone shot him dead.'

Mabel felt a cold shock flash through her. 'Who?'

'The police reckon it was a poacher.'

There was a noise as a pale figure came out of the bedroom that Frannie shared with her six brothers and sister.

'My dad's gone just like your mum,' she said in tears. Together they held each other, rocking back and forth in grief.

Later that evening, enemy planes flew overhead. 'They're bombing Exeter again,' said her aunt, standing at the window.

'For gawd's sake get under the table, madam,' yelled Cook, pulling Mabel under with her. 'There isn't time to get to the shelter.'

'I want to watch,' retorted her aunt tightly.

Despite the danger, Mabel crawled out from under the table and put her arm around her aunt in comfort. 'It will be all right,' she said.

Her aunt didn't stiffen the way she usually did when Mabel tried to show affection. 'Thank you, dear,' she said. 'Do you know, I actually think you're correct. With everyone's help, the better side will win.'

23

Mabel tried to comfort Frannie just as her friend had comforted her when she'd first arrived.

Yet, while Frannie's father was dead, there was still a chance that Mabel's papa could be alive. Mabel kept hugging this hope close to her heart, constantly asking God to make sure he was safe and promising him all kinds of things if he listened to her pleas. Always being polite to Aunt Clarissa; doing extra sums; folding her clothes more neatly at night. Yet at the same time, she felt so guilty because for Frannie, there was no hope.

At least the Colonel had organized for a tractor load of wood to be delivered to them so the fire didn't go low.

'It is very good of him,' Frannie said dully. She had lost the sparkle in her voice. She didn't even want to go swimming any more.

Mabel tried to throw herself into the war work. Before rationing made it difficult, Mama had taught her to bake cakes. Here, people had their own cows, so butter and milk were in plentiful supply. 'Your cakes are delicious,' the other women told her when she brought them down for a tea break during the camouflage netting sessions. 'Your mum would be proud of you.' Their praise made her feel both warm and sad.

Autumn was here, with blackberries bursting out on hedgerows. Mabel tried to coax Frannie into picking them with the other children after school, which her friend did, but without talking.

Mabel was beginning to enjoy the company of the other children more and more, though they were all so much better at arithmetic than she was. The teacher suggested that her aunt help her, but in truth, they both grappled with what Clarissa called 'the complex mysteries of the times tables'. The eight and nine times were definitely their least favourite.

Mabel preferred to write what her aunt called 'essays' but which she saw as stories. One day she wrote about a little girl who woke up to find that her sister had disappeared.

'Are you thinking about Annabel?' asked her aunt with a softness she usually reserved for the Colonel.

Mabel nodded.

'She's not coming back, I'm afraid,' said her aunt quietly. 'And nor is my sister.'

In the past, Clarissa had always said 'your mother'. Never 'my sister'.

'I know that now,' whispered Mabel. 'But Papa might.'

A tear ran down her aunt's face. 'Give me a minute will you, child?'

Mabel sought comfort in the kitchen with Cook. 'We've got some pheasants left over from yesterday. Why don't you take them down to Frannie's mother this afternoon? They were from the Colonel's shoot but I don't reckon he'll notice.'

Ugh! Holding them away from her, she made her way through the woods, past the cottage which Frannie had pointed out as the lacemaker's home. Her friend's words came back to her. '*She can tell people's futures.*' Was that her, digging up potatoes in the garden outside?

'I can see you're not enjoying that very much,' the woman said, looking up from her task and nodding at the birds in Mabel's hands. 'You're the girl from the big house, aren't you? My goodness, you look just like your mother did at your age.'

A thrill shot through her. Any connection to her darling mama was so precious now she was gone. 'Pleased to meet you,' Mabel said. 'I didn't know you knew my mother.'

'Well, she and her sister weren't allowed to mix with the likes of us, but I remember how kind and gentle she was. Your aunt was always very different from your mother, God rest her soul.'

As she spoke, the sky darkened and huge drops of rain began to fall.

'Come into the cottage with me. You can shelter from this storm and I'll put on the kettle for a cup of tea.'

Remembering Frannie's words ('*We're all a bit scared of her*') Mabel was about to make up an excuse. But the rain was so heavy that it was stinging her face. 'Thank you,' she found herself saying.

The lacemaker settled her down into a small but comfortable chair by the fire. Scattered round the room were several spools of lace. Mabel wanted to touch them but was conscious of her stained hands. 'You can wash them in the sink,' said her hostess, as if reading her mind.

She gave Mabel a large bar of carbolic soap. Mabel scrubbed and scrubbed but the pheasant blood wouldn't come out.

'Let me help.' As she turned Mabel's left hand over, she began tracing the lines on her palm and then gave a small gasp.

'What is it?' asked Mabel.

'Goodness me. You're going to have an extraordinary life,' she whispered.

Mabel felt as if the hairs on her arms were standing on end. 'How can you tell?'

The lacemaker's face was so close that she could smell her breath. It reminded her of cinnamon.

'You see this line here? It's very long. That means you're going to reach a good age. But challenges will come for you along the way. You will get through them, though you may doubt it at the time. Then, towards the end of your life, you'll . . .'

She stopped. Her face went pale.

'I'll what?' asked Mabel.

The lacemaker dropped her hand suddenly as if it was scalding her. 'It doesn't matter,' she said with a tremor in her voice.

'Please. Tell me.'

The woman's eyes bore into hers. 'I can't, Mabel. However, I will give you one piece of advice. You must learn what to say and what not to say. It could save your life.'

Mabel found something soft being pressed into her hand.

'Keep it and you will have peace one day. The rain's stopped now – you should go.' The lacemaker almost pushed her out of the door, the promise of tea forgotten.

Mabel ran without stopping to Frannie's cottage, the pheasants in one hand and the gift clenched tightly in the other. Just before knocking, she opened her left hand to find a beautiful piece of cream lace, which she put carefully into her pocket.

'Thank you, love,' said Frannie's mother when she gave her the birds.

'It's not from me, it's from Cook. The Colonel shot them, but we didn't think he'd miss them.'

She stiffened. 'I see.' Then she looked worriedly at Mabel. 'You're very flushed. Are you all right?'

'Yes, thank you,' lied Mabel, deciding not to talk about her experience on the way. 'How are you?'

'We must soldier on,' Frannie's mother said, gesturing at her knitting. Like many of the women in the village, she was making scarves and mittens for the brave boys on the front. 'It's what my husband would have wanted.'

A pair of heavy boots sounded at the door. It was one of Frannie's brothers.

His eyes flew straight to the brace of pheasants. 'Where did they come from?'

Frannie's mother's voice quivered. 'The Colonel and Lady Clarissa.'

'Did they indeed?' His brows knitted with anger. 'Then there's only one place for them.'

Whipping the pheasants from his mother's hands, he threw them out the back door. 'We can't have anything to do with that man.'

'Stop.' Frannie's mother's voice sounded angry in a way Mabel had never heard. 'Do you want to bring harm on everyone in this family?'

She turned to Mabel with a pleading look on her face. 'Please don't tell the Colonel or your aunt any of this.'

'I won't,' stammered Mabel. Then she remembered the lacemaker's words. *You must learn what to say and what not to say. It could save your life.*

Shaking, she walked back home. There were voices coming from the library. 'The date has been set,' the Colonel was saying excitedly. 'I've told the others. The time is coming, Clarissa!'

A date? Perhaps they were getting married. Before, she would have been excited, but Frannie's brother's angry words and his mother's look of fear made Mabel wonder if there was more to the Colonel than met the eye. If she was honest with herself, there was something about him that she had never trusted.

24

Now

'So, what happened to the Colonel and your aunt?' asks Belinda, topping up the old lady's china tea cup – part of a set that Mabel keeps hidden away in her room.

'That's for next time!' replies Mabel, pretending to sound cheerful. In truth, she is shaken by the memories, including the lacemaker's advice. Has she said too much already?

'It sounds as though you were scared of stepping out of line.'

'Yes,' says Mabel. 'I was.'

'I know how that feels.'

'You do?'

Each woman finds herself reaching for the other's hand.

'Pour me a drop of whisky, would you?' asks Mabel.

By now, both have stopped pretending it's flavoured water.

'And have a dram yourself while you're at it.'

Belinda shakes her head. 'No, thanks. I met so many women in prison who'd committed terrible crimes just because they were drunk or on drugs. I vowed never to drink again.'

Mabel raises her eyebrows, which she pencils in softly every day: a trick learned from her aunt years ago. 'What an amazing life you've lived, my dear.'

'You too,' says Belinda. She looks pensive for a moment.

'There are so many lessons to be learned, aren't there? That's why it's important for stories like ours to be told.'

Mabel leans forwards so her face is just inches from Belinda's. 'It's your turn again now. I want to know about that woman with green shoes. Was she causing mischief? Or did your husband really have a child with Karen?'

The Stranger in Room Six

A text pings through at midnight.

> The top boss is getting twitchy. This isn't just your head on the line, it's mine too. So find something, or else.

I toss and turn all night with worry until, the next morning, I hear a voice outside my door. A hoity-toity tone that can only belong to one person: Mabel Marchmont.

She's telling someone how she's decided to go to the afternoon concert 'even though I don't usually care for them'.

Bingo! I've been waiting for the old crone to leave her room so I can go snooping. It's got to be there somewhere, hasn't it?

None of the residents' rooms lock, in case there's an emergency and the carers need access. In theory, anyone could break in and go through your things, which is awkward if, like me, you possess a gun. So, when I quietly leave Room Six, I take my Colt 45 with me.

Mabel is clearly very tidy, I have to say. Her clothes are neatly hung. There's no paperwork, no bundle of letters, no mementoes. No photographs, even. Nothing that gives any kind of clue about Mabel's past, apart from a creepy old doll that must have been made years ago. It sits on a chair, staring at me glassily. Gives me the fucking freaks.

I'm rummaging through a drawer when the door swings open.

'What are you doing in here?' asks the carer at the door.

'What do you mean? This is my room.' I reply boldly. If there's one thing you learn in this business, it's to think fast.

'This is Miss Marchmont's room. You must have got lost.'

I put on my frail voice. 'Oh dear. Really? I seem to be getting more and more confused.'

'That's all right, love. Let me help you back.'

'Thank you,' I say. *When we reach my door, I insist that I'll be fine on my own. I hide my gun under a floorboard I've managed to loosen, then sink down onto my bed and heave a sigh of relief.*

My phone pings again. This time it's a voice message, robotic as if it's been funnelled through some AI system.

'This is a firm deadline. If you don't find that list by July 12, expect to be replaced.'

July the 12th is the barbecue they've all been going on about here. Why then?

But it's the final word of the message that freaks me out. Replaced. We all know what that means in this business: missing without trace.

I've got to find those bloody names. No matter who gets in my way.

25

Belinda

We're sitting in the visitors' room, reunions exploding all around us. One couple is yelling at each other. 'You promised you'd stay straight this time,' says the man.

The toddler on the mother's knee bursts into tears. 'Now look what you've done,' snaps the woman.

'That's right. Blame me as usual.'

Another couple try to hold hands until a guard shouts, 'No touching!'

I just sit, stunned into silence.

'My husband and Karen had a child?' I ask, just to confirm I'd heard this correctly.

She nods.

Then I laugh. 'You're lying; you must be.'

Penny casts a scared look around the visiting hall, ringing with children's yells and guards barking. 'It's true,' she says. 'That's why I called you just before your husband died.'

'That was you?' I gasp.

'Karen asked me to, in the hope that it might bring things to a head and push Gerald into leaving you. I was meant to tell you about their child too, but I got scared when you said you were going to report me and I rang off.' She shakes her head. 'I'm sorry it turned into such a tragedy. I never meant this to happen.'

I'm numb, trying to take this all in. A child? An affair was bad enough but this . . .

'How did they meet?' I whisper.

Penny looks guilty. 'She was a friend who needed some accountancy advice. So I asked Gerald if he'd see her and then he took her on as a client. It was clear from the start that there was an attraction between them.'

A shiver goes through me. 'Really?' I falter.

'I'm afraid so.' She shrugged as though this was inevitable. 'It was like watching sparks fly. Then two years later, Karen got pregnant and had a little boy. He's three now.'

Three? My husband had a child three years ago and managed to keep it secret?

Then I recall the many 'conferences' Gerald had gone to over the years. Had they been excuses for seeing her overnight; for being there when their son was born? Had he sat by her side in the delivery room, urging her on as he'd done when I'd had the girls? *'You're doing so well, Belinda. Keep going!'* Had he stayed on afterwards to help her in those early days?

'He kept telling Karen that he loved her,' adds my visitor, 'but wanted to wait until your girls had grown up before he left.'

I can barely speak. 'I didn't suspect any of this.'

'I guessed that, from your voice on the phone. Karen and I always assumed that you knew but were turning a blind eye. I wish now that I'd never rung.'

So do I. Gerald wouldn't have died. We could have limped on as a not-very-happy-but-not-very-unhappy couple. I feel my hands clench into fists under the table between us.

'What's her surname and where is she now?' I growl.

'It's Greaves,' she says shakily 'but I have no idea where she is. After I heard Gerald died, I called her mobile but it rang unobtainable and I was really worried. So I went round, only to find that she'd moved out, still owing rent. I was hurt, to be honest. I'd have thought she'd have told me if she was going somewhere, especially after all the support I'd given her. I even let the three of them stay in my house one weekend so they could have some time together. You and the children were in the Scilly Isles.'

I feel sick to my stomach. Gerald had left us there unexpectedly, saying he needed to get back to work early. Then anger takes over.

'Just wait until I find her,' I hiss.

Even I am shocked by the threat in my voice, but to her credit Penny sounds almost sympathetic, as well she might, given her part in all this. 'I know, I understand that.'

She glances, clearly scared, at the angry faces, the crying faces, the tension, small children yelling. 'But you're in prison. How are you going to find her, and what would you even do if you did?'

There's no way I'm going to share my dark thoughts with this woman. In truth, I haven't decided what I would do. I'm still trying to understand the man with whom I'd shared nearly twenty-five years of married life.

How could Gerald have had an affair, knowing it might break up our family? He wouldn't have made the first move, I know that. It must have been her. She probably saw a well-off man and imagined a life where she didn't have to work any more.

I'd never understood before why some wives – including my mother – silently put up with their husbands' affairs without saying anything. But now I've seen the damage it can do, I'm beginning to get it.

'If you hadn't interfered, I might not have known about them,' I blurt out.

'But wouldn't you *rather* know?'

'No,' I snap. 'Then my husband would still be alive! You need to go, now. Get out of here or I'll have to get a guard to make you leave.'

26

'What's up with you?' asks a guard when she watches me folding the sheets the next day, deep in thought about Penny's question. How *am* I going to find her?

'If you don't get a move on,' continues the guard, 'I'll give you a strike. Think you're too posh to be working, do you?'

Someone titters. 'Look at Lady Belinda with all her airs and graces.'

'Don't take any notice of them,' says a woman with a ring in her nose. 'They're just jealous. My name's Jac, by the way, short for Jacqueline.'

She might not be the kind of woman I'd have socialized with before prison. But right now, it's nice to hear some comforting words.

At lunch, Jac waves me over. She's saved a space beside her. I take it gratefully. When I ask the woman opposite to pass the salt, and I'm ignored, my new friend reaches over and passes it to me. 'Thank you,' I say to her.

'Thank you,' mimics someone else.

'That's enough,' snaps Jac. 'Give the woman a chance, will you?'

They listen to my new friend. 'Thank you,' I whisper.

'Never thank anyone,' she replies. 'Makes you look weak.'

The next day, someone pushes me out of the queue for the bathroom. Jac, who is coming back in the opposite direction, sees it. 'Fuck off,' she growls. 'Or I'll report you.'

My pusher looks suitably reprimanded. Jac clearly carries weight here. I wonder how I've never met her before.

'Come in with me,' she says when she finds me hovering at the door of the communal lounge, wondering whether to brave the cold stares and those snide 'Lady Belinda' comments. 'We could play table tennis. There are a couple of others who'll join in too. Lifers, like me. I'll introduce you.'

Playing table tennis with three lifers? Before that dreadful day when Gerald died, I'd never in a month of Sundays have thought I'd be doing that.

'Sorry,' I say, feeling the panic rising in my chest. 'I think I should go back to my cell.'

'That's OK.' She places a hand briefly on my arm. 'I remember my first time in prison. Bloody awful. But I'm here if you need a friend.'

A few days after that, Jac comes into the laundry where I've been sent to work. There are all kinds of horrible things inside the sheets. Used tampons. Turds. Skid marks. I gag, thinking of laundry back home, when on Sundays I'd change everyone's linen, comforted by the sense of order, and the lavender water I'd iron with.

'Here,' says Jac. 'Let me do that. You take a minute – go to the toilet and blow your nose.'

This time I accept her offer.

The following week, I'm sorting out the dirty pile of laundry. So far I haven't found any tampons or excrement. But what's this? A small parcel with what looks like white powder inside.

A flash of unease zips through me. I've never actually seen cocaine before, but I have seen pictures online. In fact, I'd printed out some facts about drugs to give to the girls when they were doing a project at school.

As I turn the packet over in my hand, I can hear a guard's

footsteps coming down the corridor. What if they think these drugs are mine?

'Inspection time,' comes a yell. My body freezes. I need to think fast. Hand it in and not be believed or hide it. But where?

The footsteps are getting closer. Sweat runs down my neck. Swiftly I throw the packet into the washing machine along with the soap powder and turn it on. I can feel my face burning, my heart pounding.

The guard puts her face round the door. 'Everything all right here?'

I nod, fear leaving me unable to speak.

The guard gives the room a cursory look, then marches out. When the washing-machine cycle finishes, I take out the sheets. There's no sign of the plastic bag. Maybe it's melted. Thank God! I'm off the hook.

At lunch, everyone at my table is talking about one of the girls who'd been strip-searched that morning in the drugs check. 'Bloody invasion of human rights,' snorts one.

Jac slides onto the chair next to me with an extra roll of bread. She passes it to me under the table, placing it in my lap. 'Thanks for hiding it,' she whispers.

'Hiding what?' I whisper back.

'My stuff. I wrapped it up in my bedsheet. Someone told me the inspection was happening, and I knew it would be safe with you.'

A cold horror shoots through me. 'But I put it in the washing machine,' I stutter. 'I think it melted.'

'You *what*?'

Jac raises her voice so high that everyone stares at us.

'Your girlfriend giving you problems, is she?' titters a woman with a purple crewcut.

Girlfriend?

'Fuck off and mind your own business.'

This is a side of Jac I haven't seen before.

'I'm sorry,' I whisper. 'I thought someone might blame me.'

Jac's spit flies into my face. 'Do you know how much that was fucking worth? I was meant to pass it to someone else. Now they're going to get me – *and* you when I tell them you're responsible.'

The bread sticks in my throat, making me choke until I wash it down with water.

Jac gives me a look that chills me to my bones. 'You're in trouble now. Better watch out, Lady Belinda.'

Then she stands up, tips my plate of pasta upside down on the table and walks out. The guards don't seem to have noticed.

My teeth are chattering so hard that I can feel the bottom jaw clashing against the top.

What can I do? If I report Jac, she'll deny it and maybe say I was hiding my own 'gear', as they call it. Then it occurs to me that I could go to the chaplain – I've seen the notice outside his door, inviting people to make an appointment. I've never really been a church person apart from at Christmas when we'd go to Midnight Mass. The very thought of us all being together, not that long ago, physically hurts.

For a couple of minutes, I hover outside the chaplaincy door. Finally summoning up the nerve, I knock. There's no answer. That's that then. God doesn't want to help me either. I'm in this alone.

For the next few days, I keep my head down, watching out for everyone who comes near in case I'm attacked. Thursday passes. Friday. Saturday. Then Sunday, which is always the quietest day, with limited staff available.

Jac has been ignoring me but at least there haven't been any more outbursts. Maybe it will be all right after all.

That afternoon, I go into the canteen for tea. No one greets me. Most of the others are huddled together in groups, casting hostile looks at anyone who's on their own or whom they've taken against for whatever reason.

As I queue, I wonder what my daughters are doing now. In Elspeth's last letter, she said that Uncle Derek was being very kind. Perhaps they've just had Sunday lunch round the table together like we all used to do?

'Take that,' mutters someone, cutting through my thoughts.

Looking back, I don't know how I acted so quickly. Yet in that split-second, seeing the woman with the tray of steaming tea, I realized she was going to throw it at me.

Instinctively, I push the tray back, in mid-air, towards my attacker.

There's a terrible scream as the contents fall on her. 'Christ! It's fucking boiling! Help me someone. HELP ME!'

I watch in horror as the woman's skin begins to bubble.

'GET IT OFF ME!' she yells, screeching like a pig in the slaughter.

'No chance of that,' mutters someone. 'Sugar sticks to the skin.'

I don't know what to do. The woman's face is melting like a candle before my eyes. A deafening alarm is ringing. People are screaming and rushing around in confusion.

'Who did this?' demands a guard storming in.

Jac stands up. She's pointing to me. 'Her. Lady bloody Belinda.'

27

The guard marches me to a door that says Governor Number Two. It's in a part of the prison that I haven't been to before. It's cleaner, tidier, almost like an office. It's the first room I've seen here that doesn't have bars on the windows.

'Sit down,' says the governor. 'I want to know exactly what happened.' Her voice isn't pleasant but it's not hostile either. She's wearing pale pink lipstick and I realize how much I miss small things like this, which I once took for granted.

I try to pull myself together. Everything depends on this. 'I knew that woman was going to throw hot tea at me so I shoved the tray back towards her.'

It's as though my words belong to someone else.

'I didn't mean to hurt her. It was an accident,' I add, aware that this sounds like an excuse.

The governor's grey eyes remain fixed on mine with a steady, unfaltering gaze.

'How did you know she was going to throw the tea at you?' asks the governor coolly.

'Because I'd been told to watch out.'

'Watch out for what? And by whom?'

My body begins to shake all over. 'I can't say. I'll get into trouble.'

'Trust me, Belinda. You're going to get into a lot more trouble if you don't. You're in for manslaughter. This isn't going to look good, is it?'

It's the kind of question that doesn't need answering.

The governor is flicking through my file, which is alarmingly thick. 'This is the first time you've been in prison, isn't it?'

I nod.

That unwavering gaze returns. 'Do you know what I think?'

I shake my head numbly.

'I think you've been threatened for something, that you may or may not have done. Maybe someone asked you to hide a phone or drugs. Or perhaps you've refused to share your food with another prisoner. These are the sort of things that provoke fights. Might I be right?'

The lump in my throat feels so big that I'm unable to swallow. So I nod again instead.

'I thought so. Do you want to tell me more details?'

And risk another attack? I shake my head.

'Are you scared of what might happen if you do?'

Another nod.

'I could send you to Solitary for not cooperating, you know.'

Better that, I tell myself, *than Jac or one of her friends killing me for splitting.*

'But I don't see how that would help,' the governor muses, as if having a conversation with herself. 'However, I need you to write a full statement about what happened.'

'I've already said,' I whisper. 'It was an accident.'

Her grey eyes narrow. 'You wouldn't believe how often people say that, Belinda. Please listen to me very carefully. If you're being threatened, you need to tell one of the guards before anything happens again. And if you're not being threatened, and you did deliberately mean to hurt that woman, then you should know that I will be watching you. Is that clear?'

I nod. There's something I have to ask but the words stick

in my throat through fear of the answer. 'Is she . . . is that woman . . .'

'Are you asking if she's all right?'

I nod.

'She's alive and she can still see. But she's got third-degree burns and is in intensive care. The likelihood is that she'll be scarred for the rest of her life.'

I feel myself wincing.

'I can tell this is an entirely new world for you,' says the governor in a softer tone than before. 'Just be careful who you befriend, Belinda. Very careful.'

28

When I return to my wing, it's 'association time', which is prison talk for leisure time. A group of women are huddled round a television, watching a series in which couples agree to marry each other before even meeting. Most of these women are in what I think of as friendship gangs, but I haven't been included (not that I'd want to be) so I take a seat on the outside of the ring.

'You silly bitch,' squeals the young girl opposite my cell. 'Don't do it!'

'Are you kidding,' squeaks another. 'He's a hunk. I'd give him bed-space any day.'

I walk as fast as I can, but Jac steps out and pushes me against the wall. There's no sign of an officer.

'Did you tell the governor about the coke in the sheets?' she snarls.

'No.'

'I don't believe you.'

Her elbow is pressing against my throat. I'm gasping for air. 'I promise.'

A bell rings out, marking the end of association time. Jac moves backwards. 'You'd better not be lying, or there'll be another present coming for you.'

'Jac! You're on kitchen duty. Get moving.'

It's one of the guards. Thank goodness! He turns to me. 'As for you, Lady Belinda, we'd better look out for you, hadn't we? Even your cellmate doesn't want to share with you any more. Someone who's killed her husband and scarred one of the ladies here for life? No thanks. She's requested a move, so you've got someone else. This one's been inside for a very long time. You won't get the better of her, I can tell you. She's called Mouse. Funny how names can be misleading, isn't it?'

My new cellmate has long pale hair that reaches her waist. She could pass for a child if it wasn't for the criss-cross age lines on her face, which, I'd say, put her anywhere between forty and fifty-five.

Mouse has a row of soft toys lining the edge of her bed. She looks as though she wouldn't hurt a fly.

'Good afternoon,' she says, extending a hand, as if we're at one of those boring golf lunches Gerald used to take me to.

'Good afternoon,' I reply, surprised by the courtesy.

'Please, sit down.'

She waves to the bottom bunk, which is apparently now mine. 'I hope you don't mind but I've changed it around. I can't sleep underneath someone else. Gives me claustrophobia.'

Something in Mouse's voice tells me this is non-negotiable.

I perch awkwardly on the edge. She continues to stand.

'I heard about the tea incident,' she says, looking down at me. 'Unfortunate, I have to say.'

'It was an accident; I didn't mean to hurt anyone.'

'*That's* why it's unfortunate.'

There's a chill in her voice that unnerves me. 'What do you mean?'

'If you're going to survive in this place, you don't want to tell people you didn't mean to hurt someone. You tell them it's a warning message. You have to be bold. Strong. You need to make everyone scared of you. Otherwise, they'll trample on you like a little ant. See?'

She thumps her foot on the floor, making me jump. When she lifts her shoe, I see a mangled red and black dot on the sole. 'A ladybird,' I cry. 'You've squashed it.'

'Just like you should have squashed that woman in the canteen. It would have sent out a message.'

'But I'm not like that.'

Mouse laughs, an unexpected merry tinkle to it. 'Of course you are. Why else are we inside? We stabbed a sister because she got into the sack with our man. We took a knife to our husbands because they threatened us with their broken beer bottle. We killed our children because their crying got on our nerves.'

I edge away. This woman is a psycho.

'Actually, I didn't do any of those,' says Mouse. 'But I've shared with women who have, and I know that you as good as pushed your husband to his death.'

'But –'

'No buts. The thing is, Belinda, I've been in the system long enough that I've learned how to work it. I had to, didn't I? People trod on me because I'm small, so now I make them scared of me. And that is exactly what *you've* got to do. What happened in the canteen has already got the ball rolling.'

I need to get out of here. I don't want to breathe this woman's air.

'You've got me wrong,' I whimper. 'I'm not a violent person. That's just not me.'

'Let me repeat myself,' Mouse says, tossing back her hair. 'You need to be tough if you're going to survive this. It's no good saying it's "not you". You need to create a new Belinda. A tough one. A scary one. Nasty, if necessary. It's the only way you're going to get through. And I can help you. Trust me. It's the only way you're going to leave this place with the same face that you came in with.'

29

Another letter arrives from Imran:

Please don't throw this away. If you won't let me visit, I want you to hear my words. I can't even imagine what it's like in there. You must be so scared. Just remember who you are, Belinda. You're kind and good. Try to think of nice things if you can. Remember how we used to cycle to The Trout for lunch on Sundays? You were always faster than me! Then those afternoons making love. Real love, Belinda. I haven't felt anything like it since. Something tells me that you haven't, either . . .

I screw it up and put it in the bin. How ironic that Imran thinks I'm kind and good when Mouse is telling me that the only way I can survive is to be tough and scary. Which one am I?

A week goes by. Every evening, I queue up to speak to Elspeth on the communal phones, but each time I'm blocked out. They're all in on it, elbowing their way in before me. Jac has clearly given them orders.

On Friday when it happens again, I burst into tears. 'I need to talk to my daughters,' I sob.

'Poor diddums,' scoffs Jac, hovering nearby. 'Needs to speak to her daughters, does she? What about the one who won't have anything to do with you?'

I flinch. How stupid of me to have confided in Jac. She'd been sympathetic at the time but now it's obvious I was being groomed to be one of her gang.

'The thing is, Lady Belinda, we don't care if you want to speak to your daughter. In fact, we're going to make sure that you can't. And don't even think about reporting us. We can do worse than hot water and sugar.'

Why isn't there an officer around to hear any of this?

Visiting day comes and everyone's in the hall, meaning the phones are finally quiet. At last, I can ring Elspeth.

'But I *did* apply, Mum. They said you didn't want to see me.'

'Darling, that's not true. You must believe that.'

Then the line goes dead before Elspeth can say any more. My credit has run out.

Sobbing, I run back to my cell. Mouse is there, sitting cross-legged on her bunk, reading a Margaret Drabble novel that I remember from book club a few years ago. 'I told you,' she says when I explain in tears and gasps what happened. 'They're all in it together. That guard is well in with Jac. They look after each other.'

'What do you mean? How?'

'Dear Belinda. You really are naive, aren't you? The guard gets her phones, ciggies and drink. And in return, she ... Well let's just say Jac gives her some emotional and physical support.' Mouse says the last with a wink.

'But she has no right to tell my daughter she can't visit.'

'Well, you can't prove it. But you can make a stand.'

'How? I'd do anything to speak to my girls.'

'At last! You're beginning to see reason.' Mouse jumps up, taking a notebook from the desk. 'I've drawn up a plan. It's in shorthand, of course, so no one else can read it. My own variation of teeline, dating back to 1979.'

I can't mask my surprise. 'That's right,' she says. 'Once upon a time, I lived a respectable life with a well-paid job. But then I put poison in my boss's tea.'

'Very funny.'

'I mean it. She was a right old cow. But when she accused me of helping myself from the petty cash tin – when we all knew it was her – I saw red. I only meant to give her a stomach ache but, unfortunately, I overdid it. She's buried not far from here, actually.'

I take a step back as she continues. 'Now listen carefully, Belinda. Every three months, the mobile hairdresser visits. In fact, perfect timing – they're due next week. This is what I suggest . . .'

30

I queue up with the other women but am soon shoved to the back. It occurs to me that maybe this is a good thing. All the better for giving my fellow inmates a surprise.

'Are you sure?' says the hairdresser when I tell her what I want. 'All of it shaved off? How about just a panel on either side? That's quite popular.'

'*All* of it,' I confirm faintly.

The hairdresser shakes her head and mutters something about there being 'all sorts'.

I close my eyes while she gets to work.

'You can look now.'

A different woman looks back: me but not me. This one is a tough woman. One that won't take any shit.

Yet I can't help feeling a flood of dismay as I look down at the pile of auburn curls on the floor. How often had Imran run his fingers through my hair, when we'd been young?

Gerald had never done that, never held me in that way. Had he been saving that for Karen?

It doesn't matter now. My husband is gone, along with the old me.

Feeling sick, I make my way towards the food hall. I pass the guards' office. 'Stop,' orders one as he approaches, hand on his belt as if ready to blow his whistle. Then he stops. 'Blimey. It's you.'

Ignoring him, I keep going along the corridor. I tell my beating heart to stop fluttering. If you're doing this, I tell myself firmly, you've got to do it properly. Scare the fuck out of them. Make them realize that the old Lady Belinda has gone.

Mouse's instructions come into my head. 'Harden your face, you've got to look the part.'

I set my jaw and march in. There's no one else in the queue – I'm just in time.

Jac's cellmate is dishing up and gives me a double-take. Then she recognizes me and hands me my usual small portion. It's a watery cottage pie.

'Make that a large,' I demand without my usual 'please' or 'thank you'.

'You get what you're given.'

'You owe me in arrears,' I growl. 'Now give me that large.'

'Or else?' she snorts.

I pat my head. 'Or else I'll make sure you get a haircut like this in your sleep.'

She looks as if she's going to say something but instead, she slams an extra two spoonfuls onto my plate.

I taste it. 'Not hot enough,' I say. Your food is tepid. Put it in the microwave.'

To my amazement she does.

'Better,' I say. 'And next time I expect faster service.'

Then I turn to face the sea of faces. Some are heads down, gobbling like animals at a trough. Others are staring.

Jac is sitting at the first table – the best spot nearest the radiator. She's talking quietly to the woman next to her but looks up when I approach.

'Look at you now! Lost your curly locks have you, Lady Belinda?'

'Get up,' I say.

'What?'

'I said get up. Unless, of course, you want trouble.'

Jac's mouth forms into a half-smile. 'Piss off, Lady Belinda.'

'No one tells me to piss off, Jac,' I say quietly. 'I'd be very careful if I were you.'

'You don't scare me,' she scoffs.

'I don't need to,' I whisper. 'You're scared already. Or you should be.'

I give a quick glance around. Then I tip my plate over her head.

'Ugh,' she screams.

'So sorry,' I say sweetly.

One of the guard marches over. 'What's going on here?'

'I tripped trying to find my seat,' I say. 'Unfortunately, I dropped my plate.'

'It's all over me,' screams Jac. 'Move! I need to wash it out and change.'

'You'll sit where you are until dinner is over,' says the guard. 'And move up so Belinda can sit down.'

Grudgingly she does so, and I sit beside her. 'Pity it's not shower night for another two days,' I say.

She stares at me.

'Haven't you heard? The hot water's conked out again.'

'But I can't walk around smelling like this!'

She's almost hysterical. One of the girls at the table sniggers.

'Shut up,' Jac snaps.

'You don't like getting dirty, do you? I must remember that.'

Jac scowls through the meat and potato caked on her face.

'If you don't like getting dirty,' I add, 'you'd better not play dirty. I know you're the reason my daughter hasn't been able to visit.'

It's clear from her face that I'm right.

'I'll give you one more warning, Jac. If you do that again, you'll be getting a lot worse than this. You might, say, wake up to find someone doing something to you that you'd rather not.'

'Are you threatening me?'

'Just remember what money can buy. You're right to call me Lady Belinda. I've got the means to get you in a lot of trouble if I want.'

She doesn't need to know that I have no money; that Gerald had it all.

Jac's glaring at me, then suddenly she's up and in my face. I shove a chair between us and ram it hard against her. She falls awkwardly. There's an audible snap followed by a terrible scream. 'My arm,' she yells. 'My arm. It fucking hurts!'

'What's happening here?' says a guard running up.

'She fell over a chair,' I say firmly.

'Is that right?' the guard asks Jac.

She looks at me. Fear is in her eyes. It's in my heart too, although I can't show that.

She nods.

The next day, Jac is shipped out to another prison. And that's when I know I've won: no one will get on the wrong side of me, in case I hurt them too.

The old Belinda has well and truly gone.

31

Mabel

Belinda sinks back into her chair with exhaustion. Talking about her old life has brought it all back. How had she survived?

'I need a break now,' she says.

'But you can't!' Mabel is on the edge of her chair. 'I need to know what happened next. Your life is scarier than anything on TV. I still can't get over how you scalded another prisoner. In fact, I'm going to think twice about asking you to make me a cup of tea now.'

'It was in self-defence,' Belinda points out.

'I know, dear. I was only joking. We need something to lighten the atmosphere.'

Belinda's voice comes out in a choke. 'No one knows what it's like in prison unless they've been in one.'

Tears roll down her face. The old lady reaches out, grasping both of Belinda's hands.

'It will be all right,' Mabel soothes. 'You're safe here. You'll never have to see any of those people again. Why don't we have a break? We could play chess. Do you like that?'

'Anything but crosswords,' sniffed Belinda. It felt comforting to be looked after for a change.

'Why not crosswords?'

'Because Gerald was addicted to the bloody things.'

'Personally, I loathe crosswords, so chess it is. We'll have a few walks too and maybe watch that marvellous *Who Do You*

Think You Are? programme. Then I'll continue with my story so you can have a little break. What do you think?'

'Yes,' sniffed Belinda. 'Thank you, that sounds like a good idea.'

'It's all right, love,' Mabel says, giving her a warm hug. 'It's what friends are for.'

32

1941

Christmas was approaching. There was still no news about Clarissa and the Colonel getting married, although he had said they'd 'got a date'. Mabel was glad she hadn't mentioned it.

Sometimes it felt as though she had been living in the Old Rectory for ever. At other times, it felt like a few weeks. But 'this festive time for reflecting and praying for peace', as the vicar called it, brought back memories of sugar plums, white iced rabbit-shaped sweets in her Christmas stocking; her father lifting her up in front of the roaring fire and dancing around the drawing room; her mother, clapping from her own special pink-velvet chair; the gramophone that played Vera Lynn records.

But at the Old Rectory, the festive period felt different. The jollier that people became, the worse Mabel felt. Papa was missing. He might be dead. How could people be happy?

'If we walk around with long faces, we might as well admit that Hitler has won,' Cook told her when she saw Mabel's tears drop into the Christmas pudding mixture.

'We've got to have hope, love. Miracles happen in the war. You hear about them all the time. People get dug out of buildings and . . .'

Mabel gave a sob.

'Oh, love! I'm sorry, I wasn't thinking.'

'Why couldn't Mama and my sister have been the lucky ones?'

'Oh, Mabel. Life is very hard sometimes. But if your mother and father were here, what do you think they would say?'

'Chin up,' sniffed Mabel. 'That was one of Papa's favourite phrases. Mama was always laughing too.'

'She was indeed. You've got her smile. I remember it well. We were the same age. We used to be friends, rather like you and Frannie from the cottage.'

'Was Aunt Clarissa friends with you too?'

Cook's lips tightened. 'No. She believes "everyone should know their place". I can tell you, when this war is over, things will change. I'm sure of it.'

'*What* will change?' asked a sharp voice from the door.

Mabel's mouth turned dry. 'The pudding,' she said quickly. 'When it's steaming in the saucepan, it gets more solid. Cook's been teaching me.'

'Has she indeed?' Aunt Clarissa swept her hair back haughtily. She was dressed for riding and looked, Mabel thought, very beautiful. 'Well, I don't think that's necessary for young ladies who will grow up to have cooks of their own. Now, follow me. You need to change into your jodhpurs. It's about time you came on a hunt.'

Mabel wasn't sure about hunting. She'd heard stories about it from her father, who disapproved. That poor fox with all those people after him.

'Isn't that rather cruel?' she asked, as Aunt Clarissa strode ahead to the stables.

'Absolute nonsense. The foxes need to be culled or else there would be too many. Besides, the horses need exercise.' She turned to the elderly groom. 'Right, James, are we ready?'

Before them stood the most beautiful chestnut stallion Mabel had ever seen. Its coat was positively gleaming.

'You're a very lucky young lady,' said her aunt. 'The Colonel has lent you Wellington from his own stables.'

'He's the perfect size for you, miss,' said the groom, 'and he'll go faster than old Foam. If you ride him correctly, he will obey your touch.'

Clarissa was cracking her whip. 'Right, off we go. We're meeting the others at the Hall.'

Mabel had often ridden or walked past the Colonel's home but never been inside before. As they approached, she could see a large group of riders in the courtyard. They were laughing and drinking mulled wine.

'Hello, Mabel,' said the Colonel. 'I'm so glad you could join us. May I introduce Clarissa's niece, everyone.'

It seemed from the conversation that many of the guests had travelled some distance. Yet, somehow, they all knew each other. A group of them were huddled together looking at some papers and talking in low voices. When they saw Mabel looking, they quickly folded them away and slipped them into a bag at the Colonel's side.

Wellington was getting restless, his hoofs clicking on the flagstones.

'What if the Germans drop bombs on us while we're out?' asked Mabel, nervously.

'They won't come near us,' said one man firmly.

'But how do you know?'

'Because they haven't been bombing for some time,' said Aunt Clarissa quickly.

'In fact, there needn't be a war at all if the rest of the British public saw sense,' said a man with a twirly handlebar moustache on a horse so tall that it gave her neck a crick to look up at him.

'Let's not talk politics, shall we, Bedmont?' said the Colonel, cutting in.

As they trotted past the fishermen's cottages, Mabel kept her eyes peeled for Frannie. There she was! Oh dear. How pale she looked.

'Halt, everyone,' called out the Colonel. 'We've arranged refreshments to speed us on our way.'

Again? She couldn't help feeling rather awkward as Frannie handed her another stirrup cup with a stony face. How she wanted to talk to her, but it was difficult with so many people around.

'Right, everyone!' called out the Colonel. 'Let's go!'

Wellington made to surge ahead but Mabel felt Frannie grab hold of her reins, her eyes accusing. 'It's your fault my dad was killed.'

Mabel froze. 'What do you mean?'

'That man there was talking about a "near shave",' she said, pointing at Bedmont. 'He said a poacher went to the police and that "he deserved everything he got". What did you tell the Colonel about my dad before he died?'

'Just that I'd told your family there was going to be another dinner party and . . . and that there might be some left-over food like there was after the last one.'

'That would have been enough.' Frannie's eyes narrowed. 'We've all been told to watch out for strangers in the area. Two parties in one month is downright suspicious. My dad probably went to the police and that's why they made an arrest. The Colonel was behind my dad's death. You mark my words.'

'Why would he do something as wicked as that?'

'You're either very cunning or very naive, Mabel. Go away with your loose tongue and your fancy aunt and her crowd. I thought you were different but you're not. Don't expect me to be your friend any more.'

33

'Where have you been?' demanded her aunt when she caught up with the rest of the hunt.

'I don't feel well,' said Mabel, still reeling from Frannie's words.

'You're just like your mother. Hunting made her sick too. Well, go home if you must but you'll have to make your own way back.'

Mabel did as she was told, trying to rein in Wellington. After a while, she climbed down. It felt safer to lead him on foot. As they went through the woods towards the Old Rectory, she saw a piece of paper fluttering on the ground, then another. And a third too. Mabel thought back to the papers hidden in the Colonel's saddle bag.

Curiously, she picked them up.

Are you unhappy with the running of our country? Do you want to see change? Are you prepared to stand up to the government and fight for a better future?

What kind of change? Mabel had an uneasy feeling. Before she could think further, she ripped them into tiny pieces and threw them into the river that ran down to the sea. Shaking with fear, she watched them float away.

That night she tossed and turned, wondering what to do next. There was, she decided, only one course of action. But it would take every inch of bravery.

When the cock crowed next morning, she marched up to the Hall. The Colonel always rode early.

'Mabel!' he said, when she found him in the stables. 'What are you doing here at this time? Is your aunt all right?'

She took a deep breath. 'Yes, but I'm not. You see, I saw you putting some papers in your bag yesterday, and then I found leaflets on the ground after you'd left.'

'I see,' he said, looking her straight in the eyes.

Her voice shook. 'They talked about fighting back against the government.'

'Of course they did, Mabel. We need to stand up to the politicians who are trying to take food out of people's mouths. Think about your little friend Frannie. People like that need more help.' He paused. 'What did you do with the leaflets by the way?'

'The wind took them,' she said, hoping God wouldn't punish her for telling a lie, 'and they blew away down the river.'

A brief frown passed across his face. 'That's a shame. Now if I were you, Mabel, I wouldn't say anything about this to anyone. In these uncertain times, people are understandably twitchy about perfectly innocent things. We wouldn't want anyone to get the wrong idea. Would we?'

'No,' she whispered nervously.

Mabel fretted about their conversation all the way home. Part of her would have liked to talk to Frannie or Cook about what had just happened. But something inside made her feel she ought to stay quiet.

Later that day, she heard the Colonel arrive, followed by the library door slamming shut. Standing outside, she heard low voices. 'We need to get her involved as soon as possible while there's still time . . .'

Suddenly the door swung open and Mabel flew backwards. 'Were you listening to us?' demanded her aunt.

'No,' she stammered. 'Not exactly.'

'What did you hear?'

'Something about you wanting me to get involved.'

'That's right, Mabel,' said the Colonel, stepping in. 'We thought you might like to help us make Britain great again. It might end the war sooner.'

'How?'

'It's complicated. Now, why don't you start by putting these leaflets in envelopes? No need to read them. Just fold them neatly like this.'

Excitedly, she began to do as instructed. It felt so nice to be working together round the table like this. Even her aunt gave her a little smile.

'Afterwards, if you'd really like to help, you could hide them in the woods so others can collect them,' said the Colonel.

'But why would we want to hide them?'

'It makes it more fun for people when they find them,' her aunt said quickly. 'You mustn't tell anyone what we're doing or it will ruin the surprise!'

'That's right,' said the Colonel. 'You're one of us now.'

Mabel felt a flash of pride pass through her. She liked the red-and-black pattern at the top of the letters so much that, later that night, she found herself drawing one on the lower part of the wall, which was hidden by her bed, to show she was part of the 'fight for a better future'. It was so nice when her aunt was kind like this, thought Mabel, though she couldn't help but wonder why all this secrecy was needed.

On Christmas Eve, Aunt Clarissa gave Mabel *A Child's Guide to Algebra*.

'Shouldn't we wait until Christmas Day for presents?' Mabel had asked.

'Some countries do it earlier,' said her aunt crisply. 'I thought you'd be pleased.'

'I am! Thank you.'

The Colonel, who had joined them for dinner, presented her with a beautiful bound gold-and-green book with the title *Shakespeare's Sonnets* on the cover.

'Thank you,' she said, eagerly. 'My father would love this. He used to read poetry to my mother . . .'

She trailed off as her eyes filled with tears.

'Don't start blubbing,' said Clarissa, her old, sharp voice back again. 'We can't change the past. We have to put it behind us and get on with the present.'

'But what about Papa?' asked Mabel. 'Don't you ever think of him?'

'Why should I do that?' she asked sharply.

'Because he's your sister's husband and he might be dead or in a prisoner-of-war camp!' Mabel replied, hardly daring to believe that she was speaking to her aunt like this.

'Well, of course I wish him well,' retorted her aunt coolly. 'But like I said, we have to put our best foot forward in the meantime.'

The Colonel came closer to her and patted her shoulder. 'I do understand it's not easy for you, dear.'

He'd never called her 'dear' before or patted her shoulder. In fact, he seemed so kind that she felt certain now that he hadn't had anything to do with Frannie's father's death.

He was generous too! Look how he was presenting her aunt with a pair of silk stockings.

'They're divine, Jonty,' said her aunt, flushing.

The Colonel looked pleased. 'I thought you'd like them.'

'I didn't think we could get stockings any more,' said Mabel, impressed. 'Where did you buy them?'

'Mabel,' snapped her aunt. 'I can barely believe that a niece of mine could ask such rude questions. Clearly, your parents failed to teach you manners.'

'That's not true! They did. I just meant that –'

'Don't you dare answer me back,' Clarissa snapped, before grabbing Polly from Mabel's side. 'Give this to me. You're far too old for dolls, you foolish girl.'

'No,' cried Mabel. 'Please, no. She's all I have left of my sister.'

'You can have her back in the morning if you're good. Now go to your room.'

'I say, Clarissa,' she heard the Colonel say. 'Wasn't that a bit harsh?'

That night, she woke up with a start. It was past midnight, which meant that it was now Christmas Day. But this time there was no stocking on the end of her bed. No loving kiss from her parents when she went running into their room to give them the present she'd saved up to buy them. No warm, snuggly cuddles with Annabel. Not even the comfort of Polly next to her.

Instead, she could hear a car pulling up outside. Maybe that's what had woken her. Peering through the curtains, she saw a figure run inside wearing a long beige trench coat. She went to her door and opened it a crack. There were whisperings and the sound of another door closing somewhere. Not long after that, it opened again. Looking out of the window, she could see someone running out to the car and driving off without switching on the headlights.

'Did someone come to visit last night?' asked Mabel at breakfast that morning.

'What do you mean?' asked Clarissa sharply.

'I thought I heard someone,' she replied, not wanting to mention that she'd actually *seen* someone.

'You're imagining it. Keep quiet; this is exactly how misunderstandings come about.' Then she pushed Polly roughly into Mabel's arms. 'If it wasn't Christmas, I'd confiscate this for longer. Now get ready for church. Jonty will be waiting for us.'

He was. In fact, he gave Mabel such a kindly smile that she instantly felt better, despite everything. Frannie and her mother, on the other hand, looked straight past Mabel as if she didn't exist. The lacemaker was there as well and gave Mabel a concerned glance before glaring at the Colonel. Had she been told that he was responsible for Frannie's father too? At times, he seemed honourable, and at others, scary. Was it possible to be both?

Christmas lunch was surprisingly lavish, given what her aunt referred to as 'those awful ration restrictions'. There was a huge 'bird', as the Colonel called it, followed by the raisin pudding she and Cook had made. Mabel could barely eat a mouthful; all she could think about was Frannie and her family's sad faces at church.

'May I go for a walk?' she asked after lunch.

'Good idea,' drawled her aunt, reaching for the decanter of port, her eyes half-closed as she draped herself against the Colonel's shoulder.

If they did get married, what would happen to Mabel? Maybe the Colonel wouldn't want her to live with them. Perhaps she'd be thrown out and become an orphan.

Mabel found herself walking further and further along a lane. As she did so, she heard something extraordinary: the sound of singing – soft, lyrical tones. It was another language; one she had never heard before.

34

Drawing nearer, Mabel realized the music was coming from a group of huts on the edge of the cliff. She was going to investigate when she saw one of the farmers from the village.

'Who's singing?' she asked.

'That lot's the Italian prisoners of war.'

Mabel froze with terror. 'What are they doing here? Aren't they dangerous?'

'Don't worry, miss. They're in an internment camp. Best place for them, although I have to say they're good workers.'

The melody was beautiful, even if it was coming from the enemy.

'They've got lovely voices,' she admitted.

'I suppose they have. Well, Merry Christmas to you, Miss Mabel.' His eyes softened. 'It must be hard for you after losing your family.'

'I haven't lost them all,' she said quickly. 'My father might be alive.'

'Let's pray that he is. I remember him as a young man when he was courting . . .'

He stopped briefly, as if he had something in his throat, before continuing. '. . . When he was courting your mother. They made a lovely couple.'

'Thank you,' she gulped, holding back her tears.

'It was a long time ago now, but I can still see your mother's beautiful smile. It could light up the darkest day. Everyone said so. Dainty little thing she was, just like you. Oh dear, miss. Have I made you cry?'

'It's all right,' sniffed Mabel quickly. 'I like it when people tell me their memories. It makes me feel as though she's still here.'

The farmer made the sign of the cross on his chest. 'God bless her soul and that of your little sister. Now would you like me to accompany you back to the Old Rectory?'

'No, thank you. I'll be fine. I like the fresh air.'

'Just like your mother.' He nodded approvingly. 'Well, I'll be getting on with my jobs then. It might be Christmas Day, but the animals still need feeding.'

Mabel walked on, lost in her thoughts about Mama and what she must have been like as a young girl.

'Hello,' said a foreign voice.

Mabel almost jumped out of her skin. Before her stood a young man with dark hair and moustache. Panicking, she realized that she'd missed the turn-off to the Old Rectory and had instead continued along the cliffs towards the huts.

'Please don't hurt me.'

The man chuckled softly. 'I won't. Even if I was going to, I am behind the wire and you are on the other side. But I am a gentleman, I would never hurt a lady. In fact, I would never hurt anyone.'

'Are you a prisoner of war?' she trembled.

'I am.'

'But if you wouldn't hurt anyone, why are you a soldier?'

'I was forced to enlist, just like your men in England – and some ladies too. I was a foreign-language student before that, though.'

Ladies enlisting? She hadn't heard about that.

There was the sound of a shrill whistle.

'I must go back,' he said. 'I came to get some fresh air. I am not a good singer!'

'Nor am I,' she said suddenly. 'I try but I can't seem to hit the right notes.'

'I know what that's like,' he laughed. He seemed so normal, not like an enemy at all.

Then she noticed a book poking out of his pocket, the name 'Shakespeare' just visible over the hem.

'I'm reading Shakespeare too!' she blurted out. 'I've just been given a copy of his sonnets for Christmas.'

His face brightened. 'Really? My favourite is number –'

Then a second whistle sounded. 'I must go. If this was another place and time, we could talk for longer.'

On the way back Mabel was besieged with loathing for herself. How could she have spoken in such friendly terms to the enemy? What had she been thinking? They were part of the enemy who had taken Papa.

'I'm sorry, God,' she began to pray silently as she rounded the corner to the Old Rectory. 'Please keep my father safe and . . .'

What was that shouting and swearing?

Mabel stared with disbelief as the Colonel was being bundled out of the house by two burly policemen.

Clarissa was standing on the doorstep, screaming. 'Let him go! He hasn't done anything wrong. And how dare you search our house, invade our privacy like that?'

'How can you be surprised, madam, with all these comings and goings on Christmas Eve, suspicious papers and now this stolen list? A search is the least you can expect.'

The noise was so loud it was hard to hear who was saying what. But the Colonel's voice rose above the others. 'I swear to you,' he was yelling, 'I don't know about any bloody list.'

'Just as you didn't know about the pamphlets with swastikas we found in your library. Those words about making Britain great again and fighting for a better future? They look to me like the work of a traitor. The BUF is illegal now, as well you know. You're not fooling me, sir.'

'Like I told you. Someone must have planted them there. Get off me. You're hurting me.'

'Then I suggest you go calmly,' said a second policeman firmly shutting the rear door on him. Mabel stepped back as the car shot off down the drive, sending dust flying up from the gravel as it went.

'What's going on?' she asked, running to her aunt.

Clarissa's eyes were red. 'You wouldn't understand,' she wept. 'Go away and leave me in peace.' Then she ran up the stairs towards her room and slammed the door shut.

There was only one person who would tell her the truth, Mabel thought, racing down to the kitchen.

Cook was sitting at the table, shaking. 'I can't believe it,' she kept saying. 'All those dinners . . . All those posh visitors! I could kick myself. How did I not see what was going on? I'm just trying to do my job and now I find out that we've been entertaining folk who want Hitler to win.'

Mabel gasped. 'The policeman said something about the BUF. What's that?'

'The British Union of Fascists. Members are known as Blackshirts. The BUF has been banned now, but some folk are still secretly part of it. The police accused the Colonel of being one of them.'

'Surely he wouldn't do such a dreadful thing,' Mabel stammered. 'He just wants everyone to have more opportunities and to cut down on unemployment.'

Cook's eyes narrowed. 'How do you know that, love? He didn't get you involved, did he?'

A cold fear shot through Mabel as she thought of all those leaflets. The ones that she herself had willingly put into envelopes and hidden in the woods.

'No,' she said. 'He didn't.'

35

The following morning, after a restless night, Mabel was called to her aunt's bedroom. Usually, at this time, Clarissa would be sitting at breakfast, perfectly coiffured, often with the Colonel, who would have ridden over early (it must have been early because Mabel never actually saw him arriving). They would be 'perusing' *The Times* and eating poached eggs.

But today her aunt looked pale and wan as she perched on the pink chaise longue by the window, still in her nightclothes. There were dark circles under her eyes.

'Has the Colonel returned?' Mabel asked.

'No,' said her aunt dully.

'When will he be back?' she asked hesitantly.

'I don't know.'

Her aunt turned to her. Those beautiful blue eyes were so like Mama's, yet somehow cold and hard. 'Did you tell anyone about the work we were doing? Those leaflets you delivered?'

Mabel felt herself reddening. 'No.'

Her aunt continued to stare and Mabel felt obliged to qualify her statement. Speaking in a firm voice that wasn't like her own at all, she said, 'Of course I didn't, although I don't see what's wrong in rebelling against the government if it's going to make Britain great again, like you said.'

Her aunt stood up, furiously crushing her cigarette into a shell-shaped ashtray, a wild look on her face. 'Unfortunately, there are too many people in this world who do not know what is good for them.'

As she spoke, tyres crunched over the drive outside. Mabel ran to the window. 'It's the police again.'

They stood side by side, looking down as a lone figure in uniform got out of the car and strode to the front door.

'I can't see the Colonel,' said Mabel in a quiet voice.

Her aunt was silent.

Together they waited. For the first time in her life Mabel felt attuned to her aunt. It was not a dissatisfactory feeling and she soon felt herself reaching for Clarissa's hand, but her aunt recoiled and moved away. Just then, there was a knock on the door.

It was Frannie! She must be back at work after her compassionate leave. Mabel hadn't seen her since that awful day at the hunt.

'The policeman wants to see you, miss,' she said.

'Tell him I'll join him in the drawing room when I've dressed,' declared her aunt haughtily. Her tone suggested she was back to her usual self.

'Not you, my lady. He was talking about Miss Mabel.'

Frannie's eyes were cold and harsh, and somewhat gleeful.

'Why?' said Mabel shakily.

'He didn't say.'

'I will go with her,' said Aunt Clarissa.

'He requested that Miss Mabel should go alone.'

Conscious that all eyes were on her – Cook at the door of the dining room and James the groom in the hall – Mabel followed Frannie nervously into the drawing room.

The policeman was different from the last one. This man was shorter with sandy hair and a belted raincoat.

'Please sit down,' he said, as if he was the owner of the Old Rectory and Mabel was a visitor.

'You might wonder why I want to talk to you alone.'

She nodded, too scared to speak.

'Someone has come forward to say that they saw you by the river a few weeks ago. They said you were ripping up paper and throwing it into the water. Can you tell me more about that, Mabel?'

Mabel felt her throat tighten and her mouth go dry. 'They were letters to my mother,' she croaked, thinking quickly.

The policeman's eyes narrowed. 'I was told your mother was killed in the London air raids.'

Mabel winced at his stark words. 'I still write to her. It makes me feel as though she is still here.'

'Then why were you throwing the letters away?'

'Because I realized I had to accept that she had finally gone. At least, that's what everyone seems to think I should do.'

The policeman's face softened. 'So it wasn't a leaflet encouraging people to rebel against the government?'

'Of course not,' she said, trying to sound firm. 'Who saw me?'

'Your aunt's maid.'

Frannie? How could she? Was she trying to get revenge for her father's death, even though Mabel had had nothing to do with it?

The policeman leaned in closer. 'Has the Colonel or your aunt, or maybe both, shown a leaning towards the ideologies of Hitler?'

'What does that mean?'

'Have they shown sympathy towards the enemy?'

'Not that I know of.'

'What do they talk about?'

'Hunting. Digging the land. And doing our best for Britain.'

'I see.'

There was a silence. Mabel had the distinct feeling that the policeman was waiting for her to say something but, remembering the lacemaker's words, she decided now might be a good time to stay silent.

Eventually, he spoke instead. 'Very well,' he said. 'But if you do hear your aunt saying anything along those lines, I would expect you to come to the station and tell us. Otherwise, Miss Mabel, you could be in a great deal of trouble yourself. Failure to disclose important information could be a criminal offence.'

'I understand,' she said quietly.

After he left, Clarissa called her into her room. 'What did he say?' she demanded.

Mabel gave her a shortened version.

'You write to your mother? What on earth do you do that for?'

'It helps to keep her alive in my head,' said Mabel quietly.

'I miss her too,' her aunt said after a moment. 'Sometimes I wish we had done things differently.'

'What kind of things?'

There's the hint of a sigh. 'It's too late to talk about it now. What's done is done.'

Then she dropped a kiss on the top of Mabel's head. It was so light that she barely felt it, but surely it showed that her aunt really did love her!

'Now go and play, so I can get some rest,' said Clarissa, stepping away. 'We just have to hope that Jonty returns.'

Mabel did as she was told, hoping to catch Frannie. It was time to get things straight.

'She's gone home,' said Cook. So, before she could lose her nerve, Mabel ran through the woods to the cottage.

The door was open. Frannie was scrubbing the floor. She looked up as Mabel stood there, eyes wide.

'You're still here? Didn't the policeman take you away?'

'No,' she said, deciding not to mention the leaflets. 'The

policeman just wanted to know if the Colonel had shown sympathy to the enemy.'

'I suppose you told them he hadn't.'

Mabel nodded.

Frannie snorted. 'You're so naive at times, Mabel. I bet your aunt's involved.'

Mabel thought of the kiss on her head. 'I don't think so. Besides, the only way we'll find out is if I stay here and keep an eye on her. It will be easier now that the Colonel is away. It's the least I can do after your father's death. I am so sorry; I really didn't think I had done anything wrong. If only I'd known...'

She trailed off, tears springing to her eyes.

'It's not enough,' Frannie retorted.

'I think it is,' said a voice behind them. It was Frannie's mother. 'Miss Mabel has been punished too much in life, Frannie. So have you. Both of you have lost a parent. This poor maid may have lost two, for all we know.'

Mabel's eyes stung with tears.

'You should forgive each other. We need friends in these difficult times.'

'But Dad would still be alive if she hadn't told the Colonel about that food.'

'It was loose talk, I grant you. And loose talk can cost lives. But she didn't mean to.'

'Of course I didn't,' said Mabel. 'Please, Frannie, I've missed you so much. You're the only friend I have. I vow on my life that I will be more careful from now on.'

She stepped forward to give her a hug but her friend moved back. Mabel's heart thumped with fury.

'Your dad would want you to forgive her,' her mother urged. 'If I can, so can you.'

'All right,' said Frannie grudgingly. 'I've missed you too,

to be honest. I thought you were different from the other toffs but –'

'I am,' Mabel insisted.

'I'll give you one last chance. You've got to keep your mouth shut and your eyes peeled. If you hear anything about your aunt, let us know.'

'I will,' said Mabel, breathing a sigh of relief.

'Come on then,' said Frannie, opening her arms. It was just a quick hug, but it was enough to show they were friends again.

36

On her way home, Mabel took the cliff path past the prisoner-of-war camp. There was no singing this time. In fact, the camp seemed quiet, and Mabel found herself feeling rather disappointed.

Then, when she turned into Church Lane, she noticed someone up a ladder, trimming the hedges. When he turned to look down, she saw it was the young man from the camp who had talked to her about Shakespeare's sonnets.

'What are you doing here?' she gasped, stepping backwards. Supposing he attacked her with those shears?

'We're allowed to do jobs for families in the village now,' he said, coming down the steps so they were face to face. 'I can see you are scared, but I promise I am not going to hurt you.'

'But aren't they worried you might escape?'

'Where to?' he asked, laughing. 'It is not as if we can go far. Besides, I do not want to.'

'But surely you want to go back to your family.'

His face looked sad. 'Of course, but I do not know if my loved ones are there any more. I write letters but receive no replies. I am scared that when or if I return, I may not find them. I prefer to imagine that they are here.' He looked a little shy. 'I talk to my mother in my head and to my father and my sisters too.'

'I do the same!'

'You do?'

She nodded. 'Even though my mother and sister are gone.'

'Gone?' He looked shocked.

Mabel swallowed hard. 'They were killed by a bomb in London. My father is away fighting, I pray every day that he's safe.'

The man crossed himself. 'Then I will pray too.'

'But why would you want to do that? We are your enemy. You are ours.'

'I do not believe in enemies. My family, like many, was caught up in a war we didn't want. I believe people should live peacefully together.'

'So do I.'

The church clock struck three times. Goodness, was that the time? 'I must go back,' she said.

He touched his cap. 'It was good to see you again. What is your name?'

'Mabel,' she said hesitantly.

'Me, I am Antonio.' He gave a little flourish from the ladder. 'It was lovely to meet you, Lady Mabel.'

'Oh, I'm not a lady. However, my aunt is and so was my mother when she was alive.'

'A true lady is someone who has grace. You have that. It is an honour to know you.'

So many thoughts were flying around Mabel's head that when she went in through the door of the Old Rectory, it took her a few minutes to register the wailing coming from the sitting room.

Clarissa was howling, on the edge of the sofa, bent over a glass of whisky, ash from her cigarette falling onto the antique rug.

Mabel dropped to her side. 'What's wrong?' she asked.

'Jonty,' howled her aunt, burying her face into Mabel's

lap. 'He's going to be tried for treason. If he's found guilty, he'll be . . .'

Her words trailed into the empty air.

'He'll be what?' whispered Mabel.

'He will be hanged.'

The Stranger in Room Six

I've dealt with some tough stuff in my time but this case is on another level. I have visions of my body dumped in the sea. My bosses expect results. And if they don't get them, they'll do whatever it takes to stop you talking.

So, I steel myself for certain death, whatever that might look like. Poison in my tea. A knife in the night. A muffled gunshot . . .

A knock at the door makes me jump.

I pull out my gun and, holding it behind my back, make my way to the door. My heart thumps.

But it's Claudette, the singer I've bribed to keep an eye on Mabel. Thanks to college fees and a little run-in with the law, she was more than happy to join my payroll.

'Come in,' I say, looking around to check no one's followed her. My heart's racing, as if still catching up with the sight of Claudette, rather than a masked stranger.

'I saw Mabel going for a long walk today with the new carer,' she babbles excitedly. 'It seems they're spending quite a lot of time together nowadays.'

My skin prickles.

'Where can I find this carer?'

'She's in the staff quarters on the top floor: Room Seventeen. Oh, and she's off-duty tonight but she'll be there. Never goes out much. Keeps herself to herself.'

Then she stops, looking expectantly at me. 'Ah,' I say, reaching into my pocket. 'Of course.' I hand over two £50 notes, my gun still held carefully behind my back.

'Thank you,' she says.

'There's more if you get anything else.'

It's only after Claudette leaves that I realize that I'd forgotten to ask the carer's name.

Never mind. I know where to find her.

Night falls.

I wait for the corridor to quieten. Everyone's had supper – I have mine in my room to avoid questions that might blow my cover – and most of the residents have settled down with their television for the evening.

I walk past Room Seven, Mabel's room. The door's shut; no sounds coming from behind.

I'm tempted to barge in and squeeze the truth out of this old woman to get this job over and done with. But that won't do. My boss wants me to avoid bloodshed 'if possible' because it wouldn't look good in the headlines.

The staff rooms are up a back staircase. It's not easy for me to climb but then again, it's my disabilities that helped me get my spot here as a resident.

Here it is. Room Seventeen.

I'll pretend I'm lost and ask if I can sit down because my 'good' leg is aching with the strain. Then I'll gently slip into the conversation that I've seen her with Mabel Marchmont and take it from there. I can't do too much too soon, or she might get suspicious. Of course, I've got some bribes up my sleeve. Money usually works.

I knock.

Footsteps sound on the other side. I try to look as needy as possible.

The door opens.

Her face looks as if I've just slapped it. I can only imagine the shock written all over mine.

'Belinda?' I stammer.

She sways as if she's seen a ghost, as well she might. 'What are you doing here?'

Gathering myself, I bring out my gun. My strategy has changed.

'I've come to kill you. Unless, of course, you do exactly what I say.'

PART THREE

37

Mabel

The following day, Mabel suggests they go to the library to talk. It's a much brighter and airier room than it had been in her day. It gives her great pleasure to think how the flowery curtains, which have replaced the tapestried drapes, would have horrified her aunt.

The other residents are all downstairs, listening to 'Celine Dion', as Mabel likes to think of Claudette. The sound of a love song floats up through the house.

'When did you last have sex?' Mabel asks suddenly.

Belinda gives a start. 'That's a very personal question.'

'Well, we've been talking about personal things. I'm curious, that's all. I haven't had sex since Churchill was prime minister. But I do recall feeling it was very special.'

'So you were a teenager?'

'Not necessarily. Churchill came back in the fifties, remember. Your turn now.'

Belinda flushes. 'About fifteen years ago, I suppose.'

'So you didn't sleep with Imran after he came back into your life?' Mabel laughs. 'Got you, didn't I? Now I know some of your story in advance. You probably think that old ladies like me don't talk about sex. But we do. Some of us, thank God, are still in possession of our minds too. I've got Scotch and cod liver oil to thank!'

At that, Belinda manages a laugh, despite her embarrassment. 'If we're going to jump ahead,' she says, 'please tell me if the Colonel was hanged or not.'

'No – it's your turn! You were acting all tough in prison; you'd even got Jac moved! What happened next?'

38

Belinda

Time in prison goes much slower than you think. In films, they show men carving dates into their cell walls one minute, then getting out the next. But it's not like that in reality.

Instead, you have to make a pact with yourself. You have to stop counting the days. You must stop marking the months in your mind, and think in years instead. So far, I've done three. They feel like a lifetime.

Even when those years are up, you need to convince a parole board that you've reformed enough to be released. If they *aren't* convinced, you serve another year. And maybe another. And another.

When you do get out, the world will not be as you know it, although that's another story. The point is that if you allow yourself to tick off every day inside, you will go stark raving crazy. If you're not crazy already.

I know this because Mouse has told me. She speaks a lot of sense, my cellmate. But I wouldn't want to get on the wrong side of her.

In the meantime, I'm working very hard at pretending to be scary myself. The odd thing is that the longer it goes on for, the more I begin to feel that I really *am* frightening and not just play-acting.

Meanwhile, we're coming up to Christmas. It's one of the few landmark dates that Mouse says I'm allowed to acknowledge, as I mentally count down the years to release. It would be hard not to. Staff are on leave; festive decorations are allowed, but no tinsel, which could be used for strangulation. There are more visitors in the already overcrowded hall. Everyone is upset and emotional because they want to be with their families, even if they hated each other before coming in here; in some cases even murdered them. Add menstrual and pre-menopausal and post-menopausal symptoms to the cauldron and you get the picture.

'You're different, Mum,' says Elspeth when she pays her monthly visit.

'Really?' I ask, knowing she's right. I'm doing my best to be brittle and uncaring, at least on the outside.

'You seem to have accepted you're here.'

'I have to, darling,' I say.

Seeing Elspeth is such a relief. We talk about her university studies and which career Gillian might choose and whether life is all right with Uncle Derek.

I somehow manage to ask these things despite the jealousy raging inside my heart. A jealousy mixed with fury because Gerald's affair and my own stupid actions mean that someone else is bringing up my children.

'I don't like to think of you being alone here for Christmas, Mum,' she says to me.

'I'll be fine,' I say firmly, determined that she mustn't carry my pain of a solitary December 25th in my cell: a far better option than sitting with my companions in front of the communal lounge TV.

After Elspeth has left, I am filled with such despondency that I allow myself the luxury of opening Imran's latest letter.

Dear Belinda,

I know you have my address because I put it on the last letter, but I still haven't received a reply. You can't get rid of me that easily. I'm going to keep writing because I can't bear to think that I found you again and then instantly lost you. We've been through that once before. Do you remember the Magdalen Ball? You looked beautiful, Belinda. That was the night when I said I wanted to spend the rest of my life with you. All right, I know I wasn't completely honest with you then, but I meant what I said. I just didn't explain my personal circumstances. You were right to get upset when I told you the truth. I was sorry then and I'm even more sorry now. Give me another chance, Belinda, please. I will wait for you, no matter how long it takes.

Love, Imran.

I'd thrown all of Imran's previous letters away, but this one I put under my pillow for one night only and then, in the morning, I tear it up into narrow strips. As I do so, I feel Mouse's eyes on me, leaning over from the top bunk. 'Good girl,' she says. 'Remember what I've told you. Put up a barrier and then the bastards can't hurt you.'

'Imran isn't a bastard,' I retort.

Her eyes glint. 'So that's his name, is it?'

I curse myself for having let that slip out.

'Is that why you murdered your husband? So you could go off with lover boy?'

'No,' I snap back. 'It was because Gerald was having an affair and I *didn't* allow myself to go off with the only man I've ever loved.'

Mouse, hanging upside down from her bunk like a bat, shakes her head. 'I'm not sure I get you but either way, Belinda, you're doing well. You're stronger than you think. The women respect you, but you need to work more on the staff. I'll tell you this for free. The only way to get through this hell is to make the bastards think you're on their side. Do a good deed that makes them respect you.'

'But what?'

Mouse's head is going up. She's retreated to her top bunk, out of sight. But her voice floats down.

'You'll think of something. And if you don't, you'd better start making plans for your own funeral. 'Cos sooner or later, someone will try and top you. Jac might be gone, but some of her friends are still here – and they have long memories.'

39

The funny thing is, I always liked to think of myself as a good person. I used to be on a committee that raised money for the homeless. I had been on the PTA at school, fundraising for books and playground equipment. But it's hard to do good in prison when most of us are here for doing bad; constantly terrified of being attacked.

It's Christmas Day and some of the women are claiming they're sick. We all know they're just trying to get out of their work parties. But we still have to do our usual jobs like cleaning and cooking and wiping down toilets. I'm doing the latter when I find my head being pushed down a bowl. When I'm released I look up to find the woman from the cell opposite mine staring down at me. Her name is Linda.

'What did you do that for?'

'Because you're full of airs and graces. Think you're too good for this place, don't you?'

Actually I don't but she's gone before I can say so, leaving me with wet hair that stinks of urine. I manage to rinse it in the sink and then move on to the next toilet. There's no point in complaining and getting her into trouble. I've seen women doing that before and they only get hurt.

'Wall,' says a guard, coming in. I presume she is using my surname to rile me since we are usually called by our first names. 'You're on the MBU today. We're short staffed.'

The MBU stands for the mother and baby unit, which is for mothers with babies under eighteen months. I didn't even know it existed until I came here, nor that, after eighteen months, these babies are taken away again and given to a relative or fostered or adopted.

At least I got to bring up my girls – or almost – before they went to my brother-in-law.

'This way,' says the guard sharply, leading me out of the wing and along a corridor I've never been down before.

It's as though we've entered a different world. There are murals on the wall in lemon yellow, strawberry pink and apple green. There are toys in varying conditions. In the corner is a Christmas tree, though there are no presents underneath.

Around me, women are sitting and playing with their babies. Teenagers gathered in groups while their toddlers play on their own. Some breastfeeding. Some bottle feeding. Others lying on bean bags, eyes closed while little ones crawl past. Toddlers climbing mini-slides before gliding down, beaming – blissfully unaware that they are enjoying the hospitality of one of Her Majesty's Prisons.

'Get cleaning then,' orders the guard. So I do, but I can't help stopping every now and then to look at this extraordinary family scene around me. It reminds me of the days when our girls were little and Gerald and I were all right. Not in love. But all right.

There's one little boy who keeps coming to me and stretching out his hand as if expecting me to give him something. I carry on dusting, but I can't ignore him. He keeps tapping me on my leg.

'Hello,' I say. 'What's your name?'

'Don't you dare go anywhere near my Bradley,' yells one of the girls who's sitting with a gang on the far side of the room. 'I know about you.' She gets up and pulls the little boy towards her.

I glance down at him. He has glorious blond curls. Elspeth

had curls when she was little; she still has a bit of a natural kink. Gillian's hair had always been dead straight.

'It can't be easy for you both here in prison,' I try.

'Are you kidding? It's better than being beaten up at home.'

'Is that why you're here?' I can't help asking. 'Did you fight back and get done for it?'

It was a common enough story inside.

Her mouth tightens. 'I bloody should have. Nah, I was dumb enough be a drugs mule for the no-good father of my kid.'

'I'm sorry to hear that,' I say.

The little boy has toddled off and returned with a battered-looking boardbook, which he brandishes in front of his mother's face.

'He wants you to read to him,' I say.

The girl flushes.

'I can't.'

'Why not?'

'I can't read.'

I hadn't thought of that.

'If I didn't have to clean, I would read to him,' I say.

'No way.' She puts her arms around her little boy. 'I'm not letting my Bradley near a murderer.'

I can't blame her. I'd feel the same myself.

The following day, Boxing Day, I'm instructed to report to MBU once more. The little boy toddles up to me again with the same book in his hand.

His mother comes striding across the room. 'I told you to leave him alone.'

'He approached me!'

The same thing happens on the third day, but on the fourth, when I come to clean, Bradley is lying in his mother's lap, pale and listless.

'He doesn't look well,' I say. 'Have you asked to go to the San?'

'The nurse ain't here, is she? It's her Christmas break.'

I don't like the look of this. The child's breathing is shallow. He's pale. 'Lift up his vest,' I command.

'What are you talking about?'

'Just lift it up.'

I can't do it myself or I might be accused of fiddling.

It's as I feared; there's a rash. I rush down to the office to find a guard and bring him back with me.

'This child needs to see someone.'

'What are you now, Lady Belinda? A bleeding nurse as well as a husband killer?'

'I'm telling you he needs looking at,' I hiss. 'My youngest daughter had a rash like that when she was small. It turned out to be sepsis. It can be life-threatening. He's pale too and his breathing is shallow. The nurse might be off but there's got to be someone you can call. Unless, of course, you want to risk being splashed across the headlines as the prison guard who wouldn't get treatment for a dying child.'

The ambulance comes within an hour.

No one will tell me what has happened to Bradley, even though I keep asking. I am moved away from the MBU and put back on toilets. I find myself saying prayers I haven't said for years.

On New Year's Day, I am told by a grim-faced guard to report to the same governor I saw before.

'Belinda. Sit down. I've got something to tell you.'

'Please don't tell me he's died,' I cry out.

'Who?'

'Bradley on the MBU. I told the guard to call an ambulance. He had sepsis. I was sure of it.'

'So it was you? Well done. You saved his life, by all

accounts. If the guard hadn't acted so quickly, the outcome would have been very different.'

I am crying with relief, even though it's clear the guard has taken the credit.

The governor's voice softens. 'Belinda, that's not why I called you here. I'm afraid I've got some bad news.'

A cold knife flashes through me. I know what she's going to say before she says it. In a way, I've been expecting something like this all my life. I'm the kind of person who needs to fear the worst so she can prepare herself for it.

But nothing has prepared me for this.

'I've had a message to say your daughter has been seriously injured in a traffic accident.'

'My daughter?' I am staring at her; my mouth goes dry. I feel sick. 'Which *one*?'

Am I wrong in desperately hoping it won't be my kind sweet Elspeth? But if it's Gillian, my clever studious daddy's girl of a daughter, it might be too late for us to make up.

'Which *one*?' I repeat, stamping my feet.

The governor looks nervous. 'I'm afraid I don't know. The message didn't stipulate. I wasn't aware you had more than one daughter. We'll try to find out. It may take some time owing to the Christmas staff shortages but –'

'THEN FIND OUT!' I scream, leaping to my feet and sweeping the papers off the governor's table. 'NOW!'

40

I don't know how much time has passed.

The world is caving in, disguised as shrapnel fragments. Surrounding my body, my mind, my very self in a hideous whirlwind in which nothing feels right and everything wrong. Even Gerald's death fades into insignificance. I'm hitting my head – no, slamming it – on the desk in front of me.

Alarms are ringing loudly. An officer runs in and pins me to the ground.

'Which daughter?' I yell. 'For fuck's sake, you must know.'

'Let her go,' says the governor. Her face is twisted with pity, which makes it worse. 'I'm sorry, Belinda, but I don't. The switchboard took the call and the operator has left now for the day.'

I'm aware of being helped back onto a chair. 'Ring them,' I pant, exhausted from my screaming. 'You've got them down as my next of kin.'

As I speak, I wonder which one will pick up. Elspeth or Gillian. Whichever one is still able to speak . . .

'We've already done that. Both are going through to voicemail.'

'Then call my brother-in-law,' I demand. 'They live with him.'

'We don't have his number on your files.'

I used to know it. But the digits scramble over themselves in my head in panic.

I can't even remember Derek's address. My memory used to be so sharp.

'What now?' I implore. My anger has turned to desperation. 'Sit here and wait until someone rings with more news?'

The governor's face is even more hopeless than it was before. 'I'm really not sure what else we can do.'

I try to get up again but my legs won't carry me and I feel myself crashing to the ground. I'm dimly aware of the governor calling out for help. Of guards on either side helping me right myself. Of women looking through the bars as we make our slow funereal-like procession along the endless corridors, through the double security gates on my wing and towards my cell.

'What's up with Lady Belinda?' I hear someone say. But all the time, possibilities are flashing through my head like the films Gerald used to make of the children when they were growing up. I can see those images so clearly now. Elspeth with her sweet smile. Gillian with her studious expression as she pored over her schoolwork.

'What's happened?' asks Mouse when the guard sets me down on my bunk.

'One of my daughters has been seriously injured,' I whisper. 'But they don't know which one.'

Mouse whips round to face the second burly guard. 'But you've got to bloody know,' she growls.

'Nothing to do with us, I'm afraid.'

Mouse spits on the ground. 'Communication here is fucking awful. It's more than that. It's inhumane. Can't you see the state this woman is in?'

They send in the chaplain. He's a small man with eyes that don't leave mine. 'Would you like me to say a prayer with you?' he asks.

'She doesn't want prayers,' Mouse butts in. 'She wants to see her daughters.'

'I wouldn't mind a prayer,' I venture. Another picture is coming to mind. I see myself – a younger me – taking the girls to Sunday school. Days that now seem so simple. 'Can you just say a few words?'

I catch two or three. *Hope. Forgiveness. Salvation.*

I reach out to tug his sleeve. He jumps back as if I've attacked him. 'Please could you also ask God for both my girls to be all right.'

'I will. Would you like me to pray for you too?'

I laugh hoarsely. 'I'm beyond redemption. Now go. Please.'

'But . . .'

'You heard her,' said Mouse fiercely. 'Beat it.'

I sob all night in Mouse's arms. She came into my bed when I started and couldn't stop. Her warmth is comforting. Neither of us sleeps. She doesn't say stupid things like 'it will be all right'.

At about four in the morning, we hear a blood-curdling scream. It sounds as if it comes from a cell further down the wing.

Suddenly, there's a click and the door opens. The governor stands there. I sit bolt upright. If she's surprised to see Mouse lying next to me, she doesn't show it.

'We've had an update,' she says. 'It appears that the operator who took the message confused you with another prisoner. Linda Wall . . .'

'My girls are safe?' I whisper. 'But how do you know? Suppose you've got it wrong?'

'I kept ringing your daughters' numbers until eventually they each picked up. They'd been at the theatre, apparently. Obviously, I had to explain the situation but I can assure you that both are perfectly safe and well.'

The wails down the corridor get higher and louder.

'But Linda Wall's daughter isn't,' I whisper.

'I'm afraid it's not good news,' says the governor.

'She's dead?' asks Mouse.

The governor stays silent.

'You're not allowed to say,' Mouse says slowly. 'But it's clear as bloody daylight from your face.'

'Oh God, that's terrible,' I say as the door closes behind her. But Mouse is dancing round our cell.

'Terrible?' she repeats. 'It's bloody miraculous. Your girls are all right and that cow Linda has been punished. Don't forget, she's one of those bitches who made your life hell.'

'I don't care,' I say quietly. 'I don't want anyone to have to go through the trauma of losing a child.'

'Just count your bloody blessings that yours are safe. I've told you before, Belinda. You can't afford to get soft in this place. Or they'll kill you.'

41

The following morning, I am allowed to make a private call in the governor's office. Elspeth's voice is gentle, kind, reassuring. 'It must have been a terrible shock for you, Mum.'

'It was.' I'm still shaking. 'Is Gillian there?'

'She is but she says she needs to study. Sorry, Mum.'

What would it take for my older daughter to change her mind? Perhaps if I was on a hospital bed or in the morgue? But by then it would be too late. Maybe I just have to accept that, although both my girls are still alive, one is determined to be dead to me. The pain is too excruciating to be put into words.

Meanwhile, Linda Wall has been given 'compassionate leave', which means she's allowed to 'rest' in the San and is excused from her work duties. She is apparently in 'a bloody awful state' but, still, they won't let her go home to be with her grieving husband and son.

More details filter through as the days go by. Her seventeen-year-old daughter was riding a stolen motorbike when the accident happened. She was in a race with her gang and went into a tree. I wince at every detail.

When Linda comes back to the wing, her eyes look as though they have seen things no one else has. She hunches over her meal. She stares into space. She avoids me. Does she know of the name confusion? If so, she makes no sign of it.

'I'm so sorry for your loss,' I whisper, as I find myself leaving the canteen with her one day. She looks at me as though I am not there.

Then she walks on in silence.

'You shouldn't say things like that,' says Mouse. 'I know you want to be kind, but you can't – not if you're going to survive in this place.'

A week later, I receive a form saying Derek wants to visit. Something important must have happened. Please may the girls be all right.

I take special care with my make-up.

Mouse, who's been watching, lends me her mascara. 'Fancy your brother-in-law, do you?'

'Anything but.'

'Then why are you going to all this trouble?'

'To show I'm not like the others.'

She hoots with laughter. 'Whatever you say, Belinda!'

Derek is sitting at one of the tables near the front of the visiting hall. He's on the edge of his chair, visibly nervous. This is clearly his first time in a prison.

'Are the girls all right?'

'Fine,' he says.

'Are you sure? It was so frightening when they told me that one of them was hurt.'

'Yes,' he says. 'I heard about that.'

He speaks in a clipped, matter-of-fact tone, making it clear that he loathes me.

'Do you know how terrifying that was?' I ask, riled by his lack of empathy.

'And do you have any idea how awful it is for your girls to know that their mother murdered their father?' he retorts. 'Or how difficult it is to sit opposite my brother's killer?'

'Is that why you're here?' I ask. 'To tell me how much you hate me?'

'Actually, I've come to talk about the house. It transpires that Gerald made arrangements in his will to leave the house to Karen when Elspeth turned eighteen.'

I'm speechless. How could he have snatched the roof from over our heads? Didn't he care about us at all? If not me, surely his own daughters?'

I thump my fist on the table. 'That house was in Gerald's name for business reasons only. He always said it would go to me if anything happened.'

'Well, I'm afraid that isn't the case.'

My guilt now turns to fury. Gerald leaving the house to this woman has changed everything.

'Are you aware they had a son together?' I ask.

It's clear from Derek's face that he isn't, so I tell him everything. 'The girls mustn't know,' I say firmly. 'It would be too much for them to deal with.'

He nods. 'I agree.' Our eyes meet and for a second, we are bound together by one thing: our desire to protect Gillian and Elspeth.

'Karen has sold the house now,' he says quietly. 'I've tried to communicate with her through the solicitor but she hasn't replied. Thankfully the girls have the savings from the joint account, and they can continue living with me for as long as they want.'

'Thank you,' I say, numbly trying to take this in. 'Where is Karen now?'

Her name still leaves a nasty taste in my mouth.

He shrugs. 'I've no idea. The solicitors aren't allowed to give me details. I wondered if she might have tried to make contact with you.'

'No. If she had, I'd have given her what for.'

He shakes his head at my words.

'Why are you really here, Derek?' I ask. 'You could have told me about the house in a letter.'

He sighs heavily. 'I suspect you didn't mean to kill Gerald. You're not that kind of person. Elspeth has told me some things about this place and, well, how you've changed. I've been worried about how you're coping, so I thought I would see for myself.'

I'm so surprised by this about-turn that I almost let down my guard. But if I stop pretending to be tough, I won't be able to manage. 'I'm fine,' I say staunchly. 'Don't worry about me. But there is one thing. Is there *any* way you can persuade Gillian to visit?'

He shakes his head. 'She's adamant that she never wants to see you again.'

I expected as much but still it feels as if someone has stabbed me through the heart.

Derek stands up, brushing down his trousers as if to remove prison germs. He glances around the hall, at women talking to children, husbands, partners, mothers; the distaste is plain on his face. Linda Wall is sitting opposite a man, both of them crying. Despite the way she's treated me, my heart goes out to them.

'Look after yourself, Belinda,' he says before walking away. His sudden kindness scares me. If Derek is concerned, then I really am lost.

As I'm escorted back to my cell, I pass a notice on the corridor wall. *Could you become a Listener?* it says. *Could you help with other people's problems?*

The guard sees me looking. 'It does good things, that listening scheme. The chaplain runs it with some of you lot. It seems prisoners are more likely to come along if they think that one of theirs is there too.'

'But how can I give advice to others? I've killed someone.'

'From what I hear, it's more listening than telling,' the guard replies, with a kindness in her voice. 'Sometimes prisoners just need to let their feelings out in a safe space.'

Rather like how I talk to Mouse. I hope that Linda Wall

can talk to her friends too. I count my blessings: we may have lost our house, but at least I have the girls.

That's when I realize: I need to do something good to show my gratitude.

The next day, I sign up to train as a Listener. Then I see the advert for computer classes and put my name down for those too. If I get access to the internet, I can track down Karen.

'I'm coming for you,' I whisper. 'May you curse the day you were born.'

42

Computer class is full.

'Course it is,' sniffs Mouse. 'Everyone wants to get in touch with their dealer or arrange for someone on the outside to take someone else out. We're not meant to use the internet unless we're supervised, but guards can be bribed like anyone else.'

'Can I do that to skip the queue?'

'You could but, Belinda, imagine if you're caught? Your parole might get refused and you'll be in for even longer. Is it worth the risk?'

Maybe not. Meanwhile winter is settling in. It's freezing at night. The blankets are thin and scratchy. There's ice on the windows and often we can't shower because the pipes are frozen. When it's really cold, Mouse and I have an unspoken agreement that she joins me in my bed and we put our arms around each other. It's pure survival.

Sometimes I worry that I'm too heavily under her influence. But at the same time, she's the only person here who seems to understand me.

'This is against our bloody human rights,' calls out the woman in the cell next to ours. Another set of voices takes it up further down the corridor and then another, until it becomes a chant with fists thumping on the wall. *Hu-man rights! Hu-man rights!*

Yet I can't help thinking that each one of us is in here for a reason. We've all hurt someone in some way. Non-violent crimes don't exist – the act always causes injury, whether it's physical or emotional. What about the victims' human rights? This irony appears to be lost on my fellow prisoners. I think about Gerald all the time. Of course, he shouldn't have had an affair. But he didn't deserve to die.

Meanwhile, I've started my training to be a Listener. I can't tell anyone because the whole point is that it's meant to be confidential. 'Gone all religious, have you?' asks Mouse when I get permission to see the chaplain once a week.

'Maybe,' I say.

Mouse purses her lips. She knows me well enough to realize there's more to it, but I won't let on.

'So how does the listening programme work?' I ask the chaplain at our first session.

We're sitting in his office, on comfortable chairs opposite each other. There's a table between us, with coffee and plain digestive biscuits on it. If it weren't for the bars on the windows and the alarm button on the wall, I could almost pretend I was somewhere else.

'It's what it sounds like,' he says. 'You listen. They talk. It's all anonymous. There's a screen between you and the person who comes in. I'll be there as well in case you need me.'

'So why don't they just talk to you instead?'

'Because you're one of them, Belinda. That's the whole point. They get feedback from someone who really understands what it's like to be a prisoner.'

'But what if they recognize my voice, and hate me?' I venture.

'It happens sometimes. They can then ask for another Listener, although we don't have any other volunteers at the moment. It's not for everyone. You'll find yourself taking on others' emotional baggage. Can you cope with that, Belinda?'

'I don't know,' I say truthfully.

'I appreciate your honesty. We've had Listeners in the past

who are too sure of themselves. The truth is that you'll only know if it's for you once you've got going.'

There are six weeks of training and I'm on week four now. We've done a lot of role-play. The chaplain pretends to be a prisoner and I . . . well, I listen.

'You're not meant to be judgemental,' he tells me. 'Or too forceful in telling them what you would do if you were them. Often the person asking the question will come to some kind of resolution herself. It's amazing how talking out loud can do that.'

I only wish that would work for me.

Prisoners who want to register are invited to sign up. Then, one afternoon when I'm on my laundry duty, one of the guards comes in to say that the chaplain would like to see me.

'I have someone who needs to talk,' he says when I arrive at his office.

'But I haven't finished my training.'

'I think you're ready,' he says. 'In fact, she needs to talk right now. She's new and isn't coping very well.'

Can I really do this? I follow the chaplain to his office and sit behind the screen. I hear footsteps coming towards me on the other side. The woman is sobbing. I try to remember what the chaplain has taught me. I know he's here too, but I'm nervous. What if I say something that makes her even more distressed?

'Would you like to tell me what's upsetting you?' I ask, conscious that this is a daft question. Being locked up is enough to upset anyone.

'I never thought I was the kind of person to go to prison,' she sobs. 'I didn't mean to do it. I just snapped.'

I know what that feels like, I almost say. Then I recall the chaplain's advice: *'Don't tell them your story; they are here to tell you theirs. Repeat their words back at them. It makes them feel secure, and also shows that you're listening.'*

'You just snapped? Why was that?' I say to the woman.

Her voice is raw with grief. 'I couldn't cope with Alice any more. No one would help me. My husband often works away. And I just . . .'

I wait. '*Don't jump in*', the chaplain had advised.

But she's sobbing and sobbing.

'You don't have to tell me what happened.'

'But I want to,' she says.

I'm not sure I want her to. I can't bear to think what this woman might have done to Alice, whoever she was.

Suddenly she blurts it out. 'I just walked out and slammed the door on her. Then I left the house and didn't come back for an hour.'

'How old was Alice?' I ask.

'Sixteen months,' she sobs.

'You left a one-year-old on her own?'

This is a question, not a statement. I can sense the chaplain stiffening.

'I'd have to have been there to understand the situation,' I add hastily.

'You're right,' she replies. 'If you had, you'd have understood how awful it was. I'd had enough. Alice would cry all the time and I couldn't do anything about it. I was exhausted. I couldn't sleep. When I was awake, I was a zombie.'

'Did you ask for help?'

'The doctor put me on a waiting list for counselling but I was told it could take months. I talked to my mum about it, but she lived miles away and then last year she died from a brain aneurism.'

Like my own mother had. My heart begins to soften. 'That must have been a terrible shock.'

'Yes,' she manages through another sob. 'But it got worse. I left Alice again and this time, she helped herself to a packet of tablets I'd left out. She nearly died.'

I gasp and then instantly reproach myself. Listeners aren't meant to show judgement.

'I know. It's awful, isn't it? It's why I'm inside.'

'Who's looking after Alice now?' I ask.

'My mother-in-law. She's the one who found Alice. She has her own key and visits without warning sometimes. She called the ambulance. Thank God she'd only taken one tablet and they managed to save her.'

'How long have you got in here?' I ask.

'Eighteen months.'

'Are you allowed to see Alice?'

'I've asked my husband to bring her in. He says he's thinking about it.'

'That can't be easy,' I say.

She begins to cry harder now.

'I have two grown-up girls,' I say. The chaplain gives a loud cough, indicating disapproval. I ignore him. 'One won't visit me.'

'How do you cope?' she asks.

'I tell myself that one day, she might change her mind. In the meantime, I try to take each day as it comes. Concentrate on a daily job. Keep communication going. Why don't you send Alice some pictures or maybe do Storybook Mums with the education department?'

'What's that?'

'It's when the staff help you write a story with your child's name in it and then they record you reading it aloud and send it to your children. You could ask to see the counsellor too. In fact, it seems to me that you should've had some help earlier on. Perhaps you could ask for that.'

'That's a good idea.'

'Has this helped a bit?' I can't help asking.

'I think so,' she says. 'Thank you.'

When she leaves, I know what the chaplain is going to say. 'You deviated from the script, Belinda. And you gave too many personal details.'

'So, I'm no good as a Listener.'

'On the contrary. I think you helped a great deal, even if it was in an unorthodox manner.'

'Would you want me to continue then?'

'I do. However, you need to listen to *me* more, Belinda. I know I put you on the spot by bringing you in before you were ready, but you can't share yourself like you did just then. Apart from anything else, it makes you vulnerable. The person you're trying to help might tell people things that you don't want revealed.'

A cold shiver runs through me. 'I understand.'

In the following weeks, when I'm asked to listen to others – including Alice's mother – I keep thinking someone is going to tap me on the shoulder, tell me that they know what I've done.

After all, who would want advice from a murderer?

Then the chaplain is taken ill and I find myself Listening alone. I'm sure it's against the rules but no one stops me.

And that's when I make my mistake.

43

Now

Mabel looks at Belinda, her hand on her heart as if feeling her own pulse.

'How did you cope when you thought one of your daughters might have died?'

'I just had to.'

The old lady's eyes fill with tears. 'That must have been so hard. I cannot imagine anything worse.' Then she blows her nose hard. 'A Listener in prison! I didn't know there was such a thing. I can see why you're so good at listening to me and the other residents – I've seen you. But what kind of mistake did you make?'

'I'll tell you next time,' says Belinda firmly. 'It's your turn now. I need to know if the Colonel was really hanged.'

As if on cue, the bell sounds for tea. 'It will have to wait until tomorrow,' says Mabel. She sounds nervous. As if there is something she doesn't want to tell.

The Stranger in Room Six

'Now let me in,' I hiss, before anyone sees us.

Shaking, Belinda obeys.

'You know,' I say, 'the thing about prison is that you never know who or what to believe. It doesn't surprise me at all that people thought I was dead, including you. You must have thought it was highly convenient. You never really trusted me, did you?'

Belinda has the decency not to disagree.

'I nearly did die, actually,' I add. 'It was touch and go. I was in hospital for months then they moved me to another prison. I only got out six months ago.'

'What are you doing at Sunnyside?' Belinda stammers.

'I could ask you the same.'

'I work here.'

'I can see that. I suppose no one knows what sort of person you really are then, Lady Belinda.'

Silence.

'I'm presuming you faked your DBS.'

Belinda looks scared. 'I needed a job. But please don't tell anyone.'

I love it when someone says that. It's like an open invitation to blackmail. 'Well, that's convenient, as I may have a little job for you. But this one is a bit more complicated. Your life depends on this job. And maybe your girls' lives too.'

'No,' she whimpers. 'Please don't hurt them.'

I glance meaningfully down at my walking stick. 'My employer chose me for this job because I need the sort of help that you can only get in here. And that's all thanks to you, Belinda. If you hadn't needed protecting, I wouldn't be in this state. You owe me. And now I'm calling in the favour.'

'All right, Mouse,' she says in an 'I know when I'm beaten' voice. 'Tell me what to do.'

44

Belinda

Mouse is still alive? I don't believe it. Everyone said she was dead.

Then again, poor communication in prison is notorious. Staff aren't allowed mobile phones, so they communicate through memos, landlines or the spoken word. It would have been quite easy for someone to tell someone else that Mouse had died in hospital and for it quickly to become fact.

Is it awful to admit that when I heard she was dead, I was relieved? Yes, she'd been 'looking after me' inside but we both knew that she'd expect payment one day – and I don't mean hard cash.

Now that time has come.

Mouse (who has barely changed, aside from her unwieldy walk) has got me in a corner, well and truly trapped. She knows more about me than anyone else.

I can't hand her in or refuse to do what she says or she'll tell the home that I lied on my form. Then I'll be out on my heels without achieving the one thing I came here to do.

Even worse, she might hurt my girls. She'll know where they are. People like this woman have contacts. She can do anything.

She even refused to die.

I have to face facts.

'OK, Mouse,' I say. 'You win. Tell me what to do.'

'You're friendly with Mabel Marchmont in Room Seven,' she says.

I go cold. 'I'm not hurting her.'

'I'm not asking you to. Not unless she refuses to help. She has something that I need. A list of names hidden somewhere in her room; an historic piece of intel. You're going to find it and bring it to me.'

'A list of names? Why is it so important?'

'It's a matter of national security. You don't need to know more. Just find it and get it to me. And make sure she's none the wiser.'

'It might help if I knew what I was looking for,' I urge.

She hesitates. 'Fine, but I'll slit your throat if you reveal this to anyone else.'

'I promise,' I say in a small voice.

'During the Second World War, there were some members of the British public who wanted Hitler to win because they thought he'd make Britain "great again". Apparently lists of these sympathizers were made in each county so that they could be observed and, when the war ended, possibly "taken care of".'

'Taken care of?'

'Imprisoned, executed, whatever,' Mouse says, waving her hand vaguely. 'But a lot of them weren't caught, and now *certain people* need to ensure that their relatives aren't on that list. It would be *very* embarrassing for them, don't you think?'

'But it was so long ago.'

'Mud sticks. So does blood. The list for this part of the county seems to have gone missing, and we think Mabel has it.'

'Why would you think that?' I can't help picturing the Mabel I know: her kind eyes and soft demeanour.

'Because her aunt and her aunt's lover were in on it. There's a high chance it was passed to Mabel when they died.'

Slowly, it sinks in. The war work that Mabel had described. The 'red-and-black pattern', which sounded like a swastika to me.

'Was Mabel involved too?' I ask, barely able to hide the concern in my voice.

'Possibly.'

'If she was,' I say staunchly, 'I don't believe she did it intentionally. She was only a child.'

Mouse bats away my words. 'Simply get that list off her and bring it to me.'

'How am I meant to do that? I can't walk in and take it!'

Mouse rolls her eyes. 'Use your initiative, Belinda. Spend as much time as you can with the old bird. Listen to her stories; dose her up with sleeping tablets and go through her wardrobe, her drawers, anywhere she could hide something. It might just be a scrap of paper. I don't care how you do it. All I know is that if I don't have that list in my hand before July the 12th, someone's going to die. And you don't want that to be you.'

I feel the blood draining from my face. 'July the 12th . . . Isn't that the day of the party?'

'That's the deadline I've been given. Now don't stand there. Get going. I want you to report to me on a daily basis. You can find me in Room Six.'

Mouse hobbles up to me and grasps my hand so tightly that her nails pierce my skin. 'If you treasure your girls, I suggest you get cracking.'

45

It's like being back in prison all over again. How ironic that Mouse nearly died for me. And now she's the one threatening both me and my girls.

I love Mabel. I can't help it. I've grown genuinely fond of this brave, vulnerable girl who has grown into an eccentric and feisty old lady.

But my daughters clearly have to come first. So the following day, feeling like a traitor, I arrive at Mabel's room, armed with a packet of chocolate ginger biscuits: her favourite.

'How lovely,' she says. 'Please sit down here.' She pats the chair next to hers.

'Thank you,' I say. 'You know, I've been dying to find out what happened after the Colonel was taken away.'

'Ah,' she says, her eyes looking as if they were in another place. 'That's when it really got dangerous.'

If only Mabel knew how much danger she's in now, thanks to me.

'Please,' I say, my smooth voice hiding a fast-beating heart. 'Do continue your story.'

She leans back and closes her eyes as if transporting herself to another time. 'Very well,' she says. 'It was 1943 . . .'

46

Mabel

1943

They were in the drawing room, sitting on large chesterfield sofas beside walnut tables with chequered marquetry. On the walls hung huge oil paintings, from which Mabel's grandparents peered down with stern expressions, as if they too could not believe the family scandal about to come crashing down. The Colonel had been in jail for over a year awaiting trial. He'd been refused bail while the police built their case.

'The authorities think Jonty has done something wrong,' wept her aunt. 'But he hasn't. He was just trying to do his best for King and Country. They've got it all wrong.'

Cook made a noise from the door. Mabel wasn't sure if it was because she disagreed or because she wanted to alert them to her presence.

'Lunch is served,' she said.

'I can't eat anything,' wept Aunt Clarissa.

'I won't eat either,' declared Mabel.

'You must,' whispered Cook, coming to Mabel's side. 'You need to keep your spirits up. I don't know how to say this but it's best if people don't think you're too upset about everything that's happened.'

'What are you whispering?' said Clarissa, lifting her tear-stained face.

'I suggested that Miss Mabel might like to try some of the broth I've made.'

'Go,' said her aunt, waving her hand. 'I need to be alone.'

After lunch, Frannie was still giving her cold looks despite her promise that they would be friends again.

'Will you go for a walk with me after you finish your work?' Mabel asked.

'I need to help my mam at home,' Frannie replied shortly. 'Besides, I don't want to walk with a Blackshirt supporter.'

'I'm not a Blackshirt,' Mabel declared stoutly. 'Cook has told me about them.'

Frannie turned on me, her eyes blazing. 'Then why are you so upset about the Colonel? People like him think Hitler will make them powerful. Some poor people even think they'll get better living conditions, but they're both wrong. That's what my dad used to say . . . before he got murdered. Now leave me alone.'

Frannie had to be wrong. The Colonel could be tough at times but on the whole, he was kind. Surely he couldn't be supporting that wicked man in Germany?

Mabel wandered out to the stables. She needed to do *something* or she felt her head would burst.

'Are you all right, my dear?' asked James the groom when he found her sobbing into Foam's neck for comfort.

'I'm so confused about the Colonel. My aunt says he tried his best for King and Country. But now someone – I can't say who – has told me he's on Hitler's side. I can't believe it. He's usually so nice to me. He cannot be bad.'

The groom patted her on the shoulder. 'Sometimes, bad people seem good on the outside. The Colonel is being tried for treason.' His voice rose with anger. 'That's an extremely serious offence.'

'But he loves England. He's always saying so.'

'People can show their love in strange ways, miss.'

'But if he has done wrong, why can't they just lock him up instead of hanging him?'

The groom's lips visibly tightened. 'Because an example has to be set. Now, why don't you take Foam for a ride and clear your head?'

It proved good advice. Maybe, Mabel told herself, as she trotted across the fields, the Colonel would be proved innocent and then they could return to normal. Or at least, as normal as life could be in this horrible war.

On her way home, Mabel spotted a man mending the fences around the paddock. For some reason, her heart began to beat.

'Antonio! What are you doing here?'

'We have been told to help around the village,' he replied, giving a bow. So polite!

Then he noticed her tear-stained face. 'What is wrong?'

Mabel couldn't help telling him about the Colonel.

'My father is a count,' he said. 'Depending on which way the war goes, he might too be shot as a traitor. Or hanged.'

'I am so sorry.'

'You're sorry? Even though I am the enemy?'

'I don't really see you like that,' admitted Mabel. 'You seem too nice.'

'So do you. Although you're not just nice. You are beautiful.'

Mabel flushed. No one had ever called her that before.

'Miss!' The groom was calling from the stables. 'Your aunt needs you urgently.'

Was she ill? Clarissa had become so pale and thin since Jonty had been taken.

But when Mabel arrived back at the house, out of breath after sprinting from the stables, she found Clarissa dressed in one of her best silk suits and hats.

'Get yourself ready,' she commanded.

'Where are we going?'

'To court.'

'I've said it before and I'll say it again,' tutted Cook. 'A trial is no place for a young lady.'

'Hold your tongue, or I will dismiss you,' snapped Aunt Clarissa. 'It is not your place to interfere.'

'Hah! You won't find anyone else to hire. Not with the gossip that's flying around.'

'Then I shall make my own meals.'

'I'd like to see that,' muttered Cook walking off.

'Please,' said Mabel running after her. 'Don't go.'

Cook gave her a quick hug. 'If it wasn't for you, child, I'd be packing my bags right now. But I can't leave you here. Not with her.'

The groom had the car ready. Aunt Clarissa got in without a thank you, then drove at breakneck speed to the court in Exeter.

'I need to see him,' she kept saying, urgently. 'I need to see him.'

Mabel had never been to court before. There were so many people! All shuffling and elbowing each other to get a seat on the benches. Some faces she recognized from the hunt.

'The Colonel must be a very popular man,' she whispered to her aunt.

'He was until the trouble started,' her aunt snapped. 'Now they have come to gloat.'

Someone slammed a gavel. The trial was beginning.

It was hard to know what was being said and who was saying it. At times, the lawyers' voices were drowned out by shouts from the gallery.

When the Colonel was called to give evidence, the crowd hissed and booed. Mabel could hardly hear what he was saying. He seemed to be mumbling. It didn't even look like him. This man had had his head shaved. Gone was the moustache. He slouched, too, as if he had already been condemned.

'What have they done to him?' wept her aunt, clutching the locket round her neck in distress.

Eventually the jury was sent out, only to return a few minutes later.

'Guilty.' The word resounded round the court amidst gasps and applause.

The judge was putting on a black cloth square on top of his wig. 'Lord Dashland, you will be taken from this place and hanged by the neck until you are dead. And may the Lord have mercy upon your soul.'

Clarissa let out such a terrible wail that every head turned towards them. 'Jonty!' she called out. 'Let me talk to him. Please, before you take him from me.'

But the Colonel looked right through her aunt as if he didn't know her.

'He doesn't want us to be implicated,' she sobbed.

But they weren't involved. Were they?

'What will happen now?' Mabel called out, frightened, as the crowd went crazy around them.

'No doubt the traitor will try to appeal,' said a man in front, turning round. 'But he won't get off. Not if there's any fairness. He deserves to be hung, drawn and quartered if you ask me. Sounds like most of the folk here feel the same.'

Then suddenly there was the sound of a blood-curdling scream. It was the Colonel.

'Oh my God,' gasped her aunt. 'Someone's stabbed him!'

47

Desperately, Mabel tried to follow Clarissa who was fighting her way through the crowd. But she could see they were too late. The Colonel was lying on the floor of the court, blood gushing out of his neck, his eyes open.

A man was wrestling with the police, a dripping knife in his hands. 'Traitors like that deserve to die,' he was shouting.

Clarissa was screaming hysterically. 'Jonty! He's killed my Jonty.'

Everywhere, there was panic. Some people were screaming. Others were shouting 'Good riddance' and 'Now he can't appeal against his sentence'.

'Stand clear everyone, please,' called out another policeman.

'Let's get his bitch next,' shouted someone. 'Where is she?'

'Quickly,' said Mabel. 'We need to get you away from here.'

Why was no one helping them? 'Lean on me,' said Mabel urgently. Somehow she managed to get her still-hysterical aunt back to the car.

'Are you able to drive?' she ventured nervously. 'If we don't get moving, they might do the same to us.'

Her words must have sunk in because Clarissa stopped screaming and got into the driving seat.

The gear stick made a strange noise but they were moving. 'Please don't go so fast,' begged Mabel sliding down the seat, too scared to look.

Finally, they roared up the drive of the Old Rectory, screeching to a halt. Clarissa opened the driver's door and slumped out, half-mad with exhaustion, half-mad with grief.

'I'll help you get her upstairs,' said Cook rushing to Mabel's side.

'Jonty, Jonty,' wept her aunt as she sank onto the pillow. 'How can I live without you?'

The following evening, her aunt fell down the stairs in her grief, twisting her ankle. 'What am I going to do?' she wailed to Mabel from her bed. 'Tonight is the night. Jonty told me I had to fulfil the plan, even if he wasn't here. But I can't move with this wretched pain. How am I going to do it now?'

'Do what?' Mabel asked.

Her aunt grabbed her hand. 'You asked before if you could help with the war work. Now is the time. I need you to go down to our beach and flash a torch tonight at midnight.'

'Why?'

'It's to guide in a boat containing a special person who can help us win this war.'

Surely her aunt was rambling with the pain. 'Isn't this a job for the police or the navy?'

Clarissa's grip grew tighter. 'They must not know. Jonty and I are working for a higher authority. Now go. Quickly. Three flashes. Then back here.'

Mabel hesitated.

'I've taken you in and given you a home, girl. Do you want to help me or not?'

Uncertainly, Mabel made her way down the cliff path and onto the beach. It was so dark! Scared, she held out the torch and flashed three times.

Someone was flashing back.

Mabel turned hurriedly to clamber back up the cliff path. But as she did so, she heard a shot and screams. Hiding behind the bracken, Mabel saw to her horror that soldiers were running onto the beach. There were more gunshots.

Terrified, she ran back to the house and raced up to

Clarissa's room. 'I did as you said but then the soldiers came and I heard shooting.'

Clarissa paled. 'Was anyone killed?' she rasped, grabbing Mabel's wrist tightly.

'I don't know.'

'You did your best,' she said, shaking violently. 'As a thank you, I want you to have this.'

She undid her locket and handed it to her. 'Inside is a picture of me and your mother when we were young. Your grandfather gave it to me. Wear it at all times and keep it safe.'

Mabel's eyes swam with gratitude. 'Thank you.'

Suddenly the dogs started barking madly, as if someone was at the door.

'Get back to bed,' Clarissa hissed. 'Put on your nightclothes. Quickly. I will ring for Cook to answer.'

Back in her room, Mabel couldn't help peeping through the door, trembling as two policemen marched up to her aunt's room. Their voices were loud enough to hear across the landing.

'We've received reports of an unknown boat landing on the beach. Do you know anything about it?'

'No, of course not. I have been in my room all evening.'

'Who else is in the house?'

'Just the cook and my niece.'

Terrified, Mabel climbed into bed. The knock came in seconds. 'Mabel, love,' said Cook. 'The police need to ask you something.'

'I'm sorry to bother you, miss,' said the policeman, coming in. 'We need to talk about your whereabouts this evening. Have you been here at the house all night?'

'Yes,' she managed to say, avoiding Cook's eye. What if she'd heard her running up the drive from the beach?

'And you're certain of that?' The policeman's eyes were boring into her. 'You see, we were alerted to a certain "arrival" this evening, and so were waiting on the beach. We saw a light being flashed and then the person we were waiting for drew up, as if the torch was a signal for them. Do you know anything about this?'

'No,' whispered Mabel. 'I don't.'

The policeman left. Minutes later, she heard a scream. 'Let go of me. I can't walk. Ouch!'

Horrified, Mabel stared out of her window. Her aunt was being dragged into a police car.

'They've taken her to the station for questioning,' said Cook behind her. 'Did she talk to you about this shooting?'

'No,' said Mabel, trying to hide the terror in her voice. What if her aunt confessed? Her mind went back to the whisperings at night, people coming and going; faces she'd seen once and then never again. Clarissa's insistence that she, Mabel, should flash the torch. Was her aunt guilty? And if so, was she guilty too? What if the police came to get her next?

48

Mabel tossed and turned all night, wating for her aunt to come back. But in the morning, she still hadn't returned. Unable to eat breakfast, Mabel went for a walk in the garden, only to find Antonio trimming the hedges.

He got down from his ladder. 'You are crying,' he said. 'What is wrong?'

She found herself telling him about the Colonel being assassinated, the shooting on the beach and the policeman taking her aunt away.

'The world is a strange place at the moment,' he said. 'It's hard to know who's good and bad. I mean, here you are, talking to me, a stranger who is also the enemy. But do I look dangerous to you?'

'No,' she said, flushing.

'Personally, I just want peace.'

'So do I.'

'But there is also something else I want.'

She felt nervous. 'What?'

'A proper cup of coffee like the one my nonna makes in Italy.' He looked wistful. 'I miss my family so much.'

'I could make you a cup of tea,' she heard herself saying.

'That would be very kind.'

Luckily no one was in the kitchen. *What am I doing?* she asked herself as she brought a tray back out into the garden. But it was the mention of his grandmother that had moved her.

'That's very kind of you,' he said when she returned.

'I'll leave you to your work,' Mabel said quickly, keen to distance herself.

As she walked back towards the house, she saw a police car coming up the drive. Her aunt climbed out and hobbled up the steps.

'You're home!' said Mabel running to her.

'Of course I am,' snorted Clarissa. 'As I told them, I can't be held responsible for spies who invade our country.'

'Spies?'

'It seems that the police had a tip-off about a German who was trying to land on our beach.'

Mabel gasped. 'But you said that my torch was to guide a boat in! That it was for a special person who would help us in the war.'

'It was meant to. However, there was some mistake. You must promise not to tell anyone about last night, Mabel.' Her voice lowered. 'Or you could find yourself being murdered like poor Jonty.'

Mabel shook from head to toe. Aunt Clarissa couldn't mean that, surely?

'I promise,' she said. 'I won't breathe a word.'

49

Belinda

My mouth is open in shock. 'You lied for your aunt? Why?'

Mabel shakes her head. 'I've often asked myself that. I think it's because I wanted her approval, despite everything.'

'Did they charge her?'

'No. There wasn't any evidence. Even when I heard that it was a spy that the police had shot dead, I persuaded myself that they'd got it wrong. My aunt and Jonty wanted to make Britain great again. They kept saying so. It was only later that I pieced everything together and realized they were on Hitler's side.'

Mabel grips my arm then. 'Don't tell anyone, will you? When I look back, I feel so guilty that I tried to help the enemy. I shouldn't have told you, but you're such a good listener, Belinda, and it's been so long since I've had anyone to talk to. It just came out.'

I know I should pass on this information to Mouse but I'm torn. I don't want to cause Mabel any trouble. She clearly doesn't mean harm and never has. If I can just find this list, maybe Mabel will be spared. But the locket has given me an idea. Lockets can hold pictures or even a note, can't they? Suppose the list is hidden inside? Could Clarissa have deliberately passed on incriminating information to her niece, perhaps to save her own skin if it was found on her? Heaven knows, I've searched everywhere else in this room for this list and I can't think of anywhere else it might be.

'Where's your locket now?' I ask. 'Do you still have it?'

'I put it somewhere safe but I can't remember where,' says Mabel.

'Let's have a look, shall we?' I suggest. 'It would be nice for you to have it again.'

So we search. We go through her drawers. Or rather I do, under her watchful eye. I even go on my hands and knees inside her wardrobe in case it's fallen out of a pocket. I get a chair and climb to search the pelmet in case it's hidden there. I look everywhere.

'It's very good of you, Belinda,' she says after a bit. 'But I'm sure it will turn up at some point.'

She doesn't seem very bothered about the piece of jewellery, which surely has sentimental family value. Is it possible that she's deliberately hidden it?

'Come and sit with me, Belinda,' she says. 'I'd like to carry on telling you my story.'

50

Mabel

1943

Somehow Aunt Clarissa endured the stares from the village folk. She brazenly went to church as usual. She held her head high. And slowly, Mabel heard whispers that maybe her aunt had not been involved after all. That she had been taken in by the Colonel, as indeed had they all. And no wonder! He had seemed so warm, so generous, so affable.

'I'm not fooled,' Frannie said one day when she and Mabel were foraging for mushrooms in the woods. After her cold words about the Colonel, they had managed to make up, though it wasn't the easy relationship it had been before. 'I still think your aunt knows more than she's letting on.'

'I don't,' said Mabel defensively. 'My aunt might not be an easy woman but she's not a traitor.'

'So speaks a girl who's fallen for an Italian prisoner of war,' retorted Frannie in a disapproving tone. 'I've seen you chatting to him.'

'I haven't "fallen for him",' protested Mabel, conscious that she was blushing.

Yet it was true she had spent some very pleasant hours with Antonio in the meadow, helping him bundle up straw under the watchful eye of the groom or mending the church roof. For a man who had intended to train as a doctor, he was very practical. 'My grandfather taught me,' he explained to her. 'He lived with us when my grandmother died and we were very close.'

Mabel had never had a male friend before. But it was so easy to talk to Antonio! They shared more than she could possibly have imagined, yet the most important link was that neither knew if their father was alive.

Then one morning, just as she and her aunt returned from church, they saw the telegram boy cycling up the lane. 'Dear God,' said her aunt crossing herself in a manner that was quite unlike her.

Mabel felt her knees buckle. A telegram in wartime meant only one thing. Missing or dead.

'I'll open it,' said her aunt, putting her arm around Mabel. Her tone was gentler than usual too.

'Your father is in a prisoner-of-war camp! The Red Cross has traced him. He is in good spirits.'

Mabel burst into tears of joy. Her aunt's eyes glistened too.

Cook came running out, no doubt at the noise. She began to do a little jig. 'Yes!' she whooped and for a minute, the three of them found themselves in an embrace.

Then Aunt Clarissa moved away, smoothing down her hair. 'We must remember all those who are not so fortunate,' she said in her usual stern voice. 'Now let us get on with our jobs for the day.'

'I will write to Papa first through the Red Cross,' said Mabel.

'Only when you have completed knitting your blanket squares for the Mothers' Union,' said Aunt Clarissa.

'But –'

'There are no buts. We have had our rejoicing. Now we must all do our bit for the war effort.'

'That woman has a heart of steel,' muttered Cook as Aunt Clarissa swept off.

However, Mabel knew better. Her aunt was kinder underneath than she seemed. That sharp tongue was part of her armour and she had to respect that. The most important thing was that Papa was still alive! When this war ended, they would be together again. Of that, she had no doubt.

As soon as she finished knitting the squares – after dropping a few stitches in her excitement – Mabel wrote her letter, then headed down to the private beach. As she approached, her heart lightened. Antonio was there! Then again, she'd often told him that this was her favourite place. Could he be looking for her? Her heart sang with the possibility.

'I did a little detour on my way back to the camp to see if you were here. But I can see from your face that you have had good news!' he said. 'It is about your father?'

She nodded. How was it that Antonio could read her mind?

'I am so glad for you,' he exclaimed, taking her hand.

'Thank you. He is a prisoner of war. I know this doesn't mean he will definitely come home, but I believe he will. Besides, for now, he is safe.' Then she stopped, conscious she'd just been talking about herself. 'But what about *your* father?'

His face flattened. 'No news yet. My mother and little brothers and sisters are safe, however.'

'I feel bad for celebrating when you don't know. Uncertainty is so awful.'

'Yes,' he nodded. 'It is. But I am glad for you. Verily I am, as your Shakespeare might say.'

Then somehow – she hardly knew how – Mabel found herself in Antonio's arms, his warm lips meeting hers. It felt as if she had come home. It felt so natural. So wonderful. So exciting. So right when it should have felt wrong.

'What have we done?' she asked, breaking away.

'Oh, Mabel. Nothing that is not natural. If it was not for this war, I would have declared my love for you much earlier.'

'Love?'

'I felt something between us from the minute I saw you.'

'So did I,' she confessed.

He was smiling down at her. His warmth lit up sunrays inside her that she didn't know she still possessed. 'Then that is good, is it not?'

'But you're the enemy.'

'Mabel, *amore mio*. You do not believe that. Nor do I. When this war is over, may I hope that we can be more than this?'

'Yes,' she nodded, hardly daring to hear her own words. 'Yes, you may.'

The Stranger in Room Six

At 1.56 this morning I received a message from my employer. I haven't slept since, still jittery with nerves.

> We need something fast. Remember, do NOT compromise MM's safety at present. She's a political asset.

The message is clear.

'You'd better have something for me,' I tell Belinda when she reports to me that evening, looking visibly terrified. 'Or heads might roll. And I'm not joking.'

'I need more time,' she pleads. 'It's not easy.'

'She's an old lady, Belinda. How hard can it be? You've managed much worse than that before, haven't you?'

'She's more interested in telling me about the Italian POW she fell for than connections with Hitler or the Blackshirts.'

Little Mabel could have had her head shaved for sleeping with the enemy back in the day. Her lack of patriotism would certainly dirty Harry Marchmont's reputation, which is no bad thing for my boss. Even so, we need more.

If it was me, I'd twist Mabel's arm until it snapped. I've been reading about these suspected Hitler sympathizers. Some of these traitors were imprisoned or executed. There were also rumours of local people taking matters into their own hands; sometimes cutting throats in back alleys. Bloody right too. My granddad was killed fighting up the spine of Italy, while back in this country, aristocrats and wealthy farmers were promised secure positions; the less well-off were bribed with food and clothes if they helped Hitler to invade.

If Mabel Marchmont was involved in that, I won't be sad to see her go.

'When are you seeing her again?' I ask.

'Tomorrow.'

'Then you'd better come back to me with something good. Because if you don't, I'll blow your cover. You'll lose your job but, worse, the people I work for will get you and your family. Do I make myself clear?'

Belinda shakes so much that I almost feel sorry for her. I admit, I cared for her back in the day, but my injuries changed everything. If I hadn't stuck up for her in prison, I wouldn't be in this state.

'Yes,' she sobs. 'I understand. Actually, there is something. Well, it might not be, but . . .'

'Go on.'

'Mabel's aunt gave her a locket and she doesn't know where it's gone. She said it might have been stolen or she might have just lost it in her room. I'm wondering if it's got the list in it.'

'How convenient that you've just remembered this.'

'I didn't think it was important.'

'Bollocks. You're protecting the old woman, aren't you? It sounds to me as if you're getting a little too fond of her.'

'No, Mouse. I promise I'm not.'

'We need to check out her room. Get her out of there and take a good look.'

'I have! I'll try again when she's at lunch tomorrow.'

'Right. Then get on with it. And this time, find something.'

51

Belinda

'Oh! You're already here,' says Mabel when she comes back from lunch. Hastily, I smooth down her duvet. If she'd been any earlier, she'd have caught me turning the mattress over, checking if the list or locket hasn't slipped underneath.

'Just thought I'd change your sheets.'

'They were only done yesterday.'

'Oh, I didn't know. Never mind.'

As a carer, washing clothes and bedlinen is part of my responsibilities. It reminds me of my laundry stints in prison. The two are not so different. There are stains in both worlds.

'I've been desperate to hear the next part of your story,' says Mabel, hobbling over to the chair by the window. Sometimes she needs a wheelchair but today she seems happy with a stick. 'It's got to be one of the most dramatic things I've heard. I've always wondered what it would be like to be in prison. Now, you said you'd made a mistake when you left off last. What was it?'

Her eyes are feverishly bright.

If I've broken the promise we made, how can I know she's not spilling the beans on me too? But then if I don't come up with something intriguing, she won't give me anything to share with Mouse.

The sound of a vacuum cleaner suddenly passes by Mabel's room. 'We should find somewhere quiet to talk,' I say. 'How about I take you out into the grounds in your chair and we can sit in the chalet?'

The chalet is an outdoor room where residents can look at the garden whatever the weather. I can never get enough of fresh air after being in prison for fifteen years.

Luckily there's no one else there when we arrive.

I tuck a tartan rug over Mabel's legs. It's not cold but I know that she 'feels it' in her knees.

'Come on, come on,' she says, impatient as a child. 'Tell me what happened.'

'I'd hoped to get onto a computer class so I could track down Karen,' I start. 'But then I spoke to someone who was already on it, and she said their privacy controls were so tight, they couldn't even get onto Google. So I asked Mouse for help. She told me I needed a private investigator and that she had a mate who owed her a favour.'

Mabel's eyes widen. 'So did this "mate" find her for you?'

'No. I called it off.'

'Why?'

'Because then Elspeth visited again. Just seeing her made me realize the most important thing in my life was seeing my girls again as soon as possible, and that meant being a model prisoner. If anyone had found out that Mouse's contact was doing this for me, my sentence would have been extended.'

'So that was your mistake?'

'Yes and no. I'm in two minds, to be honest. Part of me wished I'd taken the risk.'

'But what would you have done if you had found Karen?'

'I'm not sure,' I say.

She looks at me as if she doesn't believe me. I'm not convinced I believe myself either.

*

The following day, she seems to have forgotten about our conversation. 'I must get out for a walk,' she says. 'I'm suffocating in here.'

But I have to find that bloody list, which, I'm certain, is in her aunt's locket – a piece of paper hidden inside or even a message engraved. Suddenly, I have an idea.

'I need to get you dressed first,' I say. 'Let's choose you an outfit.' I open her wardrobe. 'This dress is beautiful. Do you want to wear some jewellery? Like a pretty necklace?'

'Why?' asks Mabel. 'We're only going for a walk.'

'Thought it might be nice to get dressed up, have a change,' I reply, trying to sound casual. 'Why don't we look through your jewellery box?'

'I don't have one. I decided to have a clear-out the other year and gave my pieces to Harry's daughter.'

My heart sinks. 'You said you lost your locket earlier. Do you think you gave that away too?'

Her mouth sets. 'Definitely not. It had my mother's picture inside. I would never have done that.'

'You know,' I say, 'before I went to prison and my life was normal, I used to hide my special things in various places round the house just in case we got burgled. Do you think you might have done that here?'

Mabel frowns. 'Why are you so interested in my locket?'

'I know what it's like to lose things and I want to help.' Even as the words leave my mouth, I feel terrible for deceiving her.

'You are a dear to be so concerned. I must say that there's nothing I'd like more than to find it. I've asked other carers to search too but none have had any luck.'

I feel myself panicking. 'Do you think one might have stolen it?'

'I have to admit the thought has occurred to me,' sighs

Mabel. 'I like to think that sort of thing wouldn't happen at Sunnyside. Still, I suppose one never knows. People aren't always who they seem. Now let's go out, shall we?'

As we pass the croquet lawn, Mabel leans forwards in her chair. 'My aunt and the Colonel used to play there.'

'Really? Did they have guests round to play with them?'

'Sometimes, yes.'

'Who?'

'Oh, all sorts. I can't really remember now. Why do you ask?'

'I'm fascinated by the past, thinking of you growing up here.'

'The past is gone,' Mabel mutters.

'But the memories stay, don't they?' I suggest gently.

'Yes, I suppose they do. Both good and bad.'

I park her wheelchair by the side of the lake, where there's a beautiful view to the sea.

'See that cliff?' says Mabel. 'There's a half-finished tunnel inside. It's one of the places Antonio and I would go for privacy. We –'

She stops.

'Go on,' I say, sitting down beside her. 'Please.'

52

Mabel

1943

Life was so confusing. Antonio was the enemy, wasn't he? Yet she loved him! How she lived for the brief moments they spent together, usually out in the garden, where he would work while she made them a pot of tea to share.

Often, she found him humming to himself.

'That's a lovely tune,' she said dreamily, when she came across him one morning.

'It's called "Bella Ciao",' he said. 'The resistance sing it back home in defiance of Hitler. My brother wrote to tell me.'

'Is he part of the resistance?'

'Of course. My family does not want the Germans to win any more than you do.'

So if Antonio wasn't the enemy after all, surely it was acceptable to be friends?

The following week, Antonio was instructed to work on one of Aunt Clarissa's fields, some distance from the house. Cook had gone to collect the week's rations, so no one saw her setting off with a flask of tea and a sandwich.

'This is so kind of you,' he said. As she handed the package over, his hand brushed hers.

A thrill went through her like an electric shock. Catching his gaze, it seemed he felt the same.

'Taking that lad's tea out to him in the fields again, are you?' Cook said when she returned to the house later.

Mabel nodded, aware she was blushing.

'Be careful, won't you, love?' Cook patted the kitchen chair next to her and Mabel sat down. 'It's none of my business but if your own dear mother was here, she might warn you about losing your heart to this good-looking lad. He's a prisoner of war, love. And even if he wasn't, you've got to be careful.'

Mabel jumped up, her face burning with embarrassment. 'Of course I'm careful.'

But she just couldn't get Antonio out of her head. The next day, he wasn't there and her heart felt as if it was twisting inside with pain. Then – yes! – he was back the day after. 'I've missed you,' he said when she came flying across the field towards him.

He reached out for her hand. 'When I have finished my work, can we go for a walk?'

'I could show you the disused tunnel,' she said excitedly, hardly believing she was being so daring.

'This is amazing,' he said when they clambered inside later that afternoon. Then he moved towards her and they began kissing even more passionately than they had before. From that moment on, Mabel was lost.

The tunnel became their regular meeting spot. Mabel knew she was being reckless – suppose Frannie or one of the others saw them? – but she couldn't help it. It was so wonderful to be loved! Besides, didn't everyone say that you had to seize the moment? That you didn't know if you'd be here next month, let alone next week? That's why there were so many marriages in the village church: girls not much older than her were getting wed before their men went to war.

Was it crazy to imagine being married to Antonio?

'After the war,' he told her, 'we will get married as soon as we can and have a big family. We will live in Italy, where the sun will warm our bones and all will be well.'

'But my father . . .'

'Your father can come and live with us. My family will welcome him. People will be friends again. You will see.'

Then he kissed her once more and Mabel was wrapped in a cloud of such wonder and love that all her worries disappeared.

Meanwhile, Mabel was only just getting used to having 'the visitor', an awful inconvenience involving a terrific amount of stomach cramps and blood. When it first started, not long after Mabel arriving here, Cook had noticed the stain and asked if her aunt had 'talked about it'.

'What do you mean?' she had asked.

'You know. The birds and the bees.'

'I don't understand.'

When Cook had finished telling her about men giving ladies a seed, Mabel had been astounded. 'Does it come in a packet like lettuce seeds?' she asked.

Cook had laughed then. 'You're an innocent if there ever was one.'

It was only when Cook asked if she was in need of 'more pads' that Mabel realized that she had not received 'the visitor' for ages.

'Is this normal?' she asked.

It was not a question she could put to her aunt or even to Frannie, who, despite having 'forgiven her', was still a little off.

'Not really,' said Cook. Her eyes were sweeping over Mabel's stomach. 'You've put on weight, haven't you?'

She nodded, thinking of the top button of her skirt, which would no longer do up.

'Have you been sick in the mornings?'

'No,' said Mabel, 'although it's strange that you should mention that, because I have been feeling a little queasy.'

Cook wiped her forehead, which was beginning to sweat. 'Dear Lord above. I tried to warn you before. Is it possible that . . .'

Then she stopped.

'That what?' asked Mabel.

Cook sucked in her cheeks. 'I'll come straight to the point. Has Antonio done more than kiss you?'

Mabel blushed furiously. 'Tell me exactly,' said Cook gently, 'what he has done.'

When she'd finished, Cook bit her lip. 'I see. I think we are going to have to tell your aunt.'

Now

'You were pregnant?' asks Belinda.

Mabel nods. 'I hadn't even realized.'

'That must have been so difficult, especially back then.'

Mabel feels the old sense of shame creeping in. 'It simply wasn't done in families like ours. It was the ultimate sin to have a baby out of wedlock. I was terrified by what my aunt was going to do to me. I thought she might throw me out of the house.'

Her eyes pricked with tears.

'And did she?'

Mabel was dabbing her eyes. 'She did something far worse.'

53

1943

'But I love Antonio,' insisted Mabel when she was summoned to the drawing room. 'And he loves me. When the war is over, we'll get married.'

Her aunt snorted. 'Don't be so ridiculous. This is the talk of a man who simply wanted his way with you.' Clarissa was walking up and down the room with a cigarette in her usual ebony holder. 'What in God's name are we going to do now? The village will lynch us. You are in the family way thanks to this boy.'

'The family way?' asked Mabel.

'Don't you understand?' Her aunt gripped her by both arms, glaring into her face. 'You are a girl, still in her teens, who is pregnant by an Italian prisoner of war. The villagers will see you as having betrayed the country, just as they still suspect me. We will be finished.'

Cook coughed from the doorway. 'If you will allow me to interrupt . . .'

Aunt Clarissa rounded on her. 'I most certainly will not. What are you doing, eavesdropping like this? You should not even be here. For all I know you're going to blab this to everyone we know.'

Cook drew herself upright. 'I have too much respect for your niece to do that. I was going to say that my sister lives in a small village in Cornwall. We could put out the word that Mabel needs a change of air and that she has gone to visit friends. My sister will arrange for the midwife to help Mabel when the time comes. Of course, we don't know when that will be, but the Italian arrived about five months ago. So I'd say she's at least four months gone. Then . . .'

'We will sort out the "then" when it happens,' said her aunt. Her tone had softened slightly. 'Thank you. This sounds like the best plan in a dire situation. Mabel, you must get ready immediately. How quickly can you inform your sister, Cook?'

'I will ask, not inform. And I shall write to her immediately.'

'You can telephone her for speed.'

'She isn't connected.'

'For God's sake! Well, find someone nearby who is, and ask her, then. My niece must leave as soon as possible.'

Mabel's mind was reeling. How could she have a baby without being married? What would her father say when he came home? And, most importantly, how would she tell Antonio?

Aunt Clarissa waggled a finger in front of her, as if reading her mind. 'You will not leave the house. I forbid it. No one must see you. Look at your waist! It is thickening almost as I speak.'

'But I need to tell Antonio.'

'Don't worry, miss,' said Cook quickly after Clarissa had left the room. 'Write me a note and I will get it to him somehow.'

Mabel had no option but to stay in her bedroom like a prisoner. The following day, at sunrise, her aunt drove her to the station. As they went past the camp, Mabel peered out through the window. There he was! At the wire fence, waiting for her. She knocked on the window, but the sound wasn't loud enough for him to hear. 'Don't be so stupid,' thundered her aunt.

'Look in my direction please,' Mabel whispered. Then he did! His expression turned to excitement and then dismay as they drove on.

'Antonio,' she wept. 'Antonio.'

'For God's sake,' Clarissa snapped. 'Just be grateful that when the war ends, you can reinvent yourself. In my day, we could not do that.'

'What do you mean?'

'Forget it. Now get on quickly before anyone sees you. The train is about to depart.' Then she pressed two five-pound notes into her hand. 'For emergencies,' she said.

54

The train was almost empty.

'Not many folk are travelling nowadays,' remarked a woman opposite, who was looking at her with interest.

Mabel was tempted to get up and find a seat in a different carriage but didn't want to appear rude.

'I'm going to visit my sister in Penzance for a few weeks,' continued the woman. The plastic cherries on her hat bobbed as she spoke. 'To tell you the truth, we weren't very close before the war but now everything has changed, hasn't it?'

She eyed Mabel's well-cut coat curiously. It was a hand-me-down from her aunt and at least two sizes too big but would, she'd said tartly, 'hide the bulge'.

'Was that Lady Clarissa I saw putting you on the train?'

Just my luck, thought Mabel. The woman must be local.

'Yes,' said Mabel falteringly. 'I used to work for her.'

'I see. So where are you going now? Travelling by train isn't particularly safe; those Germans could bomb us at any minute. What's your story?'

Mabel felt her chest tighten with anxiety, followed by a light flutter in her stomach.

Cook had told her this could happen. 'Sometimes it feels like a butterfly flapping its wings,' she'd said. 'I was not blessed to be a mother myself, but I've heard some tales. You'll be dead scared. You might even think you're going to die. But you won't.' Then she'd crossed herself. 'Just make sure they call the doctor in time.'

Mabel was suddenly aware of the cherry-hatted woman waiting for an answer.

'I'm going to visit a friend,' Mabel said quickly. It wasn't exactly true but it would do.

Then Mabel closed her eyes, hoping the stranger would understand and stop asking questions. But she kept going on about how awful the war was and asking whether Mabel had been unlucky enough to lose anyone.

A vision of her beautiful mother and little sister came into her mind. Try as she could, Mabel couldn't help a tear trickling down her face followed by another. 'Yes,' she sniffed.

'I'm sorry, love. I've upset you, haven't I?' The woman passed her a lacy handkerchief. 'There's me going on and on. My husband, bless his soul, used to say that I talked enough for two wives and more. You look tired, if you don't mind me saying. Why don't you have forty winks? Make yourself comfortable. Here – you can have my shawl to wrap round you. No, I insist. Which station are you getting off at? Penzance? Like me, then. That's good. I'll let you know when we arrive, although there's no chance of missing it. It's at the end of the line. And if you feel hungry on the way, I've got plenty here.' She patted the wicker basket next to her.

'I like to share what I can,' she said, taking a slice of ham out of the basket and waving it towards Mabel, who immediately felt queasy.

'Thank you but I don't feel hungry at the moment. In fact, I think I might be . . .'

She only just got to the window in time.

Ugh! Mabel began to cry with shame.

'It's all right, dear. Don't worry. Whoops! There you go again. Get it out. It will feel better that way. Here, love, let me take off your coat. We can wipe you down with my handkerchief.'

Reluctantly, she obeyed.

She cast her eyes over Mabel's stomach. 'Ah. So that's why they've sent you away. One of Lady Clarissa's maids, were you?'

Fortunately she didn't wait for an answer.

'Honestly, these people use others and then they get rid of them. Some of them, they say, even support Hitler. The woman's eyes sparked with new interest. 'Wasn't there some trouble with a colonel who lived near Lady Clarissa? Stabbed in court, wasn't he?'

'I'd rather not talk about it,' said Mabel quietly.

'Of course you wouldn't. It's not a nice thing to concern yourself with in your condition. When I was expecting, my mother told me to think of only nice thoughts. Now you just rest. My name's Beryl by the way. What's yours?'

'Mabel,' she said instinctively. Then immediately she wished she'd kept quiet. 'But please don't tell anyone you met me or that I am . . . pregnant,' she pleaded.

'Of course, I won't, love. Your secret is safe with me. Now you go ahead and have that shut-eye. Wake me if you feel hungry.'

It was a long journey. The wind was strong and every now and then Mabel jolted awake as a branch struck the side of the train.

Suddenly, she was aware of a noise from outside and of Beryl coming away from the window.

'Get down under the seat,' she said quickly. 'I can see a plane coming. From the markings, it's one of theirs.'

It flew over. Then another. And another. They held their breath as they clung to each other, crouched under the seats. The train picked up pace.

Surely any minute now, they would be bombed to smithereens just like Mama and Annabel. Mabel placed her hands protectively over her stomach. She would die to protect

Antonio's baby. 'Please, God,' she found herself praying. 'Save us both.'

'They've gone,' said Beryl, her breath coming out in a whoosh. 'Looks like they're on their way to Exeter.' She crossed herself. 'I hope to God they don't kill too many. Those poor souls. They won't know what's coming to them.'

Thinking of Mama and Annabel, Mabel began to weep.

'Come, come. You can't worry about everything now. It's all too big. Just think about what's in front of you, like your bairn. Is the father waiting for you?'

'He doesn't know yet,' whispered Mabel.

'Well, however he reacts, you'll be all right. I feel it in my bones. Us women are made of strong stuff. We cope with things that many men could not. That's why God gave us the honour of having babies. I'm blessed with four children, each with little ones of their own now, although they live miles away.' She rushed to the window again. 'Goodness me, we're nearly there.'

As she spoke, Mabel saw the sea running alongside the track. It was a different kind of sea from the one she'd just left. This was wider. It seemed to go on for ever.

'Is this friend of yours meeting you off the train?'

Mabel flushed. 'Actually, I don't know her. It's someone that my . . . that Lady Clarissa arranged for me to stay with during my confinement.'

Heavens! She'd almost said 'my aunt' then.

But when they got out, no one was there.

'I'll wait until she turns up,' declared Beryl. 'I'm not leaving an expectant girl alone.'

After an hour, still no one came.

'Do you have an address?'

Mabel passed her the piece of paper that Cook had given her before leaving.

'Let me make some inquiries.'

Mabel was left sitting on the platform, head bowed, wondering what was going to happen next. Would Cook have passed her message to Antonio? Would he escape to try and find her? If so, he would probably be arrested and sent to another camp. Or shot...

Eventually, Beryl came back. Her face was sombre. 'Mabel, I'm afraid I've got some bad news. You must be very brave. You remember those planes we saw passing on the way to Exeter?' Her lips tightened. 'They dropped their bombs on Penzance too. There was a direct hit on the street where you were meant to be staying.'

Mabel put a hand to her mouth in horror.

'I'm afraid there were no survivors. The whole road was wiped out.'

Mabel burst into tears. So Cook's sister had been killed? How terrible! Then the realization came to her that she had nowhere to go. She couldn't possibly return to the Old Rectory. Her aunt wouldn't want her there.

'You must come with me,' said Beryl, as if she could read Mabel's thoughts. 'My sister's the other side of town. We should be able to get there safely from here.'

'But you don't know me.'

'It doesn't matter. My sister will understand. It's only a modest cottage but it's right by the sea, in a small village called Mousehole. You can stay for as long as you like until your bairn is born.'

'I have ten pounds I can give you for my board.'

'Thank you, but you keep that money for yourself.'

'Why are you being so kind to me?' Mabel asked, her eyes wet with gratitude.

'I have children myself. I don't like to think of a young

girl like you being on your own. Do you want to call your mother?'

Mabel shook her head. 'She . . . She died.'

'So that's the loss you were crying about. You poor, poor girl. You can tell me more later if you want, or not at all. The most important thing is that we get you back into a warm home after this journey. Let's go, shall we?'

55

Now

Back in her room at Sunnyside, Mabel has gone frighteningly pale and her hands are shaking. 'I want to go home,' she whispers to Belinda. 'Take me back. Now. Before the bombs start again. We need to go to the shelter.'

Belinda rings the alarm. Around her, Mabel can hear voices panicking.

'Her blood pressure is up.'

'We need to calm her down.'

'You and I, Belinda,' whispers Mabel. 'We both loved and lost, didn't we?'

'What's she talking about?'

'She must be rambling,' says Belinda.

'No I'm not . . .'

Then Mabel feels a small prick and drifts back into the past again.

56

1943

Beryl's sister was called Olive. She was a taller, thinner and more angular version of Mabel's rescuer and did not seem at all put out by a stranger coming to stay. In fact, both women seemed to find it a relief that there was someone else to ease the obvious tension between them.

'Do you have brothers or sisters?' asked Olive as she led her to a pretty room in the eaves of the cottage. There was a blue-and-pink chintz bedspread, a pink rug, a sweet little dressing table and, of course, the standard blackout curtains.

'I used to have a baby sister,' said Mabel quietly. 'She was killed along with my mother when a bomb fell on our house in London.'

Olive gasped. 'Oh love, I'm so sorry.'

'I just keep thinking of Cook's sister in Penzance,' said Mabel tearfully.

'Was that who Lady Clarissa had arranged for you to stay with?'

She nodded.

'It's tragic,' said Olive with tears in her eyes.

Fortunately, Beryl's sister was sensitive enough not to ask any more questions. Instead, she took a towel out of a pine chest of drawers and showed her where the bathroom was. 'We take it in turns. There's a chamber pot under the bed.'

Mabel thought briefly of the five large bathrooms in the Old Rectory, which had been icy cold in winter.

'Thank you. I cannot believe you've been kind enough to take in a stranger.'

'It's what we do in the war,' Olive replied.

'That's what your sister told me.'

'We are more alike than we sometimes care to admit. Now you need a rest after your journey.' She looked at Mabel's tummy. 'That little one needs it as much as you.'

'Do you have children?'

'Sadly not, but . . .' her sentence drifted off, unfinished, before she shook her head. 'Anyway, I don't know what you need in the way of clothes but there are some spare clean dresses in the wardrobe that might fit you for a while. If you want something washed, please let me know. You will be safe here, Mabel.' She hesitated before continuing. 'Mousehole is a warm, friendly place but people talk, as in any small village. You haven't mentioned the father, and we don't want to pry but shall we tell people that your husband is away in the navy?'

Mabel hesitated.

'No need to say any more, dear. However, you'll need a ring to prevent questions. We'll find you one from our mother's old jewellery box.'

Mabel was too choked to speak.

'You won't be the first to have a child out of wedlock,' said Olive quietly, 'and you won't be the last. Now do get some rest.'

But Mabel couldn't sleep. Tiptoeing out onto the landing, she heard voices below her in the little sitting room.

'How could you have brought her here? To me, of all people?'

'What else could I do, Olive? The girl was destitute.'

'But what if something goes wrong again?'

'We'll just have to make sure that it doesn't.'

Mabel was terrified. *What* mustn't happen again?

Perhaps she shouldn't have been so rash in accepting a stranger's invitation. 'I must leave now,' Mabel told herself. If necessary, she'd sleep in a bus shelter. Tiptoeing down the stairs, she discovered the front door was locked, with no sign of a key.

Her chest tightened with panic, and that light flutter in her stomach returned. 'Please look after me,' it seemed to say.

Not knowing what else to do, she padded back up the stairs to her room and stared out at the sea, glinting in the moonlight. Somewhere out there was Papa. There might not have been a letter from him yet, but she prayed that there would be soon. In the meantime, she had to be grateful that the Red Cross had managed to trace him to a camp.

Somewhere out there, too, was Antonio. Please may he be safe.

'And now I have you,' she whispered, stroking her rippling stomach. 'Soon, we will all be reunited. Until then, it's just us. Sleep tight, little one. In the morning, I'll find a way for us to escape.'

After much tossing and turning, Mabel finally fell into a deep sleep in which she dreamed that she and Antonio were walking through a field. She was carrying their babe, and he had his arm around her shoulders.

The next thing she knew, Beryl was peering over her face. Mabel jumped.

'Sorry, love. Did I startle you? I just wanted to check you were all right. When you're ready, come down for some breakfast.'

It would be too difficult to leave now, with everyone up. Besides, her stomach was rumbling; she needed to eat for the sake of the baby. Mabel went downstairs nervously to find a small table beautifully laid with pretty blue-and-yellow floral china and a lace tablecloth. The sisters were sitting opposite one another, the air tight, as if Mabel had interrupted an argument.

'My sister says you need to let your former employer know that you're here safely,' said Beryl.

'My employer?'

'Didn't you say it was Lady Clarissa at the Old Rectory near Sidmouth?'

'Yes, of course. Thank you.'

'I don't have a telephone,' said Olive, 'but if you write a note, I can give you a stamp. You can hand it in at the post office. It's just over on the sea front.'

'Thank you,' said Mabel, jumping at the chance to leave without raising suspicion. She would catch a bus or a train back to Exeter, but then what?

'You can tell Lady Clarissa that you'll stay here until you have the baby, and beyond if you wish.'

'But –'

'No buts. We insist.'

Mabel went upstairs to write. As she did so, the baby fluttered again. The idea of sleeping in a bus shelter with her unborn child now seemed irresponsible. Perhaps she could ask her aunt to collect her instead.

Dear Aunt,

You will have heard of the terrible bombing in Penzance by now. Please give my condolences to Cook.

Two sisters have given me shelter but I do not trust them. One talks of why I've been brought to her 'of all people' and I fear that she has done something wrong in her past. Please come and get me. This is my address . . .

She wrote a brief note to Cook, giving the same details, in case she had news of Antonio. Then she set off for the post office.

'Ah, you're the young lady staying with Olive Fish,' said the jolly woman behind the counter.

'Yes,' she said, hoping she wouldn't be engaged in conversation.

'You'll be doing Miss Olive a favour – and Beryl too. They've never been the same since Kitty went.'

'Kitty?'

'Didn't they tell you?'

The woman took on the air of someone about to impart a tasty titbit of gossip. 'Kitty was their little sister. Shortly before the war, she was engaged to be married but her gentleman friend broke it off. She'd got into the family way by then and they tried to keep it quiet. Olive had just finished training as a midwife so it was planned they would deliver her at home. Unfortunately, things went wrong and both baby and mother died.'

Mabel gasped. 'How dreadful!'

'The doctor said he should have been called beforehand, but Olive had wanted to prove her skills as a midwife. She hasn't practised since. It's why the two sisters haven't been getting on so well. When we heard that Beryl was coming to stay, we hoped the war might bring them back together. They're good souls.'

So that's what Olive had meant by 'to me of all people'. The thought of staying in a house where a baby had died felt like a bad omen.

Maybe she should speak to her aunt – it would be quicker than the letter she'd just sent. 'Is there a telephone I could use here, please?'

'Only for emergencies, I'm afraid, love.'

'This *is* an emergency,' she faltered.

'Is it now?' The postmistress seemed to study her for a minute and then something gave in her eyes. 'Very well. The phone's in the back.'

Surrounded by piles of tins and boxes of apples, Mabel lifted the receiver and gave the operator her aunt's number.

She expected Cook or maybe Frannie to pick it up but instead she heard her aunt's crisp, well-modulated voice.

'Aunt Clarissa. It's me, Mabel. I have to be quick as I'm using someone else's telephone. Did you know that Cook's sister was killed in the bombing raid in Penzance?'

'Oh, Mabel. That's dreadful.' Her aunt seemed genuinely shocked. So the news hadn't reached them yet.

'A woman on the train has taken me in. I'm staying with her sister, Olive Fish, somewhere near Penzance, a place called Mousehole.'

'Do they know you're my niece?'

'No. I told them that I worked for you as a maid.'

'Good.' Her aunt's voice grew thoughtful. 'Send me their names and address —'

'I already have done. I posted you a letter just now.'

'Please don't interrupt. It's so vulgar. Tell them that I will send them money for your food and keep, as your concerned former employer. But on no account tell them of our blood connection. It would ruin my standing in society if this were to get out.'

Clarissa didn't even attempt to hide the disgust in her voice.

'But I don't feel right staying here,' pleaded Mabel. 'Olive was a midwife and it all went wrong when she delivered their younger sister. She says the doctor will come to me when it's my time but supposing he doesn't?'

'Now listen to me,' said her aunt sharply, as if she was

standing in front of her in real life, waggling her finger. 'Girls like you who get into trouble have no choice. You will stay where you are and save us all from shame.'

'Antonio will marry me when he receives my message.'

'You mean the note you left with Cook?' There was a snorting sound. 'I caught her red-handed and took it away.'

'But Antonio won't know what's happened!' Mabel cried.

'He certainly won't. In fact, I have had words with the camp commander, explaining that one of his men had become too familiar with a girl in the village. Of course, he was shocked. Your lover has been moved to a different camp. He won't bother us any longer.'

'Where has he gone?'

'I have no idea and I do not care. It's for your own good. The fewer people who know, the better.'

'But what will happen when the baby's born?'

'We'll sort that out when the time comes. Now, I've got a bridge afternoon to organize. Goodbye.'

57

Now

'That's so sad,' says Belinda. Her eyes are moist. She reaches out and takes Mabel's hand. The kindness makes Mabel cry even more.

'My son,' she weeps. 'I want my son.'

'Tell me as much as you can about him. Maybe it will help.'

Mabel blows her nose. 'Perhaps you're right. Can you reach the top of the wardrobe? There's a shoebox up there and I want to show you what's inside.'

Belinda pulls a chair over and reaches up for the box. The cardboard is worn as if weathered away over the years. Inside is a piece of cream lace.

'My son has the other half,' says Mabel. 'At least, I hope he does. I like to think it ties us together.'

'Where is he now?' asks Belinda gently.

'Oh my dear,' sobs Mabel. 'If only I knew.'

58

1943

It was summer, but the weather wasn't warm and the Cornish cottage was cold at night. Even so, Mabel often woke sweating from her dreams. Sometimes she was running into her mother's arms or playing with her little sister. At other times, she opened the front door of the Old Rectory to find Papa coming up the drive in his uniform. Often, she was in Antonio's arms. Or holding a baby.

'Pregnancy gives you strange dreams,' said Beryl when Mabel confided as much over breakfast.

Olive made no comment. Mabel couldn't quite make her out. Sometimes she gave firm pieces of advice, such as bedrest, and at other times she appeared to ignore the fact that Mabel was growing larger week by week.

'Lady Clarissa has sent us money for your food and keep,' said Beryl. 'Of course, we would be happy to do it for free. However, I won't deny that it helps. She sounds very kind.'

Mabel simply nodded, not trusting herself to say any more.

I feel as though I have been transplanted into another world, Mabel had written in her last letter to Antonio. *The sisters are very caring but I can tell they are anxious. Of course, everyone is. We simply don't know when this war is going to end. I can only pray that it will be soon and that our child will be born into a safer world. To give myself courage, I hum our special song, 'Bella Ciao'.*

Then she sent the letter to the Italian prisoner-of-war camp with the words *Please forward* on the envelope.

Please let someone pass it on to Antonio, wherever they had sent him! She also wrote to Papa in the camp where the Red Cross had found him.

But she didn't receive a reply from either. Nor did she dare mention it to the sisters. What would they say if she knew was pregnant with the enemy's child?

Not long after that, when she went down to the harbour, she heard the fishermen talking excitedly. 'Looks like Italy might soon be on our side, then,' said one.

'I still wouldn't trust them – not long ago, they were killing our boys.'

So Italy might not be their enemy for long! Wouldn't that be wonderful? If only these men knew Antonio like she did, they would realize how many kind Italians there were, forced to fight for their country just like the British.

Meanwhile, the doctor who examined Mabel declared himself happy with her progress. She reported this as well as everything else in her letters, still hoping they might get to their destination.

I think of you, Antonio, every day, she wrote. *I gaze across the sea and imagine that we are picking olives in the groves you told me about, drinking juice squeezed from the oranges that grow on the trees! I am helping you with your family wine press . . .*

Then she stopped. Was she presuming too much? Supposing Antonio didn't want the responsibility of a child. Was that why he hadn't written back?

Maybe, she wrote in her next letter, *you do not want a girl who gave herself so freely. I hope you do not think I am 'cheap', as my aunt says. I love you, Antonio. I thought we could call our baby after you if it is a boy. What do you think?'*

Still, there was no reply. At times she told herself the letters weren't being passed on. At other times, she thought he didn't care. Summer roses bloomed and the sea was warm enough to paddle in. But Mabel no longer allowed her heart to flutter with hope when she heard the postman's step on the cobbled street outside.

I must accept my situation, she told herself. Thankfully, Beryl had extended her stay, which meant she wouldn't be left alone with Olive.

'I don't want to be a burden on you,' Mabel had told Beryl after hearing this.

'You're not, love. I want to be here when you go into labour, but I also want to spend more time with my sister. You've brought us closer after we lost Kitty. It was too much to expect from Olive. She wasn't experienced enough to deal with the birth . . .'

She put a hand on her chest. 'Oh dear, I shouldn't have said anything.'

Mabel took her hand. 'It's all right. I know. The lady at the post office told me.'

Beryl's mouth tightened. 'Can't keep anything to herself, that woman.' Tears glistened in her eyes. 'You know, dear, you even look a little like Kitty.'

'Do I?'

Beryl brought out a dark green photograph album and flicked through some pages with a fond look on her face. 'See?' she said.

Mabel couldn't spot a similarity at all. For a start, Kitty's nose was much smaller than hers and she had dark hair rather than auburn. Maybe Beryl and Olive wanted her to be like their sister to make up for their loss.

'My . . . My former employer Lady Clarissa says that after my baby is born, it has to be adopted,' she said with a little sob.

'Does she indeed?' said Olive coming into the room. 'What gives her the right to say that?'

'She says it's because I'm too young and can't choose for myself.'

'Nonsense. She has no right to tell you what to do. It's not as if she's your mother. Besides, there are plenty of girls who start young. I saw them myself when I was training. In fact, it can be an advantage – your bones are more supple, so it'll be easier to give birth.'

This was another thing Mabel had been wondering about but hadn't dared ask the male doctor.

'How does it actually happen?'

'How does what happen?'

Mabel felt her face begin to flush. 'How does the baby come out of me?' she eventually managed. 'Is it through my tummy button? It seems very small.'

'Your tummy button, love?' Beryl burst into peals of laughter. 'Now there's an idea. The truth is, love, that it comes out from between your legs.'

'But what if . . . I mean suppose I . . . Well, what if I need the lavatory at the same time?'

Beryl's laughter turned to tears of mirth. 'You're a rum one.'

'No,' corrected Olive. 'That's a very intelligent question. At some point in your labour, you'll need to push but not until the midwife tells you to.'

'Don't worry her,' said Beryl, who had stopped laughing.

'I'm not. Am I, Mabel?'

Actually, she was, but Mabel didn't want to say so. 'I feel a bit tired now. Is it all right if I lie down?'

'Of course, love. Off you go.'

But as she went upstairs, she heard them fretting. 'I know you're trying to sound calm in front of Mabel,' Beryl said, 'but I can see you're terrified.'

'I just keep thinking of Kitty.'

'This is different. You won't be delivering the baby.'

'Because I'm no good as a midwife?'
'I didn't say that.'
'But it's true, isn't it?'
Mabel's letter to Antonio was brief that night.

I am terrified about giving birth. What if it all goes wrong? Please answer or come and find me. My address is at the top of the letter. Dearest Antonio. Don't abandon me. Ask the commander for compassionate leave. I need you. I have a bad feeling about this.

The Stranger in Room Six

So little old Mabel got pregnant by the enemy! A teenager and not married, either. It couldn't get much worse in those days.

This complicates matters, I have to say. No one mentioned a child. What if they're behind all of this? Grown up and causing havoc?

Luckily, that's not my problem. All I have to do is pass on the information.

'You did well,' I tell Belinda.

She looks uneasy. 'I don't like betraying her confidences,' she says. 'I've given you enough, haven't I? I want to stop now.'

I shoot her one of my 'don't you dare' looks. 'But you can't, can you, Lady Belinda? You're in too deep. Besides, we still need to find this list of names. Like I said, this is a matter of national security.'

She sets her chin in the way she used to in prison. 'But it isn't, is it? Otherwise, they wouldn't be employing someone like you. I think you're working for someone else. Someone shady. The question is, who? And why do they care about this list of names? What has it got to do with Mabel?'

'You're asking too many questions.'

'I just want to know the truth, Mouse.'

'Oh dear, Lady B. Do I need to teach you a lesson?'

Then, before she can answer, I raise my crutch and whack it into her left shin.

59

Belinda

The next day I return from A & E at the local hospital after being X-rayed and bandaged up. Almost immediately, I am called to Mabel's room. 'Where have you been?' she demands petulantly. 'I had another carer today who couldn't be bothered to chat.'

'I hurt my leg,' I say. 'Luckily, it isn't broken.'

'How did you do that?'

'I walked into a chair,' I lie. I can't exactly say I was attacked by the resident in Room Six. Or that it was followed by a threat of 'much worse' if I didn't 'get on with the job'.

'I haven't felt well either,' she says plaintively.

My friend, as I am beginning to see her, is hunched up in her bed, appearing smaller than usual, with a childlike 'please help me' expression on her face. I don't like the look of this. I often forget how old she is because she's still so articulate.

I lay my hand on her forehead ('That's lovely and soothing, Belinda') and check her records by the bed. Her obs (our shorthand for observation tests) seem fine.

'I'll be all right,' she says, seeing my concern. 'It's just age and tiredness. I need distraction. Will you go on with your story?'

So I do.

60

My Listener work gives me a purpose. There's nothing like hearing other people's problems to get your own in perspective. Last week, a woman told me how her brother had tried to rape her, so she'd smashed his head in with a hammer. Somehow, she's the one who's ended up in jail and he got off scot-free. Another was a forger. 'It's surprisingly easy when you learn the trade,' she says. 'Let me know if you ever need any help.'

I don't think so. But you don't make judgements as a Listener. You just lend an ear.

Then comes the day when Linda Wall turns up in the Listener's Room.

'I'm upset with you,' she says from behind the screen, in a voice that sends a chill down my spine.

I look around for the chaplain, who is back at work now. He'd been here a few minutes ago to supervise but he's disappeared.

I could ask her how she knows that I am tonight's Listener but there seems little point.

'Why?' I say.

'Because you've seen me enough times since my daughter died and you've never come up to express your sympathies.'

'But I did! Just after it happened. You ignored me.'

'I was fucking out of it with grief. But you didn't try again.'

True. This was partly because Mouse told me to keep my tough image going, but also because I felt guilty with relief that my own girls were safe.

'I didn't know what to say,' I gulp.

I hear what sounds like a snort. 'Call yourself a Listener?'

'Would it help if I said sorry now?'

'Too bloody late for that.'

There might be a screen between us but I can just picture her cold eyes locked on mine. 'You see, Belinda, grief can drive you mad. You might have tasted that for the short time when you thought it was one of your girls. But I have to live with this madness every day, every minute, every second of my life from now on. And when people say the wrong thing to me, or they don't say anything at all, they go straight onto my blacklist. Do you know what that means?'

My mouth goes dry. I try to remember my training. How you should invite people to share their emotions rather than tell them what to do.

'Would you like to tell me?'

'That's why I'm here. What it means is that I resent people like you whose daughters are still alive. It means that I wish they were dead, too, so that their mothers had to feel what I feel. It means that your daughters need to watch out. Gillian and Elspeth, isn't it? I know where they are.'

Then she names the private estate where Derek lives.

I try to hide my horror and fear by sounding aggressive. 'Are you threatening me?'

'That's what it sounds like, doesn't it?'

'I could go to the governor about this.'

'If you do, you won't just lose one daughter. You'll lose both.'

'Please, Linda,' I beg. 'There must be something I can do to stop you.'

My words sound clear but my insides are churning with fear.

'Maybe.'

I clutch at the word.

'What? Tell me. I'll do anything.'

My previous bravado has disappeared.

'You can start by giving me half of every meal.'

'Done,' I say.

'You will always let me go first in the phone queue if I am behind you.'

'No problem.'

'And you can get me a razor blade.'

'How am I going to do that?'

'It's up to you.'

'What will you do with it?'

'Do you honestly think I'm going to tell you? You've got until next Friday. Give it to me at gym.'

There's a noise behind us. The chaplain is coming back. He makes an 'all right?' face at me. I nod.

'I hope this has helped,' I say in a tone that makes it clear we are no longer alone.

'Thank you.' Linda's voice might sound normal to someone who doesn't know it but I can sense the mockery. 'You've been a great Listener.'

61

A razor blade? Is Linda planning to kill herself or someone else?

The old Belinda wouldn't have hesitated. She'd have gone straight to the governor. Then Linda would be shipped out. Simple.

Except that this is not how it works in prison. Linda Wall has friends. They would take up her cause and I would be the one who got her throat slit.

But if I don't do what she says, Gillian or Elspeth will be hurt or worse. Of that I have no doubt. Many prisoners, unlike me, have contacts outside. Linda knows my girls' names; she knows where they live. I cannot risk this.

'What's wrong?' asks Mouse when I'm quiet that evening.

'Nothing.'

'Don't give me that.'

'I can't say.'

'Can't or won't?'

'If I do, someone I love will get hurt.'

'That's got to be the girls, then.'

I've already said more than I meant to. But somehow Mouse gets it all out of me. 'Right,' she says, her mouth fixed. 'Leave it to me.'

'What do you want in return?' I ask.

'You're learning,' she says with a smirk. 'Fact is, I don't know right now. But one day I will. Maybe we'll still be in here or maybe one of us will be out. Don't worry about it now. You'll know when the time comes.'

I feel as if I've just made a deal with the devil. But I'll do anything to save my girls.

I don't go to gym on Friday because I have a migraine. That's what Mouse told me to say but it turns out to be true. It's the type that makes you vomit and see flashing lights. I never used to get them but prison makes you feel all sorts of things you didn't feel before: physically and mentally.

I am sent to the San after throwing up on an officer, who told me to 'pull yourself together'.

So I'm in one of the sick beds when the alarm goes.

'Stay there,' says the nurse nervously.

I can hear shouting and screaming and banging of doors, followed by a siren. Through the barred window, I can see an ambulance. Someone is being carried out to it on a stretcher. Then a second stretcher follows.

My chest caves in with fear.

'What's happened?' I ask when the nurse returns. Her face is white.

'I can't say.'

I'm sick again, either because of nerves or my migraine. I don't know which. Then an officer comes in. 'Did your cellmate say anything to you about a grievance with Linda Wall?'

'No,' I lie, attempting to sound genuine. 'Is everything all right?'

'No, it's bloody not.' He gives me a hard stare. 'Are you sure you're telling me the truth?'

'Of course I am.'

My migraine gets so bad that I'm told to stay in the San overnight.

In the morning, I'm taken back to a different cell. 'Why?' I ask.

'Because forensics are still cleaning it.'

Forensics? I feel nauseous again. Why won't anyone tell me anything?

'Everyone else seems to know so I might as well tell you. Your cellmate left a razor blade on the step machine. The next person happened to be Linda Wall, who trod on it and started bleeding like a pig. Apparently, Mouse then yelled, "You wanted a razor blade and now you've got it." Linda managed to pick up a weight and throw it at Mouse. You could hear the snap across the room. After that, all hell broke loose.'

I think back to the two stretchers. 'Are they in hospital still?'

'Hospital?' The guard crosses herself. 'The morgue, more like. They're both dead.'

62

Now

Mabel stares at me in disbelief. 'They killed each other?'

I nod, not trusting myself not to say that, actually, Mouse is not only still alive but here in Sunnyside.

'How awful.' Then I see an 'I get it' look cross her face. 'But how convenient for you. Neither of them can hurt you now, can they?'

If only that was true.

'It isn't that simple.'

'Go on,' she says, leaning forward in her wheelchair.

I'm reluctant to say more, but the weight of Mouse's threat feels more terrifying than ever. If I can get to the bottom of Mabel's story, it might just save me. But to do that, I have to share even more.

63

Mouse is dead? Funny, scary Mouse is actually dead? And Linda Wall too.

Linda's friends will want revenge. They'll do what Linda had threatened. Hurt my girls.

There's only one course of action I can think of.

'I need to see the governor,' I say.

'Why?'

'I can't say.'

The officer must suspect something because she makes a call immediately. 'She's in a meeting so it will need to wait until the morning.'

It can't wait. I need to ring my brother-in-law. To warn him that my daughters may be in danger. 'I have to make a call,' I say.

She allows me to use her phone. I call Derek but it goes through to answerphone. 'May I try two other numbers?'

I get voicemail for both girls.

I toss and turn all night in the San. Then, at around 10 p.m., someone is admitted with a 'stomach ache'.

It's one of Linda Wall's friends. I'm sick again, this time with fear.

When the nurse goes out briefly, she comes to my bed.

'Linda might be dead,' she growls, 'but the threat still stands.'

In the morning, I'm summoned to the office, where the governor's eyes bore into me. 'What do you know?'

'Linda threatened to hurt my girls and Mouse defended me. Now I'm worried that Linda's contacts on the outside will take revenge on my daughters. They need protection.' I look at her pleadingly. 'Please help me.'

The governor sighs. 'It's not as straightforward as that, Belinda. We simply don't have the resources to put a guard on every inmate's house because of an argument in prison. But I'll see what I can do.'

That night I weep for Mouse. I can't help it. She was my only friend in here. She helped me navigate through this crazy world I've found myself in.

I can't help but wonder if crying for her is the right thing to do. Someone out there – maybe more than one person – is dead because of her. And yet, in my own way, I loved her.

What kind of woman has prison turned me into?

I'm so upset that I find myself picking up a pen.

Dear Imran,

I can't describe how awful it is in here. Please don't write any more. I'm not the woman I used to be. Don't wait. I can never make you happy.

Belinda.

64

Now

Mabel is shaking her head. 'You silly girl, Belinda. He might have rescued you.'

'How? He couldn't have got me out of prison.'

'But he would have been a comfort to you.'

I gulp. 'I often think about ringing him. He's the only man I've ever loved. But there's no future, is there? I've messed it all up, Mabel.' Tears are streaming down my face. 'I've lost so much. My eldest daughter. My husband. Our home. Now look at me!'

'Belinda,' says Mabel sternly. 'Look at yourself, at the way you help others. You carers are angels – well, some of you. Besides, I thought you loved your job. That's something, isn't it?'

'I do,' I say. 'But I'm a graduate and I've never even used my degree. What a waste! Anyone could do what I do here.'

'How can you say that? There's nothing more important than caring for another human being. It requires particular skills that not everyone possesses. You're a good, kind woman, Belinda. Give yourself credit for that.'

How wrong she is. I may be out of prison but the old, dark Belinda still sits on my shoulders. Why else would I be deceiving this kind old lady?

'Have a cup of tea to make yourself better,' she urges. 'Take a biscuit too. That's right. Now please. Tell me. What happened next?'

65

The governor calls me in to say that the police have agreed to 'regularly patrol' past Derek's house. So I'm not surprised when he books another appointment to visit me.

'What have you done now?' he asks. His sympathy from the previous visit has clearly vanished. 'I've been told we must have protection but no one will tell me why.'

'I can't say,' I whisper, looking around in case someone is listening.

I could tell him the truth, but that would be too risky for everyone's safety. I can already imagine that the increased police activity outside Derek's six-bedroom house, built by an award-winning architect, is attracting much gossip amongst his golf-loving neighbours.

'It's not just that people are talking,' he says, confirming my thoughts. 'It's upsetting the girls. They're scared and embarrassed.'

All this is one more black mark against me, although it barely counts compared with the murder of their father.

'Meanwhile,' he adds grimly, 'we are trying to give them as stable a family base as possible.'

I want to cry at the implication (true) that I can't do the same.

'Gillian is thinking of staying on after her third year and doing an MBA.'

Really? If I'd been at home, I would have discussed it with her.

'Elspeth's in her first year at Oxford,' he continues.

'I already know that,' I say. 'We've remained in close touch.'

His face clearly disapproves. 'Have you indeed? Yet she didn't tell you about her sister. Maybe Gillian didn't want her to.'

I wince.

Derek looks round the visiting room. 'This is no place for Elspeth to visit.'

I can't disagree.

'Would you say they're managing emotionally?' I ask, trembling.

'They seem quite determined to do so.'

For a second, I sense a shared relief between us. The type you would get in a caring family. One that works together.

Then my brother in-law's eyes harden again. 'But this latest drama has set everything back, on top of losing their father.'

My eyes swim with tears.

'I miss Gerald too,' I say. 'I loved him, in my own way . . .'

'In your own way?' He stares at me with clear disgust. 'You showed what *that* was all right.' Then he gets up. 'I've nothing else to say to you.'

'No,' I say. 'Please wait. Please tell the girls that I miss them.'

Elspeth already knows this but I want to reinforce this message to both of them.

'You should have thought about that before you sent my brother to his death.'

Clearly he's forgotten his previous words about knowing I hadn't meant to kill Gerald. Suddenly, I feel furious with this man who has had it so easy in life.

'Do you know what it's like,' I burst out, 'to discover that the man you've been married to for years has been cheating and has a child with someone else?'

His eyes flash. 'It still doesn't give you permission to murder him.'

'I told you. I didn't mean to.'

'I'm beginning to wonder now. It would have been convenient to get him out of the way, wouldn't it?'

'I just lost my temper!'

'*Just?*' His sarcasm is as deadly as any knife. 'You know, Belinda, in some ways I feel sorry for you. You were never right for my brother. My parents always said so.'

I feel gutted inside. 'Why?'

'There was something about you that was different.'

'Isn't there something different about all of us?' I retort. 'What about your marriage? Is it perfect? Can you be certain that your wife has never betrayed you?'

'That's it.' He stands up. 'I'm going. You're a bad woman, Belinda. You deserve to be in here.'

'Wait! Elspeth says she's coming to see me next month. Could you ask Gillian to come too?'

I'm begging a man who hates me but I'll try anything to see my elder daughter.

'Are you joking? As I said, this is no place for them.'

I watch him looking around at the noise and the anger and the tears. The sobs punctuated by desperation. The snatches of conversation: '*The children miss you*', '*How are we going to pay the rent?*', '*When can I see you again?*'

Then he turns back to me. 'I reckon the police are watching us because you've done something to one of the other prisoners that means our family is under threat.'

'Let me explain,' I start to say.

But Derek has already walked out.

*

That evening, I call both girls on their mobiles. There's a dead sound from Gillian's. Has she changed her number?

Elspeth's goes through to voicemail again.

I go back into my cell and weep. But I have to pull myself together, I'm on Listener duty this evening.

Tonight's conversation is with a woman whose son won't visit because he's ashamed of her. The irony is so sharp that I almost tell her about my situation.

'That must be hard,' I say instead. Then I let her talk. That's what all this is about, really. Helping someone release everything inside.

Afterwards, the chaplain tells me I've done a good job. 'In fact, I'd like you to join a recruiting programme to help more people become Listeners.'

'Thank you,' I say. It's nice to feel like I'm doing something right.

Meanwhile, like everyone else, I queue for the post in the morning with my heart in my mouth, desperately hoping that Elspeth has sent another letter or – miracle of miracles – that Gillian sent one too.

There's a card for me, but the writing isn't Elspeth's or Gillian's. That small, neat script in real ink takes me back to all those years ago at university.

I cannot tell you how my heart leaped when I received your letter – and then sank when I read it. I wish you would let me visit you. I know you too well to believe bad of you.

Love Imran.

How wrong he is, I tell myself, ripping up his letter.

Then, just as I'd given up hope, a visiting request comes from Elspeth.

I'm so glad to see her that I throw my arms around her in the visitors' room, and then immediately step back, knowing that I'm breaking the 'no touching' rules.

'I would have come earlier,' she tells me. 'But it's difficult. Uncle Derek said I shouldn't.'

'I understand,' I say, not wanting to ask if he'd told her about visiting himself.

'And the police outside the house have made it so difficult to live a normal life. How long do we have to have them there?'

'I'm not sure.'

'Well, I don't want them any more, Mum. People are asking questions. I can't see my friends properly.'

'It's better than being hurt,' I whisper.

'What did you do to make this happen?' she asks.

'I can't say,' I whisper. 'But trust me. I meant no harm.'

She gives me a sad look as if she doesn't believe me. When she leaves shortly afterwards, I almost wish she hadn't come.

I could kill Karen for what she's done to my family. If only I could find her. It's definitely time for revenge.

66

Now

'Did you find Karen in the end?' Mabel asks, finishing the last chocolate ginger biscuit.

I hesitate. I could pretend. I could keep my secret close until it's time to act.

What good would it do to tell anyone?

But Mabel isn't 'anyone'. I have become truly fond of her, which makes Mouse's demands all the harder.

'Did I ever find Karen?' I repeat. Then I throw back my head and laugh, as though this is one huge, mad joke. 'Oh yes,' I say. 'I did.'

Her eyes widen. 'What did you do to her?'

Before I can answer, there's a knock on the door. It's the deputy matron. 'Belinda, you're wanted on the second floor.'

'But I'm the boss here,' says Mabel. 'I want Belinda to stay with me.'

'And I'm the matron. As we've said before, Miss Marchmont, we need to take all the patients' needs into account. Right now, Belinda is needed elsewhere.'

The Stranger in Room Six

The message is clear.

We need results. Now.

My boss is tightening the screws. I'm not surprised. The contest for the party leadership is beginning to hot up and Harry Marchmont is a favourite to become the next prime minister. Apparently, that's why the July 12th date is so important. It's the date of an important leadership debate, taking place not far from here, ironically.

If we can find that list and my boss's suspicions are correct, Harry will (hopefully) be out of the running. Job done.

Since they're tightening the screws on me, I need to do the same with Belinda. I decide to pay her a visit.

She looks knackered.

'I've just come off the dementia unit,' she sighs.

'Tough, was it?'

'You can say that again. One of the residents wouldn't stop banging her head against the window. When I tried to prevent her, she scratched my face.'

I make a sympathetic sound. 'Nasty. But not as nasty as my boss can get.'

'I'm done with your threats against me. I've tried to find this bloody list but as far as I can see, it's not there.'

'Then you need to try harder. Or do you want me to tell your beloved employer that they've got a murderer in their midst?'

Her mouth drops. 'You wouldn't.'

'Try me.'

'That would mean telling them who you are,' she points out.
'Not if I say I recognized you from the paper.'
'That was ages ago,' she stammers.

'Your release photos weren't. Scroll through the internet and you can find anything. Plus, I wasn't about to miss my good friend Lady Belinda leaving prison, was I?' I can't resist a snarl here. 'Not after everything she'd done for me. So get back to work or I will shop you. And if that doesn't work, I'll kill the old lady off. I've got nothing to lose.' (She's not to know that my boss has told me not to harm her.) 'But you, Belinda, could be in big trouble. Because my bosses will kill me if I don't deliver. And maybe you and your family too.'

67

Belinda

When I return the next morning, Mabel is ready and waiting.

'I haven't slept all night,' she says. 'My mind has been going round with so many questions. When did you find Karen? How? Where is she?' Then, in a hushed voice, she adds, 'Is she still alive?'

Now I wish I'd stayed quiet. But perhaps I can use this to my advantage, especially in view of Mouse's threat last night. I've barely slept either, visions of Linda's and Mouse's bloodied bodies on stretchers kept running through my mind. If only I could have seen then what the future held.

'I'll tell you about Karen when you tell me more of your story.'

Mabel looks rather sullen. 'I don't see why it's so interesting to you.'

I can hardly tell her that my girls' lives depend on me finding that list. I need to think of something else.

Scrambling, I say, 'The thing is, Mabel, I'm really interested in the Second World War. Remember how I was complaining about having wasted my degree? I've decided to sign up to an Open University History course to get me back on my feet.'

Mabel looks less hacked-off now. 'What a good idea. I find it extraordinary that young people nowadays know nothing of it.'

'Me too.' I take a deep breath. 'As part of my research,

I read that each county in Britain had a list of people who were suspected of being on Hitler's side.'

She frowns. 'Really?'

'Yes. After the war, some people on that list were tried and brought to justice.' I decide not to repeat what Mouse said about certain traitors being quietly stabbed in a back alley.

She shudders. 'How horrible.'

Now for the tricky bit. 'Did your aunt or the Colonel ever say anything about a list?'

'No,' she says firmly.

'So you don't have it in your possession?'

'Belinda!' She laughs out loud. 'Whatever makes you think that?'

'I just wondered,' I say, my hopes plummeting.

'Mind you,' she says, 'there are plenty of other stories I can tell you about the war that might help your research.'

I sit forward in the hope she lets something slip. It's not that I think she's lying about the list but maybe she has it without knowing. Mouse's boss seems certain it was in the family, at least at some point.

A bell rings suddenly, signalling the staff meeting. 'I'm sorry but I have to go now. We'll chat more tomorrow.'

She clutches my arm. 'Please don't.'

'I have to, Mabel.'

'Come back tomorrow,' she says imperiously. 'I want you to take me to the stables where I used to ride Foam. We can talk there. How I loved burying my face in his mane and telling him all my secrets. In fact, I'd tell them to you now if you weren't going.'

Is she playing me? She can't know I'm being blackmailed, surely? Hopefully she's just trying to persuade me to play more of this 'I'll tell you my secrets if you tell me yours' game.

Still, I can't help but worry that Mouse really will hurt Mabel.

It's not just that I've already got enough blood on my conscience. It's because I genuinely care for this courageous little old lady.

The following morning, I wheel her down to the stables and she begins.

PART FOUR

68

Mabel

1943

The leaves in the Morrab Gardens were turning burnished gold. Slowly they began to fall, one by one. 'It's nearly your time,' said the midwife when she came to the cottage to examine her.

Mabel was now far too big to fit into her normal clothes. The sisters found her some loose-fitting smock dresses.

'I made them myself for . . .' said Olive, trailing off.

But Mabel guessed. 'You made them for Kitty,' she said, giving her a comforting hug.

Olive patted her hand. 'I know we haven't talked about what'll happen after your baby's born. But I hope you know that you are always welcome to stay here.'

'Yes,' chirped Beryl. 'In fact, I'm going to stay on even longer to have more time with my sister. We'll both be able to help when the baby comes.'

'Thank you for being so kind. Aunt Clarissa said we'd decide what to do when the time comes but nothing has been arranged.'

Then she gasped, realizing what she'd just said.

'She's your *aunt*?' The two sisters stared at her. 'I did wonder why Lady Clarissa was so generous,' said Beryl slowly.

Mabel burst into tears; the relief of finally being able to be honest was overwhelming. 'I'm worried she might try to take my baby away because she doesn't want anyone in the village to know about it.'

'Well, we would be very happy for you to carry on living here.'

'Really?'

They nodded. 'It would give me great pleasure,' added Olive.

'I will visit regularly,' chipped in Beryl. 'This is a lovely place to bring up a child. And if your young man comes to find you, well I am sure we can find one of the farmers or fishermen to give him a job.'

'But if he doesn't turn up, you'll find that there'll be plenty of other so-called widows here too,' said Olive meaningfully.

'I don't understand.'

'I'm talking about young unmarried girls, deserted by their men, who find themselves in the family way. All they have to do is move to another area where no one knows them, pop rings on their fingers and pretend that their husbands were killed in the war. It happened in the Great War and it will happen again. People treat them with more respect with a ring than if they admitted they'd had a child out of wedlock.'

Mabel shuddered at the thought of Antonio being killed.

'Now don't give that any more thought. We'll sort it out when the time comes.'

But even as she spoke, Mabel felt a strange stirring inside. 'Oh!'

Horrified, she stared down at the damp rug. How could she have wet herself like that?

'I'm so sorry,' she gasped.

'Her waters have broken,' whispered Olive. 'She's early.'

'I'll go for help,' said Beryl grabbing her coat.

The pains came fast.

'Hold my hand and squeeze it when you need to,' said Olive. 'Keep taking long deep breaths.'

Beryl came rushing back in a few minutes later, her face red from exertion. 'The midwife's been called to the hospital and the doctor is with one of the land girls who got injured by a tractor.'

'Then who will deliver me?' Mabel cried out.

There was a silence.

'It will be all right,' said Olive, finally breaking it. 'Beryl, fetch me my old nursing bag, will you? It's under my bed.'

'But . . .'

'Did you hear what I said?' There was a steeliness and gritty calm that Mabel had not heard in Olive before.

Each time a wave of pain came, one of the sisters mopped her forehead until it passed.

'You're doing really well, love,' said Olive. 'Now, Mabel, I want you to push. Baby's coming much faster than we thought. He or she is clearly keen to meet you! That's right. *Push!*'

And there it was. The sound of a cry. A cry like a song of wonder and love.

'You have a little boy!'

Olive was weeping. So was Beryl. But Mabel just stared at this lovely, perfect little figure gazing up at her, eyes like a wise old man's.

'Antonio,' she whispered. 'Welcome, my son.'

He began to cry.

'Let me help you put him to the breast,' whispered Beryl, her eyes glistening. 'That's right. Oh, Mabel. He's beautiful.'

And he was. He really was.

But most of all he was hers.

And no one, swore Mabel, would ever take him away from her.

69

We have a beautiful baby boy! wrote Mabel.

He is so like you, Antonio. I suggested calling him after you in one of my previous letters but you cannot have received it. How I wish you could see him. Beryl has kindly taken a photograph of us, which I am enclosing in this letter. I have one for myself too. His skin is olive like yours and I am sure he is beginning to follow me with his eyes, which Beryl says is remarkably early. He is three weeks old now and it feels as though he has been with me for ever. The sisters say I am a natural at feeding him. He sleeps by my side in a little crib. I hum him our special song. I'm a little sore from my stitches but Olive has given me some medicine to ease the pain, though it makes me quite drowsy.

Every day, I take him out in a pram that the sisters found me and we walk by the sea. The villagers are so kind, especially the post office lady. They often stop to see how I am without asking awkward questions about a husband. Perhaps it's because so many men are away. Some say the war will end soon and others think it will be another year or more. Please come and find us as soon as you can.

The following week, there was a knock at the door. It had a different sound from the knocks that were usually made. This one had an urgent air to it.

Both sisters were out so Mabel walked as fast as she could with little Antonio in her arms, snug in his shawl.

Her heart began pounding. There was a feeling inside

her – so strong – that her love had somehow come for her . . .

'Aunt Clarissa!'

Mabel faltered on the doorstep, stepping aside just as she swept in. Behind her aunt was a tall thin man whom Mabel had never seen before.

'You failed to tell me you had had the child,' Clarissa frowned, glancing down at the little bundle in Mabel's arms. 'You broke your promise after everything I have done for you.'

Mabel's heart was racing. 'I'm sorry. I was so scared of what might happen; I want to keep my baby.'

'Of course you do.' Her aunt's voice was softer. 'You just need to sign these papers.'

'Why?'

'Because you are not yet of age. I am your guardian while your father is away.'

The drugs Olive had given her to ease the pain of those stitches below made the print swim before her eyes. Mabel's hand wobbled across the page.

'Now it is settled,' said her aunt, taking Antonio from her arms and handing him to the man beside her.

'Wait. What are you doing? Give my son back to me!'

'Be sensible, Mabel. I'm only doing what is best for you. You will realize that when you are older. Besides, you have signed away your rights now.'

'I work for an adoption society,' chipped in the man. 'Your child will be brought up by a God-fearing married couple.'

'You lied!' she screamed at her aunt.

'It's for your own good, Mabel. That's the end of it.'

The man turned to leave, his foot on the threshold.

'Wait!' Mabel raced upstairs as fast as she could and took

the piece of lace the lacemaker had given her. She hesitated for a second, before cutting it in half. Then she put the remaining piece back in her drawer, scribbled a swift note and ran downstairs again. 'Give this to whoever adopts my son along with this piece of paper. It has the name of the village in Italy where my Antonio came from. Ask them, I beg you, to give it to him when he is older with the message that I loved him and that I wanted to keep him. Please . . .'

'Mabel, enough! You are to return home with me.'

'I need to tell the sisters.'

'Don't worry about them. They know all about this.'

'No. That can't be true.'

'Isn't it? Why don't you ask them yourself?'

'They're not here.'

'Of course they're not. It's why they went out, leaving you alone. They couldn't face it. They weren't keen, I grant you that. But I explained that if they caused trouble, I would hand the older one – Olive, isn't it? – over to the authorities for committing a criminal act.'

'What do you mean?'

'When you called to say you were concerned about staying here, I rang back the number and the postmistress told me that Olive had been struck off after her sister and the child had died. She was also good enough to call me after your delivery. Not only to tell me that the baby had arrived, but also that, as rumour had it, Olive had delivered your baby after all. Be grateful that I gave you some time with your bastard before coming to relieve you. Now get into the car. We will somehow try to resume our normal lives now this little episode is over and done with.'

Mabel's wails were lost as the tall grey man carried her precious son to a car waiting outside, and her aunt led her into another.

'Please!' she called out from the window. 'Help me someone!'

Then she saw Olive and Beryl, clutching each other as they waited at the corner. 'I'm so sorry,' called out Beryl, bursting into tears. 'We had no choice.'

Her aunt reached across and pulled her back into her seat, swerving as she did so. 'For goodness' sake, Mabel. Remember who you are. You have made a mistake. You should be thanking me for giving you another chance to keep your position in society. Not every lady gets one.'

Now

Now, by the old stables, Mabel sobs and sobs as Belinda holds her. 'It still hurts, after all these years. It's the not-knowing that is so awful. What happened to my son? Is he still alive? If only I knew, I could die happy.'

Belinda tries to find the right words to comfort her friend. But they will not come. No one can replace a lost child. How was it possible for life to be so beautiful one minute and so cruel the next?

The Stranger in Room Six

'If it wasn't for your threats to my family, I wouldn't be doing this,' says Belinda when she tells me about the old lady giving up her bastard. 'Mabel has suffered enough in life. You should leave her alone, now.'

There's a big bruise on her leg where I thumped her, which makes me feel slightly guilty. But I had to make a point.

'You're getting soft,' I scoff.

'I always was until I went to prison. Then I was only pretending to be hard. That was your idea, if you remember.'

'I think you're naturally much tougher than you think. But supposing I told you that you are actually helping us to keep Mabel safe.'

'You told me she'd die if I didn't find the list.'

'But she will also live if you do. The world is a complicated place at the moment, Belinda. You were in prison for a long time. You might not have kept up with the news. Have you heard about neo-Nazi groups in Germany and other countries? It's illegal in some places. But it's real enough, and a reminder of what happened in the war. Some of those who were hurt and lost loved ones still want justice and revenge.'

I pause for a minute to take breath. I'm beginning to feel my age.

'Let's just say that Mabel will be lucky to reach her ninety-ninth birthday if it's proved that she collaborated with Hitler supporters. There are some people who would have her killed without a second's thought.'

'But it was so long ago!'

'Don't you get it? That's the thing about history. The past never really goes away. Just like we'll never get prison out of our heads.'

I can see from her face that I've hit a nerve there.

After Belinda leaves, I make a decision. Perhaps I should take matters into my own hands. Of course, it's a huge risk, especially as my boss told me I shouldn't hurt her. But it's time I got really tough.

70

Mabel

Mabel wakes with a start. It's pitch-black outside, although she can hear the sea roar as the old diamond-paned windows rattle in the wind.

'Alexa, what's the time?' she asks.

'The time is 12.43 a.m.'

Such a clever invention!

Mabel tries to get back to sleep but it's no good. Something feels wrong. She can sense it. Perhaps it's just the wind.

Then she jumps. What's that sliding noise? It's as if a drawer is opening somewhere, a rustling sound.

'Who's there?' she whispers.

Silence. Is she having one of her bad dreams again? Mabel pinches herself. No. That hurts, and pinches don't hurt in dreams, do they?

There's a creak and a shuffle.

Mabel sits bolt upright. That sounds like a floorboard. Mabel knows the creaks of these floors well. Hadn't she herself crept from room to room back in the days when she'd listened in on Clarissa?

'Who's there?' she repeats, this time with a catch in her voice.

Nothing.

It must be her imagination, she tells herself, or perhaps the temperature. Floorboards make noises when it's too hot or too cold and this place can get so stuffy even at night. Old people need to be warm, and the heating is always on high.

There's another creak.

Mabel feels her pulse racing, her heart banging out of her chest. Then she remembers what Frannie taught her in case the Germans invaded. *'Don't look or sound scared.'*

'Reveal yourself,' she demands. 'Or I'll take a pistol to you.'

She doesn't have a pistol, of course, but the words capture a bravado that Mabel doesn't feel.

Is that someone breathing? Mabel's fingers fumble for the emergency alarm cord. Where is it? And why can't she find the wall light switch? Then to her relief, her hand closes round the spiky hairbrush that she keeps by her bed so she can do the fifty strokes that Mama taught her all those years ago before the bombs came.

Then with all her might she throws it out into the darkness. There's the sound of it hitting something, followed by a grunt.

'Don't you fucking do that to me,' growls a voice.

Mabel can feel someone's breath on her face.

'Who are you?' she asks, trying to keep her voice steady. Something Frannie once said comes into her head again. *'Stand up to evil.'*

But what if you were evil yourself? Has Mabel's comeuppance finally arrived?

'You don't need to know my name,' replies the voice. 'I'm not going to harm you, provided you give me what I want. Where are you keeping the list?'

That bloody list again.

'I don't know about any list,' she says.

'I don't believe you.'

The breath is right above her now.

Frantically, Mabel fumbles in the dark for the emergency cord again. Where is the damn thing?

'If you don't give it to me right now, I'll –'

Thank God! She's finally found it. The alarm is ringing, siren-like, along the corridor.

'Fuck you, Mabel Marchmont,' snarls the voice. 'I'll be back. You'll see.'

Mabel can hear something dragging on the ground, as if the stranger has a stick. Then the door opens and slams back on itself again.

'Help, help!' she calls out.

Nothing. Where the hell is everyone? Then again, there are only two staff on night duty and alarms are always going off. It seems like an age before someone finally comes. She'd hoped it might be Belinda but it's one of the new night staff.

'Everything all right, Mabel?'

'No, it bloody isn't. Did you see someone going out of my room?'

'No, dear.'

'Don't "dear" me. It was a woman. At least I think it was, although she had a deep voice. She said she wanted something.'

Instinct tells Mabel not to go into details.

'There, there. I expect you were having one of your nightmares. Let me give you something for it.'

Too tired to argue, Mabel sinks into a deep sleep into which her past comes too; each memory jostling with another in its impatience to get out.

When she wakes the next day, Mabel can't wait to tell Belinda what happened. But her mind feels fuzzy and she can't quite grasp the memory. As the morning passes, she begins to wonder if everything was quite as she remembered.

Had someone really asked about the list? What would any intruder want with her, after all?

Perhaps she should keep quiet about the stranger in the night, in case they think she's lost her marbles and dose her up again.

So instead, when Belinda comes on shift, Mabel continues her story from where she'd left off.

71

1943

Mabel felt numb with grief at the thought of returning to the Old Rectory. The fact that it was nearly Christmas, a traditional time of celebration, made it worse. She had left with a child inside her and now she was returning with an empty heart. Somewhere out there in the world was her little Antonio, being brought up by a properly married couple.

Now she was expected to get on with her life, as though she had never given birth to him. Never held him in her arms. Never felt his downy little cheek against hers or his rosebud mouth sucking at her breast.

'Why did my love desert me?' she asked herself on the long drive back to the house, her breasts leaking now that they had no baby to nourish. 'Surely some of my letters must have arrived.'

Cook took one look at Mabel's face and put her arms around her.

The two women sobbed.

'I am so sorry for your loss,' said Mabel, thinking of Cook's sister.

'You dear child, always thinking of others. I am so sorry for yours.' She spoke as though the baby was dead. In a way he was.

'Is there any news of Antonio?' Mabel asked hopefully.

'I'm sorry. Like I said when I wrote to you, he was moved to a different camp and then moved again. But no one seems to know where.'

Cook stopped as footsteps approached.

Her aunt's face was furious. 'This is highly inappropriate of you, Cook, to comment on a personal situation. Besides, Mabel is a grown woman now. She needs to learn to be responsible for her actions and their consequences.'

'If I am now a grown woman,' retorted Mabel, 'why couldn't I have kept my baby?'

'Because I am not allowing an illegitimate child to grow up in this house. Now stop this impertinence and go upstairs.'

Gladly, thought Mabel as she climbed the stairs and snuggled down under the counterpane in the hideous Red Room. There, she rocked herself back and forth, weeping at the thought of little Antonio crying out for her, and for his father who had clearly deserted them.

Slowly, Mabel's return to the Old Rectory established an unfamiliar pattern as the days went on. Christmas Day was miserable. Her aunt, after insisting she went to church with her 'to keep up appearances', immediately retired to her room, leaving Mabel to have lunch alone in the dining room.

Although her stomach was rumbling with emptiness, she could barely eat for grief. 'I would suggest you sat in the kitchen with me, love,' said Cook, 'but your aunt wouldn't be pleased if she came down to find you there.'

'It's all right, thank you,' Mabel said numbly. 'I'm not hungry anyway.'

She spent that afternoon walking in the woods or sitting on the private beach, trying to keep away from people. A couple of times she tried to sing her and Antonio's special song. But the tune would not come out.

'Does anyone know I had a baby?' she asked Cook later that day when her aunt was safely out of the house and no one else was around.

'Lady Clarissa told everyone you needed a break in

Cornwall because you were so anxious about your father. If anyone does suspect, they won't say anything for fear of your aunt. As a landowner, she still carries a lot of weight around here, despite everything that happened with the Colonel.'

'What do you mean?' asked Mabel.

'Let's just say that although the police didn't arrest Lady Clarissa, there are still quite a few who think she knew what the Colonel was up to. When the war is over, she may well be brought to account.'

'Brought to account?'

'I have said enough already. Now, I hope you don't mind but I thought you could do with some company of your own age. So I asked Frannie if she'd like to come up to see you.'

'But she'll be with her family. Anyway, she won't want to.'

'Actually, love, I think you'll find she will.'

When her friend arrived that afternoon, Mabel flung her arms around her. To her relief, Frannie did the same. 'I had a baby,' she sobbed, 'and my aunt gave him away.'

'My mam and I wondered if something like that had happened,' muttered Frannie, stroking her friend's hair. 'You poor thing.'

After that, Frannie came to sit with her every day after her work was done, sometimes walking with her down to the sea.

'I wish I knew where Antonio had been sent,' Mabel would say again and again as if the refrain might bring him back. 'I don't understand why he hasn't contacted me.'

'Some men are like that,' her friend responded sagely. 'My mam says that war gives them an excuse.'

Was that true? Antonio had seemed so genuine, but maybe she had been too naive. Perhaps he simply didn't love her any more. Perhaps he never had.

72

1944

Spring had arrived. Her son would be sitting up by now. Maybe crawling someday soon. The thought broke her heart.

Mabel had taken to spending more and more time at the cottage with Frannie. Fortunately, her aunt didn't seem to notice, constantly 'busy' in the library. Indeed, she seemed so obsessed with 'paperwork' that she hardly mentioned the Colonel. 'Some folk do that when they're grieving,' commented Cook. 'It's the shock. They need to do something practical.'

On one occasion when Mabel went in, she saw her aunt tearing up documents that had fallen out of a file. Rushing to pick them up, Mabel saw that one was headed 'Confidential'. 'Leave that alone, girl. Haven't you caused me enough trouble?'

There were also some photographs, she noticed, but her aunt was tearing those into tiny fragments, making it impossible to see who they were of.

'She doesn't seem to care how wicked she's been,' said Mabel to Frannie's mother. 'How could she make me sign the adoption papers when I was in no fit state to do so?'

'I know, love, it's unimaginably cruel,' she replied, giving Mabel a big motherly hug.

That afternoon, as Mabel walked back to the Old Rectory, she saw a large black car outside. It didn't look dissimilar to the car that had come to take little Antonio away from her in

Mousehole. Perhaps they were bringing her son back to her! Breaking out into a run, she tore up to the front door, only to hear raised voices coming from the library.

It was her father! She would have known his voice anywhere. So he was back, released from the POW camp. He was alive!

But it sounded as though he was having a terrible argument with her aunt. 'Let me get this right. My daughter had a child and you made her give it up for adoption?'

'It was the best thing, George.'

'Don't you have a heart? Don't you remember –'

She cut in. 'That's exactly why I did it.'

'My poor little girl,' he shouted. 'What in the name of God have you put her through?'

Mabel could not wait any longer.

Turning the stiff library doorknob, she flew into the room and into his arms. 'Papa!' she cried. 'You're safe!'

As she hugged him, she could feel his bones under his coat.

Eventually, he stepped back, facing her as if he too could not believe that she was there. 'A sympathetic guard helped me to escape. However, it took me time to get here.'

'I heard you talking about my baby. Please find him for me,' she begged.

Her father looked grim. 'The documents have been signed. There is nothing that I or anyone else can do. You will have to be brave, my darling, although I do believe that it is time you learned something else about our family.'

'No,' said Clarissa, tugging his arm. 'You can't do this, George.'

He shrugged her off in a rough manner that didn't belong to the Papa Mabel knew. 'It should have been told long ago.'

'What should have?' she asked, scared.

Papa's mouth tightened. 'When your aunt was your age, she found she was expecting a baby herself.'

'Who were you married to?' asked Mabel.

Her aunt turned away, her face pale.

'That's just it,' thundered Papa. 'You weren't married, were you Clarissa?'

'No, because I was still in love with you.'

'You knew perfectly well that we were over by then,' he snapped. 'My heart belonged to your sister.'

Shocked, Mabel interrupted. 'But you were in love with my aunt before you married Mama?'

Her father went red. 'It was a brief infatuation.'

'Not on my part,' snapped back Clarissa.

'You recovered enough to find someone else and carry his child.'

'You had married my sister,' whispered Clarissa. 'I was hurt. But if we're going to come clean about what happened, you should tell Mabel the whole truth.'

'What whole truth, Papa?'

'*Papa?*' snorted Clarissa. 'Ha!'

'I don't understand,' said Mabel confused.

Her father put his hands over his face for a minute. 'I think you'd better sit down, darling.' He took the chair next to her and sighed. 'When your aunt revealed she was pregnant, she also said that the man in question was not willing to marry her. So your grandparents sent her away to give birth. They then suggested we should adopt you. That way we could keep the child – you – in the family. Clarissa agreed.'

'I had no choice,' said her aunt bitterly.

'So you're not my real father?' gasped Mabel. 'And Mama was not my real mother?'

'It makes no difference. I can promise you that we loved you as our own, especially as it then took us several years to conceive Annabel. We were so happy that you could have a sister.'

He tried to hold her, but his embrace did not feel the same.

'Who *was* my father?' she asked in a small voice.

They stopped still. Silent.

Then Aunt Clarissa opened her mouth and suddenly Mabel knew what she was going to say before the words came out.

'Jonty,' she said. 'It was Jonty.'

73

The Colonel? The Colonel with his twinkly eyes, who could be so charming and kind one minute, and yet so scary and strict the next?

The man who had been much kinder to her than her aunt, only to be convicted of treason.

He had been her father? The Colonel who had been stabbed to death by a local man intent on 'handing out his own justice'. At least, this was how the newspapers had phrased it.

And Aunt Clarissa . . . The woman who had rarely shown her any warmth, who had failed to give her the love that one might expect towards a motherless child. *She* had given birth to her?

'You are my mother?' she said with disbelief in her voice.

Aunt Clarissa looked away. She said nothing, but the blush crawling up her cheeks was enough.

'I didn't want you to hear it this way,' said Papa. 'Mama and I loved you as our own. You must know that.'

Mabel wanted to believe this, but how could she? He had lied to her for so long. He held out his arms to her, but she stepped away.

'Please, darling,' begged Papa. 'It is love that makes good parents. Not birth.'

This was all too much. She turned away.

'Where are you going?'

'I need to think,' said Mabel.

Stunned, she walked through the woods towards the sea.

A figure came towards her. It was the lacemaker, on her arm, a basket full of mushrooms. She looked at Mabel's face.

'So you discovered the truth about your parents,' she said.

It was a statement and not a question. Mabel shivered. Any doubts she'd had about the lacemaker seeing into people's minds now disappeared.

'Does everyone in the village know?' she asked.

'There were rumours, but then they died out. No doubt folk were threatened. People like your aunt think they can hide their secrets. But truth will out in the end.' She touched Mabel's head lightly. 'You will survive this, my child,' she said.

'I just want my baby,' sobbed Mabel, unable to keep her secret any longer. 'They sent him away for adoption.'

The lacemaker nodded. 'I guessed as much. It is very hard on you. But we cannot always have everything. I will say one thing. Your father – the one who brought you up – is a good man. Sometimes we do not tell the truth because we do not wish to hurt others. Forgive him. Now carry on with your walk, Mabel. The sea will give you peace. As for your aunt, her time will come. Believe me.'

The tide was out. Mabel sat for some time on the rocks below the cliffs, staring out across the sea. 'I loved you, Mama, as if you were my own,' she said. 'And you, too, Annabel.'

'We are still yours,' the waves seemed to whisper.

Eventually, she stood up and walked back to the Old Rectory.

Her father (how false that word now sounded) was pacing up and down the hall, the dried mud from his boots flaking off onto the antique rug. 'Thank God you're back,' he said, relief flooding his face. 'I've been out looking for you everywhere.'

He took her into his arms. 'You will always be my little girl.'

She sobbed into his coat. 'Would you have told me the truth one day?'

'That's a question your mother and I discussed constantly. She thought that we should but I was scared that you'd feel deceived. And then the war broke out. The world became so uncertain that we did not want to put you through any more distress.'

'Did you love Annabel more than me?' asked Mabel, staring up at him with fear in her heart.

'Of course not. We loved you both the same. Blood does not need to be an essential factor of parenthood, or indeed childhood. Your little baby will find that out. He will be loved too, God willing, by his adoptive parents.'

Mabel flinched. 'But that means he will never know me.'

His face tightened. 'Your aunt was very wicked to take him away from you. I hope she pays for it one day.'

'Where is she now?'

'In the library. She instructed that when you were back, she wished to speak to you.'

Her hand shaking on the door handle, Mabel went in.

'Ah,' said her aunt – it was impossible to think of her as her mother. 'There you are.' She spoke coolly, as though this day was like any other.

'No doubt you think badly of me,' she said, blowing out a wisp of smoke from the cigarette in the ebony holder. 'However, I hope you will understand from your own experience that these things happen. Sometimes one gets – how can I put it? – swept away by the waves of passion.'

'But at least you had the opportunity to watch me growing up,' retorted Mabel. 'I cannot do that with my child.'

'Trust me,' said Clarissa. Her voice sounded cracked now.

'That is harder. Do you not understand how agonizing it was for me? It's why I couldn't bear to visit you in London. Time and time again I wanted to tell you the truth, but I'd promised your parents that I wouldn't. It was part of our agreement. They felt it would break you. Eventually I kept my distance, until the war changed everything and you had to come here. It's been agonizing to see my lovely daughter every day and realize how much I had missed.'

Lovely? 'If it was "agonizing", as you put it, why have you always been so horrible to me?'

'It was my way of dealing with it,' said Clarissa wistfully. 'If I had allowed myself to be a kind, loving aunt, it would have been all too easy for me to have told you how much I love you as a mother.'

'*Do* you love me?' Mabel asked, taken aback.

Clarissa moved towards her, wrapping her arms around her briefly before stepping back as if shocked by her own actions. Mabel was shocked too.

'Of course I do,' she said quietly, red spots on both cheeks. 'You are my daughter. Jonty was proud of you as well. Again and again we spoke about what might have been.'

'Why didn't you just get married when you knew you were expecting me?'

'Jonty's parents wouldn't allow it,' she said. 'They wanted what they called "a more suitable match". Her lips tightened. 'They said they would cut him off without a penny.'

'But you're a Lady? Wasn't that enough for them?'

'A titled Lady without much money,' said Clarissa drily.

Mabel was still confused. 'But I was told that the Colonel was a bachelor.'

Clarissa laughed bitterly. 'His fiancée died from pneumonia before the wedding. By then, I had given you away to my sister.'

'Why didn't Jonty ever marry? Why didn't you? Why didn't you marry each other when you were older and could do what you wanted?'

'We discussed it. Perhaps it was the guilt of giving you away that stopped us. I do not know. And then this awful war started. We all got so busy and, well . . .'

Then she turned away. 'It doesn't matter now. It is all in the past. Jonty is dead. You, my daughter, quite rightly hate me because I gave you away. And I have now given away *your* child. Perhaps it was wrong of me. But now it is all too late.'

There was no answer to that.

When Mabel went back to find the man who was no longer her father, she found him ready to depart again. 'I have to rejoin my troop,' he said, cupping her face with his hands.

Mabel stepped back.

'My darling daughter, please do not be like this.'

'But I am not your daughter.'

'Your words are breaking my heart. You *are* my daughter. You always will be.'

'But what do I call you now?'

'Papa,' he said. 'Always Papa.' Then he held her again. 'I will be back. I promise you. Remember that I love you. Your mother loved you too. I am not talking of the wicked, cold woman in the library. I am talking about the woman who raised you. Who loved you. Who constantly told me how lucky she was. You must believe me. Please.'

'I'll try,' choked Mabel.

'Thank you,' he said. 'I'll return as soon as I am allowed.'

Slowly, Mabel closed the door without waiting to wave him off. Instead, she ran up to her room and opened the locket around her neck. Slowly with her finger, she traced the face of the woman whom she'd thought was her mother. 'I will always see you as my mama,' she whispered.

Then she looked at the photo of Clarissa. Part of her wanted to rip it up. But something stopped her. So instead, she shut the locket firmly with a click. If only she could do the same with the past.

74

'So you know,' said Cook quietly when she went down into the kitchen.

'You knew too?' asked Mabel.

'Some suspected but no one said anything. But that was in the old days. The war is changing everything. People are more accepting of women who have babies out of wedlock.'

'Including me?' whispered Mabel.

'Including you, love,' she said, giving Mabel a floury hug.

At dinner that night, the table was empty. 'Your aunt is in her bedroom,' said Cook. 'She has asked me to give you her apologies.'

Your aunt. It seemed as though everyone else was going to continue this pretence.

Thank goodness Clarissa was not present. Mabel did not know how she could possibly have a normal conversation with her after this. She lay awake all night, tossing and turning. Thinking back over her life. Remembering her mother who was not her mother, calling her 'special' again and again. About her little baby, Antonio, whose own adoptive mother was perhaps also calling him 'special' that very second.

Outside, the wind was whipping up. Branches were falling. At one point, there was a particularly loud crack as though a tree had fallen.

At 5 a.m., still unable to sleep, she got up and went down to the library. Reading often helped her sleep but she couldn't think what to turn to at a time like this. A book was sticking out from the others as though it had recently been read and then replaced unevenly; Mabel pulled it out and flicked through it.

It was written in a foreign language that Mabel didn't recognize. She was reasonably fluent in French thanks to her governess in London, but this was different. Then her blood chilled as she took in the printing details on the frontispiece. There was one word there that she did recognize: *Berlin*.

As she held the book in her hands, a photograph fluttered out. Mabel gasped at a younger Clarissa, standing alongside the Colonel and a tall, imposing man with a moustache. There were others next to them, waving placards saying 'Make Britain Great Again'. Then she turned it over. There, in her aunt's writing, were the words 'Our first march with Oswald Mosley.'

Wasn't he the leader of the British fascists? The man who openly supported Hitler before the war? So, her aunt had been involved after all.

The following morning, the breakfast table was empty.

'Where's my aunt?' she asked.

Cook looked concerned. 'I don't know. She's not in her room. I went up with a cup of tea earlier.'

She couldn't be walking the dogs either. They were in the kennels, on their hind legs, barking. Clearly they hadn't even been out.

'I'll see if she's in the gardens,' said Mabel.

'I'll come with you,' said Cook. 'You take the route to the tennis courts and I'll head for the stables. Maybe the groom has seen her.' The 'garden' was so vast that it would take all day for one person to search it.

Mabel had almost reached the courts when she heard the scream.

Running as fast as she could, she followed the yell to the lavender bank. Cook was bent double, standing over what looked like a pile of red rags. Then she realized it was a body, drenched in blood.

Cook was too hysterical to speak.

Shaking, Mabel knelt down, forcing herself to turn the body over. Her aunt's glassy eyes stared back at her, a bullet hole in her chest. Beside her lay a stone and underneath a note with one word.

TRAITOR.

'Help,' screamed Mabel. 'Help!'

Belinda

Now

I draw a sharp breath. 'Did one of the locals kill her?'

Mabel's voice is flat. 'There was a rumour that Frannie had done it in revenge for her father's death. But I don't see her as a killer.'

'Who do you think did it, then?'

'Well, quite a few murders happened during the war. It was easier to cover them up when bombs were falling everywhere. The whole village disliked my aunt.' Mabel shudders. 'It could have been anyone.'

Then her voice changes. 'I don't want to say any more. It's too horrible. What I *do* want to know is where Karen is and what you did to her to make her pay.'

Luckily, a bell sounds. 'It's time for tea,' I say brightly.

She puts on the sulking face I've grown to know so well. 'I don't want any. I'd much rather hear your story.'

'Mabel, you might own this place but I'm afraid you're not the only resident I have to take care of. Tonight, I'm on tea duty.'

To be honest I'm not looking forward to it. There's one woman who chucks food at everyone although she can be as sweet as sugar at other times. Butlins Bill isn't my cup of tea either; he's too loud and raucous for my liking.

Mabel makes a long-drawn-out 'Ohhhh', like a petulant child.

'I'm sorry, but I'll continue my story next time.'

'Promise?' she asks.

'Promise.'

The Stranger in Room Six

Mabel's confessions via Belinda are building up into a possible nice front-page headline. Any stain on Harry Marchmont's name will help, even if it's through association rather than a personal involvement. Yet it's not enough.

So I get one of my old contacts to find out where Belinda's eldest daughter Gillian lives and follow her. Then I instruct him to 'bump into' her on the Tube to work and deliver a verbal message.

It works. Belinda comes knocking on my door that night.

'It was you, wasn't it?' she yells.

'Inside,' I say, pulling her in before anyone hears her. She's hysterical. 'Gillian rang to say that a man knocked into her and said that her mother needed to "do what she was told" or something would happen to the whole family. Then he showed her a knife. She wanted to know what I'd got mixed up in.'

'What did you say?'

'I said I didn't know what she was talking about but she didn't believe me. Now Elspeth is doubting me too.'

'Then you'd better get Mabel's secret out of her, hadn't you? Or else we might just have to carry out that threat.'

75

Mabel

Belinda is late, observes Mabel crossly, glancing at the grandfather clock in her room. She can still remember standing on tiptoes as a child, admiring the silver moon and stars on its face.

The two of them had arranged to chat after lunch today, when the residents have their quiet time. But she isn't here.

Mabel isn't just bored; she is scared. Last night, a familiar nightmare reared its ugly head: the one where she found Aunt Clarissa's bloody body on the ground, moments before it stood up and started to scream. Mabel has had this nightmare – or variations of it – ever since Clarissa died. It terrifies her, despite the fact that some would say her aunt deserved it.

Thank goodness for Belinda's story, which helps to distract her from her own horrors. Now where *is* she?

Crossly, Mabel rings the emergency bell.

It takes a while for someone to answer it.

'This isn't good enough.'

'What's wrong, Mabel?'

'I need Belinda.'

'She's looking after someone else at the moment. Mabel, you know we have to look after everyone and that we don't have enough staff as it is.'

'I don't care. Go and tell Belinda that if she doesn't come now, I will tell on her.'

'And say what?'

'Just give her the message.'

Belinda arrives, breathless, fifteen minutes later. 'You can't do that,' she gasps. 'Someone needed me.'

'I need you more.'

Belinda looks scared. 'I was warned that you'd "tell on me".'

'It was only a joke.'

'It isn't funny. Now they might suspect me of something.'

'I'm sorry,' says Mabel, feeling a little guilty now. 'But I'm so bored when you're not here. Just tell me what happened to Karen.'

Belinda sighs. 'I have to tell you more about the prison first for it to make sense.'

76

Belinda

Nearly five years have gone by since I was sentenced. Elspeth has graduated from Oxford with a 2:1. I'm bitterly disappointed not to be at her graduation, although she does bring in photos, which she's thoughtfully had printed out. Gillian has been promoted at work; I have continued my Listener work, but all I want is to turn back the clock and be with my girls.

Gillian got married four years ago. I only found out from Elspeth that her sister was expecting a baby. A baby! A grandson or granddaughter whom I wouldn't be allowed to see. A child who would one day discover the appalling secret that their grandmother murdered their grandfather.

Every morning when I wake up, I think of Karen. How can I find her? How can I make her pay?

Part of me knows I should let it go, but I can't. I will find that woman, even if I have to wait until I'm released.

Some months drag so badly that it's like being stuck on a calendar page, unable to turn the date.

At other times, it goes faster, especially now I'm helping to train others as Listeners. The chaplain says I'm a 'natural'. It's been a long time since someone praised me.

Then Gillian gets married. I only find out after the event, in a letter from Derek. *She doesn't want you to know any details.*

I write back, asking for a photograph, but I don't receive a reply.

I don't like to press Elspeth for information on her sister's wedding; it wouldn't be fair on her. And yet, I am desperate for any snippet of news.

I've told myself that I will block my hurt in order to protect myself, but I can't.

More time goes by. I've stopped counting the months and just note the years instead. It makes my sentence feel more do-able.

Instead of using her law degree to become a solicitor, Elspeth has taken a job in the charity sector.

'I want to help people,' she says when she visits.

'That's wonderful, darling. You know, there's a charity called Koestler Arts that runs competitions for writing and painting in prison.'

'Really? Have you entered?'

'Not yet,' I say. I don't tell her that I briefly considered entering the life-story category but then dismissed it just as fast. My life so far is loud enough in my head as it is. Writing it down would feel too real.

Then, one evening when I'm on duty as a Listener, a young-sounding girl comes in. 'I've been given twelve years,' she sobs. 'How am I going to get through that?'

'You will,' I say softly.

'But how?'

'Take each day as it comes. Keep your head down. Don't annoy anyone. Toe the line.'

'They've taken my kids away,' she weeps. 'My mother-in-law won't have them. They're being adopted. I'll never see them again.'

'I'm so sorry,' I say. 'Do you have a mother who could help?'

'She's got twelve years too. We were in it together. She said it was safe.'

I don't ask what the crime was. It's an unspoken rule here. 'Write to your children,' I say. 'Ask the officers to send the letters to the social worker or the probation officer so that one day, when your kids are old enough to read them, they will realize how much you missed them.'

Another prime minister comes and goes. And another, followed by a war with implications for 'home security' as *The Times* puts it. (I'm the only one who reads it.)

It's almost impossible to describe the agony of wasted years. All I can do is keep my head down. Do the right thing.

The women who have threatened me before have long moved on, though that isn't to say they've forgotten about me or my family.

How did I get by? Looking back, I don't know. I just concentrated on my Listening work and hoped I was doing some good. It would never make up for killing my husband and depriving my girls of their father. But it was all I could do.

Sometimes I got letters from women I'd helped, including the girl whose three-year-old I had saved.

I don't know what id have dun without yu, she wrote.

I put that letter on my noticeboard in my room, along with others.

I never forgot Mouse. If it hadn't been for her wise words, telling me not to count the days, I wouldn't have got through.

But at last, my sentence is almost up. At the parole hearing, it is decided that, thanks to my good behaviour and dedication to my Listening, I will be released immediately. I have to live at an approved address in a hostel, which my probation officer has found for me.

Elspeth, bless her, offers to take me in. But that wouldn't be fair on her. She has a steady boyfriend and, although she's told him about me, I'm aware she needs to live her life, without her ex-con of a mother under the same roof.

On the morning of my release, they give me a plastic bag containing my belongings. The beige skirt suit I was wearing when I was sentenced is now so loose that it almost falls off me. How my life has changed since that day.

They order a taxi to take me to the hostel, which is just five miles from here. As I wait, a car draws up.

Elspeth! She has come, despite me telling her not to.

But as I see the driver, my heart does five hundred flights to the moon and back.

It's Imran.

Now

The supper bell sounds.

'You can't leave it at that!' protests Mabel. 'I want to know if you go off with Imran. And you still haven't told me about Karen.'

The door opens and a new carer comes in. The next shift has started.

'I'm sorry,' I say, getting up. 'We'll have to continue this conversation tomorrow.'

I bend down and give her a kiss on her soft cheek. The action takes us both by surprise. I'm getting too fond of this old lady. I need to take care. Or both of us will get hurt.

77

Mabel

Mabel hasn't been able to sleep all night. 'So what happened next?' she asks as soon as Belinda arrives with her breakfast.

'It's actually your turn.'

She finds herself thumping her fist on the arm of the chair. 'But I want to know about Imran and Karen.'

'And I'd like to know what happened after Clarissa died,' says Belinda. 'In fact, I've a feeling you need to get it off your chest.'

Her new friend knows her all too well. 'Yes,' whispers Mabel. 'I suppose I do.'

1944

The weeks after her aunt's murder were hazy. Later in life, Mabel couldn't decide whether she had deliberately blocked them out or was simply too shocked to take everything in.

Clarissa shot to death, killed in cold blood. The note beside her body declaring her aunt a traitor.

The aunt who was really her mother.

The chief constable came to interview her about finding the body (perhaps an ordinary policeman wasn't high-up enough for a well-known figure in the community), but all Mabel could say was that she had no idea who could have committed such a terrible crime.

If it hadn't been for Cook and Frannie's mother, and the others in the village who had gathered around her, Mabel would not have coped.

'You don't think I was involved too, do you?' she asked Cook after the chief constable left.

'Of course I don't, love,' she said, taking Mabel in her arms. 'No one does. You mustn't worry about that. But there's a lot of folk out there who might be guilty; the ones who thought she was a Hitler sympathizer like the Colonel was. I even heard that Frannie was questioned.'

'Frannie?'

'She was often heard bad-mouthing Lady Clarissa. But they can't have anything on her 'cos she's walking round the village now, her head high. There isn't much else for the police to go on.'

It was true. The note had been in big capital letters, leaving no indication of who might have written it. And despite extensive searching through the grounds, there was no sign of the gun.

Mabel tried to send word of Clarissa's death to Papa (she still saw him as that, despite everything), but received a reply to say he had now been sent on 'special duties' to Jerusalem. What could he be doing there? The war was drawing to a close. Everyone was saying so.

I am so sorry, he wrote in a scrawl that seemed rushed and most unlike his usual tidy script. *This must have been a terrible shock. Hold tight, my darling. I will be back when this is all over.*

But would he? There seemed no certainty in life any more. As for Antonio, no one knew where he had been taken. But the one person she missed most of all was the person she'd barely got to know. Her son.

'One day,' she told herself, as she threw the final clump of earth on her aunt's coffin (a ceremony attended by only her and Cook), 'I will find you, my precious boy.'

Later that week, when Mabel was summoned to the local lawyer, she was stunned to discover that Clarissa had left her the Old Rectory as well as a considerable sum of money. Then again, her aunt had no one else to leave it to. Now this beautiful home was owned by the Marchmont family. Gone were the stains left by the Sinclairs. She might have Clarissa and Jonty's blood in her body but Mabel still saw Papa and Mama as her parents.

'Will you sell it?' asked Cook when she told her.

'No. I want to do something good with the place. We'll offer it to those returning from the war who need somewhere peaceful for a break. We can invite their wives too. And their children.'

'That's a lovely idea. Mind you, it will be a lot for us to manage.'

'Actually,' said Mabel. 'We don't need to worry about that. Clarissa didn't just leave me the house. She left me quite a lot of money as well.'

Cook sniffed. 'Maybe the woman had a conscience after all.'

'The best part is that this means all your jobs are safe and we can afford to employ more staff to take care of the convalescents.'

'Will we need to provide medical help?'

'No. I see it more as a holiday refuge.'

'You're a good girl.'

Tears sprang in Cook's eyes, making Mabel cry too. 'I just want to try and put something back into the world. It's the only way I'm going to cope without my baby.'

Then she broke into big, juddering sobs.

Once more, Cook put her arms around her, until she

stopped. To Mabel's relief she didn't come out with platitudes like 'it will be all right'. Because it couldn't be. Not unless she found her son, and even then, he would already have been formally adopted. He could never be hers now.

'What about your young man?'

Mabel blushed. 'When I went to the camp, someone thought he'd been sent on from the one he'd been transferred to.'

'He might be on his way home now.'

Mabel's heart swelled with hope. 'Please may that be true. In fact, I did wonder if I might try to get to Italy somehow. He told me the name of the village he came from.'

'You'd go there on your own?'

'Why not?'

'You're plucky, I'll give that to you. Just like your mother.'

Mabel gave her another hug. How she loved it when people compared them. It helped to keep Mama alive in her heart.

78

1945

When peace was finally declared, it seemed unreal and too late. So much damage had been done, not just to the landscape but to the hearts and souls of everyone all over the world.

Mabel showed her face at the village VE-day party in May but left early to pack.

'You're still going to Italy?' asked Frannie.

'Yes,' she said. 'I have to see if Antonio's still alive and tell him about his son.'

'Good luck,' said Frannie. 'I'm leaving too.'

'Where are you going?'

'I want to go to London. Live a bit. The war has shown me that I need to widen my eyes a bit more.'

Part of Mabel wondered if this had anything to do with those rumours about Frannie's involvement in Clarissa's death.

'Good luck,' she said.

'You too,' Frannie said, hugging Mabel warmly.

'Thank you,' said Mabel, a lump in her throat. Frannie had been such an important part of her life since coming down here. How would she manage without her?

'Promise me you'll come back to the Old Rectory one day?'

Frannie seemed to contemplate the question for a bit. 'I can't be certain of that. But I can promise something else.'

Then she spat on her finger.

'Do the same,' she said to Mabel. 'Now rub your finger against mine. It's a pledge that we'll always be friends.'

They hugged again, then Mabel stood and watched Frannie walk away, until she disappeared from sight.

Mabel had butterflies in her chest as she took the train to London, then another train to Dover, followed by a boat and then another train all the way through France on to Italy.

It meant changing trains several times and, once, the carriage was full of people speaking in languages she didn't understand. Some were laughing, some silent, some weeping. Some well dressed. Some in rags. Perhaps they were refugees.

Naturally, she gave some of the food she bought on the way to children in her carriage. Always children. On one occasion, a woman came through with a baby in her arms and began to feed it. Mabel couldn't keep her eyes away. Eventually she could bear it no longer and moved into another compartment. She had fed Antonio like that before he'd been torn away from her. How devastating it must have been for him to be given to another woman without milk in her breast.

Eventually, she reached the station that, according to her Baedeker Guide, was the nearest to Antonio's village. With the help of a phrasebook plus a few words Antonio had taught her, such as *destra* or *destro* for 'right' and *sinistra* or *sinistro* for 'left', plus *dove* for 'where', she managed to communicate with the stationmaster, who told her to wait in the dusty town for another bus.

By this time, she had been travelling for five days and four nights. Mabel was aware that she was smelly and dishevelled. What would Antonio think of her? What if he didn't love her any more? What would he say when she told him they'd had a son who had been taken away?

Eventually, the bus stopped. The driver indicated that this

was the place. Mabel stood and stared. There was not one building left standing; just low, open-to-the-sky walls that appeared to have once been part of houses.

No. This couldn't be right.

'My husband came from here,' she said in what she hoped was understandable Italian from the phrasebook.

'*Andati tutti,*' he kept saying.

Mabel consulted her phrasebook: *They are all gone.* Her eyes filled with tears.

Poor, poor Antonio. What must he have thought when he returned home to find his town razed to the ground? Had he lost his mother and his father and his sisters? Please God, no. Where would he have gone after he saw these terrible sights?

It was hopeless. She would never find him. Just as she would never find their son.

'You have come on a fool's journey, Mabel Marchmont,' she told herself. 'Go home and help Cook get the house ready for people who need it. Do some good instead of harking after the past.'

It was the only way to go on.

Now

Belinda nods. 'I've learned that too. When life is tough, if you can make it better for others, somehow it helps you feel better too.'

'You help me by listening,' says Mabel. 'I wasn't sure I'd feel like that at first. But you do. You may have killed your husband but in my view, you're a good, honest woman.'

'Honest?' Belinda blushes with shame. 'How can you say that when I've told you – the owner of this home – that I got a fake DBS certificate.'

'I was rather disturbed about that,' admits Mabel. 'But I didn't say anything at the time because I could see why you did it. I might have done the same in your position. Besides, sometimes there's a fine line between right and wrong.'

'I know exactly what you mean,' says Belinda quietly.

Silence falls between the two women. Both want to say more. Both wish they hadn't said anything at all.

79

1945

When Mabel got back to England, she was physically and emotionally drained, hardly able to put one foot in front of the other. Thank heavens for Cook and her warm welcoming hug.

But then her old friend (she was so much more than staff) looked at Mabel nervously, before handing her a telegram. 'It arrived a few days ago but I didn't like to open it.'

Heart thumping, Mabel tore open the envelope.

Delayed in Jerusalem but escaped terrible bombing. On way back. Have surprise.

Papa was safe! As for the surprise, was it possible that maybe he had somehow found Antonio? Although he had said there was 'nothing we can do' to trace her son, it wasn't inconceivable, was it, that he had come across the father of her child? There were so many stories about people being reunited.

Mabel could scarcely breathe for excitement. The following week, shortly before their first guest was due to arrive at the newly converted Old Rectory, a large shiny black car crunched up the gravel drive. Her father got out, but before she could run towards him, he opened the passenger door. A tall, elegant woman emerged and took his arm.

Together they walked up the steps of the Old Rectory.

'Mabel, darling.' He held her in his arms and then stepped back. 'Allow me to introduce my wife.'

'Your wife?' she gasped.

'We met in Jerusalem,' the woman gushed.

Her father had his arm around her. 'Diana was working in the special forces team. We got along famously, didn't we, darling?'

Papa didn't even sound like Papa. He seemed like a besotted young man. 'I could not believe it when she did me the honour of accepting my proposal. The war has made me realize that you have to seize happiness when it comes along.'

'Yes,' said Mabel numbly.

'I'm sorry,' he said. 'How thoughtless of me. Is there any news of Antonio?'

He spoke as if Diana knew all about him. Mabel couldn't help feeling surprised that her father had moved on after Mama's death. This woman, with her coquettish air and glamorous clothes, was so different.

Briefly, Mabel described how she had just come back from Italy, looking for him. 'I'm afraid you are one of many who can't find loved ones,' commented Diana.

How unfeeling! 'The worst of it was that I don't know if his family survived,' said Mabel sharply.

'I'm so sorry,' Papa said, giving her a brief hug. 'Now, I've spoken to Diana and she would be happy for you to live with us. She has a house in Cheyne Walk.'

'Yes,' her voice tinkled. 'Miraculously, it survived the war.'

Mabel winced, thinking of their own ruined home with Mama and Annabel's bodies underneath.

'Thank you,' she said. 'However, Clarissa left me the Old Rectory and we're opening it up as a convalescent home for those who have suffered in the war.'

Diana looked horrified. 'Strangers? But you don't know what kind of people you'll get.'

'People who need love and comfort,' said Mabel firmly.

'I'm very proud of you,' said her father, and for a minute Mabel got a glimpse of the Papa she had known.

'Darling,' whined Diana. 'May we go inside and rest? I'm exhausted.'

'Of course,' he said, as if he, rather than Mabel, owned the house. 'Let's all go in, shall we?'

'Well,' said Cook when they left two days later. 'If there's any proof that a man can lose his head, we've just seen it. Are you all right, love?'

Mabel nodded, still stunned by Papa's 'surprise'. Naturally she was happy for him but she couldn't warm to Diana.

'Good. Then let's continue with what we were doing before, shall we? We've only got a week until our first guests arrive!'

Now

They pause while Belinda brews some tea for Mabel in a proper pot, pouring it into her special gold-and-silver Limoges china cup because it 'tastes so much nicer'.

All this talking is thirsty, tiring work. Mabel had felt herself dropping off at times but now she can't wait to shed this burden that has sat inside her for so long. It's as though her friend (who is so much more than a carer) has revealed a door that Mabel had kept locked for years, but which is now ready to be opened. And it seems Belinda feels the same.

'I've been thinking about Karen and forgiveness,' says Belinda. 'I know I should try to forgive her but I can't. None of this would have happened if she'd stayed away from a married man, no matter which one of them had made the first move. I know it's different but how did Britain manage to forgive after the war? How quickly did you all learn to even talk to Germans again or trade with them?'

'Good question,' replies Mabel. 'It took some longer than others. I knew people who refused to buy German cars for years afterwards. Yet you must also remember that there were many Germans who didn't support Hitler. In the end, I realized that you just have to move on.'

'But what if you can't forgive someone who hurt you and your family?'

'The anger and bitterness gets to you in the end. It eats you up. You must let it go. Or you'll kill yourself inside.'

'Easier said than done,' says Belinda.

'True. To be honest, I'm still working on it. There is one thing that . . .'

She stops.

'That what?' asks Belinda.

Mabel gives what seems like a little shudder. 'It doesn't matter. In fact, I can't even remember what I was going to say. That's the thing about getting older. A thought can slip out of your head before it reaches your mouth.'

But she's lying. Belinda is sure of it. There's something in Mabel's past that she is keeping to herself. And, somehow, Belinda must get it out of her if she's to protect her own family.

80

1946

Mabel's decision to run the Old Rectory for respite care proved to be one of the best of her life.

Looking after these poor souls who needed love and care after the war gave her a sense of purpose. Yet it could never ease the pain of not knowing where her son was (he would be three by now) or if his father was still alive. Mabel had, of course, written to the Red Cross to see if they knew where her love might be, but there was no trace of him. All over Europe, families were still desperately trying to reunite. But it was equally possible that Antonio had returned to Italy and made a new life for himself.

Meanwhile, Mabel had come to terms with her father's new situation.

From his letters, he seemed very happy His wife was even expecting a baby. 'I hope you can share in our joy,' he wrote. His words were like a punch to her stomach. This baby would be his real flesh and blood – not like her.

'Grow up,' she said to herself. 'You're almost twenty now. Be happy for them and get on with your own life.'

So she threw herself into her convalescents, who seemed to be finding peace at the Old Rectory.

'How did a young girl like you come to live in a beautiful place like this?' asked a discharged soldier one day, as he sat in the conservatory, staring out at the sea. He had one leg propped up on a stool. The other ended just below the knee.

'My aunt left it to me,' she said. Of course, she could have told him that the aunt had really been her mother, but that wasn't something to be shared with strangers. Mind you, this man did not seem like a stranger. From the moment he entered the doors of her gracious home, he had seemed different from the others. Her instinct told her that, like many, he'd been wounded emotionally as well as physically.

Yet there was also a steadiness about him that reassured her.

'Did your parents live here too?' he asked.

'Actually, my mother and baby sister were killed in the London Blitz.'

'I'm so sorry. How dreadful for you.'

Mabel bowed her head in acknowledgement. 'I was sent to live here while my father went off to fight but then . . . Then my aunt died just as the war ended.'

The image of finding Clarissa's body crumpled on the ground was imprinted on Mabel's mind: the word *TRAITOR* under the stone; the blood from the gunshot. No sign of a gun.

'So you live in this big place on your own,' he said, bringing her back to the present.

'Not at all. I'm surrounded by people who care for me.' As she spoke, she saw Cook bustling across the lawn, handing a plate of warm scones to a young couple. The man was an amputee, his plane having been shot down over France. This was their honeymoon. But the girl was laughing as if all her dreams had come true. Mabel would feel the same if Antonio came home, however badly injured he might be.

'What about you?' she asked, trying to regain her composure.

He spoke without emotion, in the way people sometimes do when they're hurting inside. 'My father was killed in an air raid too. My mother passed away from tuberculosis when I was a child.'

'I'm so sorry. Do you have brothers or sisters?'

'No, but I do have my work.'

'What do you do?' she asked, having mentally put him down as an engineer or maybe a teacher.

'Before I was called up, I was a scientist.'

Mabel had never really understood science, either at school or when her aunt had been helping her. In fact, they'd skipped those particular lessons together.

'How very clever,' she said, impressed. 'I'm afraid my education suffered horribly during the war, although I do read a great deal.'

'So do I,' he said eagerly. 'I'm enjoying a wonderful book at the moment, by an author called Hermann Hesse. Have you heard of him?'

'He sounds German,' she said hesitantly.

'Half-German, actually. But that shouldn't stop us reading good books.'

Mabel agreed. 'I'm reading a book by Virginia Woolf. It's called *To the Lighthouse*.'

'I've never read any of hers.'

'Well, you must borrow my copy if you'd like,' she said.

'Thank you. I'd like that.'

Over the next fortnight – the usual period of a guest's stay – Mabel began to spend more and more time, checking that the young man, whose name she learned was Michael, was comfortable and enjoying his visit.

Although she sensed a vulnerability under that assured manner, she didn't like to ask what had happened to him in the war. But one day, as they took a slow walk down to the sea – he was coming to grips with his crutches now – Michael began to tell her.

'You've been very good not to inquire into my situation, but I would like to tell you.'

'Only if you want,' she said quickly.

'I do.'

He took a deep breath. 'I joined the RAF before the call came out. It gave me a wonderful freedom. As a child, I used to think that my mother was in the clouds, and even as an adult, I liked to imagine she was still there.'

I understand that, thought Mabel.

'Then one night, our plane took a hit and we had to bail out over the sea. I was rescued by some Norwegians. They hid me for a short time but then word came out that the Germans would kill anyone who assisted the enemy. So I gave myself up and was sent to a POW camp until the end of the war.'

'What was it like?' she asked, thinking of Antonio's camp and how he was able to come and go as he pleased.

Michael's lips tightened. 'Horrible. I tried to escape but was shot in the leg, which explains this.' He glanced down at his crutch. 'When the army were on their way to liberate us, one of the guards shot himself in front of me. His brains splattered around us. I knew I should feel grateful he couldn't hurt us any more, but I also felt sorry for him. This war . . . it's conjured so many mixed emotions.'

'I know. I feel the same.'

He reached out for her hand. 'Please forgive me if this is too forward but I can't help telling you how much I admire you. I've been watching how kind you are to everyone and thinking about how marvellous it is that we can talk so easily. I'm aware we haven't known each other long but the war has taught us all that life can be short. The truth is that I have fallen in love with you, Mabel.'

Mabel stepped back. This was the last thing she'd been expecting. She'd seen Michael as just another young man who needed help and comfort.

'I'm so sorry if I've given you the wrong idea,' she stammered. 'But my heart belongs to someone else.'

His face dropped. 'I should have known. A beautiful girl like you would be taken by now. Who is the lucky man?'

Someone who might have tried to kill you during the war? The enemy? How could she tell him that?

'His name is Anthony,' she said, not wanting to give his Italian name. 'He's been caught up in the war.' She swallowed hard. 'I have no idea where he is.'

'I'm sorry to hear that.' He was standing a good distance from her now. 'Well, Anthony is a very lucky man. I wish you both happiness if he returns.'

Later, as she went down to the sea to clear her head, Mabel noticed the door to the lacemaker's cottage was open. Mabel recalled her words at their last meeting. *'But we cannot always have everything.'*

Yet surely she could have some happiness?

Tentatively, Mabel went in.

The lacemaker was sitting at the table, as though she was expecting her. Although no one knew how old she was, she seemed to have aged in the last few months, her movements slower and hair greying.

'How nice to see you, Mabel,' she said.

'I hope I'm not disturbing you.'

'I never mind being disturbed by you. Your kind smile is so like your mother's.'

Mabel felt the warm glow she always got when someone commented on their likeness even though Mama was actually her aunt. She was also glad that the lacemaker, even though she knew the truth, continued to keep up the pretence.

'Please, take a seat. Are you here to talk about your young man? I suppose you're wondering if you'll ever see him and your child again?'

Mabel nodded. 'How did you know?'

The lacemaker tapped her head in answer, smiling softly at Mabel. Then she closed her eyes, as if in a trance. Mabel's mouth was dry with hope and fear as she waited.

'I'm sorry,' she said eventually, 'but I cannot see anything this time.'

Mabel felt her heart plummet with bitter disappointment.

'But there is one piece of advice drumming away in my head.'

She looked unflinchingly at Mabel. 'The truth always finds us out.'

Now

'Was she right?' asks Belinda. '*Does* the truth always come out?' She looks rather pale and tired, Mabel notices.

'I'm not sure,' says Mabel. How can she admit that she is still waiting for that knock on the door?

The Stranger in Room Six

'Is that all you've got?' I thunder. 'That Mabel spent the rest of her life pining for the kid she gave away and some Italian she met during the war?'

'Give me a bit more time,' pleads Belinda. 'I think I'm close to something.'

'Are you sure you're telling me everything? This fortune teller — "the truth always finds us out". Sounds like a load of nonsense to me, Belinda.'

'I promise, I'm telling you everything.'

But there's a little quiver to her chin as she speaks.

'For your sake, I hope that's true. I've already given you an ultimatum but I'll give it again. It's not long until the party. If you don't come up with the goods by then, you and your girls will end up like your husband. Got it?'

Belinda whimpers, and I remember there's something else I've been meaning to ask her. 'One more thing. Did you ever find your husband's lover? Karen, wasn't it?'

'No,' she says. 'I didn't.'

'Ha! Your face says otherwise. Where did you put her, Belinda? The bottom of the Thames? A rubbish tip somewhere? Should I be telling the authorities about that private detective you wanted to hire to kill Karen?'

Her eyes flash at me. 'It was your idea, Mouse. Besides, I changed my mind. Do you want me to do this job for you or not? If so, let me get on with it.'

I love it when Belinda gets mad. I've taught her well.

'Then go. And this time come back with something better.'

81

Belinda

I find Mabel sitting by the French windows in the lounge. She's wearing a vivid turquoise jumper and sleek black slacks. Her elegance sings out across the room. From a distance, I can see the young girl she's been describing to me. The girl who has been through so much. All I want to do is help her find Antonio and her child, but I know I have no choice. If I want to save my loved ones, I need to find out more about the past.

'Shall we go outside for a walk?' I suggest.

She shakes her head. 'I've got a bit of a headache. I'd rather go back to my room if you don't mind.'

I'm not surprised. The music is hurting my head as well. Everyone takes turns at choosing the radio channels in the community lounge. It's usually a mixture of sixties and present day. But today it's rap, chosen by a seventy-two-year-old resident called Dylan who claims to have once sung on *Top of the Pops*.

I wheel Mabel back to her room. Someone has opened the window, letting in a nice summer breeze. But the old feel the cold in their bones. 'I'm freezing,' says Mabel. 'Can you shut it please?'

There's a lovely vase of freesias on the table. 'They're from my brother Harry,' says Mabel. 'Well, he's actually my half-brother. He's a lovely man.'

'I had wondered when you'd tell me more about him.'

'Later,' says Mabel. 'It's your turn.'

I'm aware that if I don't get something to Mouse soon, she'll run out of patience.

'Mabel, have you ever heard of the BUF?'

I see her stiffen.

'Of course. Why?'

'Did you know anyone who was a member? I believe they were known as Blackshirts.'

I see a colour rising in her cheeks.

'No. I didn't.'

She's obviously lying, but I'm not sure where to take it from here. It's clear already that the police suspected her family of working with the BUF, but I need proof, names, conspirators. I have a feeling Mabel knows exactly what I'm after.

Then, as if someone has flicked a switch, her mood changes. That earlier nervous demeanour is replaced by sparkling, mischievous eyes and she claps her hands, as if waiting for a performance to start. 'Belinda, I'm no fool. I can see you're not ready to tell me about Karen yet. But I will respect that and ask instead that you tell me about the day you left prison. Did you get into the car with Imran or not?'

82

Of *course* I want to get into Imran's car.

But I'm aware that my hair is greasy; that the skirt suit I wore for my court appearance is now hanging off my bones; that I smell because the soap ran out in our showers last week; and that there are grey streaks in my hair.

More importantly, I am not the Belinda he once knew.

As he climbs out, I see that Imran has gone grey too. His face has also filled out but his eyes are the same. They hold my gaze as steadily as he held me in bed all those years ago.

'Before you say anything,' he says, 'it was Elspeth who told me you were being released today.'

'I didn't know you and she were speaking.'

'I had to find out how you were. You wouldn't respond to my letters, so I got one of my people to find her.'

'I can't believe we're having this conversation,' I say. 'I don't want you to see me like this.'

'You look as beautiful as ever,' he says.

I take him in. His handsome face. His aquiline nose. 'Where's your wife?'

'We divorced by mutual agreement, as I told you.'

'Divorced?'

'You didn't read all of my letters, did you?'

'It would have hurt too much,' I blurt out. 'Besides, it's too late.'

'You and I still have time,' he says urgently.

'No,' I say. 'We don't. Time has changed me. *Doing* time has changed me.'

'Please don't say that, Belinda. Take a while to think about it, if you need to, but don't rule me out.' He presses a card into my hand. 'Here are my details if you want to get in touch.'

'I won't,' I say, sounding firmer than I feel inside.

Another car pulls up, it's my taxi. Before I can change my mind, I get in and give the cabbie the address of the hostel my probation officer has arranged for me. As we drive away, I can't resist turning back to look at the only man I've ever loved. But we've turned the corner and he's out of sight.

Now

Mabel gasps. 'Why didn't you take him up on his offer?'

'Because too much had happened. I couldn't make Imran happy. Not after murdering Gerald.'

Mabel shakes her head. 'I spent years looking for Antonio,' she whispers. 'I would have fought for his love if we'd found each other, even if he hadn't liked the person I'd become.'

'What do you mean?'

'Never mind,' she says briskly. 'Now tell me about Karen. I've waited long enough.'

83

I've never been in a hostel before. But at least it's not a cell. I share a room with a junkie who spent five years in prison and is now 'using' again. 'Don't tell anyone,' she hisses as she lights another pipe.

There's a communal bathroom, carpeted with used tampons and dirty towels.

The kitchen is crawling with cockroaches and there's grease everywhere. But I have freedom. I can go out. I can walk around. I can breathe in fresh air.

Best of all, I can see Elspeth. It doesn't matter that my probation officer comes too, as a condition of my release on licence.

I can hold my daughter's hand. Hug her. Tell her how much I love her. Tell her how sorry I am. 'Please don't, Mum,' she says. 'I can't talk about it any more.'

We sit in silence for a bit. 'How is Gillian?' I ask. The answer is still the same. My eldest daughter doesn't want to see me. There are some crimes that cannot be forgiven. Murdering her father is one of them.

'May I see pictures of my grandson?' I ask her. I glance at her phone. 'You must have some.'

She looks embarrassed. 'Gillian says she doesn't want you to.'

'Tell me what he's called, at least.'

'Gerald,' she says quietly.

Gerald? My eldest daughter has named her son after her father: the man I killed? The pain is so acute that I have to concentrate on my breathing to calm down. That's something I learned in prison. It stopped me hitting my head against the walls or thumping someone else's.

I try to distract myself by concentrating on the practicalities. For a start, I need a mobile phone. My daughter goes with me to the shop, but getting a contract isn't as easy as I thought. My bank account no longer exists and the young man looks uneasy when I give him the hostel address. In the end, I buy a cheap model from a supermarket. Elspeth also comes with me to the doctor's, where I have to give a previous address. Reluctantly, I name the prison, and the receptionist visibly backs away. But, by law, she has to give me a doctor. I make an appointment for what they call a 'general assessment'.

Elspeth takes me shopping and to the hairdresser. Afterwards she drops me back at the hostel, where she is clearly horrified at what she sees.

'Our charity has a flat that might be available. I'll come with you to your next probation meeting and we'll talk about it.'

A fortnight later, it's agreed. The flat is in a part of east London I've never been in before. But it's clean and near a market where people are friendly. Where no one asks me questions. At first, the speed of life, the traffic that goes so fast, the people who push by, is all too much.

Often, I climb into bed at 7 p.m. and go to sleep, revelling in the luxury of clean sheets. But every morning I wake at 5.30 a.m. sharp, waiting for the ping of the electronic doors and the jostling queue for the bathroom. When it doesn't come, it dawns on me that I am free.

Now that I have a phone and a laptop – Elspeth gave me her old one – I try to find Karen.

But I don't know where to start. Technology has moved on so much in the last fifteen years.

I ask my daughter for help. 'Mum,' she says. 'This isn't a good idea. You know it isn't.'

But I have to. I need peace of mind. I must find out exactly what happened. Only then can I attempt to forge ahead with my life.

At least, that's what I tell her. The truth is that I want to make Karen pay, whatever the cost.

In the end, it's easier than I thought to find a private detective online. When I explain, the woman at the other end seems to think my request is quite normal. I pay her with the money Elspeth has given me, plus my state benefits.

A month later, when I am at the universal credit office, my phone rings.

'I've found her,' says the woman. 'Karen Greaves is in care, due to early onset dementia. You can find her at the Sunnyside Home for the Young at Heart.'

84

Of all the scenarios I've imagined (Karen marrying again; Karen moving abroad; Karen dying), this one has never crossed my mind. I think back to when I saw her in the street, just after I pushed Gerald. She looked at least ten to fifteen years younger than me, which would put her in her early fifties now. Yet I know that dementia can strike people earlier and earlier these days.

I Google the home, which appears to be in Devon. There's an advert running down the side, looking for staff. I know that I can't apply until I've passed my probation. So I wait.

I become a model ex-prisoner. Then, when the time is up, I apply. Sunnyside seems desperate for staff: I'm interviewed on the phone and then asked to provide a DBS certificate to show I have a clean record. What am I going to do? Then I remember the forger whom I'd helped as a Listener in prison. She had insisted on giving me her phone number 'in case you ever need it'. She's been released now and is happy to oblige for a fee. My DBS certificate duly arrives. I send it off to the home, convinced they'll realize it's a fake.

But within days, an email pings to say I have been successful in my application for a job as a carer.

It's as simple as that.

Now

Mabel's expression is as though someone has just stolen her last chocolate ginger biscuit, only to give her a whole packet instead.

'Karen Greaves? That woman who throws food at people one minute and is all sweet the next, is *your* Karen?'

I flinch. 'Not mine.'

'Your husband's, then. Sorry, I don't mean to sound insensitive.'

Not for the first time, I'm wondering why I've laid my soul bare to someone I barely know. Yet maybe that's why; it's a relief to tell someone who doesn't seem to judge me. Besides, I *do* know Mabel, in a way, through her stories.

'I don't believe in coincidences,' says Mabel. 'I think it was meant to be that you found Karen and then almost immediately there was a job going here at Sunnyside. Fate can be very clever sometimes.'

Her eyes sparkle with interest. 'I was watching you with her last week. I noticed that when she reached out her hand for support, you didn't want to take it. I thought it was out of character, but now I know she was the woman who had gone off with your husband, I understand.'

Mabel may be almost ninety-nine but she's frighteningly quick on the uptake. Then her eyes narrowed. 'Is that why you came here with that fake certificate of yours? To hurt Karen?'

'I want to talk to her,' I say, skirting round the question. 'I need to know every single detail, such as when their affair started and if she really had a child. Recently, she said she didn't have any.'

'Maybe she's just confused.'

'Does she have any visitors?'

'I haven't seen any,' says Mabel. 'Then again, that doesn't mean she doesn't have family. There are plenty here who just get dumped.'

I've seen it. Some of the residents get jealous when they don't get visitors and others do. It's impossibly sad to watch.

'Do you know what I would do if I found Karen when she's a bit more with-it?' asks Mabel.

'What?'

'I'd ask her to tell me *why* she had an affair with your husband. There's usually a reason behind someone's actions.'

'Hah,' I scoff. 'Clearly, she saw Gerald as a money machine and zoned in. The fool fell for it – he even left her the house in his will.'

Mabel tilts her head quizzically, suggesting I might want to think twice. 'You could be surprised,' she says. 'People don't always act in the way you might think. Now, what are we going to do about Imran?'

We?

'You're getting older,' she continues. 'If you don't allow yourself to be loved now, will you ever?'

'I don't know,' I whisper.

'Send him your address and phone number,' commands Mabel, patting my hand. 'You need to take that leap. Listen to what happened to *me* next, and you'll understand.'

85

Mabel

1950s

The Old Rectory, in its new form as a convalescent home, helped to distract Mabel from her broken heart. Together, she and Cook ploughed their energies into helping those who were damaged.

But when children visited – especially small, ruddy-faced boys who were the same age as her son would have been – Mabel found herself retreating to her room.

'I understand, miss,' Cook would say at the end of the day, giving her a warm hug. Mabel had noticed that she'd begun calling her that instead of 'maid' or another endearment. Perhaps it was because she was now in charge. 'Please,' she said. 'Let's not stand on formality.'

Cook looked both flattered and concerned at the same time. 'If you say so.'

Meanwhile, Mabel kept writing to the authorities – both British and Italian – to see if anyone knew where Antonio and his family were, but she had no success. And despite her pleas, the adoption society confirmed that she was not allowed to know where her son was.

She had to accept that they were both gone for ever. The only way to cope was to try and help others.

After a few years, the demand for convalescent homes began to ease off. People had to get jobs. They were expected to 'get on with it', even though the after-effects of war would never go away. Then Mabel had an idea.

They would open up the Old Rectory to families who had not necessarily been hurt by the war, but simply needed a rest. To her delight, they were given a 'rejuvenation' grant by the authorities, to add to what was left of Clarissa's money.

'You must keep some for yourself,' said Cook.

'But I don't feel I deserve it.'

'Nonsense. Of course you do.'

If only Cook knew her secret, thought Mabel guiltily, then she might think differently.

Meanwhile, she continued to make sure that Frannie's mother and her remaining children at home had plenty of fuel and food.

'You're a kind girl. When are you going to settle down? You'd make a good wife.'

'I'm happy the way I am,' Mabel would say. No one could replace Antonio.

Over the next few years, Mabel continued to find comfort and pleasure in those who found rest at the Old Rectory. Many called her 'auntie'. Some returned again and again.

To her surprise, she also found solace in someone else. Until now, Mabel had seen little of Harry – her father and stepmother's son. Every now and then, Mabel would get the train to London and have lunch with Papa, but always at his club. 'It gives us time to talk,' he'd say. Yet Mabel had the feeling that Diana was jealous of her husband's previous family.

As Harry grew older, and reminded her less of little Antonio, they began to form a closer connection. Harry had grown into a strapping lad who loved cricket and riding. Foam had long passed on and James the groom had retired, but there was another horse now called Sparkle, whom

Mabel looked after herself. Harry often came down in the holidays, sometimes without his parents. They had wonderful days riding and walking by the sea.

And that's when it happened.

Now

Mabel pauses at this point and stares into the distance, although there's nothing there.

'What is it?' asks Belinda.

'I'm sorry?' murmurs Mabel.

'You just said "That's when it happened".'

Mabel looks scared, shrinking in her chair. 'I shouldn't really tell.'

'Please,' says Belinda. 'Let it out. You'll feel better. I promise.'

86

1961

Mabel had been looking forward to the summer. Somehow, it had become part of the year's pattern that Harry, now fifteen years old, would come down and spend a month at the Old Rectory. He was away at boarding school and often wrote to say how much he was looking forward to his time with her. Papa and Diana had not had any more children, and Mabel got the feeling that coming down to the sea was a welcome change for the lad. It was the same for her too; her time with Harry made her feel as close to being a mother as possible. Although thankfully, now she was thirty-five, most people had stopped asking her when she might get married.

Despite the fact they weren't related by blood, Mabel saw a lot of herself in her 'little half-brother', as she called him. He loved the open air and riding. He was also keen to please.

When the old Red Room needed redecorating, he offered to help. She could, of course, have paid someone in the village to do it, but Harry insisted that they could do it themselves. 'I enjoy practical things like this,' he assured her.

They started by scraping off the red peony wallpaper on opposite sides of the room. Then she heard a cry. 'Look,' he said, pointing to something low down on the wall. Is that what I think it is?'

'Yes,' she said numbly. 'It's a swastika.'

'Why would anyone have painted that here?'

'My aunt must have had something to do with it,' she said, crossing her fingers. How could she tell him that she had drawn the pattern on the wall herself as a teenager, in her enthusiasm for 'the cause'.

'Why?' he asked, clearly shocked.

What should she say now? How much had his father told him of the family history? Should she ask him first? Yes, that seemed the right thing to do.

But Harry was standing right in front of her, demanding answers.

'Sit down,' she said. Enough lies had been told in life.

So they sat, side by side with their backs against the wall. It was easier not to face him as she told him everything of her childhood at the Old Rectory. Well, not all of it, obviously, but enough.

'You mean that Clarissa, the woman you thought was your aunt, was actually your mother, and that she was one of the fascists who supported Hitler?'

'I'm afraid so.'

'And your father was murdered for it?'

'Yes, but I didn't know he was my father. Of course, back then, I thought *your* father was my father, until he came back from the war and told me.'

Harry squeezed her hand. 'That must have been a real shock.'

'It was. But I still see him as my father. He was the man who brought me up. Besides, he and your mother have given me a brother,' she said, squeezing his hand back.

'Did you know anything about Clarissa and the Colonel's activities then?'

'No,' she said, trying to keep her voice steady. If she told her beloved Harry that she had been a crucial part of those activities, he might not understand it had been well intentioned.

'But who killed her?'

'We don't know. As everyone said at the time, it could have been anyone in the village. She wasn't liked, and by the end of the war, there were definite rumours that she was pro-German.'

He shuddered. 'The Nazis did such wicked things. I can't believe people were so cruel back then.'

'Nor could we. But it is frightening how anger and ambition can take over some people.'

'It must have put you in a very difficult situation,' he said.

'It did,' said Mabel. It was on the tip of her tongue to tell him about Antonio but he would be shocked to know she'd fallen in love with the enemy, let alone had a child. She and Papa had agreed long ago not to tell him.

'My poor sister.'

She leaned her head into his shoulder. It was so comforting. At times, she could almost imagine that he was her son.

'I will always be here for you, Mabel. Always.'

'You are a good, kind boy,' she said, almost choking with guilt. 'I am so lucky to have you.'

Then she struggled to her feet and looked down at the evil sign on the wall. 'Now let us obliterate this loathsome thing.'

Now

'You mustn't blame yourself,' says Belinda. 'You were so young. You just wanted to please your aunt.'

Mabel is looking away, as if not wanting to meet her eyes. 'No one will know how ashamed I am. I didn't mean to tell anyone this. It just came out. But it's such a relief to confide in you.'

Then Mabel grasps Belinda's hand. What a strong grip for someone so old! 'Promise you won't tell anyone this?'

'I promise,' says Belinda, feeling terrible. But she has to tell Mouse. Because if not, her girls might die.

87

1966 onwards

Mabel was as proud of Harry as if he were her blood brother. When he got into Oxford to read History, she told everyone.

By then she was having to slow things down at the Old Rectory. Cook had long since retired and had to be looked after, which Mabel was very happy to do until Cook sadly passed some years later.

As she had done before, Mabel threw herself into work, hiring more staff and continuing to give free refuge to those who needed it. As time went by, Mabel couldn't help noticing what a variety of visitors they had. More wars had broken out; more refugees were desperate for somewhere they could come for a break. Or sometimes it was simply people who couldn't make their pennies stretch and were beyond grateful to find kindness here.

When Harry graduated – a ceremony Mabel attended with pride bursting in her heart – he declared that he wanted to enter politics.

'Are you sure?' said Papa. 'That's a very unstable business. You need a job to support you. How about the law? I know someone who might be able to offer you a pupillage.'

Then, two weeks later, Diana rang in hysterics. 'It's your father. He's . . . He's dead.'

At first, Mabel couldn't believe it. Papa had seemed so well at the graduation. But Diana managed to explain through her cries that it had been a heart attack out of the blue.

Mabel went straight to bed – something she never did during the day. All she wanted to do was put the covers over her and sob, but then she thought of Harry. She briefed the staff as quickly as she could and got on the train to London to see her brother.

'I am the head of the Marchmonts now,' she told herself. It was a strange feeling. She didn't feel old enough at forty to be at the top of the tree; Papa's death, for some reason, made it feel as though her mother and Annabel were drifting further and further away in her memories.

Papa had been her rock. He had been trying, through his connections, to track down her son but it seemed impossible. The adoption society had closed down and she didn't know the name of his adoptive parents. Their only hope was that he might find *her* one day, but although Mabel lived in hope of a letter or phone call, it never came.

Meanwhile, she had long given up hope when it came to her lover. As a prisoner of war, Antonio would have been released some time ago. If he truly cared, he would have found her by now.

By the time Mabel reached her seventies, Harry had achieved his ambition of becoming a Cabinet minister. His next ambition was to become prime minister one day – a goal she was sure he would achieve. Her own little brother!

But her excitement was cut short when she broke her hip a week later, tripping on the staircase. It was enough for Harry to declare that she couldn't continue the way she was.

'I'm not going into a home,' she told Harry firmly when they discussed the 'options'. 'This place *is* my home.'

'Of course it is,' said Harry. 'But I have an idea. Why not turn it into a residential and nursing home? You can be the first resident!'

'Oh my dearest, I'm not sure. It would be such a huge project! We'd need to change so much in the house to make it accessible.'

'We're going to need to do that for you, anyway,' he pointed out gently.

'There will be so many rules and regulations to follow.'

'We can find the right people to help us.'

'What about staff?'

'We'll go through agencies and word of mouth to find the best.' Harry's eyes were shining. 'Think about it, Mabel. You'll be able to stay in your own home and be looked after, without giving up the business. We'll make sure it's the crème de la crème of care by the sea.'

'I don't think we've got the money to do this and we might not be able to get a grant.'

'I'm happy to use some of Dad's money if you like and be an investor. He'd have liked that.'

The idea was beginning to grow on her. 'But I want it to be a happy place for everyone,' said Mabel. 'We need a cheerful name. How about . . . Sunnyside?'

'Sunnyside Home for the Young at Heart,' finished Harry, hugging her. 'It's perfect.'

Although Mabel couldn't admit it, she hoped it would dispel any of the evil left by Clarissa and the Colonel. She still felt sick to the core when she thought of the things that had taken place here during the war, and what would happen if anyone found out.

Within a month of opening, the home was full. One of their first residents was a lovely man who was visited regularly by his equally kind daughter, Anne. Their surname was Marples. 'A bit like Miss Marple, the detective,' they joked.

She could not have been happier.

If only she'd known what lay ahead.

88

Belinda

Mabel's suggestion that I find out *why* Karen had an affair with my husband, is haunting my mind.

People don't always act in the way you might think.

I'd presumed that my husband's mistress was just a foolish young woman who saw an older man and, with him, security. For Gerald, on the other hand, it must have been sex. Is that my fault? He'd never turned me on, not after Imran. Yet it takes two to tango and two to stray. It also takes two to talk about marital problems, which is something Gerald and I had never done; perhaps because we were too scared of the inevitable outcome.

I will only rest when I know more about what happened between them. Then, I'll be able to heal, or at least make sense of it all. I'm just hoping she can tell me. Karen might have dementia, but she still has her cognitive moments. I discovered that the day that I met her at Sunnyside.

The private detective I'd hired had sent me a photograph of her. It looked like a passport shot, her hard eyes staring out at me. This was a woman who didn't care about breaking up a family to get a wealthy man. I have no doubt that's why she got pregnant – to seal their relationship further and give him no choice but to financially support her. 'You knew exactly what you were doing,' I said to the photo. 'Didn't you?'

On my first day here, I was put on breakfast duty and given the list of residents expected in the dining room.

Karen's name, I saw with a jump of both excitement and fear, was on it.

But despite the photograph, I hardly recognized the woman in front of me. Her sunken eyes and long grey hair made her look more like seventy than fifty as she was wheeled into the dining room by another carer. She sat up at the table, stared down at the bowl in front of her and hurled it on the ground.

'You put nails in my cereal,' she screamed at the woman next to her.

'Don't be so bloody daft,' snapped her neighbour, still in her nightdress. 'They're just raisins in the bran flakes.'

'No, they're not.' Karen stood up then, her eyes wild. 'Someone here is trying to kill me.'

Everyone looked at me. The carer who brought her in had disappeared, no doubt to do the million other jobs that need doing round here, like changing soiled sheets and answering emergency calls.

'Don't worry,' I said nervously, in case she recognized me. 'Let's get rid of it, shall we? I'll get you a fresh bowl of cereal.'

'Thank you!' She grabbed my hands. 'You're new, aren't you? What's your name?'

My heart pounded. 'Belinda,' I said. Surely, she would twig now. I'd briefly considered changing my name before coming here but it was too complicated: all my identification documents are under Belinda Wall.

'Belinda,' she repeated. 'That rings bells but I can't remember why.' Then she beamed at me. 'I like you,' she said. 'You took away those nails. Please. Stay with me.'

And that's how I came to have two admirers: Mabel, whom I have genuinely learned to love, and Karen, the former mistress of my dead husband, whom I loathe.

I have so many questions I want to ask the bitch but her mind is all over the place. Sometimes she talks about the *Antiques Roadshow* (her favourite TV programme) and at other times she insists she was the first woman on the moon. 'I planted flowers there, you know.'

Then a few weeks ago, it all came out. We were doing one of Butlins Bill's jigsaw puzzles together. The picture was the Eiffel Tower. 'I went to Paris once with my husband, Gerald,' she said out of the blue.

I froze.

'Did you?'

'Yes. It was wonderful. We stayed in a place called Montmartre. But then we had to come home because of his wife.'

'You just said you were his wife,' I managed to say.

'His other wife.'

Suddenly she pushed the jigsaw puzzle off the table and it fell apart. 'I don't want to do this any more!' she screamed. 'Get me out of here. Get me OUT!'

One of the nurses gave her a sedative and took her back to her room.

Later, I tried to ask her more questions, like how long she'd known Gerald for. But she just kept chattering on about planting flowers on the moon.

I might not understand her mind, but I have come to know her body intimately. One of my duties is to help her shower. I want to retch as I help her under the hose. To think that these now-scrawny breasts were the once-firm bosom that Gerald found so alluring.

She looks at me, smiling. 'Soap,' she says. 'I like lavender soap. He used to buy me that.'

I could drown the bitch my husband destroyed our family for here and now. I could push her and claim she just fell.

I could direct the shower nozzle straight at her mouth and stop her breathing.

When I dry her, I want to do it roughly. I want to scratch her skin so hard that it bleeds.

But I find I cannot. Instead, I pat her dry and get her dressed for the day.

'You have to do better than this,' I keep telling myself. I need to know what happened between her and Gerald. Otherwise, I will never move on.

So, over the weeks, when I'm not with Mabel, I volunteer to go along with Karen to all the activities. I sit with my husband's old mistress as the children from the local primary school come to sing. I even go with her to the theatre when there's a group outing. I try to befriend her, through silently gritted teeth. Everyone tells me how good I am with her. Karen is known for her outbursts.

She doesn't seem to recognize me, but then again nor would anyone who knew me back then.

When it's visiting time, we sit together in the lounge while everybody else talks to their relatives. She looks at them enviously.

'Do you have any children?' I ask.

'No,' she says. 'I wish I had.'

Is that the dementia speaking or could it be true? Had Penny, Gerald's receptionist, been lying to me? Was it possible that Karen sent her to see me in prison with some concocted story about a child just to make me feel worse?

Did I kill my husband for nothing?

But then something happens that pushes Karen clean out of my mind.

89

I can tell something's wrong with Mabel the minute I arrive. Her face is pale and her words stumble over each other.

'I received something in the post this morning.' She hands over an envelope with a shaky hand.

Inside is a note in large capital letters.

FASCIST TRAITORS MUST DIE. YOUR SINS WILL BE PUNISHED.

My heart begins to thud. 'Who sent this to you?'

'I don't know. But I do know that I'm not a fascist.' Mabel's eyes fill with tears. 'I was just a naive teenager. I didn't know what I was doing. You're the only person alive who knows about Clarissa roping me in. Have you told anyone?'

'No, of course not.' I tell myself that the snippets I'd passed to Mouse didn't necessarily imply that Mabel was a traitor.

'Have you shown this to anyone else?' I ask.

'I briefly thought of telling Harry but he's so busy with this political campaign that I don't want to bother him.'

'Political campaign?'

'Don't you know? He's in the running for PM.'

During my time in prison, I avoided the news and the habit has stuck. 'What's his surname?'

'Like mine, of course. Marchmont.'

Harry Marchmont! I'd seen pictures of him on the front of newspapers when he'd been appointed deputy PM a while ago. A good-looking man with kind eyes. The public seem to like him.

'Why haven't you mentioned that your brother's a famous politician?'

'Well, I sort of did,' Mabel says vaguely. 'But Harry has always told me to play it down. It might put off residents if they don't share the same political values.'

I can see that. But what will it do to his prospects if it's discovered that his half-sister was unwittingly involved with people who wanted Hitler to win. And more importantly, what would it do to Mabel? Her safety could be threatened.

The jigsaw pieces are slowly beginning to fall into place.

'Give the note to me,' I tell Mabel. 'I'll sort it out.'

'Do you think I'm in danger?'

I hesitate, not wanting to frighten her. 'Just don't accept any visitors or phone calls until we know more.'

90

I storm into Mouse's room and find her slumped in front of the television, watching a daytime quiz show.

Slamming my hand down on the remote, I wave the note in front of her.

'Mabel received this in the post today. Anything to do with you?'

My old cellmate reads it out loud.

'FASCIST TRAITORS MUST DIE. YOUR SINS WILL BE PUNISHED.

'Of course not,' she says. 'But you've done well, Belinda. I'll pass on this information.'

'To who?'

'I've told you. I can't say.'

I try to snatch the note back but she's too quick for me.

'OK. I'm going to tell the police.'

Alarm crosses Mouse's face. 'You can't do that. It could send us back to prison.'

I shudder at the thought. 'Then tell me what's going on.'

She sighs. 'The boss – and I mean, the *big* boss – wants to bring Harry Marchmont down.'

'So why do you want this list?'

'You don't need to know that.'

I run out of the room, shaking. I won't let them get my family or Mabel, whoever 'they' are. There's only one thing to be done. It's a big risk but I have to tell Harry Marchmont about the note. I would do anything – well, almost anything – to protect Mabel's life.

The Stranger in Room Six

The threatening note was my idea. I'd hoped it might push the old lady into confessing all. But so far, nothing has happened. Still, at least Belinda has given me some useful information about Mabel's part in the war. If only we had the list too.

I'd brushed her 'So why do you want this list?' question away because my bosses have told me not to reveal anything to outsiders. In fact, the list is a collection of names, all of whom were 'persons of interest' to the authorities back during the war. Some were members of Mosley's British Union of Fascists, and many were sympathetic to Hitler, hoping a German victory would 'make Britain great again'.

Different counties had different lists. The Devon one was stolen from the county archives near the end of the war and never found.

'Surely they had a copy?' I'd asked my boss.

'Just a paper one, which they think was stolen too.'

'So why didn't the thieves just destroy it?'

'It was proof that they were loyal to Hitler's cause. This would have helped them if Germany had won the war although it could have led to imprisonment or death if the English had been the victors, which, thank God, they were. Get it?'

Of course I got it. People think serving time means you're stupid, but they underestimate me.

So, who stole the list? The thief was Lord Dashland, also known as the Colonel. How do we know? Because Lord Bedmont, who was also on it, revealed this on his death bed to his grandson. And how do we know that? Because the grandson is my boss. And I mean the big boss. He's also a billionaire businessman, who can't afford for Harry Marchmont's politics to make their way into Number 10.

It feels like a lot of fuss over nothing, right? Wrong.

I need to find that list so that Bedmont can remove his family name, save his reputation, and then ruin Harry Marchmont in the process. Two birds, one stone.

That's why I'm here at Sunnyside. Lord Jonty Dashland hands this list to his lover Clarissa, and who does she pass it on to? Her one living relative: Mabel Marchmont. So, this old lady is my client's last chance.

Or should I say our last chance? Because if Belinda and I can't come up with the goods, we'll be taken out. It makes sense. We know too much.

In the wrong hands, that list could be dynamite. Memories of the war still rankle and some whose relatives were killed might well carry grievances. But they've had eighty years to do so, I point out to my boss. Why start now?

'Because of the rising profile of the neo-Nazis,' he tells me. 'It has all kinds of implications for society, businesses and politics. That's why your information about Mabel Marchmont being involved is so crucial. It will discredit Harry Marchmont's name, which is just what my boss wants to save his business. We're about to leak it to the papers now. Meanwhile, keep looking for that list. The powers that be are terrified of being outed.'

Two hours later, my phone bleeps with an online news update. The shit has hit the fan.

BREAKING NEWS

It has emerged that ninety-eight-year-old Mabel Marchmont – the half-sister of prime ministerial contender Harry Marchmont – worked for Hitler during the Second World War. Miss Marchmont grew up in a Devon mansion, which she now runs as a luxury nursing business, the Sunnyside Home for the Young at Heart.

However, we have learned that the house was a base for members of the illegal BUF movement (also known as Blackshirts), many of whom supported Hitler. These are said to have included Miss Marchmont's own parents Lady Clarissa Sinclair and Lord Jonty Dashland who, unusually for the time, were not married.

The same source insists that Miss Marchmont worked underground with illegal BUF campaigners, delivered anti-government propaganda and helped a German spy land on English soil.

How much of this did Harry Marchmont know?

This is a man who has personally invested in Sunnyside, which, as he must surely be aware, was built on blood money left to Mabel by her pro-Hitler parents.

Does the country really want a prime minister whose blood is stained by evil – and whose success is built on fascist money?

And would you, our readers, be happy to put your loved ones into a home that holds some of the Second World War's darkest secrets?

91

Belinda

The article in the next day's newspaper is on the front page. I feel sick to my stomach when I read it. Everything in it – the leaflets, the parties, helping a spy to land – was given to me in good faith by Mabel. To protect my girls, I passed it on to Mouse for her boss. And now he must have fed it to the press.

When I force myself to think about it, I suppose I always knew this couldn't have a good ending. But when Mouse found me here in Sunnyside, I didn't love Mabel in the way I do now. Love is a strong word but it's how I feel. Mabel is funny, brave and courageous. She was just a teenager back then, used by Clarissa and Jonty.

Once more, I have wounded someone close to my heart.

What will Mabel say when she sees the papers? She'll know that all the information came from me. Will she think I'm the anonymous source?

Despite these headlines, what I'm really worried about is the hate note she received. I'm still trying to contact her brother so he can protect her. But it's not easy.

Unsurprisingly, it's impossible to get through to the deputy PM's office. I've tried phoning and emailing. Each time I receive a polite 'we'll get back to you'.

In desperation, I go to the manager's office in Sunnyside but she's on leave and her deputy is in a meeting.

'I think Mabel is in danger,' I tell one of the nurses. 'She's had a threatening note.'

'Then perhaps she should have been more careful in the past,' the nurse snaps back.

Judging from the rumblings amongst the residents, huddled round the newspapers, she's not the only one to think this.

Then Elspeth calls. 'I've read the news about Sunnyside. Has this got anything to do with the man who bumped into Gillian on the Tube?'

'I can't say,' I whisper. I'm in the dining room when she calls and I shouldn't even have my phone on me.

'Are you in trouble again?'

'I'm simply trying to protect you all.'

'What do you mean?'

'Trust me,' I whisper again. 'Sorry, I have to go.'

Later, when I'm in my room, Imran rings. (I'd followed Mabel's earlier advice and sent him my address and phone number.) Instantly, I'd regretted it and have been ignoring his calls, just as I ignore this one. If I needed any more proof that I shouldn't get close to people, this is it. The sooner he sees that, the better.

Just as I decide I'll go to the police about the note, even if it means they'll check out my background, news arrives. Harry Marchmont is coming to visit his sister.

92

Mabel

'Thank goodness you're here,' says Mabel, flinging her arms around her brother.

Harry sits down on a chair opposite her with a serious face. 'Mabel, there's great sensitivity around the issue of neo-Nazism at the moment. Obviously, this is abhorrent. My enemies are using my connection with you – the daughter of two Hitler sympathizers – to bring me down. Please tell me the truth. Some newspapers are claiming that you were involved with Clarissa and Jonty's work.'

Mabel is speechless. The only person who knew about this was Belinda, and she would never tell on her.

'Were you or were you not involved with their work?' Harry says.

'No,' stammers Mabel nervously. 'Not exactly. Well, sort of.'

Harry looks at her in a way she hasn't seen before. 'What do you mean?'

'Well, when I lived with Clarissa, she wasn't very nice to me, as I've already told you. But then she and the Colonel asked if I would do some "war work" with them. I presumed it was to help Britain. So I did things like put letters in envelopes and leave them in the woods . . .'

Mabel trails off.

'Carry on,' says Harry tightly.

'I also drew that picture of the swastika that you found

as a boy. I was too embarrassed to say I had done it. At the time, I didn't know what it meant, you see.'

Harry looks as if he has swallowed something nasty.

'And did you really help a German spy?'

'Clarissa just told me to flash a torch down on the beach. She said I would be helping to win the war.'

He groans. 'Mabel, I need you to listen carefully. During the war, people made lists of people who they knew, or suspected, sided with Hitler. Many were British citizens. The plan was that after the war, they would be punished. But the local list here went missing and it's widely believed that traitors stole it to protect themselves. My enemies have been spreading rumours that Clarissa passed this list on to you.'

So that's the list everyone's been talking about, realizes Mabel. As if she was a traitor. That's ridiculous.

'Well, I can assure you that she did not.' Mabel snorts. 'The only things Clarissa ever gave me were books at Christmas and then her locket, but really that was only because she thought she was about to be arrested.'

'A locket?' says Harry, sitting forward. 'Where is it now?'

'I wanted to throw it away when I found out that the two of them were traitors,' says Mabel. 'But something inside wouldn't let me. So I put it somewhere safe. The thing is that I can't remember where. In fact, I've been looking for it myself.'

'Really?' says Harry.

But she can tell from his eyes that her beloved brother isn't sure whether to believe her or not.

93

Belinda

I wait outside Mabel's room. It's my only hope of catching Harry Marchmont. Amazingly, there isn't a bodyguard. I just pray that Mouse doesn't come out of Room Six and see me.

The door opens.

'Mr Marchmont,' I say. 'I help to look after your sister. She received a threatening note. It said "*FASCIST TRAITORS MUST DIE. YOUR SINS WILL BE PUNISHED*".'

I'm aware that I'm babbling in my fear of not getting it all out.

'May I see it?' he asks.

I can't tell him Mouse snatched it from me but I've prepared my story. 'Someone stole it from me.'

He looks shocked. 'Who?'

'I don't know. I kept it in my room to hand over to the manager when she was back but then it disappeared.'

I feel awful about lying but I don't know what else to do.

It's clear that he sees me as either a nutcase or a suspect. 'What's your name?'

'Belinda,' I say. 'Wall,' I add reluctantly.

'We will look into it. Thank you. I expect the police will want to talk to you. You're not going anywhere, are you?'

I feel even worse now. What if they find out that I supplied the information to Mouse? If it wasn't for my daughters' safety, I would confess everything on the spot.

But now I've put myself right under the microscope. The police will investigate my background – it's what they do to people who give information, isn't it? I've just risked my family's life for an old lady who might be as guilty of breaking the law as I am.

Mabel

'Who could have given the papers that information?' Harry asks.

It's on the tip of her tongue to say 'Belinda' but she knows her dear friend wouldn't do that.

'I don't know,' she says.

'One of your carers mentioned the note you received. It appears to have "disappeared", rather conveniently. I've just telephoned the police but they say they can't do anything without physical evidence. You should have come to me first.'

'But you're always busy with work,' she protested.

He makes a 'you're right' gesture. 'Please stay in your room, Mabel, for safety.'

Yet she can't bear it. She needs fresh air.

But everyone stares at her wherever she goes. The dining room. The communal lounge. The games room. The gardens. 'I'm not living in a place with Nazi connections,' says one woman.

Residents start to talk of leaving. Mabel gives a radio interview with Harry next to her, explaining she had no idea that her parents were working underground for the illegal BUF but not denying this fact either. She also added that she had not even known they were her parents at the time.

Numbers look set to plummet. 'Sunnyside's going to go into the red at this rate,' Harry says when he visits again.

Mabel squeezes his hand, wanting to say something. But all she can think of is Clarissa's body, the word TRAITOR under the stone beside her.

Supposing someone tries to kill her too?

The Stranger in Room Six

My phone pings with another text from my boss.

> Newspapers are asking for physical documentary proof. We need that list of names in order to erase Bedmont's name before someone else finds it. You've got twenty-four hours.

That's it. He doesn't say any more. He doesn't need to. I've seen what happens to those who don't deliver.

They are found in car scrap yards. Discovered at the bottom of lakes. Or they disappear without trace.

Mouse, *I tell myself, in a voice that sounds like my mother's,* you've bitten off more than you can chew this time.

I almost feel sorry for myself. But hell, twenty-four hours is twenty-four hours. I can do something in that time. I've got to.

Outside, they're putting up the banners for tomorrow's summer barbecue, which is always held on Mabel's birthday. But through the window, I can hear grumbles.

'I don't know why we're doing this for her.'

'We don't know for sure that she's guilty, do we?' *says another.*

'My family are still coming. They want to have a nosy around, especially after those headlines.'

For me, the barbecue could be the break I need. Parties, barbecues, dances – any kind of community crowd – are always good for hiding crimes. People are too busy enjoying themselves to notice what's going on.

Even better, everyone will be outside, including the hostess.

Tomorrow will be my last opportunity for a good snoop around this house. And despite what my boss said about no bloodshed, I'll take my gun. Just in case.

94

Belinda

The Day of the Barbecue

The bunting is up. The trestle tables are being laid for those who wish to eat outside, and there are banners everywhere.

HAPPY BIRTHDAY TO MABEL AND TO SUNNYSIDE HOME FOR THE YOUNG AT HEART!

Despite the bad press we've had – or maybe because of it – the place is packed with visitors oohing and ahing at the grounds and the house. I can't help but notice how many glance Mabel's way suspiciously.

'Isn't she the woman who supported Hitler during the war?'

'We're thinking of taking my mother out of here, to be honest.'

'Us too. My great-uncle was a POW. It doesn't feel right to keep him here.'

Meanwhile, I'm still waiting for the police to interview me.

Mabel is sitting in her wheelchair beside a huge birthday cake. The cook – a young man from Ukraine – has made it in the shape of Sunnyside. She only just manages to blow out the candles. Claudette strikes up 'Happy Birthday', but not everyone joins in.

'I'm not singing for someone who was on Hitler's side,' says one.

'I've always thought Mabel Marchmont was up herself, just because she owns this place,' says another.

Mabel's head is sinking onto her chest.

'Are you all right?' I ask, hurrying over to her.

'Actually, dear,' she says listlessly, 'I'm very tired. I think I'd like to go to bed.'

One of the other carers takes her. I have to be here on duty. Now I won't be able to search her room, though I suspect I wouldn't find anything. I've already looked enough times already.

Karen is there, all dolled up in some cheap-looking sequinned dress and trademark red lipstick, which she keeps smudging by running her hands over her mouth. If Mouse is going to finish me off, then this is my last chance to find out the truth about Karen and Gerald, and whether they actually had a son or not.

Meanwhile, Claudette is asking the residents for their favourite songs.

'"Twinkle, Twinkle, Little Star",' Karen calls out. 'My husband Gerald used to call me Twinkle. He said it was because I made him feel twinkly inside.'

'Ahhh,' coos the audience.

Husband? How dare she call him that? As for the 'twinkly' bit, that makes me feel sick. He'd never given *me* a pet name.

My blood pounds as Claudette strikes up the tune and everyone joins in. I watch Karen singing, her eyes closed in rapture. My chest hurts with fury. I might not have loved Gerald, but he had no right to destroy our family. And nor did she.

Afterwards, Claudette takes a break. My prey is still there in her wheelchair. I wander up casually.

'Why don't we go for a little walk, Karen? It's such a beautiful evening.'

She turns to me, beaming inanely. 'Yes,' she says. 'I'd like that.'

95

Mabel

Mabel has told everyone that she was tired. It might be her birthday but she wants to go to bed early. 'No,' she says to the carer who comes with her. 'I'm quite capable of undressing myself, thank you.'

In truth, all she really wants is to be alone so she can have another search for that bloody locket. It's the only way she can prove to Harry that she's telling the truth.

She knows she put it somewhere safe. But where?

The problem with getting old – well, one of them – is that you can remember the past as clearly as if it was yesterday. And yet you can't remember something you did three seconds ago.

She manages to get down on her knees and push her stick under the bed to feel if anything is there. Oh – her back! But she can't feel anything. Then she pokes her stick into the back of the cupboard. Nothing. Then again, her locket was small enough to have got hidden in a dress pocket. Anywhere.

'Alexa?' she says out loud. 'Where the bloody hell is my locket?'

'OK. Here's storage box. Sorry. I'm having trouble accessing your storage box skill right now.'

So it's in a box but Alexa doesn't know where. How frustrating!

Mabel carries on with a renewed energy, tossing knickers out of her underwear drawer and books out of the bookcase.

Nothing.

Maybe her earlier fears were correct and one of the carers has stolen it. Please don't let it be Belinda. She's been acting very strangely recently.

Eventually, she gets into bed, but finds she can't settle. Something isn't right. Is it because she's finally reached ninety-nine and is still lonely, even though she's surrounded by people?

'Alexa,' she says. 'I'm sorry about getting cross earlier. Please talk to me.'

'Where is the list?'

This doesn't sound like Alexa's voice. It's deeper and gruffer. Perhaps this is another one of these weird dreams.

'Give me the list, old woman, or I will cut your throat.'

If Mabel was younger, she would have leaped up and confronted such audacity. Instead, she manages to ease herself onto her elbows so she can face this person with a black hood over his face.

'Young man,' she says. 'That's if you *are* young. It's difficult to tell with that thing you're wearing. I have lived through a war. I dug through rubble in an attempt to find my mother and sister during the Blitz. I have lost a child. I have lost the love of my life. Alexa . . .' Here she stops for a moment, gathering her breath. '. . . is now my only friend. I am not scared of anything. If I had this bloody list which everyone keeps asking me for, I might give it to you just to get rid of your unpleasant presence. But I don't.'

'Then I'll shoot your brother instead.'

That's it. It's one thing being threatened yourself, but another where Harry's concerned.

Mabel would kill for him if necessary.

Swiftly, she presses the alarm button, which immediately sets off a shrill siren.

'What the fuck . . .'

At the same time, she reaches for her walking stick and lashes out.

There's a resounding, hollow noise. 'You've done it now,' the man says, clutching his head and coming towards her. The gun in his hands glints in the evening sunlight through the curtains.

Mabel hears the shot before falling to the ground.

PART FIVE

96

GUN ATTACK ON DEPUTY PM'S HALF-SISTER

FURTHER INVESTIGATIONS TAKING PLACE INTO POSSIBLE LINK TO PRO-NAZI MOVEMENT IN OLD PEOPLE'S HOME

Mabel

A voice is hovering above her. 'Mabel?'

It's Harry, her brother. She's sure of that.

'Are you all right?'

'I think so. Where am I?'

'In hospital, under observation. You had a nasty blow to your head when you fell but, thank God, the bullet missed you.'

'Who tried to shoot me?'

'We're not sure yet but from what she's admitted, she was working for someone else.'

'I thought it was a man. He wanted the list. I don't know why everyone keeps asking me for it.'

'Who?'

'Well, just one person actually. Belinda, my carer.'

'Does she now?' Harry appears thoughtful. 'Look, Mabel. I know I explained this before, but the thing is that there are some pretty important people who might be implicated by that list. They'll do anything to destroy it. At least, this is what I've just been advised by Special Branch, who, unknown to me, have been watching over you.'

'To spy on me or to protect me?'

He looks embarrassed. 'Both. Apparently, they needed to make sure you were telling the truth. And if you were, they needed to check you weren't targeted by the people who are after this list. The man who shot your attacker – and saved you – had been working undercover as the entertainments organizer here.'

Mabel feels her jaw drop. 'Butlins Bill?'

'I believe that was his nickname.'

'Was? Is he all right?'

'Luckily he wasn't injured.'

'Thank goodness for that.'

'Mabel,' says Harry, taking her hand. 'We really do need to find that list.'

'But I've told you. I don't have it. You do believe me, don't you?'

He hesitates.

'You don't, do you?' whispers Mabel. Her eyes fill with tears. 'I think I'd like you to leave now. I'm feeling very tired.'

97

Belinda

I'm called to Room Nine, which I've never been in before. To my knowledge, it's always been empty, but now I see there's electronic equipment everywhere. Harry Marchmont is there and – to my surprise – Butlins Bill.

'I'm afraid I had to deceive you all,' he says. 'My real name is Garth. I'm from Special Branch, here to keep an eye on Miss Marchmont. We have recently learned that you were in prison with Amanda Smith, also known as Mouse. It's all right. You're not going to get into trouble for failing to mention your earlier conviction, providing you can give us some help.'

I swallow. 'First, can you make sure that my daughters are safe. Mouse said they'd be in danger if I didn't get her the information she was after.'

'So that's why you got so close to Mabel. I wondered as much.'

'Actually, I really care for her,' I start to say but he gives me a 'who do you think you're kidding?' look before continuing.

'As for your girls, we'll see what we can do. In return, I want you to think very carefully. You spent a lot of time with Miss Marchmont. Can you think where she might have hidden that list?'

'I've no idea.'

'Please,' says Harry. 'My sister's life might depend on it.' He puts his head in his hands before looking up at me again.

'My enemies hope that the connection will ruin my career. But we're more concerned that Mabel is becoming a target. Someone has already tried to kill her.'

I shudder. 'Mouse threatened my girls' lives if I didn't give her the list.'

'Well, at least you don't need to worry about that any more,' said Garth.

'What do you mean?'

'Amanda Smith – Mouse, as you call her – died on the way to hospital.'

98

Mouse is dead. And this time it's true.

I can't believe it, but I have to admit I'm relieved. She could have killed us all. Unlike last time, I don't shed any tears.

Meanwhile, Mabel is back in her room at Sunnyside. She seems more shocked by Butlins Bill than by the shooting. (I thought that Harry would stop me from being with Mabel but he wants me to continue as her carer in case she says something important. So I've gone from having one master to another.)

'He's such a clown! I'd never have had him down as a member of the Special Forces.'

'I agree but, Mabel, we really need to find that list. It's of national importance.'

'So they keep telling me. But I've no bloody idea where it is.'

It's been a while since Mabel swore. Is it frustration or guilt because she is indeed hiding it?

'They think your aunt gave it to you.'

'I told you before. The only thing my aunt gave me was a locket but I don't know where it is now.'

Her eyes fill with tears. 'I'm tired of this. It's not the way I want to end my days. My brother suspects me of supporting a pair of Hitler sympathizers when in fact they were the ones who ruined my life. Someone tried to kill me and, for all I know, someone else might try to do so again.'

'It's all right,' I say, holding her. 'Just let it out, love. I believe you.'

And I do.

For a few minutes we sit there. Mabel in bed. Me on the eiderdown next to her, holding her hand.

'I want to sleep now,' says Mabel. 'Can you give me my doll?'

I hand her over. 'Polly,' murmurs Mabel, clasping it to her chest.

Within minutes she is asleep.

The doll stares up at me, sending shivers down my spine. Then Mabel moves and Polly slips precariously out of her grasp. I grab her before she falls and go to put her on the bedside table.

Then Mabel's words come back to me when she'd described Polly, after rescuing her from the rubble of the Blitz. '*She was so soft and warm.*'

I take off the doll's elaborate dress, which has become quite grimy over the years. Her body underneath is made of cloth, which appears to be stuffed. I recall Mabel vehemently refusing suggestions that it should be washed 'in case it disintegrated with age'. There's a seam down the side of her body. All I need is a pair of scissors.

99

I am about to slit open the doll's body when something makes me stop. Am I right to interfere with possible evidence?

So I call Garth on the private number he'd given me 'in case you think of something important to tell me'.

'Don't touch it,' he says firmly. 'I'm on my way.'

When he arrives, he insists we wait until Mabel wakes up so we can 'see her reaction'. Then he puts on a pair of latex gloves – the kind you see in films, so no one contaminates the evidence.

Harry, who has also been summoned, goes pale. 'I hope to God this isn't what we think,' he says.

I watch Mabel's body rise and fall with each breath. I've truly grown to love this woman. I don't want her to have committed a crime, willingly or not.

Eventually, she stirs.

'What are you all doing here? Why have you got Polly?' she demands. 'You'll hurt her with those sharp scissors!'

There's a collective gasp from us all as we peer over Garth's shoulder while he unpicks the seam. Then, using a pair of tweezers, he carefully extracts a folded piece of paper from the stuffing inside.

Garth unfolds it. He whistles.

'Look.'

We all lean over it. The heading is *CONFIDENTIAL. SUSPECTED NAZI SYMPATHIZERS AND PEOPLE OF INTEREST.*

Then there is a list of names. He reads it out.

Lady Clarissa Sinclair
Lord Jonty Dashland
Lord Henry Bedmont

There are more.

And right at the bottom is *Mabel Marchmont*.

There's a collective gasp.

'Why would anyone have put my name there?' protests Mabel.

Harry sighed. 'You've already told me that you helped Clarissa and Jonty. Someone in the village must have suspected you but didn't have evidence. That would have been enough to have made you a "person of interest".'

'But how could this document have got into my doll? Unless . . .'

She stops, as if remembering.

'Clarissa used to confiscate Polly when she was annoyed with me. Maybe she put the list in her then.'

She looks at the faces around her: the one that doubts her (Garth) and the ones that desperately want to believe her (me and Harry).

'I remember Clarissa and Jonty being accused by the police of hiding something too.'

They still don't look convinced.

'It's true,' she says, wringing her hands. 'Although there is something else I should tell you.'

'What?' says Harry, a fearful tone in his voice.

'I've kept it quiet for years, but please understand that I'm being honest about all of this.'

I want to believe the woman who has become my friend. I really do, but this doesn't sound good.

'If you look under my bed,' says Mabel, 'there's a floorboard which is slightly looser than the others.'

Garth's face stiffens.

'It's why I insisted on staying in the Red Room when the house was made into a home, even though I never cared for it. I wouldn't let the builders alter it like the other rooms.'

Garth is already on his knees.

'I've got it.'

He prises it open and brings out a small badge.

'I found it when I was helping Jonty and Clarissa with their paperwork,' says Mabel. 'I picked it up by mistake and then was scared of giving it back, so I kept it.'

Garth's face is grim. 'I've seen this design before. It was a distinction award given to certain members of the Blackshirt movement.'

'It belonged to one of the guests who visited,' adds Mabel.

'I think,' says Harry, 'that we should stop right here until I've called my lawyer.'

Garth's mouth tightens. 'In the meantime, I'm afraid I cannot allow your sister to leave Sunnyside.'

Harry is physically sweating. 'But even if my sister had been part of the Blackshirt movement, that's not a crime any more.'

'No. But we have to keep her safe from the public. She's already had one anonymous threat and an assassination attempt. There are plenty of people out there who would be happy to take revenge.'

'But I didn't mean to,' wails Mabel. 'I just did what Clarissa and Jonty told me to do.'

'I'm afraid that's not an argument that will save your life.'

Traitor or not, I can't help putting my arms around Mabel to comfort her, grateful that she hasn't made the connection between the headlines and me. Then I leave to give her time with her brother.

As I walk away, down the corridor, the manager catches me. 'Belinda? You have a visitor.'

My heart leaps. Elspeth? Imran? Despite me telling him to go away, I yearn to see him. Be in his arms.

'His name is Stephen Greaves,' says the manager. 'Says he's Karen Greaves's son.' She narrows her eyes. 'I hope he isn't going to complain about something.'

100

Stephen Greaves? Karen's son? My heart feels as if it's beating overtime as I walk down the corridor, past the community lounge where two residents are arguing over a jigsaw.

I push open the office door with a trembling hand. A man is standing with his back to me, looking out of the window and over the croquet lawn. He turns to face me.

I gasp. A young Gerald is standing before me.

'Belinda Wall?' he asks.

I nod nervously.

His face breaks out into a smile. 'My mother kept saying she had a lovely carer called Belinda. I wanted to thank you for being so kind to her.'

Phew! So he has no idea who I am.

'It's funny,' he adds. 'My mother also told me you reminded her of someone. When I asked the manager if I could talk to you, I also asked what your surname was.'

My mouth goes dry.

'I know this might sound silly, but my mother used to know a Gerald Wall who was married to a Belinda. Of course, it's a common-enough name but . . .'

He stops. This is where I tell him that there is no connection. But he gets in first.

'The thing is, Mum also told me what you'd said to her last night at the barbecue. I was meant to have been there but got delayed by work.'

I pretend to act dumb. 'I've no idea what you mean.'

His eyes are unwavering. 'I think you do.'

My mind goes back to those seconds just before we heard the shot inside the home, not knowing it was Mabel who was being attacked.

'*My husband Gerald,*' Karen had said.

'*No,*' I'd snapped. '*I was Gerald's wife. Not you.*'

'Your mother has dementia,' I say now. 'The other week, she told me she didn't have any children, and yet here you are. So I'm afraid we can't believe everything she says.'

'Sometimes she doesn't recognize me, but I assure you that I am her son. Your husband's name is on my birth certificate too.' Then he brings out a newspaper cutting from his pocket. 'And this is you, isn't it?'

I stare in shock at a much younger me, the newspaper article headed 'Mother jailed for murdering husband'. The picture had been taken on that holiday in the Scilly Isles. Had Derek given it to the paper?

'My mother used to read it out loud to me over and over again. "This is the woman who killed your father," she would say. It's how I know that you're the same Belinda Wall. There's still a similarity.'

On any other occasion I would be flattered. Instead, I know I've lost.

His voice hardens. 'Did you track down my mother or is it a coincidence that you found a job here?'

'I paid someone to find her,' I stammer.

His voice sharpens even more. 'Did you plan to hurt her?'

'I was curious,' I say, evading the question. 'I wanted to find out more about their relationship and if she really had a child. Years ago, a friend of your mother's came to visit me in prison and said that Karen had a child, but I never knew if it was true.'

'That must have been a shock.'

I'm surprised by this sudden sympathy. Is it a ruse? Either way, I need to seize this moment.

'Tell me,' I say hungrily, 'exactly what happened between your mother and my husband. I had no idea they were together, or that they'd had you, until just before he . . . he died.'

'My mother just told me that she fell in love with an accountant who was doing some work for her. She said that he had a lonely marriage –'

'Lonely?' I burst in. 'He had me. His girls. His responsibilities. His bloody crosswords.'

'Mum also said that he wanted to wait until Gillian and Elspeth had gone to university. This upset her. She wanted him to move in and be a proper dad to me. It sounds as if he was trying to please everyone. It couldn't have been easy for him.'

'Then he shouldn't have had an affair,' I shoot back. 'My eldest daughter won't talk to me. Your mother divided our family. She even took our house from us.'

Stephen shakes his head. '*You* divided the family by murdering him.'

'I lost my temper, but he deserved it.'

It's not until I hear the words leave my mouth, that I allow the real truth – the one I'd been hiding from myself all these years – to finally come out.

At that moment when I'd pushed Gerald, I had indeed wanted to kill him. More than that. I'd wanted to smash his adulterous skull.

Wasn't that why, deep down, I had gone along with the lawyer's advice to plead guilty?

'Is losing your temper an excuse for murder?' asks Stephen coldly.

It's a question that doesn't need answering.

There's a long silence before Stephen continues. 'For what it's worth,' he says, 'I don't think it was right that Mum and I got the house. He should have looked after you as well – and my father should have told you the truth.'

'Thank you,' I say, quietly.

'I just wish I knew more of him,' Stephen says, a regretful note in his voice. 'I have a vague memory of a man picking me up in his arms. That's all, though I do have photographs.'

He reaches inside his coat and pulls out a packet of prints. And there it is. Indisputable evidence. Here's Gerald with a little boy on his knee; Gerald holding hands with Karen in another shot. And here's Gerald by a beach with both Karen and the same little boy.

'I never thought Gerald was the kind who would have a mistress,' I whisper.

'My mother wasn't a mistress.' His voice is firm. 'She loved him. He loved her. Look.'

He hands me a letter. Gerald's precise handwriting shouts out at me.

My dear son,

I felt moved to write to you in case, one day, I am not able to explain the situation of your birth myself. I was – still am – married to another woman. However, I fell in love and you are the wonderful result. You may think I am weak but I cannot, at present, summon up the courage to leave my family until my girls have become adults in their own right. But I wish you to know how much I love you and your mother.

You may wonder what I mean by not being able to explain all this. The truth is that I have a serious heart condition, which has only just been diagnosed. The outlook does not look good.

Why hadn't Gerald told me that? Then I think of the way his forehead would sweat when he did the crossword. How he could never walk far without getting out of breath. If I'd been a more caring wife, would I have picked up on the signs?

'He was returning from seeing the consultant that morning,' says Stephen. 'My mother had gone with him.'

His words come back to me. '*Sorry, dear, I've got a meeting to go to.*'

In fact, it had been a hospital appointment and he'd taken her for support – not me.

That hurts. So too does the realization that he might have died anyway, even if I hadn't pushed him.

'I shouldn't have done it,' I whisper. 'Nor should he.'

'My mother wasn't blameless either,' he says quietly.

We say nothing for a moment or so. Then he takes me by surprise. 'I'd like to meet your daughters – they're my half-sisters, after all. I think Dad would have liked that.'

'No,' I say fiercely. 'That's too much.'

His eyes turn wistful. 'I always wanted a proper family. It was hard growing up without a resident dad. Hard for Mum too to be a single mother.'

'Not as hard as it was for us,' I shoot back. 'My girls had a mother in prison. And now I'll have to go back behind bars.'

'Why?'

'Because you will tell the home about my past. They'll find out I lied on my forms. I'll be taken before the court and –'

'I'm not going to do that,' he says.

'Why not?'

'I think we've all suffered enough, don't you? I just want to know one thing. Are you safe to look after my mother?'

It dawns on me that my resentment is beginning to subside

now I've heard the full story from her son. Besides, I am no killer. Not an intentional one, anyway.

My time in the prison has also taught me to forgive. I've seen what rancour can do if you don't. I've also seen a different side to the Karen I thought I hated. She's no longer my husband's lover who broke up our family. She's a woman whose mind is going and who needs looking after.

'I will never hurt her, if that's what you mean.' I almost add 'not now' but decide that's best left unspoken.

'Having met face to face, I'd like to believe you.' He gets up. 'Shall we go?'

'Where?'

'To Mum's room. I think it would be a good idea if we both saw her together, then perhaps she might accept you, depending on her state of mind today.'

'Her? Accept me? Shouldn't it be the other way round?'

'I think it will take two of you.'

So I go, with this young man who looks so like Gerald and, come to think of it, Gillian. It seems the right thing to do.

101

Karen is sitting by the window with a photograph album in her lap.

A picture of Gerald beams out at me. Part of me would throttle him if he was still here. But there's also a small voice that says '*Come on. You were never suited. Besides, you always loved Imran.*'

She looks up at us.

'This is my son!' she says, beaming at me as if introducing us.

'I know,' I say.

Stephen crouches down by her side. 'Does Belinda look after you all right, Mum?'

He is scared, quite rightly, that I might try to hurt her. Who can blame him?

'Oh yes,' she says. 'We have some lovely chats.'

Then her forehead wrinkles. 'Apart from the night of the party.'

I stiffen.

'What happened then?'

'I told everyone how my Gerald would call me Twinkle. I don't think she liked that. Belinda took me for a walk, and then we heard a shot.'

She giggles as if it's funny. 'We were both a bit scared, weren't we, Belinda, when we heard that gun go off?'

'Yes,' I say. 'We were.'

'Do you know, for a moment, I thought you had shot *me*.'

'Why would I do that?'

'It might have had something to do with a man I once knew called Gerald.'

She speaks as though she hadn't just been talking about him. I've learned that lost conversational trails are common in dementia sufferers.

Stephen cuts in. 'Gerald was Belinda's husband, Mum. My dad. The man you had an affair with. So I have to ask you something. Are you really happy for Dad's wife to look after you here?'

Karen's eyes narrow. She's glaring at me. 'But she's not his wife, is she? Not really. He loved *me*.'

I'm about to say that of course I was his bloody wife. But then I stop. What kind of marriage did Gerald and I have? It was a sham. I have a feeling that Stephen was right when he said his parents really did love each other.

'I like Belinda,' Karen is saying, stretching out her hand to me. She's switched moods again. 'She's a good listener.'

I can't say I like her back because I don't. But at least I no longer feel like I want to kill her. When I think of her as a woman who has been struck too early by this cruel disease, I can't help but feel sorry for her. Then I remember Mabel saying that there's always a reason for someone to do something. Karen's reason for stealing my husband was that she really had loved him. And I hadn't.

'I can assure you, Mr Greaves,' I say stiffly, 'that I would never harm your mother.'

'If you did, you'd end your life in jail.'

'I don't need reminding of that.'

'Then let's move on to other family matters, may we?' His voice softens. 'My mother always told me that my father wanted me to meet my sisters one day.'

'Half-sisters,' I remind him sharply.

'I'm sorry. That's what I meant. Do you think you could ask them?'

Why on earth should I do that?

'I can't ask Gillian because she hasn't spoken to me since her father died,' I say. 'I'm in contact with Elspeth but I don't know whether she would want to see you.'

'They're the only family I have left now, apart from Mum.' His voice has turned from tough to desperate. 'Your girls and I don't just share your husband's blood. We share memories of the same man. I have no one else to talk to about that. Please, will you just ask them?'

There's a longing and vulnerability on his face that moves me, despite everything. And beneath it all, I worry that if I don't make it happen, he will tell the manager about my past. Then they'll check my DBS, discover it's fake and sack me. I would find it hard to get a similar job without references. But most of all, I would lose people whom I've grown to love and care for: especially Mabel. I just hope I'm not going to lose her anyway with my betrayal.

'I'll ask my daughters,' I say reluctantly. 'But I can't make any promises.'

'Thank you.' He hands me his card.

'You're a dentist?' I ask, impressed.

'Yes. That's my private number. You can get in touch with me any time.'

That's when I notice something.

'You're wearing Gerald's watch.'

'Dad left it to me in his will.'

I want to say that's not fair. I want to ask if he'd left my girls a special gift too. I want to ask Gerald what the hell he was playing at, having two families.

But dead men give no answers.

102

Elspeth is furious, especially as I have to explain how this all happened.

'Karen is a resident there?' she asks appalled. 'You went to Sunnyside to find her? I thought we agreed that you wouldn't try and track her down.'

'Actually, that was your opinion,' I point out. 'Not mine. I needed to know the full story if I was ever going to move on.'

'Well, I'm definitely not meeting some man who claims to be Dad's son. I know Gillian would feel the same without even asking her. She's still furious that you were involved with all that political stuff.'

I'd given the girls a brief version without going into too much detail; explaining I'd been asked to keep a special eye on Mabel Marchmont as her carer and that the assassin had tried to get at her through scaring me. It's not far from the truth.

With trembling fingers, I call Stephen. 'I'm sorry,' I say. 'They don't want to meet you.'

'I see.' There's a pause.

'I suppose you're going to shop me now?'

'No,' he says. 'I said I wouldn't, and I meant it. Besides, my mother seems comfortable in your presence, and she likes talking to you.' He gives a short laugh. 'Ironic, isn't it? Well, thank you for trying.'

He seems, I have to admit, a decent man. I can only hope he sticks to his word.

As I put down the phone, there's the sudden sound of glass shattering.

People are running down the corridor screaming.

'Someone threw a brick through the dining-room window,' I hear one of the nurses yell. 'It was a kid from the town – I recognized him. Call the police!'

Mabel isn't the only one who's not safe. None of us are.

103

Mabel

The police arrive to take statements about the broken window. Then Mabel is interviewed by more official people whose questions make her head spin.

Afterwards, Belinda brings her lunch in her room to avoid the other residents' staring eyes. 'I'm not hungry,' Mabel says.

There's a knock at the door. It's Harry.

'I'm so glad you're here,' says Mabel tearfully. 'I'm so confused.'

Belinda gets up. 'I'll give you some privacy.'

'No,' says Mabel. 'Please sit with me and hold my hand. It makes me feel comforted.'

'Yes,' says Harry. 'It might be helpful if you stay. Now let me try and explain all this as simply as possible.'

He takes a deep breath.

'There's a prominent business tycoon who's been pressurizing the government to pass new tax legislation that will help large companies like his but make it much harder for small businesses. According to our sources, he saw an advertisement for Sunnyside while looking for a home for his own mother. He spotted that it had originally been in Lady Sinclair's family before passing to the Marchmonts. The name "Sinclair" rang a bell because his grandfather had been a friend of Clarissa and Jonty.'

'What was his name?' asks Mabel.

'Bedmont.'

'I remember him.'

'His name was also on the list in your doll,' says Harry grimly.

'Bedmont then discovered that you, Clarissa's niece – or so he thought – are not only living here but also own what was known as the Old Rectory. He knew from his parents and grandparents that there was a list of all the prominent names involved in supporting Hitler but that this list went missing years ago. He suspected that as the sole family survivor, you might have it.'

'As indeed I did, without realizing,' chips in Mabel.

'Exactly. He feared that if the names were released, he'd lose his business. It's struggling badly at the moment and is dependent for its survival on securing a large contract in the Middle East against fierce competition. Any stain, even if it's from the past, could tip the balance away from him. At the same time, he wants me out, in the hope that Parliament will support my rival's bill to give tax relief to companies like his: something I've been fighting against.'

'How *can* he get you out?' asks Belinda.

'Through Mabel, I'm afraid. His people have been spreading rumours in the press to say that I was aware of your "support" for Hitler during the war. We are also concerned for your safety.' He shivered. 'You could have died if Garth hadn't saved you.'

He puts an arm gently around Mabel's frail shoulders. I can see how much she means to him.

'Luckily,' he continues, 'you mentioned Alexa, which came out as a command word. As a result, part of the following conversation was recorded in the history section of your Alexa app. So we have legal evidence. We also recorded what Amanda Smith said on her way to hospital. Unfortunately, she confirmed my worst fears about her source . . .'

Mabel gasps. 'Who was it?'

Harry looks straight at her companion. 'Belinda Wall.'

The air goes very still for a second. Belinda looks at the ground as Mabel stares at her in disbelief.

When Harry continues, his voice is cold. 'It seems that your favourite carer had been feeding information to Amanda about your work for Clarissa and Jonty.'

'No,' cries out Mabel, dropping Belinda's hand. Was it really possible that she'd been betrayed by the woman she'd told her life story to? The only woman who knew the truth about her?

'I thought you cared for me, Belinda,' she chokes.

'I do, Mabel. I really do. I can explain –'

'GET OUT!' Mabel startles herself with the sound of her own voice. 'Do you hear me, Belinda? I never want to see you again.'

If it wasn't that Belinda knew so much about her, she'd dismiss her on the spot.

After that, come more headlines. There's no mistaking them: every time Mabel is wheeled into breakfast, ignoring Belinda's pleading face, she sees the other residents poring over the papers and giving her hostile looks.

99-YEAR-OLD OWNER OF OLD PEOPLE'S HOME HID LONG-LOST LIST OF HITLER SYMPATHIZERS, INCLUDING HER OWN NAME

Of course she didn't hide it, Mabel wanted to say. She didn't know it was there. But who would believe her? Then, at the end of the week, comes the final nail in the coffin.

As Mabel arrives at breakfast, there's the usual group hovering over the papers.

'In those days, it would have been a scandal,' she hears one say, before looking at her with contempt. 'My father was a prisoner of war in Italy. I don't want to be in a place where the owner had an affair with one of them.'

Mabel's blood runs cold as she leans towards the group.

They move aside, their faces shooting daggers.

The picture is of a young couple who are clearly in love.

Gently, Mabel runs her finger over the black-and-white picture on the front page, stroking the young man in uniform, as if doing so might bring him back. 'Antonio,' she whispers. 'My love.'

Below the picture is a caption.

Proof that Mabel Marchmont, half-sister to PM candidate Harry Marchmont, socialized with the enemy. This man was an Italian prisoner of war.

Below is another picture. This time it is Mabel holding a baby.

And this was their child.

104

'How did it happen?' demands Harry after leaving a Cabinet meeting to find out what 'the hell is going on'.

'I loved him and he was kind,' says Mabel staunchly.

'I understand that,' says Harry more gently. 'But who took the pictures?'

'One of Antonio's friends in the camp took a couple of us together before I was sent away. I kept one and he had the other. The picture of me with my baby was taken by the sisters I stayed with in Cornwall. I sent a copy to Antonio but I never knew if he received it.'

'How did they get into the hands of the papers?'

'I've no idea. I hid them in a shoebox on top of the wardrobe.'

'Let's get Belinda in here,' says Harry grimly. 'My bet is that she stole them. Perhaps she stole your locket too. You said she kept asking about it. Maybe she found it and sold it. I said you should tell the manager and get her sacked.'

'I can't,' says Mabel, who's had time to think a bit more clearly now. 'I know she's betrayed me but she had her reasons. I'm still angry but I don't want her out of a job.'

Although this is true, it isn't the only reason but she can't tell her Harry that.

When Belinda comes in, she is adamant that she didn't steal the locket. 'You do believe me, don't you?'

'I want to,' Mabel says, but the truth is that Mabel doesn't know who to trust any more. Least of all, Belinda.

105

Belinda

I take myself off for a walk through town. In the past, I haven't had a spare moment to get down here, but since Mabel no longer wants to see me, I seem to have a lot of time on my hands. After all, I used to spend many of my hours off with her before all this happened.

I pass an Oxfam charity shop, a greengrocer's and then a jeweller's, which I've never been into because what use do I have for jewellery? However, today it has a CLOSING DOWN SALE: 80 PER CENT OFF sign in the window so, on impulse, I go in, hoping I might find Mabel something small to say sorry. I don't have much money but it's worth a look.

The owner is about my age and immediately starts telling me how sad he is to be shutting up. 'My dad started this place and I took over. But now I feel it's time to retire.'

He runs his hands through his hair. 'He kept paperwork going back years. I'm still trying to sort it out. You wouldn't believe how many people have left jewellery here and forgotten to collect it. I've got a pile of tickets with names but no contact numbers.'

That's when I have a lightning-bolt moment. 'I don't suppose you have a locket under the name of Marchmont, do you?'

Sometimes, things are meant to be. When I have paid the cost of the repair for the broken clasp, I bring it back to Mabel.

Her eyes narrow when she sees me and get even harder when I hand her the locket.

'So you've decided to return it have you?'

I was worried she might say that. But I have proof. 'I found it in a jeweller's shop. Here's the repair ticket. It has your signature and the date from twenty years ago.'

Something dawns in her eyes. 'Yes . . . I remember now. I knew I'd left it somewhere safe, but my memory isn't what it used to be. I took it in when the chain broke.'

She opens it. I'm beginning to think I should have called Garth in case there are more surprises inside.

There's a photograph of a woman on either side. They're both classically beautiful, their hair in chignons above swan-like necks. 'This is my mother,' says Mabel softly, 'and then this is my aunt.'

'What's that underneath the photograph of your aunt?' I ask, glimpsing a tiny edge of something white.

It's a photograph of a baby. On the back are the words *Our darling daughter.*

'That's my aunt's handwriting,' whispers Mabel. 'But why put it there if she didn't want anyone to realize she was my mother?'

'Perhaps,' I say, 'she wanted you to know that she really did love you.'

Then Mabel bursts into tears. 'Thank you, Belinda, for finding this. You've made me very happy.'

It's not forgiveness. I don't deserve that. But it might be a start.

106

That afternoon, another brick is thrown, this time through Mabel's window. More people withdraw their loved ones, but Mabel refuses to leave Sunnyside, despite Harry's pleas to find a safer place.

'I'm innocent,' she says. 'Why should I hide? Besides, this has been my home since I was a child.'

I can see the writing on the wall. Sunnyside won't be able to survive this.

Imran texts again.

Are you all right? I've seen some of the messages on social media. They're scary.

I don't reply. I shouldn't have given him my number.

The following day, I'm in the reception area when a taxi draws up. A smart, stout woman in a velvet coat climbs out, supported by a wooden cane. She looks around curiously, then hobbles cautiously up to the front door.

'Who are you visiting?' asks the receptionist through the intercom.

'Mabel Marchmont.'

'Can you give me your name please?'

'Certainly. It's Dame Frances Buss. But Mabel may remember me as Frannie.'

PART SIX

107

Mabel

Mabel is sitting in her chair by the window overlooking the old croquet lawn. The sun is bright today. She can see Antonio in her mind, trimming the hedges. Feel his lips on hers.

BANG!

The gun sounds as real as if it had been shot just now. The carpet in front of her turns to lawn, her aunt's bloodied body lying face down with the word TRAITOR on the ground next to her.

'Stop,' she tells herself firmly. 'All that was years ago.'

But it's not over, is it? It never can be.

There's a knock on the door. Then it opens before she can reply. Mabel holds her breath. Despite her outer bravado, she's been extremely jumpy since that horrible attack. She could have been shot. And now Harry has made it very clear that it could happen again.

A woman walks in, leaning on an ornate wooden cane. She is tall and imposing and wearing the most beautiful coat. Something about that firm nose and no-nonsense expression stirs Mabel's memories. No. It can't be.

'Hello, Mabel.'

That broad Devonian accent. The slightly deeper tone.

'Frannie,' cries Mabel. Then she stands up, wobbles a bit, and finds herself being caught by Belinda, who sits her down gently.

'Careful,' says Frannie. 'Neither of us are spring chickens now.'

'How did you know I was here?' asks Mabel, stunned.

'I think half the country is aware,' replies Frannie. 'I'm surprised that brother of yours hasn't moved you somewhere safe.'

'I won't leave my home,' says Mabel.

'I understand.' Frannie's voice goes soft. 'I went to see our old cottage on my way here, but it had gone. There was a block of glass-fronted apartments there instead.'

'Things have changed around here. But more importantly, how has life treated you?' asks Mabel. At first, she'd thought Frannie didn't look her age but now they're close up, she can see the blue veins on her arms and swollen legs.

'Well, thank you. I went to work as a secretary for a lawyer in London. She encouraged me to train as a barrister and eventually I became a judge, although I'm long retired now.'

'You know,' says Mabel slowly, 'I was shocked when you left so suddenly. Why did you?'

Frannie's mouth sets in a firm line. 'For years I'd hated working for your aunt. The final straw was when I was dusting the library and came across a photograph of the Colonel and your aunt on one of Mosley's marches.'

'I saw it too,' murmurs Mabel. So that's why it had been sticking out of a book. Frannie had found it first.

'It made me realize that I couldn't stay in a place that was tainted by Clarissa and the Colonel, even if they were both dead. I hated the way they treated you. I knew you were helping them – I overheard about the leaflets. I was going to turn you in, to be honest. But my mother stopped me. She said you were just a young girl who didn't know what she was doing and that you were being groomed by that pair. You were desperate for love and you thought they were giving it.'

'The trouble is,' says Mabel sadly, 'that the newspapers and the public don't seem to believe that.'

'That's why I'm here. I don't want to boast, Mabel, but my word carries weight now. I have several contacts including the editor of a well-known national newspaper. What do you think about me going on record to say that, in my view, you were an innocent pawn in their wicked game?'

'You'd do that for me?'

'I think I owe you.'

'I don't understand.'

Frannie sighed. 'Remember my brother who threw those pheasants out of the house? He was convinced you were working with your aunt and the Colonel to help the Nazis. He'd seen you in the woods and thought you were leaving messages for other sympathizers.'

'I didn't know that then.'

'I believe you but he went to the police. He said he didn't have any firm evidence but you were put on their list of "people to be observed".'

Mabel thought back to when the police had questioned her.

'I thought I was helping the country.'

'I believe you. That's why I'm going to help you now.'

To Mabel's amazement, Frannie spits on her finger.

'Do the same,' she orders.

Mabel does as instructed, and they rub their fingers together.

'Now, remember what we promised each other all those years ago?'

'Friends for ever,' murmurs Mabel.

'Exactly. And it seems that I've also returned to the Old Rectory, just as you'd asked me to. Now let's get to work, shall we?'

*

It was a risk, both the lawyer and Harry argued. What if it went against them? But it didn't. Frannie, or Dame Frances as she was known after being honoured for her services to the legal profession, was right. She *did* pull weight amongst all sections of society.

There was a long editorial in one of the Sunday papers, where Frannie likened Mabel's situation during the war to that of a child being groomed by criminals.

Frannie described her childhood friendship with Mabel: *Although traumatized by her mother and sister's deaths, she tried her best to fit in and help with the war effort, giving food to the poor (myself included), fundraising, knitting socks and making camouflage nets. In 1945 she opened her home free of charge to convalescents and then families who simply needed a break by the sea.*

It struck a nerve amongst readers. *Mine was one of those families*, wrote Doris from Bexhill. *Mabel Marchmont was kindness itself. I came from a family of eleven. We'd never seen the sea before. Those two weeks at the Old Rectory are still some of the happiest days of my life.*

Then there was an anonymous letter printed in one of the broadsheets. *My mother was recruited into the Blackshirt movement. She wasn't posh like Mabel Marchmont. She didn't have two pennies to rub together. They offered her new clothes if she'd run errands for them. Later, on her death bed, she confessed this to me. She was deeply ashamed. I now carry that shame of having a mother who could have been responsible – if things had gone the other way – for us being invaded. So I don't blame this old lady. She was taken in just like my mum was.*

More letters came flooding in. It was consoling to find there were others who had to live with the shame of parents or relatives who'd supported the enemy.

Sure enough, other papers joined in, and there was a slew

of articles supporting Mabel and condemning the hate she had suffered.

The ebb of residents leaving the home began to slow. It looked as if Mabel's reputation – and that of the Sunnyside Home for the Young at Heart – was slowly being restored.

108

Belinda

Despite my efforts with the locket, Mabel ignores me as I go about my care duties. I've lost my friend. A woman who, a year ago, I hadn't even known. But Mabel has become such an important part of my life that I cannot bear to see the distrust in her eyes.

A week later, I go to the manager to hand in my notice. It's only right that I leave Mabel to live out her last years in peace. Hopefully my short experience here will help me find another job, although I'm nervous about using the fake DBS certificate again; I might not be able to fool another home so easily. Besides, I don't want to lie any more.

'She's in a meeting at the moment,' says the manager's secretary. 'Please wait in her office. She won't be long.'

As I wait, the phone rings. No one comes in so I answer it. 'Hello?'

'Is this the manager I am speaking to please?'

'Err –'

'Ciao! My name is Isabella. I have seen the online photographs from the 1940s of your Mabel Marchmont. I believe I am her great-granddaughter.'

My heart skips a beat. 'Her great-granddaughter? Can you prove that?'

'Well, I have copies of the same photographs, and also a small piece of lace my grandfather has had since he was adopted.'

'Lace,' I repeat excitedly, remembering what Mabel had told me. 'Could you hold on a minute?'

I run to get Mabel. Something tells me that the caller is genuine.

109

Mabel

Mabel can't quite believe what this woman is telling her.

'You're my great-granddaughter?' she says over and over again. 'But how is my Antonio?'

'He is good. I live near him in Italy.'

'But how? Where?'

'I will tell you all, my bisnonna, when I arrive.'

'Bisnonna? What does that mean?'

She laughs merrily. 'It is Italian for great-grandmother.'

Mabel's head is spinning. 'You are coming here?'

'But of course. If you would like me to.'

'Yes! Yes, I would. Please. Be quick. I need to see you before it is too late.'

Sunnyside Home for the Young at Heart is waiting. News has got around. A room is made up for Isabella in the visitors' wing. Mabel spends hours putting on her make-up and trying on different clothes. Belinda is on duty so she helps with this task, although Mabel barely talks to her. If it wasn't for the fact that it takes her for ever to get dressed on her own nowadays and that there are not enough staff to go round, she wouldn't have had Belinda in the room. The air is tight.

And then there's a knock on her door.

'Please open it,' she tells Harry, her heart thumping so hard that it rings in her ears.

A tall, olive-skinned woman stands there. She is pushing an elderly man in a wheelchair.

'My bisnonna,' she cries, running to Mabel.

But Mabel's eyes are on the man.

'Antonio!' she cries out. 'My love. I knew you were still alive. At last, you have come to find me!'

110

Of course, the man in the wheelchair is her son, rather than her old lover, Mabel tells herself after hearing Isabella's story. She had been confused on the phone when she'd asked her great-granddaughter how Antonio was, because both father and son had the same names.

When she thinks about it, the figures would never have added up. Her beau Antonio had been ten years older than her, which would have made him almost 110 by now. Possible, perhaps, but not likely. Her son, who is now in his eighties, looks just like his father. Yet he is staring at her as if he has no idea who she is.

'My grandfather – or nonno as we say – has dementia,' Isabella says. 'He understands things sometimes, but not often.'

Mabel swallows the lump in her throat. How cruel that they should find each other too late.

Isabella is sitting by her chair, holding her hand. 'I have been trying to help Nonno to trace his family for years. When he reached twenty-one, his parents told him he was adopted. He contacted the adoption society but some of their records had been destroyed in a flood.'

'I tried to find him too,' Mabel says quietly. 'I didn't know which society Clarissa had used.'

'Who was Clarissa?'

Mabel feels her jaw clench. 'My mother, who I'd thought was my aunt. She made me give away your grandfather.'

'I'm so sorry.' She feels the woman's slim hand take hers; the warmth heats her. 'Shall I go on?'

'Please.'

'My grandfather left for Italy to try and find his father. The authorities had the name of the village he came from.'

'I remember putting that on the letter I gave the adoption man,' says Mabel, 'along with the lace.'

The girl beams. 'I brought it with me.' She opens her haversack and brings out the strip the lacemaker had given Mabel all those years ago.

'Look,' cries Mabel, 'I still have my half!' She opens her bedside drawer and pulls it out.

'They match,' breathes Harry.

Antonio, she notices, seems to be watching her every move without saying anything. Her heart wants to break. Her poor sweet boy.

Her great-granddaughter continues. 'When my grandfather went to Italy to find out more about his roots, he discovered that the village had been destroyed by the Germans.'

'Yes. It was the same when I went to try and find him after the war.'

'But in Nonno's day, they were beginning to rebuild it. His relatives had come back to help with the restoration and welcomed him as if he had been born there. He married my grandmother – a local girl.'

'But what about *my* Antonio – your great-grandfather?' asks Mabel urgently. 'Did anyone find out what had happened to him?'

Isabella's gaze falls to the ground. 'I'm afraid he was drowned on his way back to Italy after the war ended. The boat struck a drifting German mine in the English Channel, even though peace had officially been declared.'

Mabel closes her eyes. So Antonio had died. Not recently but nearly eighty years ago. Wasted years that she'd spent hoping that one day he would come back.

'After his death, the British authorities sent some of his possessions back to his parents. They included the letters that you had written to him but which he had never received. We think they were sent to a different camp from the one he was in.'

'So he never knew he had a son,' chokes Mabel.

'I'm worried this is too much for my sister,' cuts in Harry.

'No,' says Mabel sharply. 'I need to know everything. Don't you see?'

Easing herself up on her stick, she gently rests her cheek against Antonio's. 'My darling son. I have thought of you and your father every day of my life.'

He does not move or speak, but she can feel his cheeks are wet.

'He is crying,' whispers Isabella. 'Don't weep, Nonno. It is all right. At last, we have found your mama and my bisnonna. We are all together.'

Then she looks pleadingly at Mabel. 'I know this is a lot to ask at your age but, please, will you come back to Italy with us for a visit? My mother, she wants you to. She thinks that in his own environment, Nonno might show us some of the clearer moments he had before.'

'Yes,' says Mabel without even needing to think about it. 'Of course I will.'

Isabella claps her hands joyfully. 'You can also meet my six younger sisters! We joke that our parents had kept trying for a boy but my papa says he is blessed to have so many women around him. My next two sisters down each have four children but I am single. I have not yet found the right person. My mama says I am right to wait because marriage can last a long time.'

She says all this with a lilt to her voice and a sparkle in her eyes.

Mabel gasps. 'So I have great-great-grandchildren as well!' Sad as she is about her son and his father, she feels a burst of excitement too.

Harry looks both relieved and sad. 'I'll miss you,' he says, kneeling at her level, and putting his arms around her. 'But I think you might be safer there until things have died down a bit.'

'Are you ready?' Mabel asks Polly who is perched in the basket of her wheelchair. 'We are going on a big adventure!'

III

Belinda

I find myself lonely after Mabel leaves. I hadn't realized how much her companionship meant to me, until her room was empty. I thought that my job was to listen to her. I would have done so even if I wasn't being blackmailed by Mouse. But in fact, Mabel listening to *me* has meant just as much.

Maybe it really is time to leave now. But then I overhear one of the other carers talking to an elderly gentleman who's just arrived and is feeling low in spirits. 'You need to chat to Belinda. She's a good listener.'

Those words make me feel useful. Valued. I still have a job to do.

When people move into a care home, their past is the most important luggage they can bring with them. After a busy life, they now have the time to dissect it. To look back and think what they should and shouldn't have done. It's a difficult journey. Mistakes have been made that can't be rectified. Wonderful times have gone that they can't recreate. They need someone to share this with. To listen. And not all have relatives close by to do that.

But it can take its toll on the person listening too; it can also encourage that listener to re-evaluate their own life. To learn lessons from those who are one step ahead in the chain of life and death.

Now I am staying on, I decide to spend more time with Karen. I'm not trying to find out anything new now. I've learned what I needed to from her son. When Karen refers to 'Gerald, my husband', I no longer boil with anger. In some ways, he was her husband more than he was mine.

I remember Mabel's words about forgiveness. I'm not quite there. But I'm slowly moving towards it.

'I know who stole those photographs from Mabel,' Karen whispers to me one day.

'Of course you do,' I say. I'm used to Karen's wild ramblings.

'It was that Claudette. The singer. I overheard her telling someone that she'd made a mint by selling something to the papers.'

Is this Karen's dementia speaking? Still, I tell the manager and she calls the police, who question Claudette and she confesses. I worry about what will happen to her. She's only nineteen and she did it to pay her tuition fees, although that's no excuse. But she gets let off with a suspended sentence and a fine.

Elspeth and I see each other about once a month. Sometimes she links her arm through mine. When I ask how Gillian is, she simply says 'fine'. It makes my heart ache. Just as it aches for Imran.

It might have been different if I'd been brave enough to get into the car when he came to collect me from prison. But the longer I am free, the more I realize how far apart we have grown. Imran will never see the prisons where I spent my sentence. He doesn't know that I still wake in the night, screaming with terror in case someone is coming in to attack me with boiling water. How can we make a life together when his has been so different?

I try explaining this when he rings. I've ignored him for long enough and I need to be straight with him.

'Please, Belinda,' he says. 'Just give me a chance. Let me come and take you out for the day. We can talk properly.'

My weekend off is coming up. I could spend it wandering round this seaside town alone, or I could accept Imran's offer.

I don't take long getting ready. I dab on some concealer and tie my hair into a chignon to try and hide the grey strands. Then I put on the dress Elspeth bought me last Mother's Day. 'Going somewhere nice?' asks the receptionist.

'Just seeing a friend,' I say as casually as I can.

But underneath, I am shaking. It's been a year now since I was released. A year since I turned down Imran.

How will he feel about me? How will I feel about him?

I wait outside in the visitors' car park. Imran isn't here. I'm early, of course, but I persuade myself he's not coming. A twitch of a curtain makes me aware of a figure standing at a window, peering out at me. It's one of the residents on the ground floor. They always watch everything. To them it's a world acted out beyond their lace curtains. The stage on which they used to play a bigger role.

A sleek blue car pulls up noiselessly. I hold my breath. It's a different car from last time but the driver is the same. He gets out, as tall as ever.

His eyes lock with mine. He holds out his arms and envelops me. I feel like a lost jigsaw piece that has finally been found. Then he releases me briefly and looks down at me. 'It's going to be all right, Belinda. Trust me. It's going to be all right.'

But will it?

112

Imran drives me along the coast towards Lyme Regis. 'I thought you'd like a change,' he says.

We've been talking but there have also been silences. It's the measure of a good relationship that you can have comfortable gaps. With Gerald they had always been awkward.

We walk along the Cobb, where Meryl Streep had been filmed in *The French Lieutenant's Woman*. 'I love it here,' he said.

'I didn't know you knew this part of the country.'

'Only since you came here. Sometimes I'd drive past Sunnyside and hope to catch a glimpse of you. Then I'd walk along the cliff path and wonder how on earth I could get you to see me. In the end, I realized I just had to wait.'

He takes my hand in his. We haven't so much as kissed but this feels even more intimate. That and the knowledge that he really has been waiting for me.

We walk past a news placard.

TYCOON BEDMONT ADMITS NAZI FAMILY TIES – CHARGED OVER PLOT TO MURDER DEPUTY PM'S SISTER.

'Mabel could have been killed,' I say, shivering.

'You really care for her, don't you?'

I nod. 'She's lived through so much, yet she could always see the better side of everyone. She told me to take a chance on you.'

He looks amused. 'Is that how she put it?'

'Not exactly. She just said there was still time to make a life together.'

'There is, Belinda.' He stops; cups his hands around my face. Looks me straight in the eye. 'We might not be the same people we were at university. But we still share that kernel of understanding. That love. We are made for each other, Belinda. Please give me a chance. What have you got to lose?'

I think of the lie I'd told him at university when he'd said he had to return to an arranged marriage. I told him that was fine because I wasn't ready to settle down. I hadn't meant it. I just didn't want to make it harder for him than it clearly was. But I'm not going to lie now.

'What have I got to lose?' I repeat. 'The independence I have built up.'

'But are you happy? Don't you miss something?'

A sob escapes from my lips. 'Yes. I miss Gillian and I want to see my grandson.'

'I will help you,' he says.

'You can't. They're gone from me for ever.'

He holds me as I weep. People might be looking at me, but I don't care. Imran is holding me. For the first time in years, I am beginning to feel safe and loved.

'Live with me in London,' he says.

'I can't. I have a job to do,' I reply. However, as I say it, I realize that my time at Sunnyside is up. If Harry Marchmont knows the truth about my past, it won't be long until management does too; not to mention the residents. They will all view me with suspicion.

'We could open something together, Belinda,' Imran says, as if reading my mind. 'We could start a project, perhaps.'

My voice wobbles. 'It's too soon.'

'After forty years?' he asks, his eyebrows raised. 'Please, Belinda. We let each other go at university. We can't do it again.'

Then I hear Mabel's voice in my head as if she is standing next to me.

'*Call yourself a Listener? Isn't it time you listened to your own heart?*'

'Yes,' I say.

He looks alarmed. 'You mean, yes we can let each other go again?'

I stand on tiptoes to put my arms around his neck. 'No.' I am half-laughing and half-crying. 'I mean yes, I will live with you.'

113

I hand in my two weeks' notice.

'We'll miss you,' says the manager. 'No one else listens like you do.'

'I'll miss you all too,' I say. It's on the tip of my tongue to confess, but what would that do? Imran and I have been talking about what our own business could look like: a charity for women starting out on their own – something that I could have done with after leaving prison. It feels good to give something back, though I will always carry my guilt about Gerald and now Mabel.

Shortly afterwards, Stephen turns up to visit Karen at the same time as Elspeth comes for lunch on my day off.

Of course it was bound to happen one day. But here they are. Arriving in the reception and signing in one after the other, without knowing they are half-brother and sister.

I could keep quiet. I could just nod at Stephen and go out for lunch with my daughter. But I don't. Instead, I tell her who he is.

'You've set this up,' she says furiously.

Why are adult children so condemning?

'No. I didn't know he was visiting at the same time as you.'

Then Stephen turns. I watch the realization dawn on his face.

Elspeth gasps. 'You look just like Dad,' she whispers.

'So do you,' he says.

I go and wait in the car park, leaving them to talk or not talk, whichever they feel more comfortable with.

When Elspeth gets into the car, I can see she's been crying.

'I'm sorry,' I say. 'I honestly didn't know he was going to be there.'

'It's all right, Mum,' she sniffs. 'I'm glad we met, actually. It helps to put it all together.'

I don't ask if they have plans to meet up again or introduce him to Gillian. I reckon that's their business.

But a few weeks later – just before Christmas – I receive a text from Elspeth. Can I meet her at the Regency Hotel on Christmas Eve?

'Would you like me to come with you?' asks Imran.

'Not quite yet,' I say gently.

As I go into the reception area, I see a tall, strapping fourteen-year-old who has my nose. Next to him, is my daughter Gillian.

'Hello, Granny,' he grins. 'I've been wanting to meet you for ages.'

My grandson! 'And I've been wanting to meet you too, Gerald,' I choke through tears.

'Actually, I'm known as Gerry.'

I can't help feeling relieved.

Gillian doesn't hug me. She doesn't even take my hand.

'We've all been talking,' she says stiffly. 'We thought we ought to try again, for everyone's sake.'

'Thank you,' I gulp. I make to hug my eldest daughter, but she hesitates. Instead, I reach my hand and slowly, very slowly, she stretches out hers. I feel the touch of her warm skin. Just briefly. But it's a start.

114

In January I receive a postcard from Mabel. It shows sunny blue skies and a matching sea. She writes in that spidery writing that the elderly appear to have perfected:

I think of you a lot, Belinda. I am coming to terms with your betrayal, and I forgive you now. I hope you can find peace as I have. I don't think I'm coming back. At this time of my life, my body is only made for a one-way journey. Besides, Britain is too cold for my bones. Harry is coming out to visit shortly. I feel guilty that he lost his seat but he says this was not necessarily due to the scandal and that it was time for him to leave politics anyway. He's going to dedicate his time to voluntary causes now.

I put the postcard on the mirror in the room I now share with Imran, next to a photograph of my grandson.

Gerry and I often go out for lunch together. He doesn't seem fazed about what he calls 'the family skeleton'. 'I mean it's not cool that you killed my granddad but Mum says you didn't mean to.' His eyes seem to gleam with curiosity. 'What was it like in prison?'

'Awful,' I say. 'Make sure you never do anything illegal. It's not worth it.'

He laughs as if I am joking.

'I mean it,' I say firmly.

Then I receive a text from Stephen.

It's wonderful to have found my sisters. They're my only link to Dad.

I don't question my girls about it. I reckon that if they want to tell me, they will. But they don't. Maybe it's easier that way.

Despite her 'ought to try again' words on Christmas Eve, I never hear from Gillian directly. Perhaps I just have to accept that some crimes are too big to forgive.

115

My own story would not be complete unless I told you how Mabel's ended. After her decision to remain in Italy permanently, she and I wrote several letters to each other. My first was a long apology, explaining again how I hadn't known what to do: the only way to keep my girls safe was to betray her. Once the air had cleared, we talked about family. In my case, Gerry, my girls and, of course, Imran; in hers, her son and her great-granddaughter.

But Mabel's last, in that shaky, spidery writing, was different. She knew she was going to die, yet her writing was decidedly lucid:

If I do not see you again, dear Belinda, I want you to know how grateful I am to you for listening. I won't pretend that I wasn't hurt by you. But that is all over now. Thank you for being so kind and sympathetic, knowing exactly when to ask a question and when to pause. You helped me heal. Most importantly, you gave me the great privilege of letting me into your own life and secrets.

My eyes blur with tears. I should be thanking *her*. I hear Mabel's voice in the letter. It makes me feel as if she is still here, sitting right next to me. I may have helped her, but Mabel's story taught me to forgive.

I like to think we both benefited from each other's company, and dare I say it, love. The special kind of love that can only exist between two kindred spirits. For that's what Mabel and I were. Two women who had done wrong in the eyes of the law. But who lived and learned to tell their tales.

Epilogue

Mabel

I have had a lot of time to think here in Italy.

It is wonderful – oh, so wonderful – to have my enormous extended family (as they call it nowadays) around me, but I wish Belinda was here. There is one thing I did not tell her and it's rubbing on my conscience. Indeed, it scorches my skin.

Not long after we met at Sunnyside, Belinda said that it's important for stories like ours to be told.

She was right, but it wasn't the time to tell all of mine then and I'm not sure it is now. But if I don't, it might become too late.

So I think back further, as if rummaging through an office index of cards, to the morning I'd found the photograph of Clarissa on Mosley's march.

I went straight up to her bedroom and when she didn't answer, walked in. Her bed was still rumpled but no one was there. Her bathroom was empty. Perhaps she was walking the dogs. But no. They were sleeping quietly in their baskets. I tiptoed past, shutting the back door gently behind me so as not to wake Cook, and went out into the grounds. Where could she be? Eventually, I found her by the lavender bank.

She seemed distressed, walking around still in her nightdress and talking to herself. I caught names. My mother's name. The Colonel's. Even my own.

When she saw me, she started like a spooked horse. 'What are you doing here?'

'I am looking for you,' I replied.

'No. I mean what are you doing here?'

'I live here.'

'You can't. I gave you away. I made a terrible mistake. So did Jonty. He should have stayed by me. We could have kept you if we'd been braver. We would have been a family. Now it is too late.'

That's when I saw it. The gun in her hands.

'Don't,' I said, despite everything. 'Please don't.'

'But I must. Don't you see? They will find out sooner or later.'

She thrust the gun into my hands. '*You* do it.'

'No!' I looked with horror at the weapon in my hands. 'I couldn't possibly. I'm not a murderer.'

Then she gave me a look I will never forget. 'Trust me, Mabel. None of us are who we think we are. Shoot me. They are coming for me. I feel it in my bones. I don't want to be assassinated like my Jonty.'

'Maybe you deserve to die,' I said.

'But not that way,' she pleaded. 'I gave you life. If you have any compassion, please end mine for me.'

'What about *your* compassion?' I demanded. 'You took my baby away.'

'That was different,' she scoffed. 'The father was a lowly Italian prisoner of war from a country about to switch sides. I wasn't having a child like that in the family.'

And that's when I pulled the trigger.

As soon as I fired the shot, I realized *I* was a murderer. I was no better than the bombers who had targeted innocent civilians. My aunt had been a traitor, but who was I to hand out a death sentence? I should have let the authorities take her.

I knew they would come for me unless I could disguise my crime.

Shaking, I wrote one word:

TRAITOR.

I weighed the paper down with a stone beside her and ran down to the sea, where I flung the gun as hard as I could into the waves.

'I won't tell anyone,' I vowed to myself. Not until my dying day – and maybe not even then.

Then I ran back into the house and told Cook that my aunt was missing.

As the villagers said at the time, almost anyone could have done it. Everyone had a grievance against Lady Clarissa. But no one, as far as I know, ever suspected me of killing her.

This is my story, which I have told no one. No one, that is, except my great-granddaughter, and only her because I know I do not have much time left and she deserves to know the truth.

'Do you think I'm wicked?' I asked Isabella as she sat by my side, taking all this in.

'Of course not,' she said. 'Your act was a crime of passion. It was a difficult time and you were young. I would love to write about it. May I?'

My great-granddaughter wants to be a novelist. It's not an easy profession, but one day, I know, she will make it.

'Yes,' I said. 'Just wait until I'm dead.'

'I hope that won't be for many years,' she said, putting her arms around me in the kind of warm, all-encompassing, truly loving embrace that I'd thought I'd never have.

Now I know that if I die tomorrow, I will die happy. Because at last I have a family.

Two Years Later

ITALIAN AUTHOR'S DEBUT NOVEL, BASED ON HER GREAT-GRANDMOTHER'S LIFE STORY, ATTRACTS SIX-FIGURE BIDS IN WORLDWIDE AUCTION

Author's Note

Two years ago, after the launch of *Coming to Find You*, a man came up to me.

He said he wanted to tell me a little-known fact about the Second World War. His uncle had been a policeman in those days and had told his nephew about the existence of 'lists' in certain counties.

These lists named locals who were suspected of being sympathetic to Hitler and/or posing a threat to national security.

Many of these were members of the British Union of Fascists, led by Oswald Mosley.

Anyone on the list was put under surveillance and some were sent to jail.

The BUF was made illegal in 1940, and Mosley himself was imprisoned.

However, there were still pockets of British nationals who secretly supported Hitler.

After the war, some of these people were punished. In some cases, according to my source, locals wreaked their own retribution by brutally harming those who they suspected of being on the other side.

It's true that three men were executed as traitors; however, my character Jonty Dashland was created from my imagination.

As military history author and lecturer Jonathan Walker told me: 'Certain members of the aristocracy, whilst not necessarily supporters of Nazism, saw Hitler as a bulwark against communism. Their fear of a Bolshevik-inspired revolution in Britain was paramount.'

During my research for *The Stranger in Room Six*, I also interviewed Andrew Chatterton, an historian specializing in the Second World War. He said: 'It's possible that any connection with pro-Hitler sympathies in the family, however long ago, could seriously stain and damage people's reputations today – especially with the revival of antisemitism. Social media is partly responsible. It can make rumours go viral. Such stains could ruin businesses, reputation and family ties.'

These lists, which could blow a family apart, were generally kept in county archives.

I do not know if there was a list for Devon, but I couldn't help but wonder what might happen if one of those lists went missing. 'This is also possible,' said Andrew. 'There weren't necessarily copies at that time; there wasn't the technology there is today.'

This led me to conceive another strand of my plot. When I worked as a writer-in-residence at a high-security male prison, I used to walk past a door marked 'Listeners' every day and often wondered what happened behind it. I made inquiries and found it was a sort of 'Samaritans' where prisoners volunteered to listen to other prisoners' problems, often under the auspices of the chaplaincy service. It struck me as a very worthwhile and noble cause. Indeed, Samaritans often go into prisons to train Listeners.

There is one other factor I must add, and that is about Sunnyside itself – known as the Old Rectory in Mabel's childhood.

My grandmother died of cancer during the war, and my then nine-year-old mother was brought up by a very strict aunt (a former debutante). She and her more genial husband lived in a rambling old rectory in Gloucestershire and, as a teenager, I was sent down to stay there during the summer holidays.

The atmosphere was fairly forbidding, although I got through by reading the entire collection of Jane Austen.

After my great-aunt (whose beliefs were far removed from those of Clarissa Sinclair!) died, I discovered that her seemingly tough exterior owed much to a series of miscarriages. As Mabel would have said, people always have a reason for being the way they are.

However, I am very grateful to her for inspiring the picture of Sunnyside Home for the Young at Heart: a gracious home with secrets oozing from its wooden stairs, high ceilings and grand chandeliers.

This apart, all characters are fictitious and any resemblance or similarity to real places, people or events, past or present, is entirely coincidental. Sunnyside Home for the Young at Heart is similarly a figment of my imagination.

Acknowledgements

I had no idea until I became a published author several years ago, how many people were needed to nurture a book from the first word on my computer to the first copy off the printing press. Nowadays, with social media, teamwork has become even more important.

I could come up with lots of different ways to express my gratitude but instead, I'm just going to say 'thank you very much' to the following, with the odd pertinent remark!

Kate Hordern, my wonderful agent, who accepted my initial thriller *My Husband's Wife* before I'd even finished it and who then sold it to . . .

Katy Loftus, my first brilliant editor at Penguin, who found me in her submissions pile and taught me so much.

The wonderful team at Penguin including my talented editor Rosa Schierenberg; Olatoye Oladinni; Ellie Hudson; the brilliant sales team; my publicists Jane Gentle and Rebecca Gray; Natalie Wall; and Leah Boulton.

My meticulous and indispensable copy-editor, Trevor Horwood (only one of us can work out dates and it's not me).

Proofreaders Sarah Barlow and Sally Sargeant.

Thanks to Anne Marples, whose name has been used for a fictional character in aid of the annual auction run by Young Lives vs Cancer.

Grace (Erin Grace), whose parents bid for her name to be used as a character in aid of The Children's Project.

Booksellers in all formats.

Bloggers (love your posts!).

Readers (thank you for your fabulous messages).

Reviewers (I used to be a staff features writer on women's magazines so I love it when I'm on the page!).

Andrew Chatterton, Second World War historian and author.

Jonathan Walker, military history author and lecturer. Any historical 'tweaks', such as dates of events, are mine.

Richard Atkinson of Tuckers Solicitors who gives me legal advice. Any mistakes or stretches of my imagination are down to me entirely.

Peter Burnside, for helping me with technical content.

The fantastic Betty Schwartz who inspired me at the beginning.

My family.

You can find me at www.janecorryauthor.com. Also on Instagram, Facebook, Twitter and TikTok. Please follow me if you'd like details of my next book.

blood sisters

THREE LITTLE GIRLS. ONE GOOD. ONE BAD. ONE DEAD.

Kitty lives in a care home. She can't speak properly and she has no memory of the accident that put her here.

At least that's the story she's sticking to.

Art teacher Alison looks fine on the surface. But the surface is a lie. When a job in a prison comes up she decides to take it – this is her chance to finally make things right.

But someone is watching Kitty and Alison.

Someone who wants revenge for what happened that sunny morning in May.

And only another life will do . . .

Praise for Jane Corry

'A fearsomely good thriller'
Nicci French

'I raced through this'
Teresa Driscoll

'So many brilliant twists'
Claire Douglas

the dead ex

HE CHEATED . . . HE LIED . . . HE DIED.

Vicki's husband David once promised to love her in sickness and in health. But after a brutal attack left her suffering with epilepsy, he ran away with his mistress.

So when Vicki gets a call one day to say that he's missing, her first thought is 'good riddance'. But then the police find evidence suggesting that David is dead. And they think Vicki had something to do with it.

What really happened on the night of David's disappearance?

And how can Vicki prove her innocence, when she's not even sure of it herself?

Praise for Jane Corry

'Compulsive, edgy and fabulous twists!'
B. A. Paris

'Few writers can match Jane Corry'
Cara Hunter

'Totally hooked me'
Peter James

I Looked Away

**YOU MADE A MISTAKE.
BUT THEY'RE SAYING IT'S MURDER.**

Every Monday, 49-year-old Ellie looks after her grandson Josh. She loves him more than anyone else in the world. The only thing that can mar her happiness is her husband's affair. But he swears it's over now and Ellie has decided to be thankful for what she's got.

Then one day, while she's looking after Josh, her husband gets a call from *that woman*. And – just for a moment – Ellie takes her eyes off her grandson. What happens next will change her life forever.

Because Ellie is hiding something in her past.

And what looks like an accident could start to look like murder . . .

Praise for Jane Corry

'Sensitive and thought-provoking'
Adele Parks

'Thrilling, emotional and pacy'
Claire Douglas

'Dark, sinister, compelling'
Nicci French

I Made a Mistake

IT STARTED WITH A KISS . . . AND ENDED WITH MURDER.

In Poppy Page's mind, there are two types of women in this world: those who are faithful to their husbands and those who are not. Until now, Poppy has never questioned which she was.

But when handsome, charming Matthew Gordon walks back into her life after almost two decades, that changes. Poppy makes a single mistake – and that mistake will be far more dangerous than she could imagine.

Someone is going to pay for it with their life . . .

Praise for Jane Corry

'Gritty, real, interesting and clever'
Gillian McAllister

'Clever, compulsive and twisty'
Claire Douglas

'Absolutely brilliant'
Angela Marsons

The Lies We Tell

**YOU DID WHAT ANY MOTHER WOULD DO . . .
AND NOW SOMEONE ELSE'S SON IS DEAD.**

Sarah always thought of herself and her husband, Tom, as good people. But that was before their son, Freddy, came home saying he'd done something terrible. Begging them not to tell the police.

Soon Sarah and Tom must find out just how far they are willing to push themselves, and their marriage, to protect their only child . . .

As the lies build up and Sarah is presented with the perfect opportunity to get Freddy off the hook, she is faced with a terrifying decision . . .

Save her son . . . or save herself?

Praise for Jane Corry

'Everything I love in a book'
Lisa Jewell

'Jane Corry's best yet'
B. A. Paris

'Brims with suspense'
Louise Candlish

We All Have Our Secrets

YOU KNOW SHE'S LYING . . . BUT SO ARE YOU.

Two women are staying in Willowmead House.

One of them is running.
One of them is hiding.
Both of them are lying.

Emily made one bad decision and now her career could be over. Her family home on the Cornish coast is the only place where she feels safe. But when she arrives, there's a stranger living with her father.

Emily doesn't trust the beautiful young woman, convinced that she's telling one lie after another. Soon, Emily becomes obsessed with finding out the truth . . .

But should some secrets stay buried forever?

Praise for Jane Corry

'Clever, gripping, nuanced'
Phoebe Morgan

'An unputdownable read'
Emma Curtis

'The twists just keep on coming'
Celia Walden

Coming to Find You

**YOU CAN RUN AWAY FROM YOUR LIFE
BUT YOU CAN'T RUN AWAY FROM MURDER**

When her family tragedy is splashed across the newspapers, Nancy decides to disappear. Her grandmother's beautiful Regency house in a quiet seaside village seems like the safest place to hide. But the old house has its own secrets and a chilling wartime legacy . . .

Now someone knows the truth about the night Nancy's mother and stepfather were murdered. Someone knows where to find her. And they have nothing to lose . . .

**So what really happened that night?
And how far will she go to keep it hidden?**

Praise for Jane Corry

'A compelling read'
Shari Lapena

'Deliciously dark'
Claire Douglas

'I couldn't put it down'
Heidi Perks

I DIED ON A TUESDAY

THERE'S THE STORY EVERYONE BELIEVES...

The victim: Eighteen-year-old Janie leaving home for a new life.

The criminal: World-famous rockstar, Robbie, who harbours a shocking secret.

The protector: Witness support officer, Vanessa, desperate to right the wrongs of her past.

They tried to bury that fateful day.
Now it's back to haunt them.

... AND THEN THERE'S THE TRUTH.

Praise for Jane Corry

'Gripping and multilayered, I couldn't put this down'
Sarah Pearse

'Nerve-racking, spine-tingling and heart-warming in equal measure'
Nicci French

'A clever, twisty story with a huge heart at its core'
Andrea Mara